PEOPLE LIKE US

CAROL ANN EASTMAN

Copyright © 2024 by Carol Ann Eastman

All rights reserved.

No part of this publication may be reproduced, distributed, or transmitted in any form or by any means, including photocopying, recording, or other electronic or mechanical methods, without the prior written permission of the publisher, except as permitted by U.S. copyright law.

The story, all names, characters, and incidents portrayed in this production are fictitious. No identification with actual persons (living or deceased), places, buildings, and products is intended or should be inferred.

"We will never have true civilization until we have learned to recognize the rights of others."

(Will Rogers)

My bleeding, open, and accepting heart dedicates this book to all marginalized, oppressed, and browbeaten individuals who've ever been forced into believing they are less than or unworthy due to their lifestyles, their choices, and their beliefs. Someday, hopefully in the very near future, we will all unite and learn to embrace one another based on the beauty and love that grows in our hearts and not based on how we expect others should act, feel, believe, or think. Until then, keep fighting the good fight, stand up for yourself and for others, and never—ever—let anyone tell you what to think, what to feel, what to do, and whom to love. Don't let anyone force you into a box or category in which you don't belong. As individuals, we are here to shine and fly. So keep soaring and never stop being yourself. I believe in you. And I will forever be on your side. You have a friend and ally in me. Enjoy this book that was inspired by my students who have endured living in a world that hasn't always been kind or welcoming. This is your book, your validation, that you are loved, needed, and appreciated. And above all else, you matter.

I can't believe this is happening. Vicissitude Maddox, rule follower, the girl voted most respected and admired by her graduating class is now all alone, heading for the border for a chance at survival. With Authority on my tail and ready to arrest me—or worse. They say you learn a lot about yourself during your senior year. I learned a lifetime's worth about myself in less than six months. I just hope I live long enough to talk about it and use what I learned to save more people like me.

PROLOGUE

Long ago, in the time **B**efore, society was beaten, battered, and broken after a plague contaminated the world. All countries suffered. All people were impacted. Nobody was safe. Worse yet, nobody had the answers to save the individuals from this catastrophe. Those who tried were ridiculed and ignored. Those who didn't try either suffered and died from the plague or annexed off to follow their own belief system. Quickly, the fear and anger spread worse than the contagious plague that threatened innocent lives. Divisive and hostile, the **C**razies and the **L**oonies fought for control, fought to be the guiding authority in a world ripped apart. The battle continued while animosities skyrocketed. Soon, nobody could be trusted, and the states that were cohesive crumbled. But the Authority united and created a world—a world in which the fighting ended and peace was finally restored—a world that is **N**ow in the country of **Eka**.

CHAPTER 1
VICISSITUDE

"If civilization is to survive, we must cultivate the science of human relationships—the ability of all peoples, of all kinds, to live together, and work together, in the same world, at peace."
(Franklin D. Roosevelt)

My moms were right. My green eyes match my emerald dress perfectly. They're typically always right. They're smart women who know what's up. And I'm extremely thankful they're mine. Most girls my age don't value their relationships with their mothers, but I do. And I'm not afraid to admit it.

"Oh Cissy, you're stunning. My gracious, every girl at that dance is going to be green with envy when they lay eyes on you," Mama compliments, tucking one of her long braids back behind her ear.

"That's all they better lay on you, Vicissitude. Those girls only want one thing," Mom says.

"Will you stop? She only has eyes for Marjorie. Haven't you seen how she looks at that girl? They'll be together forever; I just know it," Mama sings.

I roll my eyes at them in the mirror. "Will you both stop? This isn't a big deal. Since when is it a big deal for a bunch of ladies to be in one room dancing and acting a fool? It's what we do literally every single time we're together."

My moms have been co-mingled for almost 25 years. It took a long time for them to get permission to have me. They filled out an application every year for seven years before Authority granted them permission for insemination. But when Mama finally got approval, and she was inseminated, my moms were nearly 35 years old. They were running out of time. Authority doesn't allow anyone over the age of 37 to carry a child.

When Mama got pregnant with me, they got quite the surprise. She was pregnant with twins. They were thrilled. Finally, they were getting the family they'd always wanted in one fell swoop. That was right up until the twins they were having ended up being one girl and one boy. Mama was devastated. Poor Mama was never permitted to hold, snuggle, or smell Cleave before they handed him over to his dads. And she laments about it every chance she can.

"Are you picking up Marjorie or is she driving—?"

I sigh, closing my eyes for a beat. "For the hundredth time, she is coming here." Just as I finish my sentence and slip my foot into my shoe, the doorbell rings. "Speak of the villain." I take one last look in the mirror and feel pretty good with what I see. Taking a deep breath, I spin one last time for my moms and grab my handbag to leave.

∾

"I feel like you're bored or something," Marjorie whispers in my ear as she traces a finger down my bare back. I hate when she tries to tickle me like that.

"Not bored at all. Just slow dancing with my girlfriend," I say, pulling back to look her in the eyes. Marjorie has entirely too much makeup on tonight. I know it's our final dance, and we're supposed to go all out, but I bet she used every bit of makeup she owns tonight. It's caked on. I'm tempted to use my long, painted nail and see if her face scrapes off. I don't though. She'd lose it if I ever criticized her in any way. Her moms do that enough.

Her long blonde hair is piled beautifully on top of her head with some loose curls cascading down and framing her face. She really is gorgeous—and she knows it too. We are definitely the power couple at Case Academy. Every girl here vies for our attention, and the girls never even try to hide the fact that they'd do anything to take Marjorie from me. They want her. These girls are like dogs in heat when she's around.

"Have I told you tonight how sexy you look?" I ask, twirling a strand of her curls around my finger.

"Actually, you haven't," she admits. "I was beginning to think that I shouldn't have gone with hot pink. Blonde hair and hot pink seem so cliché."

"Ummm, since when?"

"Don't you remember those girls' toys from Before?" Marjorie says with her eyes wide.

"Uhhh no, and neither do you. Those are urban legends," I groan, pulling her against me. "I tell you that all the time. No way people would make toys that look like that, so girls all over the world would try to look the same. That's not a thing."

"Hmmm, I don't know. My moms swear they were real," she says. "Sometimes, you're too trusting and accepting. For real Cissy, you need to start asking some questions and thinking every now and then."

I stop. Pushing away from her to look her right in the eyes, I ask, "Excuse me? I'm sorry I just don't believe all the crap your moms come up with. How would they even know? They weren't around for it, and these are the same moms who tell you daily that your beauty is all that you have?" I watch her face fall while her eyes glisten. My shoulders slack, knowing that I shouldn't have fought back. Marjorie is so sensitive. I know better than to pick a fight with her.

Marjorie's moms are the worst. I couldn't live in her house. Everything is pristine and white. You're legit not allowed to sit on her couches. What are couches for if you can't sit on them? All they ever talk about is how pretty or how thin someone is. It's ridiculous. They notice if Marjorie or her sister gains one pound—and they tell them about it. Look them right in the face and comment on their weight gain. These girls are the thinnest students at Case Academy.

I wonder what Marjorie's moms think of me. I'm not built like Marjorie or her sister, Mallory. They're all muscles and bones. Marjorie's ribs are prominent, and her abs are clearly defined. I'm sure I have abs somewhere under my curves and fleshy parts, but I'm not about to eat less or exercise more than I have to. Exercise is not my jam. Don't get me wrong. I'm not overweight; nobody is. It's not allowed. Well, men are given a little more leeway than women. They're allowed to be more robust than females are. I've actually never seen an overweight woman before. I heard about them though.

Julia Parsons was gaining weight once; we all noticed. But one day, she was no longer at school. Two months later, she came back with her weight fixed. I don't know what happened to her or what they did to her, but it clearly worked. I like that we are granted a doable weight range that we can be. I think it would be strange if all of us were the exact same size with the same body type. Some of us are curvier and fluffier than others, but nobody takes it to the extreme. I like that. I would hate it if anyone I knew were unhealthy just because she ate too much. I can't even imagine that. Why would anyone eat beyond being full? I think it's another one of those urban legends we always hear about.

"I don't know why you hate them so much." She frowns.

"I can't figure out why you love them so much," I counter.

"They're my moms. Of course, I love them. They only want what's best for me and want me to be the best. Why is that so wrong?"

"How can you think that forcing you to not eat, to exercise beyond our requirements, and to belittle you for not looking hot is what's best for you?" This is our typical fight. We have it all the time. It's exhausting and old. Noticing the tears in her eyes, I'm wrought with guilt. I always do this to her. "Listen, I want to have fun tonight and not fight."

"Oh, can we leave and make up? I love our make up sessions." Marjorie winks.

I'm starving. There's no way I can forgo dinner. Not tonight. "I'm definitely down to play later, but I have to eat first. Let's go to Gino's and get some pizza." I watch her face and add, "Or just some salads." Her eyes brighten.

I'm not just getting a salad. According to my digital readout, I still have 900 calories to consume, and woman, I plan to devour each and every one of them. Tonight, I won't even care if my alarm goes off in the restaurant, and people hear me nearing my 1500-calorie limit. It's a special night. I deserve it.

CHAPTER 2
RIOT

"Ignorance of the law is no excuse in any country. If it were, the laws would lose their effect, because it can always be pretended."
(Thomas Jefferson)

"Nice work, gentlemen! We're going to destroy Woodruff Prep this weekend," Coach Cox yells, his whistle signaling the end of practice.

Just as the whistle blows, the electronic readout on my wrist reveals that I'm at goal for exercise and calories burned. It's lower than yesterday's. Thank Authority that coach went easier on us today.

I take off my helmet, dropping my lacrosse stick on my bag. I hate sports. But even worse than that, I hate being good at sports. If I would've known those evaluations I had when I was eight years old would mean I'd have to play a sport year-round, I would've pretended like I couldn't run, jump, throw, or catch. Now, I'm stuck in an endless cycle of running, jumping, throwing, and catching. Lacrosse is my favorite of the four sports they make me play though. I like hitting people and knocking them around. My best friend thinks I have anger issues. Maybe I do.

I guess playing sports is better than the alternative. I'd hate to spend four hours after school solving math equations or building things. One class of math a day is definitely enough for me. The last time I tried to build something, I hammered a nail right through my finger. My dads freaked.

"Riot, wait up!" Nigel yells, grabbing his bag. "We going to Gino's? I'm starving."

Nigel and I eat after every practice. We're supposed to. It's part of the rules. Good thing too, because I'm always ready to eat my helmet by the time practice ends. My dads don't really cook. They're always at work. Nigel's dad does, but Nigel usually eats twice. Something with me and then something when he gets home. He's a goalie, so he has approval to eat more than I can. Goalies need to be bigger and more hearty.

"We always go there. Can't we hit somewhere else?" His frown tells me that we're going to Gino's no matter how much I don't want to go there again. He's nutting bad for one of the servers there. If he doesn't make a move soon and ask him out, then I might make a move on him just to piss Nigel off. Now, that would be fun.

"Hey Riot, I heard McCarthy McCorum is dying to get in your pants," Nigel says, getting into my car. His red hair is slick with sweat, hanging in his eyes. He shakes his head, swinging his hair to the side to see. His freckles are the exact color of his hair.

"Yep, heard that too. Not interested," I say, starting the car.

"Dude, you can have any guy at Lakeward. What are

you doing—and I know what you *aren't* doing," Nigel says, pushing the buttons of the radio.

"No chance. My car. My podcast," I say, pulling out of the parking lot. "Just because some guy is interested in me doesn't mean I have to screw him."

"I get it. You know me; I'm a one man guy," Nigel says, checking out his reflection in the mirror.

"Yeah right, a guy you've never gotten up enough nerve to even order one refill from," I joke, turning up the audio.

"Hey, are we rolling through Male Monument Center on our way?"

I groan, turning my blinker on, indicating we aren't going near Male Monument Center today.

"Don't you want to see that dude?" Nigel asks, pointing in the other direction.

"Not even a little bit," I admit.

"You're no fun," Nigel complains, reclining in my car seat and placing his sunglasses over his eyes.

"Yeah, sorry dude, I just have no desire to gawk at Authority's latest execution," I explain. "And it's disturbing that you always want to go see their most recent victims."

"Criminals, not victims," Nigel corrects.

"Says Authority," I argue. "What'd this one do anyway?"

"They found animal carcasses in his freezer. They think he hunted small animals and ate them." Nigel crinkles his nose in disgust.

"They think?" I ask, needing clarification.

"Well, he denied it."

"And let me guess; Authority Selects came in and killed him anyway."

"I can't believe your dads didn't tell you all about him," Nigel sounds surprised.

"Oh come on!" I exclaim. "You know they don't tell me anything."

Nigel and I have been friends since we were nine years old. When we were 12, we tried hooking up. It was weird. Felt like I was kissing my brother. Not that I have any brothers, but it was just odd. He agreed, so it didn't mess with our friendship. We decided that we were better as friends and that was it. The guys around here are so dramatic, starting and ending relationships faster than I can score a goal. I decided a few years ago that I just wanted to finish high school before I really got into anything with anyone. The guys here are all too predictable and clingy. Not interested. I'm just going to kick ass on the lacrosse field and study hard.

My dads are all about me following in their footsteps. My dads own a law firm, *Logan and Logan Associates*. My sperm father, or active father, Luther, is all about the law to an extreme. He doesn't let us break any laws. Dude doesn't even go one mile per hour over the speed limit. At the top of his law class, he knows the law inside and out and never budges on it. He'll be a judge someday, I bet. His broad shoulders, piercing blue eyes, and bald head make him an ominous opponent in court. If you saw my dad in a dark alley, you'd fear for your life. When other lawyers realize that they're facing off against Luther Logan, they shake in their shoes. Admittedly, I shake in my shoes when my father admonishes me. He's a scary dude.

My sperm father caught me drawing in a notebook once and immediately burned it. I was five-years-old. I'd never cried harder. I was only trying to stay awake until my other dad got home. I started doodling without even thinking about it. Man, my father blew up. He's never seen me do anything like that again. I hate disappointing him.

My passive dad, Atticus, is a public defender, so he's always on the defensive for me. He sticks up for me—even when I'm wrong. He once tried to fight the school, because I wanted to take a season off of sports. He tried to set up a meeting and fight the good fight for me, but that didn't fly. Dads aren't allowed to make rules or try to run the school or athletics—unless they actually work for the school. Nobody would even listen to one word my father said. He tried though, and that meant a lot to me.

Everyone wants Atticus Logan on his side. The man's a giant teddy bear of love and devotion. He often pushes the limit on his size. Twice now, Authority has put him on caloric deficit when he started rounding out a bit. To me though, I like him soft and cuddly—it suits him well. My dad and I both push the limits on the length of our hair. Men in Eka can't have hair that touches their ears or middle of their foreheads. My dad taught me how to use a little hair product to make my hair styled in a way in which it appears shorter than it is. My dad even cut his hair pretty short when he tried to set up a meeting at the school. He was ready to prove how professional and persuasive he could be. However, he got nowhere. The school and Authority shut him down before he could get any facts or research to them.

I've heard that parents used to have a big say in what went on in schools. Supposedly, they used to have clubs that parents and teachers were a part of together. That's just wild. It's probably just a myth. No way would parents try to say what a teacher does. How would they even know? You can't just walk into a teacher's classroom and automatically know how to do the job better than he can.

"Just ask him out," I grumble, grabbing my card out of my wallet.

"What? I can't just say, 'hey let's go out sometime.' He'll laugh me right out of here." Nigel shifts in his seat, glancing quickly behind him. Our server, Decarion Rattler, graduated from Lakeward two years ago. Nigel's been drooling over him since we were in middle school. "And let's not forget. I'm a damn ginger. I'm no Riot Logan with those piercing and brooding blue eyes or that mop of sexy black hair," Nigel jokes, mussing my hair.

"Dude, don't make me break that hand," I threaten. "Listen, have you ever paid for French fries here?" I ask. He shakes his head. "Do you always get a large milkshake for the price of the small?" He nods. "And last but definitely not least, did Decarion leave you his number last freaking year?" Nigel's head drops onto the back of the booth as his eyes flutter closed.

"You don't get it, man. I can't," he says, his head pounding against the booth. "What if we go out and he hates me—or I hate him? Or worse. What if it's perfect?"

"I never know what the hell you're talking about," I say, slurping the last of my caramel chocolate shake as I stand. "Why would it be worse if it's perfect? That makes no sense."

"Says the guy who's never had his heart broken. It sucks," Nigel groans.

Nigel doesn't know anything about my heart or the shards of heart I have scattered all over this place. "Listen, you and Curtis broke up two years ago. Yeah, it was messy, gruesome actually, but screw him," I say, whispering down into his ear. "You can't let him win by never trying again. Curtis was a prick. Everyone knew it, but you. You couldn't see anything beyond his perfect hair and chiseled body."

I don't blame Nigel. Curtis destroyed him. Nigel was in love, and Curtis just played him—used him whenever he could. I thump Nigel on the back, trying to pump him up. "Now, take Decarion for a test drive. You might like it."

Nigel glances at his wrist, checking the time on his secured tracker. "It's almost time for the women to get here, and the females to take over the shift. I'll catch him next time," Nigel says, grabbing his backpack.

"We have plenty of time before we have to clear out for the females. Go ask him—" The blare of the alarm cuts me off.

"Attention all males in Gino's. You have 20 minutes to finish your meals and exit the premises. Gentlemen, please pay your outstanding balances before departing the establishment."

"Twenty minutes? That's it?" Nigel says, looking around. "I can't be rushed if I'm going to do this."

"Hey Nigel, those shoes are lit," a voice booms from behind him. Nigel's eyes widen as he turns around. Decarion is within arm's reach from him, holding his jacket, ready to leave. We're his only table that hasn't cashed out yet.

"These? These old things—" Nigel stammers, pointing at the brand new shoes he's been bragging about for the past four days.

Decarion takes a breath, his eyes darting to the ceiling. "Listen, I've been waiting for over a year for you to ask me out, dropping hints nonstop. I'm not waiting anymore," Decarion states firmly. "You guys play Woodruff on Friday, right?" Nigel nods like a bobblehead on a dashboard. "Why don't we come back here after close, and I make you one of my specialty pizzas? It's an early night for the females, so we can have the place to ourselves. Gino won't care."

"Sounds...sounds—" Nigel stutters.

"Sounds great. He'll meet you outside of the locker room after the game, Decarion," I confirm, shoving my shoulder against Nigel, hoping to jolt him out of his stupidity. No such luck. Nigel just nods, wide-eyed and terrified. The dude's all talk.

Walking out of the restaurant, Nigel is floating on cloud nine. I haven't seen him this happy since Curtis bought him a ferret. Why anyone would want a ferret or buy another human being a ferret is beyond me, but it sure made Nigel happy. I like seeing him like this. And if he's this giddy, then maybe, just maybe, he'll get off my back about dating someone.

As we leave the restaurant, I notice the females are barricaded on the other side of the partition. I can clearly hear them giggling and chatting. They sound excited. I heard through the grapevine that their big dance was tonight. Supposedly, girls love a good reason to get all fancy, show off their clothes, and dance. Thank Authority that I don't have to do that—ever. Can't even imagine it.

I know I'm in the minority, but I wouldn't care at all if the females ate with us or around us. We're just people. I'm not sure why we have to separate out like this. My dads said the authorities of Before found this to be the best way for us to exist. Supposedly, men and women can't coexist together, because men are the superior beings, and women just hold them back. And Authority knows, my sperm father would never let us break one of the Laws of Life and Liberty.

CHAPTER 3
VICISSITUDE

"Sometimes the strength of motherhood is greater than natural laws."
(Barbara Kingsolver)

"This salad is everything," Marjorie moans. "I was starving, but needed to make sure my dress zipped today."

"Let me get this straight, your pile of spinach and kale, covered in lemon juice is everything you've ever dreamed of?" I ask, sauce dripping down my chin as I stuff yet another bite of pizza into my mouth. I love pizza, but I really wish the sauce wasn't so messy. It's basically just bread with tomato sauce. They say that Before, pizza was so much better. Covered in cheese. No way that could be good. I'd never eat anything that came out of an animal. The thought's repulsive. We do have many forms of cheese now, but nobody puts it on a pizza. Mainly, our cheese is made from birthing mother's breast milk. Yeah, not eating that either.

"Don't even start," she says, reaching over to dab at the sauce on my face.

I bolt backward. "Nice try, Mom, but I can wipe my own face. Shall I ask you to wipe my ass when I go to the bathroom too?"

"Oh, I love when you talk dirty." She laughs, before taking a drink of her water. She runs a stockinged foot up my leg, but I scoot my legs away from her. "Boo, you're no fun," she flirts.

"I'm fun. I'm lots of fun—just not in the middle of Gino's with half of our class sitting here," I explain. Marjorie rolls her eyes and takes another nibble of her scrumptious pile of grass.

"Hey Cissy, how's your mom?" Celeste Peltzer asks, grinning from ear to ear. I give her a "thumbs-up," indicating that she's just great. "Tell Ruth I miss working with her." I nod as my lips dip down, and my eyes narrow. Ever since Celeste volunteered on my mom's floor at the hospital, she's been obsessed with my mom. I catch a mumbled "MILF" as she walks away.

"I'm so jealous of that," Marjorie whines. "Nobody likes my moms."

"Are you seriously jealous of the fact that our friends want to hook up with my mom?" Marjorie and I are like hamsters on wheels. We just have the same conversations —or fights—over and over again.

My egg-release mom, Ruth, is the charge nurse on the cardiology floor at Female General in town. She busted her butt to be Integral Nurse, which is the closest thing a woman can be to being a doctor, but she failed the final evaluations. Now, Mama just runs the entire floor and oversees all the other nurses and volunteers. She really wanted to perform surgeries, but only Integral Nurses can do that.

My mom can do everything else, but operate. It drives her crazy.

Once, when one of our neighbor's appendix burst, my mom had everything she needed at our house, so she just took it out. The woman was fine, the scar minimal. My mom was still charged with "Activity Unbecoming of a Woman," and had to donate her next three paychecks to Male General. She was livid. It makes her absolutely bonkers when women do not receive the same health care and health choices that men do. Women aren't the preferred gender of Eka, so oftentimes, our health and longevity of life are jeopardized. Ekian Authority will do everything in their power to save a man, but a woman doesn't receive the same. As a child, I struggled with this notion, but as I get older, it does make sense to me. Men run Eka; we just live here. It seems fair to me that they prioritize men over us. They are the stronger and smarter sex. But, we should all be granted equal health care.

My passive mom, Gloria, is a teacher at Female United Elementary. She absolutely loves her job. It doesn't even bother her that she has to work seven days a week, ten-hour days. She loves it. She doesn't care at all. Teachers are the only professionals that aren't permitted to take time off of work. Mom loves kids, though, so she doesn't mind.

It's sad that Mom couldn't be impregnated, due to being a teacher, because she'd need time off to recover from birth. So, Mama carried Cleave and me. It does make sense to me; not all students can attend school every day. Schools need teachers there for whenever students can attend. Sometimes, kids get sick or have other plans, and when they do, they need to make it up. It's up to the teachers to be at the school whenever students need to come and make up that time and education.

I heard the male teachers do not have to do that. As long as a male teacher coaches a sport, he is permitted to take the weekends off as well as any other days that he may need to get his athletes in shape. Mama agrees with that completely, because she wants to make sure the athletes don't get hurt. She's always worried about everyone's safety and well-being.

I worry about Mom's safety and well-being. I think they should figure out a way to give teachers a break. Even when we are on break from school and have weeks off, Mom has to go in to the building to make her lesson plans, get them approved through the Authority, study and research more, and help students who are struggling. I am so glad I've never had problems in school. Assigned academics during breaks would kill me; I just know it.

Marjorie's eyes widen. "Babe, Celeste Peltzer thinks your mom is hot."

"We just establish—"

"That means, she thinks **you're** hot. I'm doomed. You're definitely going to leave me for her." Marjorie pounds her head on the table just centimeters from her rabbit food.

"First of all, Celeste Peltzer is not my type," I explain. "Secondly, I'm not going anywhere. And third, how did you even come up with that?"

"You look just like Mama. You have the same green eyes, gorgeous mocha skin, and perfectly sectioned and braided hair. You're twins almost!" she screeches, and then immediately covers her mouth. "Sorry," she mumbles.

"It's fine. I am a twin. It's no secret," I say, shrugging.

"I know, Cissy, but you hate talking about him in public. You always end up—" I wipe the corners of my eyes and shake my head. "Crying," she finishes.

Marjorie slides out of the booth and slides in next to me, wrapping an arm around my shoulder.

"I'm fine," I say, taking a deep breath to compose myself. "It is what it is."

"Oh, it is not. You hate that phrase. It's right up there with 'sorry, not sorry,' so I know you're not okay." She pushes against me in a playful nudge.

"I do hate those sayings." I laugh, closing my eyes as I refuse to let more tears flow. "I just hate—hate—"

"Hate that you can't see Cleave whenever you want," Marjorie finishes my sentence. "It's dumb. I totally agree with you. But look on the bright side; you do get to see him once a month. At least Authority passed that law a few years ago."

"Oh yeah, so lucky about that. Gotta love our 30-minute supervised visitations," I say, as my eyes roll to the ceiling. "It makes no sense. And it's even worse that Mama is never allowed to see him. So stupid."

Marjorie shrugs. "Those are the rules. We can't do anything about it." She glides the wand of her lip gloss across her lips and then puckers them.

"What happened to the Marjorie who just told me to start asking questions?"

"You know what I mean. We can't change the laws, but you can at least start to wonder about life Before," she says. She takes one of my braids in her fingers. "Ready to get out of here?" she asks, winking at me.

"Ummm, yeah, sure," I say, taking a final bite of my pizza just as my tracker screeches a warning bell, signifying that I have ten more calories left for the day.

I'm a rule follower. It's what I do—what I've been taught to do. But for the life of me, I cannot understand why I can't spend more time with Cleave. I also cannot understand why that time has to be supervised either. What are we going to do? Cleave is the only male I've ever spoken to.

Once, I was walking into Gino's and a guy came out of the restaurant late, because he was in the bathroom. He was rushing so fast to get out of there. My guess is he didn't want to pay the fine for being in there past male occupancy —or he needed to get to another bathroom after eating something expired at Gino's. He was so oblivious to anyone around him that he crashed into me throwing me backwards against the wall. He mumbled a pathetic "Sorry," and that was the extent of me speaking to a man. Thrilling. Now, they ensure that the entire building is cleared out before the employees are even permitted inside.

There was a huge march years ago at Authority Central demanding that men and women be permitted to congregate in the same areas, but that backfired. They only tightened the reins more. We were just recently granted permission for siblings to interact with strict supervision from a male Authority officer.

Cleave is fascinating. I love talking to him. His dads seem so much fun. They're older. They'd both tried to donate their sperm for years, but something stopped them from being productive. They got lucky when Mama had him. They had to sign an airtight contract that they'd never attempt production again if they were given a baby. His dads agreed immediately. So many people think that they need to be genetically connected to be considered family. That's not even remotely true. Family is created with love, commitment, time, and respect. Even I know that.

When I first met Cleave, I was so nervous. It was the only time in my life I understood what it meant to feel butterflies in my stomach. Actually, they felt like hornets trying to sting their way right out of my belly. I'd never been around a male before, let alone one I was supposed to talk to face-to-face, one-on-one with. I was terrified.

Needless to say, my fears were heightened and on edge the moment we met on Authority grounds. Cleave took one look at me and said, "Thank Authority, I got the good looks. You must have the brains." His smile spanned from ear to ear, the same smile that I'd seen daily in the mirror. His mocha skin is the same shade of mine, his hair more unruly than mine, but his eyes have more of a mischievous sparkle than I could ever dream of. He's the male version of me. And, I'm not afraid of myself, so why would I be afraid of him? His dig was just the icebreaker we both needed. Our friendship, our sibling bond, was solidified right in the moment.

~

"Are you even with me right now?" Marjorie asks, waving her hand in front of my face. We're tangled in the sheets of her bed, legs intertwined, dresses askew on the floor.

"Of course," I say, kissing the end of her nose. "Where else would I be?"

"You seem a million miles away right now. Are you thinking about Celeste Peltzer?" She laughs, rolling on top of me, pinning my arms above my head. "Because I think I can take her. Have you seen my muscles?" Marjorie flexes. Although she is petite, her biceps look like grapefruits bulging right out of her upper arms.

"Oh yeah, you got me. Celeste's everything I've ever wanted in a woman. I'm thinking about asking Mama if we can share her," I take a stab at humor. Jokes and humor aren't my things.

"That's just disgusting." Marjorie grimaces. "But seriously, what were you thinking about?"

"I'm not sure if the truth is any better," I admit.

"Try me."

"Cleave," I answer, knowing that she hates when I get sentimental about my brother.

"Ewww, your lips were on me, and you were thinking about a boy? That is worse," she says, sliding back off of me. She pretends to gag, choking back fake vomit.

"Not like that," I say, rolling my eyes. "I just wish there was a way that we could spend more time together, do things together, and just, you know, be."

"Well, there isn't, so just get over it, and get back on me," she says, tugging at me.

"It's not that easy," I say, rolling out of her reach. "What if you couldn't see Mallory anymore? What if one day someone told you that you and your sister could no longer hang out, eat meals together, or sit up all night and talk?"

"Would I get to keep all of her clothes and makeup?" she asks.

CHAPTER 4
RIOT

"A man's mind stretched by new ideas may never return to its original dimensions."
(Oliver Wendell Holmes Jr.)

"Why are we talking about this now?" I ask, sick of the cycle of this conversation. "I don't want to be a lawyer. Never have. Never will."

"Your resume is abysmal, Riot. You have to start thinking about your future," my father says, rubbing his bald head in frustration.

"Why? You think about it enough for both of us," I quip. The fire in my father's eyes proves that I've gone too far. Yet, again.

"Luther, come on. Riot's fine. He doesn't need to know what he wants just yet." My passive dad is always coming to my rescue. His light eyes glisten. Even his eyes are kind. I'm so thankful my dad does most of the parenting, and my father does most of the grumbling and complaining. The nights that my dad and I are alone are my favorite nights.

We bond and make memories like best friends. People say you shouldn't be friends with your parents, but I challenge anyone to meet my dad, Atticus, and not immediately want him as a confidante.

"College starts in five months. He needs a plan," my father argues.

"He has a plan. He's going to college. That's enough for now. He's only seventeen. Why does he have to have his entire life mapped out already?" my dad reasons.

"Because Atticus, he has no motivation, no drive. He's going to end up living with us for the rest of his life," my father yells, pounding on the table. The vein in his forehead is bulging right out of his head.

My dad and I both jump as my pasta bowl dances on the table from the force of his fist.

My dad looks at me and asks, "Are you sure there isn't anything that really interests you, something that you can see yourself doing for the rest of your life?"

There is. There definitely is, but I would never tell either one of them. The law is their life. Authority knows; they'd never let me do one thing to break that law.

"I mean, maybe I could teach—or coach lacrosse." I shrug.

"Coach? You hate lacrosse," my dad states firmly, knowing the truth about that at least.

"You wanted an answer. I gave you an answer." I grab my backpack and head out of the house.

"Riot! Get back here!" my father yells as I slam the door behind me.

How do I look my two law-abiding fathers in the eyes and tell them that what I want to do is illegal? That would go over real well. My dads fight for laws and rights, but I don't think they fight for what's *actually* right. Things they taught me that I certainly didn't learn in school are to think and to ask questions. Things I can't even do at school, at home, or anywhere, really. My dads know information about Before, but they never share it with me—no matter how much I ask and beg. It's against Authority to discuss the past. None of what goes on makes sense to me. Why do they teach me to think and ask questions if they never tell me anything? I wish I had access to real knowledge. I'd love to read and know more about Before. I have little to no access to books. They've been completely restricted—or totally destroyed. And technology (where the real answers are) is illegal to anyone under the age of 25. Apparently, the human brain isn't fully developed until 25. I think that's bullshit. But even then, Authority is monitoring every single thing on technology, so I bet that isn't even all that accessible.

I park at a local car charging station, plug my car in, and pay for a four-hour charge. Grabbing my backpack, I head down the road toward the forest—vigilant of any cars that pass me. Not many pass today, which helps even out my nerves.

As I walk into the woods, I look around, making sure nobody is watching. I'm not allowed in the forest today. It's an even numbered day, so only females can take hikes, climb trees, or have picnics. But the place I go to is so secluded that nobody notices me when I'm there. It is deep in the woods on the other side of the mountain that separates our community with the female community. The females have the modest, and if we're being honest, the poor part of town. It's in an area that if men were permitted to go to, they wouldn't step foot in. The Female Faction is desolate and drab.

Now, the Male Faction is luxurious with beautiful

homes, lavish swimming pools, and upscale architecture. Men live large in Eka. Women live with bare essentials, but they make it work. I've never heard of any female complaining or even trying to change their living environments. Women are just happy spending time and chatting with other women. They don't need money or extravagant things to be fulfilled. They're just always pleased with whatever they have.

Nearly tripping over a root and off the ledge, I grab a jagged piece of a boulder on the mountain to maintain my balance. It's quite a trek to get to this area, and there are some dangerous edges to the walk. Once you get past the swimming hole, picnic area, and easy-to-hike trail, the route gets a little more treacherous, so I'm typically the only person who ventures out past the public domain. Back where I go, nobody is ever there. It's quite the hike and not easy for people to navigate. I've been coming out here for ages, so it's a breeze for me—unless I'm not paying attention, and I stumble like I just did.

Occasionally, I see this one girl, but she's never seen me. I've watched her from time to time. All she ever does is lie on her back and look up at the sky. She always looks deep in thought, but from what I've heard, very few girls have original thoughts.

I make my way to my favorite spot, a tree canopied area, plush with vegetation near a small cave on the mountainside. I go deep into the briars, getting pricked half a dozen times before reaching my hand in the little cave and pulling out my concealed wooden box. Just the sight of the mahogany rectangle relieves all of my tension and anxiety. The cedar box has a pungent woody scent that with just one whiff releases the tightness in my shoulders. As I open the box, I marvel at all the vibrant colors. The law that men cannot paint, draw, or create any form of art is absurd. I wish my dads would battle Authority to allow me to do what I love—and what I'm the best at. But they don't know my secret. It's one of the many things that I cannot share with them. My only—and I mean only—joy is creating beauty from nothing or creating fear and pain from scratch. I can do anything with my hands.

I take out a scroll of paper and a piece of charcoal, knowing exactly what I'm going to draw today. Color is out. Darkness and doom are in. Beginning to scrawl all over the paper, I thank Authority for Jase Johnson, a teammate on my lacrosse team. He can get anything—for a price. I have no idea how he secures our forbidden items, but without him, I'd have no outlet for my pent-up feelings and cravings to create. We have a solid agreement. He gets me what I need. I pay him exorbitantly. And neither one of us ever rats the other out. We'd both get fined and charged with "Activity Unbecoming of a Man." My dads would have my ass.

I love drawing her. Her features are still so clear in my head. I know eventually my memories will fade. I'll forget the vibrancy of her hair, the curve of her jawline, or the gleam in her eye when she came up with a mischievous plan. But for now, I relish in the memories and draw the perfect portrait.

Just as I finish my masterpiece, a booming voice echoes in my ears. "What the actual--?" The tree-gazing girl. Her voice is shrill and terrified. Fuck. Not again. I'm done. Screwed. It's all over.

I jump up, stuffing all of my materials into the box. I can't put it all back in the briars without her seeing it. "It's cool. I'm leaving." I scramble around trying to get away as fast as I can.

"Don't come near me!" she screams, backing away, grabbing a stick. Her eyes are wide, riddled with fear.

I'm nowhere near her. I'm moving backwards, not breaking eye contact with her. "I'm not. I'm outta here." Stuffing the box into my backpack, I know how truly dangerous that choice is. This box cannot come home with me. I turn to leave.

"Did you kill her?" Her question stops me dead in my tracks. "Don't lie! I saw whose face that was on that picture."

It's a punch to the gut, a pain I've felt for months, the worst months of my life. The loneliest six months of my life. "Kill her?" I ask, turning around to face the accusation. I feel the bile rising in my stomach, the burning sensation familiar and welcome. "Yeah, I guess I did," I admit right before I vomit.

CHAPTER 5
VICISSITUDE

"Those who deny freedom to others deserve it not for themselves." (Abraham Lincoln)

I totally hated dance class. All females are required to take dance classes from the age of three until they are nine-years-old. I was downright terrible. No rhythm. No grace. No coordination. Nothing. Supposedly, dance makes us strong, lithe, flexible, graceful, coordinated, and as always...thin. My dance teachers loved my look, my exotic features and long, thick braids. So, when I started dance, I was front and center with this beautiful, fiery, redheaded little girl. We became instant friends. However, little by little, I found myself in the back left corner of every dance routine we did. At some of the shows, they had me so far to the left that my moms couldn't see me behind the curtain. I'm pretty sure it was intentional to tuck me way back there. Yeah, I was really bad.

Lizzie Griffin stayed front and center. Not only was she beautiful, she was an incredible dancer. Her feet legit looked like they never even touched the floor. This girl glided through air—even as a toddler. She was a natural. We all noticed it even before we acknowledged that we couldn't compete with her. Moving in the back of the line of competent dancers ended up forcing a wedge between us. Her moms treated me like my ogre-like abilities were contagious, and she might catch my lack of rhythm. It wasn't long before our friendship fizzled out. However, I always liked Lizzie, and she always liked me. Our circles just didn't cross anymore.

Last year, everyone noticed how happy and full of life she became. Lizzie was always sweet and kind, but she was pretty reserved, very serious about dance. Then suddenly at school, she was different. The quiet and serious Lizzie morphed into a lively, fun, and upbeat teen girl. There was a positivity to her that none of us had ever witnessed before. Woman, her bliss was infectious.

Then, the unthinkable happened. Lizzie was dead. We were devastated and confused. When the news hit, it shook our entire community. Suicide. Lizzie Griffin hanged herself in the woods—in the same spot I go every chance I can to stare up at the vastness of the sky. Her moms were immediately arrested.

Parents are held accountable if their children end their lives. It's imperative that parents check in on the well-being and mental health of their children on a regular basis. Females are required to attend at least a one-hour therapy session each month, starting at ten-years-old. Lizzie's moms should've been cued in on her depressed state. It's a privilege and honor to be permitted to parent. If parents fail to raise their children with love, understanding, and forgiveness, then the child's failure is on them. Mrs. and Mrs. Griffin will serve five years in our Women's Confinery —separated from one another. The Authority dissolved their partnership the moment Lizzie's body was removed from the tree.

My moms and I felt terribly for them. Sure, they were elitist when it came to dance and treated me like a filthy pariah, but woman, did they love Lizzie. She was their entire world. There's no part of me that believes they're to blame for Lizzie's death. But to be honest, I never believed she completed suicide either. Marjorie and I could never wrap our heads around the fact that the happiest, giddiest girl we knew would end her life, knowing her moms would be separated and confined for five years, and Lizzie wouldn't receive any sort of burial or end of life ceremony. The Lizzie I knew wouldn't do that. Whether she was focused and reserved or gleeful and giddy, Lizzie would never do such a thing to her parents.

"Get away from me!" I scream. "Murderer! Help!" I start running for the opening in the brush when I'm yanked back by my jacket, catching a branch. I fly back and thud hard against the chest of the very murderer I'm running from.

I open my mouth ready to bellow as loudly as I can, when his hand covers my mouth. "Shhh, please," he whispers in my ear, his breath hot on my neck. I squirm, trying to escape his grip and my imminent doom. "I want to let you go, pretend like none of this happened. Can I trust you?"

I nod, my body quaking with fear. He loosens his grip, and I break from his clutches, whipping around and clocking him right on the side of the head. His lack of pain and shocked expression spurns me into overdrive as my shoe connects powerfully with his groin. The muffled yelp as he doubles over gives me the courage to plow my knee right into his nose. He crumples to the ground. Just as I'm about to kick him again, I notice it. A gold locket escapes the collar of his shirt. A gold locket I've seen many times in my life as she danced around the stage, the locket glittering in the spotlight.

Lizzie's locket.

"You stole her fucking necklace too," I scream, hysterically as I kick him again right in the head.

Seconds before my foot meets his skull, he muffles a painful, "I loved her."

I never realized how long people lay there, corpse-like, when they're knocked out. But jeez, this male is out. He's breathing, so I'm off the hook there. A woman would lose her life if she injured a male in any way. Lizzie was probably the one getting him those forbidden art supplies. No wonder he loved her. Or thought he loved her. You'd have to love the person breaking the Laws of Life and Liberty for you and risking her life, so you can be a criminal. Disgusted, I want to kick him again. How dare he use her like that? Loved her? Yeah right.

Men do not love women in these parts of the world. I heard that they do in other countries, but definitely not in this one. Once we united and became Eka, many restrictions were put into place. Technology was the first to go. Second was the integration of men and women. And the third one was travel. I would love to travel. I've heard so many stories about these other communities, but I never know what to believe. If a teacher tells me, then I tend to believe it. But when Marjorie or Cleave tell me things, I just basically feel like they're just trying to make themselves sound smart and worldly.

Supposedly though, there are places that have snow, white fluffy, cold fuzz that falls from the sky. And it's right here in Eka, but much further north. I would love to see that. But, we're only permitted to live where we're born.

There are, however, a few exceptions to that. Authority can reposition people to other places if they are needed somewhere else. It's very rare. My moms know people who have been relocated for their careers, but I've never known anyone who left or who showed up where we are. After travel was banned, people stopped being curious about other places and other lives. People just worry about themselves now and their own environments. They couldn't change the covenants anyway, so why bother? However, that didn't stop Authority for making all sorts of new guidelines and rules. Every fifth grade student, male or female, has to memorize the Laws of Life and Liberty:

1. No person under the age of 25 shall be permitted to use, activate, control, or view any form of technology. Individuals over the age of 25 will have controlled access to technology based upon his/her occupation, mental health, and necessity.
2. Males and females are prohibited from congregating, conversing, cohabitating, or co-mingling. All individuals must remain their birth gender. All individuals must adorn their bodies in gender-appropriate clothing.
3. A person's geographical status may never change after his/her birth.
4. Every person from the age of 10 and up will be required to learn the proper techniques in handling and using firearms. All individuals are permitted and encouraged to carry a firearm at all times.
5. Occupations will be based upon a series of evaluations, competencies, and familial status.

No person will obtain a career that does not fall into his/her gender at birth.
6. No male will earn a living less than any female in Eka. Only females will be required to pay taxes on items and properties.
7. Animals will remain as pets or free to roam their own habitat. Animals will never be used as clothing, food, or entertainment.
8. Any form of alcohol or mind-altering substance is prohibited for all females and controlled for all males.
9. No individual is permitted to worship any false idols. Authority is the only guiding leadership of Eka.
10. Authority may add, omit, or amend any governing Law of Liberty at any given time for any given reason without approval of the people of Eka.

Those were the first ten. Since I was in fifth grade, they added sixteen more of them. I'm required to know them by heart, but there is no test for me to recite the laws in front of an evaluation board. I feel sad for the fifth graders now, because there are just so many—and they even added subcategories under the main laws. Authority added our trackers and our weight control six years ago. I cannot even fathom a world without trackers. How would anyone ever find another person?

We are permitted to leave our trackers off each week for a total of 12 hours for charging and maintenance. I never take mine off though. My moms would freak if they couldn't locate me any second they so desired. And so would Marjorie.

I'm totally fine with the Laws of Liberty. I mean; I'd love to spend more time with Cleave and see this snow I've heard rumors about, but other than that, the laws all seem fair to me. Why would my moms need more money than they have? We're fine. I know Authority has our best interest in mind. They're the entire country's parents in a sense. They know what's best for us.

"Fuck," he grumbles, applying pressure to his head. "Where'd you learn to fight like that?" I jump up, holding his backpack firmly against my chest.

"Start talking, dick stick," I grit through my teeth. "What happened to Lizzie Griffin?" He rolls over onto his side, spitting blood out of his mouth. Whoa. Blood? I'm pretty badass.

"You know what happened. Everyone knows. She killed herself." He coughs, pushing up onto his hands and knees.

"Then how'd you get her locket? Did you just happen to rip it off her cold, dead body?" I ask, my voice shrill. "Did you kill her for it?"

He sits back on his knees, his hands gripping his face and head. "Lizzie gave it to me."

"Fuck off, I'm taking this to Authority," I say, shrugging his backpack onto my back. I'm so pissed. I'm always carrying my firearm. Today, I just wanted a peaceful day in the woods—alone. I didn't want to carry my backpack. And of course, the day I need it is the day it's on my nightstand. Now, if he comes after me, I'm dead.

"Cissy, stop!" he screams. "Please, you can't. I'll tell you everything."

CHAPTER 6
RIOT

"Life beats down and crushes the soul and art reminds you that you have one." (Stella Adler)

The first time Jase secured some paint supplies for me, I was terrified. I kept them hidden inside my mattress for weeks. Then one day, I just decided to put them in my backpack and head out into the woods. I'd always liked going out here, but it wasn't the norm for me. I figured I could tell anyone who saw me that I uncovered the supplies in the forest, shrugging it off as if they were some girl's who left them. It was a perfect alibi.

I was painting a picture of my lacrosse team's logo, when Lizzie Griffin walked right up to me, and said, "That's pretty boring—and flat. It needs dimension." Lizzie plopped right down next to me as if it were perfectly normal for a man and woman to talk to one another. "If you're going to break the Laws of Liberty, then you need to put your whole heart and soul into your craft. I'm an art 4 student. I can help you." My jaw hung as my eyes widened.

A girl.

A girl in the forest.

A girl in the forest was talking to me.

A girl in the forest was talking to me, and she wasn't afraid about it one bit.

I was mesmerized by her audacity, courage, and honesty. And her eye for art. I could use her help, because I had no idea what it meant for my painting to be flat.

And what the hell was "dimension?"

Truthfully, I'd been waiting my entire life, well my entire teenage life, for someone to challenge me, for something to catapult my feelings of complacency in this humdrum existence of Eka. And there I was, face-to-face with the very catalyst that was going to ignite all of my pent up frustrations, questions, and anxiety about this community that we all blindly succumbed to like sheep following their shepherd.

Our friendship was immediate. Lizzie was a powerhouse. She was smart, articulate, brave, and unbelievably talented. She'd dance for me with her long red curls swirling about her as she glided through the forest, light and graceful on her toes. I could watch her for hours. And I did. She'd dance, and I'd draw or paint. Time didn't exist when we were together. I never cared about what time I needed to be home, if I had homework, if I needed to be at lacrosse, or anything. All that mattered was spending time with her, being with her.

I didn't understand it. Nigel and I have fun together. The joking and jibes never stop. He's my man, my ride or die. But being with Lizzie was everything. I could be myself —never had to try with her. There were times when we couldn't stop talking, telling, or recapping stories. Every word would just flow right into the next one. There was never a moment of uncomfortable silence or awkward pauses. Other times, it was silent and serene, comfortable and familiar. She'd dance. I'd create. No words were spoken, but yet, everything was understood. I couldn't wrap my head around this type of friendship, this comfort and fulfillment. I'd never experienced it before. Neither had Lizzie.

Her death destroyed me. And I couldn't talk about it ever—to anyone. Not Nigel. Not my dads. Nobody. Our friendship was forbidden, so my emotions were taboo. I couldn't cry. I couldn't feel. I couldn't do anything, but go out into the woods and pour my feelings and thoughts into whatever creative outlet I'd chosen for the day. And now, I'm screwed. This crazy as shit girl is threatening Authority on me. It's truth and die or grovel and lie.

"How in Authority's sake do you know my name?" Cissy asks, bringing me back from my reverie, her eyes narrowed to minute jade slivers.

"You sucked at dance," I say, my shoulders lifting slightly, hoping she catches the nonchalance in my voice and backs off a bit. "By the way, I'm Riot."

I didn't think her eyes could get any smaller. "First of all, I didn't ask, nor do I care. And how would you even know that?" she asks, her words gravelly and precise.

"We talked about everything—and anything. That's what friends do; that's what we did," I say, my head falling back onto the tree behind me. "We even talked about you."

"Why me?"

"Because you were here, looking up at the damn sky like you always do," I say as my eyes close, remembering Lizzie's words. "You were her first friend and the first friend her moms drove off, because 'you weren't good enough for Lizzie.' Apparently, you were the first of many," I explain, finally looking directly into her eyes.

The green eyes staring back at me are wide, full of

surprise. "Lizzie Griffin was friends with a boy? No way! She'd never break the Laws of Liberty like that."

"'Fraid so." I click my tongue, running my hand through my hair. My shirt sticks to my body, damp with sweat. It's not even hot. My body always betrays me like this when my nerves are in overdrive.

"No way!" she says again, her head shaking back and forth emphatically. "How? How can that possibly be? We aren't supposed to talk to boys at all."

"Do you follow every Law of Liberty?" I ask, surprised.

"Ummm, yes!" she says, puffing her chest in pride. "And so should you." My laugh escapes me before I even have a chance to stop it. "You think that's funny? Are you trying to end up in the Male Confinery?"

"There's no doubt in my mind I'll end up there someday," I say, standing as Cissy's features blur. I grab the tree to stabilize my wobbles. "Whoa, you've got quite the strength in those legs. Ever consider soccer?" I don't know how I'm going to explain a concussion to my dads or my coach.

"Very funny. You know girls can't play sports," she says, backing away from me.

"You sure could." I walk toward her. "Now, may I please have my bag, so I can get home?"

She looks at my backpack as if she forgot she was holding it. She tosses it at my feet. "Here, but you really should get rid of those paints and charcoal."

"No chance," I say, unzipping the pack and securing the wooden box into the hidden compartment of my backpack.

"Hey," she asks, twisting her fingers around each other.

Lizzie was right about her. This Cissy girl does have soft, kind eyes—even when she's throwing punches and low blows to the groin. Her features are strong; her dark skin looks soft and smooth. The long braids give her an attractive edge, bordering on threatening. I'd like to paint this girl and highlight the beauty that she probably can't see with her own eyes.

I stop, raising an eyebrow. "Yeah?"

"Do you know why she did it?"

"That's not my story to tell," I admit, dropping my head and retracing my steps out of the woods.

∽

"Tell me everything," Nigel says, getting into my car. "Oh my Authority, don't leave anything out."

"Dude, there's nothing to tell. I got a mushroom sub to go. Decarion asked me if I wanted a drink. I said, 'no'. He threw in a bag of chips, and I left."

"That's it? Did he say anything about me at all?"

"Not one word."

"Did it seem like he was looking for me? Like over your shoulder? Expecting me to be there?"

"Nope."

Nigel is losing it. He hasn't heard from Decarion since their date Friday. Granted, Nigel hasn't tried to contact him or anything. It's been the most annoying 48 hours of my existence. Nigel wants so much out of life, but he does nothing to go get it. He just sits and waits for everything to happen to him or for him. Makes me crazy.

Nigel just bangs his head on the dashboard, mumbling, "Crap. Crap. Crap," over and over again.

"Oh wait, I forgot," I say, turning to look at him. "I told him that you had a blast the other night. And he said that he did too. He may have also said that he's dying for you to show up at work tonight when he gets off to hang out at his house later."

"You're a total ass, you know that right?" Nigel's smile is infectious.

"Oh, I'm an ass? The one who scored you date number one **and** two is an ass? Let's not forget how you've been just waiting around for him when all you had to do was stop into Gino's and get what you wanted."

There's so much life to live; yet so many people just walk the straight and narrow and never take any risks. It blows my mind. I want so much out of life. I'm not just going to sit around and wait. "And Nigel, please don't screw this up. Decarion is great."

"I know that," he says. "It's just scary. You don't get it, man. You've never been in love, never hurt like I did after Curtis. It sucks."

I was sitting in Statistics and Probability when my instructor announced that there'd been a completed suicide. The murmurs in the class drowned out his words. I heard "female," but nothing else. They wouldn't release the minor's name. It was four days later that I learned that it was Lizzie. And Nigel thinks I don't understand pain. How about pain that you can't even talk about or express?

CHAPTER 7
VICISSITUDE

*"I learned to question everything. But I feel like everything is so divisive now. Going against the grain would be to **not** be divisive and be inclusive. That's the disruptive way to go about it."*
(Mike Dirnt)

"Moms, can I talk to you?" I sit down on their bed. Mama puts her word puzzle away, while Mom barely looks up from her grading. Mama leaves the hospital at the hospital. I love that she doesn't have to bring her work home with her. Poor Mom is always grading papers, doing her lesson plans, making bulletin boards, or changing her classroom all around. Mom would be beautiful if she had time to be. Sadly, she always looks so frazzled, worn out, and overwhelmed. Her blonde hair is always a mess—either in a ratty bun or hanging down and scraggly. In the last few years, she's really aged. Her eyes are sunken; she's so tiny—nearly emaciated. Teaching does her in. Truthfully, I've never even seen a beautiful or well-put-together teacher. They all looked burned out like Mom does.

I have to ask them about men and women. Can they be friends? I cannot imagine a world where men and women interact cordially and fondly. That's not reality here—literally unfathomable. And yet, I haven't stopped thinking about that Riot guy since the day I knocked him out. If he is telling the truth, then my heart aches for him and his loss. Lizzie was a loss for everyone.

"Of course honey, what's up?" Mama asks, looking at me over her glasses as they slip down her nose.

"Have you ever—have either of you ever had a male friend before?"

Mom tucks her light hair behind her ears and releases a long, huffy breath. "We have." She clears her throat. "Well, Mama has."

"I have," she admits, shifting in the bed. "Don't look so surprised, Cissy." I feel like I can pick my jaw up off of my lap. I figured they'd probably talked to men a time or two for one reason or another, but to formulate a friendship with one is absolutely unheard of. "We're in our late 40s, of course we've done and seen things that you know nothing about."

"And things that we'll never tell our daughter," Mom adds in.

"Listen Cissy, you don't spend over 40 years on this earth without stepping outside of the rules, without trying new things every now and then. We can't live here our entire lives without meeting all walks of life no matter how hard Authority tries," Mama says.

"Ruth, I don't think now is the ti—"

"Gloria, how long are we going to protect her from the truth? She's about to graduate from high school for Authority's sake. It's time she knew," Mama says, patting the bed next to her. "I'm going to make this as painless as possible."

"What do you mean 'painless'—?"

"She means for her," Mom says, reaching for Mama's hand. "Are you sure, Ruth?"

"I'm sure. It's time, Gloria. Long overdue," Mama says, pulling a breath in, closing her eyes, resting her head against the headboard, and finally releasing a slow, slow breath. "I had a sister."

Mama's sister, Portia, was five years older than she was. Portia treated Mama like she was her baby, always taking care of her, coddling her, doing everything for Mama to the point that Granny Meredith would often remind Portia who the mother was.

After Portia's first year of college, she got a job as a server in a restaurant. Granny Meredith didn't want her working during her time off, but Portia insisted that she needed her own money, her freedom, and her chance at growing up on her own. One night, during the shift change, a fire broke out in the restaurant, all hands were needed on deck to save the restaurant. There was a little girl stuck in the bathroom. Her mother couldn't get the bathroom door open, and the flames were spreading fiercely and furiously.

The sirens for the fire were being drowned out by the alarms for the gender shift change. Women needed to evacuate, and the men were due to enter. The door to the bathroom wouldn't budge. The flames were breathing down Portia and the mother's back. Portia was screaming for someone—anyone—to help them. The men stood at the barrier, refusing to break the Laws of Life and Liberty.

Until one man did.

Alex Jackson grabbed a chair, charging the door and crushing against it as mightily as he could. The doorjamb splintered, and Alex was able to kick the door the rest of the way in, freeing the little girl from the bathroom. He threw the little girl over his shoulder and bolted for the door just as Portia's arm was engulfed in flames. Portia screamed. Alex nearly tossed the girl to her mother, grabbed a coat, threw it on Portia, and tackled her to the ground. Once the flames were extinguished, he cradled Portia in his arms and brought her outside. The gasps from the onlookers were deafening. A woman was in the arms of a man.

Portia couldn't resist the feeling that overcame her. Immediately, she knew that she'd never feel for a woman the way she felt about Alex Jackson. In his arms, Portia felt secure—and for the first time ever in her life—complete. She knew by the way his eyes penetrated her entire being that the feeling was mutual. Portia and Alex hid their feelings, telling nobody. But every night when she got off of work, he was waiting to go in. Alex was biding his time, trying to figure out a way to talk to her yet again, to hold her as he'd dreamed about for months. Meanwhile, Portia couldn't stop thinking about the man who saved her.

After four full months, Alex simply left a note on her car that read "If you're ready for an adventure, meet me at 2423 Delilah Ave tonight at midnight." It was signed "Your Fire Extinguisher." Portia was more than ready.

That night, she snuck out. She had no idea where Delilah Ave was, so she stopped at a charging station store and bought a map, a map she had no idea how to read. She was determined to figure it out on her own. It was time she used her wits and stopped relying on everyone else to navigate the paths of her future.

An hour later than she was supposed to arrive, Portia knocked on the dilapidated door of 2423. A man with a long, gray beard and kind eyes asked, "Can I help you, Little Missy?"

Terrified, Portia spun on her heels, ready to flee. "Wait!"

The voice she'd heard in her dreams for months stopped her in her tracks. Alex had waited for her. And now they were together. Again.

"The Delilah," it turned out was an underground sanctuary for men and women to be together. Nightly, there were over ten brave couples who couldn't resist their desires to be together.

For nearly a year, Alex and Portia worked the system and searched for ways to be together when society so fiercely had forbidden their love. Sadly, the unthinkable happened. Authority uncovered the truth about "The Delilah" and demolished the entire building. There were no protests to save "The Delilah," because nobody would admit that they knew of its existence.

Alex and Portia concocted a plan to head north and leave Eka for once and for all. They'd heard that north of Eka was a country where men and women could love one another openly and safely without the threat of punishment or death. Just a few miles before the northern border, Alex and Portia were caught and detained. Both were placed in Confinery. But Authority needed to make a statement, a statement loud enough for the entire country to hear. Heterosexuality would not be tolerated in Eka. Alex and Portia were publicly executed, and both sets of their parents had to serve seven years in Confinery for not raising their children to adhere to and respect The Laws of Life and Liberty.

"Mama! Why'd you never tell me this? I'm so sorry." I wrap my arms around her, tucking my head under her chin.

"Baby, I've always wanted to tell you about Portia, but it's hard to talk about—and illegal to speak of the past." She runs her hand along my head, comforting me. "I loved her so much. And I didn't want you to ever think badly of me—or my family. Portia made some very bad decisions. But to know about Portia, you have to know her whole story."

"Heterosexuality is forbidden in this country, Cissy," Mom says, "but that doesn't mean that people don't have those feelings. It may be wrong in the eyes of Authority, but to those who feel that deeply for another person, it only feels right to them. Does that make sense?"

"Don't you think being linear is gross?" I ask.

"It's not our place to decide that. Portia and Alex loved each other just as much as your mom and I do. What if people thought we shouldn't love each other like we do?" Mama says, gripping Mom's hand harder. "Love is love, baby."

"Yeah but—"

"No buts, it's true. I just wish Portia and Alex could've made it out alive. I'd love to know they were living up north with a family of their own."

"Right, like anyone would allow a man and a woman to raise a baby together," I say, rolling my eyes. "They'd never grant Portia permission to be inseminated."

Mama and Mom look at one another. Mama bites her lip just as Mom lets out a giant laugh. "That's a story for another day, Cissy," Mom says, rubbing her eyes and shaking her head.

"Or for now," Mama says, "she's about to graduate, you know? She's way too young to be this naïve."

"Authority help me," Mom groans, resting her head on the headboard, "it's going to be one long night."

CHAPTER 8
RIOT

"Honesty is often very hard. The truth is often painful. But the freedom it can bring is worth the trying." (Fred Rogers)

"Riot! Get your head out of your ass!" Coach Cox bellows, banging his knee against his clipboard.

"Dude, what's up?" Nigel asks, shoulder bumping me. "Get in the game, would ya?"

I brought my lacrosse stick to the woods once with me. Lizzie wanted to know more about the sport and how to play. She was enthralled by the stick, but she couldn't catch or throw the ball at all. I guess Authority is right; women belong nowhere near a sports field or court.

Once, she swung so hard to catch the ball that she spun around and fell to the ground. I ran toward her and stumbled over the same stump that tripped her up. Landing next to her with our faces just inches apart, I knew that I would find a way to be with her every day. Being with her was the only thing in my life that ever mattered to me. Don't get me wrong; I love my dads. They're really great men. But my time with Lizzie gave me reason to get up in the morning.

The days that I knew I was going to see her breathed life into me that I'd never felt before. And then, out of nowhere, that breath, the life force, that oxygen was cut off. No warning. No goodbye. Nothing.

Now, things that shouldn't even remotely remind me of Lizzie remind me of her. Like lacrosse. I can't get my head in this dumb game, because I'm thinking about how terrible she was at it. My head won't stop reminding me of how she used the lacrosse stick for everything—other than catching and throwing a lacrosse ball. It creatively became her make-believe air guitar, a microphone, a rifle, and even a squirrel catcher. Thankfully, that squirrel was way too fast for Lizzie.

I miss another shot. Braxton Anderson grabs my helmet, pulls me close, and grits through his teeth, "What the fuck, Logan? What're you, some linear plugger?" He shoves my head back. "Stop playing like a girl, you plugger."

That's it. That's all I can take. I dive at Braxton, ripping his helmet off, and plowing my fist directly into his jaw. He flies backward, and I pounce on him, letting all of my anger, sadness, and frustration loose. Every punch more powerful and deliberate than the next. I want to kill him, end his fucking life. He doesn't know me—doesn't know one thing about me.

Suddenly, all I feel is pain, a shooting, excruciating pain that shakes me to the core. Unable to move or react, my body shakes and stiffens as it tumbles to the ground. Teachers and coaches use tasers on the regular, but I'd never been tased before. Until now.

Just as I'm getting my bearings back, I hear Braxton say, "Now Coach?"

"Yeah, get it over with Anderson," Coach Cox says.

I brace myself, knowing what's coming now. Braxton kicks me hard in the ribs. I groan, bringing my knees to my chest in the fetal position, thinking that's the worst of it. But then, Braxton's fist collides with my nose. I hear the crack and feel the warm liquid explode from my nose. Another punch lands on the side of my head. I hear "asshole" right before everything goes black.

~

"LUTHER, come here. He's waking up."

"He's going to wish he was still out cold," I hear my father growl. I don't want to open my eyes and face this.

"Gentlemen, you need to stand back, so I can take his vitals," an unfamiliar voice says. I feel a cold object on my chest. "If you can hear me Riot, take a deep breath." I inhale and groan with pain, choking the air back out. "Okay, okay, looks like we missed something." My shirt is lifted and the hospitalist presses on my sides.

"Oh no, Luther, look at that. Our poor boy," my dad says, his voice shrill and full of fear.

"A few broken ribs never killed anyone. But me, I'm going to kill him," my father says.

"Mr. Logan, that behavior and those comments aren't helping your son," the hospitalist scolds. He injects something into my IV. "This should help with the pain."

"And what're you doing? I'll sue this whole damn place. You said you missed it. Those bruises and marks don't look too hard to see if you ask—"

"Luther, why don't you go get us some coffee? I'll stay here with Riot and speak with the doctors and hospitalists," my other dad says. I hear my father's voice getting further away as they speak. I love when my dad interjects and calms my father down. He's like the father whisperer—and he's usually whispering thoughts that make it, so my father doesn't kill me.

I open my eyes and look at the hospitalist staring back at me. By all normal standards, this guy is gorgeous. Everyone would fall over for this man. His muscles are nearly popping out of his tight t-shirt. The stethoscope he wears around his neck can't even hang properly due to how big his pectoral muscles are. The hospitalists are the nice ones; they take your vitals, cleanse you, give you pain medicine, and just make sure you are comfortable and well cared for. It's the doctors who are always all businesslike and stoic—with very little empathy or compassion. If my dads weren't lawyers, my sperm father could've been a doctor, whereas my passive dad could've been a hospitalist. I can't see my sperm father being anything but a cold, judgmental, unwavering dick.

"Mr. Logan." Dr. Davis walks in looking at my chart. "Seems to me that you shouldn't be picking fights on the lacrosse field."

"I didn't—"

"According to the results from your CT scan, looks like you just scored a concussion on top of a previous concussion."

My dad walks back into the room alone. "Dr. Davis, Riot hasn't had a concussion ever in his life."

"Not according to these tests." Dr. Davis looks over my chart. "With the latest technology, we can see everything. This shows that not only does he have a pretty severe concussion right now from today's brawl, but also suffered a minor concussion a few days ago."

"Riot, what's he talking about?"

"I have no idea," I lie.

Dr. Davis raises his brow, like he knows I'm lying. "Well, I'm not about to get in the middle of a family blowout. But Riot, I would highly suggest no lacrosse the rest of this season."

"But it's his last year; he's a senior," my dad says, trying to persuade the doctor into letting me play.

"Listen, it's against my better judgment to have him in any more games this year. But, you're his dad. You ultimately get the final call. Today's concussion was pretty significant." He looks back over my results. "I don't advise that he plays again this year." My dad slumps down in the chair, putting his head in his hand. "But, I also understand the importance of competitive sports, so you both can decide. Just to be safe, we are going to keep him overnight for observation."

Dr. Davis walks out of the room, and my dad stares at me, eyes narrowing. "What aren't you telling me?"

"Man Dad, I don't tell you a lot. This could take a while," I say, faking a smile and wincing at the pain. "Well there was the time Nigel and I tried your whisky."

"This isn't funny, Riot." My dad pulls his chair closer to my bed. He props his elbows on the mattress and leans in. "Start talking."

"Immunity?" I ask.

"Partial, depending on what you're about to say."

"Anderson called me a 'linear plugger,' because I was playing like shit," I admit.

"Crap."

"Sorry, I was playing like crap," I correct. "I don't know, Dad. Something came over me, and I just snapped."

Calling someone a "linear plugger" is the ultimate insult in Eka. It's unacceptable and unheard of for a man to want physical intimacy with a woman. Heterosexuality is

53

so shunned and repulsive here that to have desires so repugnant is grounds for public ridicule—and sometimes torture.

"Since when do we let what other people say provoke us like that?" my dad questions. "That's not really like you, Riot. What's really going on?"

I want to be honest with him. I want to tell him everything. Lizzie was so important to me and if he knew, then maybe, he could help me get out of this funk. He's good like that.

"You know son," he starts, "graduation is a scary time, especially for someone like you."

"Someone like me?" I ask, trying to find a comfortable position on the bed.

"You know, 'big man on campus,' 'king of the world.' When you go to college, and you *are* going to college, you have to start all over again. Prove yourself again. Show everyone that you're smart, athletic, and a born leader. You go back to the bottom of the totem pole."

"What's a totem pole?" I ask, never hearing the phrase before.

"Oh, ummm," my dad stutters. "Nothing, just something of the past."

"The past? Like Before?"

"Don't worry about it," he says, standing up. "I get why you're nervous and acting up. You'll be leaving us soon and going out to prove yourself all over again. It's a lot. But you've got to keep it together for a bit longer, Riot."

"No Dad, that's not it—"

"And Riot, we can tell your father that Dr. Davis said no lacrosse whatsoever if you want out of the rest of the year," he says, patting my leg over the blanket. "I just think you should try to finish out the season. Remember, you'll never get to play again for the rest of your life."

"Yeah, whatever. I'll do whatever you want," I say, dropping my throbbing head back down onto my pillow. The medicine is kicking in. The weight of my eyelids is too cumbersome to bear any longer. My eyes fall closed.

I hear him walking toward the door, probably to meet my father downstairs. "I just loved her so much," I say, feeling myself fall deeply into a medically-induced euphoria.

～

"Take it easy, Riot. You're off school and the field for the rest of the week," my active father says, putting a cup of water on my bedroom nightstand. "I talked to Cox. You're starting next weekend, so make sure you rest up."

"Luther," my dad groans. "Don't you think he should take a few games off? He hasn't even been home from the hospital a week yet."

"No way! It's the championship. Lakeward can't beat Crane Hill without him. You know that as well as I do." My father turns to leave and adds, "And don't think this is over. Once you're feeling better, we'll discuss the punishment for going off on Braxton at practice like some barbarian who doesn't know any better." He looks at my dad and asks, "Ready? We have to get out of here."

"Babe, I already told you. I'll meet you at the office. I've got an appointment uptown with a potential client."

"That's right. Damn it. I was going to have you drive while I looked over a brief. Alright then, be careful." He kisses my dad and rushes off without even a glance back at me.

Once we hear my father's car start, my dad looks at me, narrowing his eyes. "Start talking, buddy."

I look around the room, confused. "Huh?'

My dad sits on my bed and leans closer to me. "Right before you went to LaLa Land, you said, and I quote 'I just loved her so much.' What in Authority does that even mean, Riot?"

"Huh? Dad, I have no idea—"

"Riot James Logan, you are the worst—I mean worst—liar I've ever met. Start talking."

With a sigh and a fear unlike any I've ever experienced before, I ask "Dad, have you ever known any women or been friends with one?"

"No Riot, I have not," he admits, shaking his head as his lips turn down.

I'm so disappointed, but not surprised. I don't know how else to broach this topic and really talk to him about it.

"But I know many men who have," he says, shifting on the bed. "I've even known men who've loved and been intimate with women before."

My eyes widen. "You have?"

"Of course. I've lived over half a century. I've seen and heard a lot of things you know nothing about."

"Because you guys never tell me anything," I groan, closing my eyes and shaking my head.

"Riot, our job is to keep you safe and make sure you're a law-abiding citizen and a productive member of society. We're not going to go around and put all kinds of thoughts into your head that may tempt you to do things that negate the Laws of Liberty."

"I just feel like I'm trapped in a world that doesn't let me do anything, know anything, or feel anything."

"Go on."

"I just want more."

"More what, Riot?"

"Ummm freedom, I guess," I say. "They're called the Laws of Life and Liberty, but they've taken all of our freedom. Liberty literally means freedom, and yet, we have none."

"I've done this long enough with you—and with clients—I know when someone is stalling and not telling me everything. Who is the 'her' in your drug-induced confession?"

I end up spilling my guts to my dad about Lizzie being my friend who completed suicide—omitting all the details about my art. My dad thinks I was in the forest on a female day on a dare from a lacrosse buddy.

"You say you 'loved' her," he says. "Loved her like how?"

"We were friends, best friends. I could tell her anything."

My dad sighs, relief washing over his face. "Oh thank Authority. I was afraid you were going to say you loved her like I love your father. I can handle a lot of things, but I'm not sure I could've handled that."

I laugh, uncomfortably and a bit unnaturally. "Nah, not like that. Like I love Nigel, I guess."

"Oh son, I'm so sorry you had to deal with her death all alone. That had to be awful for you. But don't you see now why Authority put this rule into place? Men and women can't be together, not even as allies. The pressure of your friendship drove that poor girl to end her life."

"Dad, I don't think that's why—"

"Of course it is. Breaking the Laws of Liberty brings about more pain and suffering than you'll ever understand." He stands up, adjusting his tie in the mirror. "I hate to say this Riot, but it's probably for the best. Now, you can focus on school and your future. And maybe even lacrosse."

My shock must be evident, because he adds, "I know you're hurting now, but it'll get easier with time. People like us can handle anything." My dad pulls my blanket up and actually tucks me in like I'm a child. "Let me know if you need anything." He starts to leave. "And Riot, let's not tell your father about any of this. He'll lose his mind just knowing you went into the woods on a forbidden day."

When the front door slams and I know he's gone, I grab my pillow, cover my face, and just scream. I have nobody. I'm in this alone.

CHAPTER 9
VICISSITUDE

"Having siblings is like making music, some high notes, some low notes, but it is always a beautiful song." (Jesse Joseph)

"Thank you, Colonel Sumter." I nod, keeping my politically correct gender distance, as I walk over to the picnic table that Cleave and I are permitted to sit at while we have our supervised meetings.

Colonel Sumter always stays at least ten feet away from me. He dons a helmet and a full-body suit at every meeting. He looks like he's going to war in a forest green one-piece zip-up suit. It's quite atrocious. His suit proves he's a low-level Authority officer. If he were mid-level, he'd be all in white and silver, head to toe. The white suit officers aren't too ominous when you look at them, but they're lethal. Supposedly, their motto is "Shoot now—ask questions later." But the worst are the Authority Selects. The top of the top, the Authority Selects, get all black suits that are terrifying on sight. The Selects are unforgiving and ruthless.

Colonel Sumter probably wants to be a Select, but I can't imagine that. He does nothing. I've never seen his face or even the color of his eyes. I'm certain he's male, but I'd truly have no other proof.

"Colonel, my ass," Cleave scoffs, rolling his eyes. "That dude's never served Eka or anything other than a plate of fries to someone." I throw my head back and laugh. I swear whatever Cleave says makes me lose it. I don't know what it is about him, but his personality and jokes always seem like the perfect medicine for me.

"Why do you look so good?" I ask, checking out his hair and fit. "New shoes, new jeans, and your hair is on point. Spill it."

"Date." He grins.

"Oh my Authority, are you finally going out with Nicholas Lavery?" I squeal.

"Nah, it ain't like that. That's old news."

"What in the world? Last month you were going on and on about 'making babies with Nick Lavery.' I wanted to rip out your tongue if we're being honest."

"Well, I'm being honest now, and Nick said that there was no way, and I quote, that he'd ever go out with a dickbag like me."

"Whoa. Harsh," I say, getting snacks out of my bag and offering him a chip.

"Yeah, it was harsh. So, I'm biting the bullet and going out with Carson Gables." He shrugs, taking more than a handful of chips out of the bag. As we watch, more chips fall to the grimy picnic table than into his hand, he adds, "I heard he's wanted me for years. It's about time someone wanted me for a change and not the other way around."

"Cleaveland Shaw, don't you dare tell me that you're settling. You are way too goo—"

"Hold up, I'm not settling. I mean Nick's a wet dream—don't get me wrong. But, Carson's a good guy. Abs for days.

And his calves. Holy Authority, I've got ideas for those legs tonight." He shakes his head and sighs dreamily.

"Alright, that's pretty convincing—and disgusting. So, what's the plan for tonight?"

"Tonight is just low-key. We're just hanging out at his house. Nothing major. A little get to know each other time." Cleave smiles and winks at me. I fake gag. "But Friday, we're going to the lacrosse game. Let the world see us together. It sucks though. Riot Logan's on the DL, so Crane Hill might actually beat us. There are some rumors flying around that Riot may play. But I'm not sure. Man, I hope so. We need a W."

"Did you say Riot?"

"Yeah, he's the Lakeward golden boy. Every guy either wants him or wants to be him. Lacrosse doesn't even exist without him, really. He's a stud on field. Has a mean temper, but uses it wisely."

"Oh I'm sure he does," I say, feeling my lunch stirring in my stomach.

"Nah really, he's a good guy. The silent, brooding type. I'd do him in a heartbeat. He wouldn't give me the time of day, but he's never been an ass or anything to me." Cleave takes another handful of chips and catches them in his mouth before more fall to the picnic table. "Why do you care anyway? You don't know him, do you?"

"Of course not. How would I possibly know him?"

I cannot believe Cleave just said that Riot was a good guy. He can't be. Can he? That day in the forest, he seemed so distraught and worried that I was going to turn him into Authority for painting when I was straight up accusing him of murder. If what he said was true about being friends with Lizzie, then how horrifying for someone to think he killed her. That someone is me.

Cleave shrugs. "Crazier things have happened."

"Like what?" I ask, feeling my cheeks pinken.

"I don't know. Caterpillars turn into butterflies. That's crazy." Cleave laughs and bits of chips come flying out of his mouth.

Are all males gross like this and lack any form of depth? Is it always just sports and sex with them? I don't understand how an entire gender can be obsessed with just two things like that. I mean, they can't all be this way, right? I just want to have a profound conversation with Cleave sometimes, but our talks are always just so superficial and really rather ridiculous.

"Don't you wish you could come to the house and see Mama?" I ask, like I always do.

"For what? She get a new hairstyle or something?" And there it is. He always says something stupid like that. The guy lacks all compassion and emotion.

"Well, Mom and Mama are having their 5th Recommitment Party next week. It would be great if Authority would permit you to go and celebrate them with us."

"Come on Cissy, like that would happen," Cleave says, shoving a stick through the wooden slat of the picnic table. "It's kind of dope though that they made it 25 years together."

"I know," I agree. "I know so many moms of girls at my school who don't even sign up again after the first five years."

"You chicks are lucky; you get the recommitment every five years. We have to go seven before we re-up our marital contracts." He shoves the stick the rest of the way through the slot, and it disappears under the table. "Women are way luckier than men."

"Oh my Authority, you've got to be kidding me?" I say,

shaking my head and narrowing my eyes at my brother. "We have two years less than you, and you think that's good news?"

"Well of course it is. We have those final two years. That's where that 'seven-year-itch' comes from. Those last two years are supposedly tortuous, Cissy. Imagine spending an extra 730 days with someone you don't want to be with any more. 730 days. That's outrageous."

"Did you do that math on your own, smart guy?" I ask, trying to lighten the mood.

Cleave laughs so loud that I jump. "Nah, a bunch of us were just talking about it at school the other day, so I remembered the number. We all agree though that you ladies have it better than we do."

"Imagine if we lived Before," I respond. "How'd you like to spend 'until death do you part' with someone you didn't like or want?"

"Authority, don't get me started," Cleave says, shaking his head and snorting. "What idiot made that up in the first place? I can't believe it's even true. The happiest day of your life, and they said crap like poor, death, sickness, and faithfulness. Why would they bring the whole celebration down by talking about stuff like that?"

"Look at you, getting all worked up and even getting a little serious. I like this side of you," I admit, smacking his hand.

Immediately, the whistle blares.

"Infraction," Colonel Sumter shouts, walking over to us. "Ms. Maddox and Mr. Shaw, both of your parents will get demerits for this physical infraction. Ms. Maddox, your mothers will be required to pay a two hundred dollar fine. This is your second time reaching for Mr. Shaw. If it happens again, that will be the last time you two will be permitted to collaborate."

"Yes sir." We nod, in unison.

Not being able to be a real sister to my brother drives me crazy. I should be able to reach out and touch him, feel him, and really get to know him. The fact that I cannot hug him like I hug my moms is ludicrous. Affection is so important. Who cares if he's male and I'm not? We should be afforded the luxury of human touch. They say that after a global pandemic of some sort that personal touch and affection fizzled out. People were reportedly force to stand at least six feet away from each other—even from their spouses and children. That is just bonkers. If I couldn't touch my moms, due to some deadly plague, I'd hug them and love on them anyway. Nobody is going to tell me that I can't be around my moms. I guess three of us would just all go down together. Truthfully though, I think it's another one of those legends of Before. That cannot possibly be true. Who would willingly not want to caress the arm or back of her loved one?

"Listen Cleave, I have an idea," I whisper, leaning in to emphasize the gravity of my proposal.

Cleave's eyebrows shoot up, excitedly conspiratorial. "Oh yeah, whatcha got for me?"

"What if we figured out a way to sneak you into the Recommitment Party as a surprise to Mama on her special day?" I can feel my lips spread in anticipated excitement as I deliver my mischievous idea.

"Ummm for what?"

"As a surprise! To get you and Mama together in the same room!"

"Listen Cissy, I love our visits. They're a nice break from Testosterone Town and all. But, I've got no desire to go to a women's brunch party. Men don't 'brunch.' Brunch is a woman's thing and not really something I want to try," Cleave says, scowling, looking as if he just ate the most sour-tasting food ever.

"Cleave, she's your mom!"

"Is she though?" he asks, side-eyeing me. "She's no more than the incubators at the Birthing Center. Literally, any person with a uterus can hold a baby for nine months. It's not like it's a big deal." Cleave stands up. "I'd rather just hang with Carson and eat breakfast and then later some lunch—not cram them together in one silly meal." He throws his left leg over the bench and then the right, extricating himself from the confines of the picnic table. "Give your moms my best. Take care, Cissy!"

With that, he walks away. I'm sitting there like he punched me in the gut and left me choking back the pain of his delivery. How do you share a womb with someone and end up miles apart?

CHAPTER 10
RIOT

"Each friend represents a world in us, a world possibly not born until they arrive, and it is only by this meeting that a new world is born." (Anais Nin)

"Riot, over here!" Nigel waves me over to the far side of the field. Decarion is sitting on the bench, wearing sunglasses, sport shorts, and nothing else. He's definitely taking advantage of this beautiful day —and flaunting it all for Nigel's benefit. I like it. Decarion definitely has a body worth worshipping, and Nigel clearly does. They're happy together and that in turn makes me happy. Nigel deserves this.

"Hey guys, what's up?" I ask, dropping my lacrosse bag and setting my water bottle down on the bench.

"I'm just getting pumped for our game Friday. This is going to be epic," Nigel exclaims, bouncing on his toes like a kid waiting for the ice cream truck to meander down his road at a snail's pace. "Still can't believe the Logan dads are letting you play, Riot." Nigel runs his hands through Decarion's hair.

"I'm just getting pumped watching my man get all sweaty and hot," Decarion says, pulling his sunglasses down, eyeing Nigel from head to toe.

Nigel grins and swats at him. "Stop, you're making me blush."

"Guys, save it. We've got a lot to do before the game this week. Nigel, things have been getting by you left and right. You've got to get your head in the game."

"Weren't you playing like shit a few weeks ago, and I said the same thing to you? And so did Braxton. Maybe you don't remember, because you hit that lug of a head too many times," Nigel counters.

"Touché!" I turn and look at Decarion. "Isn't there some incentive you can offer him to keep him focused?"

"Oh, I do like this," Nigel says, turning back to Decarion. "What will you do for me—or give me—if I don't let anyone score on me Friday night?" Decarion's eyes narrow as he starts to think. Then, his face lights up as he motions Nigel over. When he whispers into Nigel's ear, Nigel's face reddens while his eyes widen with excitement.

"I do not want to know," I say, tightening my shoelace before grabbing my stick. "Alright loverboy, let's see what you've got." We head over to the goal.

"Do your thing Riot, because ain't nothing getting by me—"

"That's one for me," I shout, scoring on Nigel while he's trumpeting his athleticism. "And none for you—or you, Decarion." I laugh, scooping another ball into my stick's pocket. "Stop thinking about Decarion's shaft and more on your stick's shaft, man. We've got a championship to win."

"Boo!" Decarion yells. "Come on, Nigel. I'm counting on you."

"I got you! That's the last time he's scoring on—fuck man," he yells as a ball whizzes by his head.

∽

"Are they really giving us all of this for free?" I ask Decarion as the server at Gino's puts a smorgasbord of food down in front of us.

"When male workers come in on their days off, we eat for free. Whatever we want," he says, biting into a garlic knot.

"And the women?" I ask, curious of the ins and outs of male vs. female employment.

"Nah, they get 40% off their meals," he says, shrugging. "Seems fair though. They don't need as much money as we do."

"How do you figure?" I ask, twirling my pasta around my fork. "Don't they have to pay for the same things in life that we do?"

"Well, I guess, but nobody cares if they're poor or not. Men are judged by how big their wallets are. Women aren't."

"And that wallet in your pocket is bulging in all the right spots," Nigel says, staring at Decarion's crotch.

"Enough," I say, rolling my eyes and chuckling. "I'm starving and don't want to ruin my appetite."

Decarion clears his throat. "Speaking of appetite Riot, where is yours? Where's your thirst, if you know what I mean?"

"No Decarion, I don't know what you mean," I say, downing my entire glass of water.

"You're never with anyone. And we just have to know why. You're too hot to be alone." And before Nigel can say anything, he adds, "Not my type though. I like my men bigger and broader with a little ginger spice." Nigel smiles and snuggles into Decarion's side.

"Should I vomit now or wait until after I eat?" I ask, faking gagging at their blatant display of affection. "I can feel it coming up right now."

"Oh I feel it coming up too." Nigel laughs, winking at me.

"Do you ever stop?" I ask, rolling my eyes.

"Do you ever start? Seriously Riot, we have got to get you laid."

"I'm fine; thank you. I don't need any help."

"I guess with your hands readily available and consenting at all times that you really must not need anyone," Nigel shoots back.

"Listen, that's the first thing you've gotten right all day. I don't need anyone, Nige. I'm fine. I actually like being alone and not worrying about making someone else happy all the time." I stab my tofu ball and dip it in more sauce before shoving the entire ball into my mouth.

"Hey, guys! Sorry, I'm late. My car wouldn't start, and of course my dads insisted that they fix it right then and there. And they know nothing about cars, so that was fun," McCarthy McCorum says, sliding into the booth right next to me. "Finally, I just left in my dad's car. They'll figure out I'm gone once they come out from underneath my car."

"Umm, no problem, McCarthy," I say, narrowing my eyes at Nigel and Decarion.

"McCarthy, it's awesome that you could meet up with us," Nigel says. "This is Decarion. He graduated a few years before—"

"Oh, I know Decarion," McCarthy says. "Basketball legend." He opens a menu and looks straight at Decarion.

"That championship was off the chain. You drained ten three-pointers in the second half alone, breaking records all over Eka. Man, nobody could guard you that game."

"Yeah, look where it got me." Decarion rolls his eyes, arms splayed out wide. "A server at Gino's while I go to school to be a damn coach. Dare to dream."

"Or, it got you right here with me," Nigel says, wrapping his arm around Decarion's shoulder.

"I'm just saying all the training and crap that they put us through to make us these basketball machines for their entertainment is just ridiculous. Back in the day—"

"You mean Before?" Nigel asks.

"Yeah, people played for fun. And now, we're just a bunch of show ponies for Authority's entertainment, hoping to make bank." Decarion takes a long swig of his drink. "I trained my life away—literally. And now, I've got nothing to show for it."

Nigel pulls him in closer and places a light kiss on his temple.

"It sucks that athletes as talented as you have one shot for college or pro ball and that's it," McCarthy says. "Can't believe you blew out your knee during that Elite Evaluation." McCarthy turns toward me. "What about you, Riot? You going to the Elites for Lacrosse?"

Nigel barks out a laugh. "Dude can't quit LAX fast enough. After Friday's championship, he's probably going to burn his stick in celebration."

"Seriously? " McCarthy looks back and forth between Nigel and me.

"Yeah, I'm ready to be done. Thirteen years of nonstop sports is enough for me," I say, throwing my napkin onto the table.

"McCarthy, are you going to the game Friday?"

"Wouldn't miss it," he says, glancing up at the expectant server. "I'll just have a medium pizza and some cranberry juice."

"We're thinking about all going up to the lake after the game. You in?" Decarion asks.

"For sure," McCarthy says, "as long as my car is fixed."

"No worries. Riot's driving up. You can ride with us. Right, Riot?"

"Huh?" I ask, looking around at them.

"After the game," Nigel nods in McCarthy's direction, "you'd be more than happy to drive him up to the lake. Right?"

Nigel eyes me carefully. McCarthy inches a little closer to me. Decarion is smiling from ear to ear.

Unbelievable.

How am I this dense? This is a set-up. I thought maybe it was just a coincidence, but now I know for sure. I will kill them. I expect this crap from Nigel. All he ever does is butt in to things that are none of his business. But Decarion is much more civil than Nigel is. I wouldn't expect this from him.

"Oh yeah, I forgot to tell you guys. Dads aren't letting me go. After the concussion and my little hospital stay, they want me home after the game, so they can keep an eye on me."

"What? But we have my uncle's cabin. It's going to be epic," Nigel whines.

"It's gonna have to be epic without me," I say. "Listen, it's good to see you, McCarthy. But, I gotta get going." I slide closer to him, bumping his hip against mine, hoping he gets the hint and lets me out of the booth. I'm suddenly feeling trapped and ready to suffocate.

"Will I see you again?" McCarthy asks, staring right into my eyes.

"I'm sure I'll see you around," I say, shooting my deadliest glare at Nigel. The disappointment on McCarthy's face is evident. I feel like shit, but this is so far from being my fault. This is all on Nigel and Decarion. Don't get me wrong. McCarthy is extremely good-looking. He's fun. He's smart. He's a powerhouse on the soccer field. He's a great catch for any guy—just not me.

~

THE FOREST IS the only place that feels like home to me. Even my own house doesn't feel all that welcoming—or forgiving. The struggle is real. I haven't any idea how people really confide in their parents. It's like they're these judgmental assholes that are just waiting around for you to screw up. And when you do. BAM! They're ready to pounce —even on the most minuscule mistake. I know my dads love me. I also know that it isn't all that unconditional as they say. There are definitely conditions. Every time I screw up, I think the love lessens. The conditions are there though: do homework, get good grades, get into college, dominate on the lacrosse field, keep the bedroom clean, clean up after myself, come in before curfew, and a long list of other expectations they have for me.

Today, the woods are perfect. The sun is hot and unyielding, which is a bit early for it to be this hot. Most people love the glaring, blazing sun. I prefer the cooler months. Living here, I get very few cooler days. They say that up north, it's much more tolerable. It even snows. I'd love to see that, but with the travel ban, it's just a pipedream. My best chance would be if my dads needed to try a case up north or got transferred up. A long shot. Ain't going to happen.

I extract my mahogany box from the canopy of trees. Thankful that I was able to get it out of my backpack and house and back into its hiding spot without getting caught. My dads would go ballistic if they saw all of these illegal items in their home.

I don't know what I'm creating today. Haven't even thought about it yet. I was worried that Tree Gazer was going to be lying out on the ground, deep in thought when I got here. Not sure why I'd think that, considering it's a male day and that girl wouldn't break a Law of Liberty if her life depended upon it—and it sort of does.

Visually, there are so many similarities and differences between Lizzie and Tree Gazer that I want to create a portrait of the two of them melding together as one--a Venn Diagram of two people becoming one. I want to accentuate their differences and flow their similarities together.

Sometimes, I feel like all the girls I've ever seen rather look alike. Sure, Lizzie's milky white, porcelain, freckled skin looks nothing like Cissy's light mocha skin. But the few times when Cissy's hair was unbraided and long as she was sprawled out on the blanket staring at the sky reminds me of the soft, spiral swirls of Lizzie's fiery red hair.

As I begin to surrender into my art, I get lost in the details of Lizzie, remembering every curve of her body, every angle of her face, and every feel of her touch. Recreating her never does the true Lizzie justice. Lizzie couldn't be captured and locked in on a two-dimensional picture. She was vibrant, full of life, energy, and presence.

Suddenly, I notice the details of the portrait. I've portrayed Lizzie in all black and white, a fuzzy, faded picture of the past. I didn't even blend the hues of red and orange to accentuate her hair. But, what I've done with Cissy is indescribable. Cissy is full of vibrant color, details, and clarity—almost like she's sitting right next to me. How does art do that? Why would I even draw her at all? I don't even know this girl. I know nothing about her. And I certainly will never get to know her.

No way.

Not a chance.

Not again.

I grab the matches out of my backpack, because this portrait, this picture, this creation will receive the same fate as all of my others. I strike the match, take one last look of the two girls, one who changed everything for me and one who silently waits in the periphery, and slowly ignite the forbidden females in the flames that will destroy them.

Like I always do. Like it always does to my heart.

CHAPTER II
VICISSITUDE

"We cannot really love anyone with whom we never laugh."
(Agnes Repplier)

The first time I met Marjorie, I was like every single girl at our school. I was mesmerized, even as an eight-year-old little girl. It was the first day of school. My moms never bought into that whole "First Day of School" pictures and new clothes business. I looked just like I looked every day. We didn't go all out. We didn't feel the need to chronicle the entire day with pictures, signs, and banners. School was school, and I was just a normal student starting school.

We were in our first-ever cooking and sewing class, and I noticed her immediately. She was so put together, but at the age of eight, I didn't quite know what I was looking at or thinking. I just knew that she had perfect hair and great clothes and that my shirt had my morning orange juice on it, and my hair was in desperate need of a rebraiding. Then, I noticed that she had long, glittery pink nails, and my nails were caked with the dirt from our garden. Three days earlier, I'd helped Mom plant basil and mint. I'd been lying about taking a shower, so I knew how long that dirt had been under my nails. Self-consciously, I'd begun to dig the grime out from under my nails with my teeth, while raising my hand to ask if I could use the washroom before making the muffins we were about to mix. Simultaneously, I was angry with my moms for not insisting that I put forth some "first impression" effort into my clothes, hair, and hygiene.

As soon as I got into the bathroom, I splashed water on my face and washed the syrupy crust from my breakfast pancakes off my chin. When I opened my eyes, Marjorie was staring at me. "You need to do your hair." I nodded, frantically agreeing with her. "Once you do your hair, you can be my friend." She turned on her heel and walked right out of the bathroom.

That weekend, Mama took me to get rebraided, and she let me get my ears pierced as well. Walking into school on Monday, I felt so confident and full of pride, showing off my new beaded and braided hair—as well as my new fake diamond earrings. I was the talk of Gabriella-Grace Elementary. Marjorie found me at lunch and sat right down next to me. She gave me one long look and said, "Now, you look like someone who could be my friend."

I should have been offended. I should've told her that my looks shouldn't determine if I was worthy enough to be her friend. But at 8-years-old, I was flattered and so excited to be Marjorie Allen's friend. As time went on, our friendship bloomed. I went from being Marjorie's friend to being her best friend. It just made sense that we blossomed into more than friends.

Throughout middle school and the start of high school, we ebbed and flowed. Sometimes, she was dating someone. Sometimes, I was. But we were always friends—as close as close could be. Then, at the end of our tenth grade year, Marjorie broke up with Cali Deeds at a weekend dance party. Cali was devastated and left the party. Marjorie hadn't thought twice about her actions or whom she just destroyed. Instead, she was on the dance floor having the time of her life, moving to the music without a care in the world. I wanted to be her in that moment. I wanted all the weight of the world that I carried on my shoulders to vanish, so I could feel the lightness Marjorie was portraying. It didn't seem strange or odd to walk over to her and just begin to move with her to the music—to hear it and feel it from her vantage point. We were best friends, after all.

Marjorie beamed at me, wrapping her arms around my neck with a natural and confident ease. She pulled me closer, and with no hesitation whatsoever, she kissed me. And I was right, in that moment, I did feel lighter, more confident, and invincible. That kiss sealed our promise to one another. We both pretty much knew in that moment that it was the two of us from then on out.

"Are you even listening to me?" Marjorie asks, taking a sip of her drink.

We're on my back patio, sunning ourselves and decompressing from a week of midterms and projects. When spring hits, teachers go wild with tests and at-home group projects. It's just awful. I've asked Mom about it before, and she just says that teachers need breaks too. She's always said that if it's a hard week for students, then it's an easy week for teachers. And the opposite is also true. If it's one of those weeks filled with parties and activities, then it's overly hard for the teachers.

"Of course, I'm always listening to you," I say, sitting up

in my chair and looking over at her. For the record, I was actually zoning out. I'm not sure what she said at all.

"Do you think your moms would let us stay alone in a cabin for a long weekend after graduation?" she asks, leaning in conspiratorially. "Wouldn't it be wonderful, just the two of us for three long days alone in the wilderness with nobody nagging at us and all we have is just you and me?"

"Ummm, yeah, sure. That would be pretty great," I lie. I truthfully cannot imagine all that alone time with Marjorie. I'm fairly certain we'd kill one another. "I don't know though. They're pretty set on me just focusing on higher learning right now."

"Right, but once you get your acceptances, they'll lay off, and we'll spend all weekend with one another," she says, smiling. Then she adds, "Clothing optional, of course."

"Listen Marjorie, I don't know that they're going to let me do that," I say.

"Dummy, you don't tell them we're going to be naked all weekend." She laughs, putting her sunglasses back over her eyes and lounging back on the chair.

"No, I mean, they're never going to let me go to the lake cabin for an entire weekend—especially if we're unsupervised."

Marjorie sighs and sits up. She looks strange to me—not angry, not sad. Just blank. She slips her feet back into her sandals. "I'm out."

"What? Why?" I ask, following her to the front yard.

"Listen Cissy, you know I love you." She looks around and sighs deeply. "It's just, you haven't touched me in weeks."

"That's not true," I counter, shaking my head in disagreement. "We literally held hands the entire walk to

Needlepoint and Crochet today. Then, we kissed before going to our seats."

"I grabbed *your* hand. I kissed *your* lips. You never, like ever, reach for me," she says, taking off her sunglasses and wiping away tears that spilled from her eyes. "Quite frankly, I'm sick of being the one who always has to initiate everything. It's exhausting."

"Marj, I'm so—"

"I'm legit beating Celeste off with a bat on the regular, because she wants me so badly. But my own girlfriend won't touch me with a ten-foot pole."

"Uhhh what? What're you talking about? Celeste's been hitting on you?" I ask, shocked and suddenly, feeling very territorial and possessive.

"Don't look so surprised. My Authority, don't you realize that there are girls who want me, girls who want to DO things to me? Things that you haven't done in ages. My gracious Cissy, it's like we're back to being best friends and not in a relationship anymore. Can't you see that?"

The first time Marjorie and I hooked up was in her moms' room when they were at their friends' recommitment party. It was fun, but it wasn't passionate and pleasurable. We were mainly just curious and wanted to know what all the fuss was about. I don't think either of us really enjoyed the whole thing. But after that first time, we got the hang of it and knew what each other liked or wanted.

But she's right. We haven't been intimate in a while. I'm not sure why either. We just haven't. I don't know if she hasn't been into it or if I wasn't. I just know we haven't done much lately.

"Okay, you're right. I'm sorry. I haven't been affectionate lately. I promise, I'll be more touchy-feely—"

"Don't you get it? I don't want to remind you to want

me. I just want you to want me. Is that so hard?" she asks, turning around and getting into her car. I stand there confused, not knowing what to do or say. Her window comes down. "I just think we need a break or something. You need to decide what you really want. Because right now, I don't think it's me."

Marjorie starts her car and drives off, leaving me alone in my driveway, watching her grow smaller in the distance. I'm stricken with guilt. She's right. I haven't been in this relationship in a while. I've just been going through the motions. It's strange how that can happen. One minute, you're all in and feeling all the love and joy. Then suddenly, all the romance, butterflies, and excitement diminish, and you're left with a feeling of empty numbness, wondering if you'll ever find that bliss again.

Standing in my driveway, I realize I only want to do one thing right now. I run back into my house and straight into my bedroom. Rummaging through my old tote, I find everything I need. I cram it all into my backpack and head out. Then, I remember my tracker and put it on the charger, leaving a note for my moms.

I write:

Ran to the school for a study group. Be home for dinner. Tracker is charging.

Walking into the woods on a "Male Day" feels strange, ominous almost. I've never broken a rule like this before. Granted, I've touched Cleave during our visits, but I've never deliberately done something like this in my life. It feels like I'm someone else, living a life that isn't really mine. But, I'm not going to lie. It's exhilarating to be out here, walking the trails in the forest, without permission from anyone to be here.

But the real question is: what in the world am I doing here? There is no reasonable explanation for why in Authority's power that I would risk my life or my moms' lives breaking a Law of Liberty for this. I can't even wrap my head around it. Yet, here I am doing just that—and for what?

I smell the smoke before I see the flames. Finally, the fire is in full view, maintained and safe, but burning nonetheless. Then, I make out Riot's eyes through the smoky air. There are tears puddling in the corners of his eyes. I'm not sure how to approach this situation. From what I've heard, men do not like to talk, to share, or to even feel. So, I doubt I can just walk over and ask him why he's crying. That's probably not a thing in the male world. I need another strategy.

I make my way through the covered brush, stomping my feet a little louder than I normally would, ensuring that he hears me before he sees me. "Jeez Riot, you trying to burn down the entire forest?" I ask, taking my water bottle out of my backpack. I pour the entire contents of my jug onto his small bonfire.

"Cissy! What're you doing here on a Male Day?" he asks, jumping to his feet abruptly, wiping his hands on his pants. "Didn't figure you for the rebellious type." We stare together at the remnants of the fire, watching the embers fizzle out.

"Apparently, I'm saving the world from a wildfire that may kill us all."

"I had it under control."

"Said no man ever." I laugh, kicking some dirt onto the remaining embers.

"How would you know?" he asks, grinning, definitely coming out of his funk.

"You were legit sitting in front of a giant fire watching it as it prepared to destroy our entire wilderness."

"I wouldn't really call it 'giant.' I wouldn't have let it get that bad," he says, sitting back down. "So what're you doing here anyway?"

"I have an apology gift for you," I say, reaching into my bag. Riot is staring at me. "Stop looking so apprehensive."

"Sorry, I'm not thrilled to see you. Last time we were face-to-face, you plowed your shoe right into my nads," he says, hinging at his waist and blocking his groin from me. I'm not sure if I should be reaching for my Glock or running for the hills."

"Very funny," I say, pulling everything out of my bag. "I realize that I wasn't all that kind the last time I saw you, so I came with a peace offering." I hand him a bag with all of my markers, colored pencils, crayons, and paints. "I thought you might want these. I can get more super easy, so I figured you could use what I have."

"Uhhh thank you?" He eyes me wearily without saying any more. His gratitude is more of a question than appreciation.

"Stop being so suspicious. Can't a girl do something nice for a man?"

"Not in Eka they can't," he says looking around, "unless we somehow teleported back in time or something."

"Was that supposed to be a joke, because it definitely needs some work," I jab, clearing the leaves on the ground with my foot.

"You could sit if you want," he says, eyeing the spot I just cleared.

"Nah, I can't stay. Just finished some cleaning of my

room and thought I'd donate some supplies to the less fortunate. You know, good deed and all."

"Oh okay, so now I'm the 'less fortunate,' some needy guy who can't get by without the help of some woman—"

"No, I was just tea—"

"Joking with you, Cissy. Calm down. Take a seat," he says, motioning to my now-cleared spot. "There's plenty of room." He starts rummaging through all the materials I gave him. His eyes widen with more excitement every time he pulls something new out of the bag. "These look cool. What're these?"

"For real? You don't know what a colored pencil is?" I ask in utter disbelief. We live in a society that a nearly grown man has no idea what a colored pencil is, and I've used, broken, and rebought over a thousand colored pencils in my seventeen years of life. That's just insanity.

"I made sure my name and address was on them—and on the bag. That way, if anyone catches you with them, you could just say you found the whole bag here," I offer, finally sitting down across from him with the fire's smolder between.

I pick up a stick and start breaking pieces off of it and toss them into his pile of ash. "So what did you burn, anyway?"

"My art," he says, shrugging, staring at the ash.

"Holy Authority, if you're that good, then why do you have to burn your art?" I would be so mad if I created something that gorgeous and watched it go up in flames. If I'm going to make something, then I'd want it known, appreciated, and maybe even celebrated.

He looks at me like I'm some strange entity that he cannot quite figure out. "That's a pretty dumb question.

The same reason that you thought to write your name on everything. Nobody ever gets to see my art."

"Thanks for calling me dumb," I say, rolling my eyes and shaking my head. "I'm far from dumb, thank you very much. I just meant why can't you just bring it home and hang it in your bedroom? It's not like Authority hangs out in there. Right? Or do they?"

"Actually, it's worse than that," he admits. "My dads are lawyers. Their whole lives revolve around upholding the law and seeing to it that the their son is the most law-abiding citizen in Eka."

I vividly remember a time a few years ago that I wanted to see what would happen if I overate my caloric intake. My tracker went off, blared like a fire truck siren nearing a traffic intersection. The sound was piercing. I ignored the screech and kept eating. My moms came running in. Mama looked horrified, but simply said, "If you're going to overeat, then just charge your tracker while you're eating the extra food." She shook her head and walked out of the room.

Mom walked over to me, unlatched my watch, and brought it to my room to charge. I looked at the food, took one more bite with my stomach aching from the gluttony, and scraped the rest of the food into the trash can. The whole thing was rather anticlimactic. I thought it was going to be exhilarating eating all of that food and breaking a Law of Liberty. Turned out, it wasn't so exciting.

"Are you sure they'd freak out? They're your dads. I'm sure they'd love to see just how talented you—"

"All they care about is how gifted I am on the lacrosse field. That's it. They just want me out, out of the house and out of their lives. They're counting down the days until I go to college."

"I'd bet all of my art supplies that you're selling them short. They love you and want you to be happy."

"Listen Miss Sunshine & Roses," he says, running his hands through his hair. "You really don't know anything—about me or my dads. Not everyone has an easy and perfect little life."

"Excuse me? At what point did I say or ever insinuate that I had a perfect life?"

Are all men like this? Do they really think they know everything? So far, Cleave and Riot are both really... really... I don't even know the word for it. Is there a word for men thinking that women are just these fragile, silly beings with no brain, and they're these big, bad, superior intellectuals?

"I didn't say that you were—"

"I came here to be nice, to give you something that I know you can't get easily. I also felt a bit guilty for beating the crap out of you—"

"You didn't—"

"I'm speaking right now, and I'd appreciate it greatly if you didn't interrupt me while I say my speak."

Riot clamps his mouth shut quickly while his eyes widen in surprise. Clearly nobody—or no woman—has ever spoken to him as such.

"I know you've spent a lot of time with Lizzie, but Lizzie isn't every female. We're not all these talented powerhouses with moms who'd move mountains for their daughters." I stand up and brush off my pants. "Some of us just have normal, everyday parents. I'm sorry if it annoys you that I've never had any major hardships or that I get along with my moms."

I start to walk back toward the path. But before I disappear deeper into the woods, I turn around and add, "Ya know, Riot? I don't break laws. I follow my moms' rules, because truthfully, rules are put into place for a reason. I'd like to believe that Authority understands what's best for us. But ya know what? Authority doesn't know everything. I saw a flaw, recognized it for what it was, and decided to break a law. I broke a pretty big law for you Riot, a guy I don't even know. But I felt it was worth it. With your talent and your passion, you should be celebrated. I'm sorry if something in your life messed you up so badly that you can't even see kindness when it kicks you in the balls."

Riot scrambles to get up, nearly falling back down as he does so. I start down the path. I don't need to listen to any man explain to me how I'm wrong, or how I don't understand. The last thing I need is some guy telling me anything. I'm not sure what propelled me to come here, but it was probably the poorest choice I've ever made. Things were spiraling out of control with Cleave and with Marjorie; I just wanted to do something different, be a part of something that wasn't the same old thing, day in and day out. This was clearly not the answer.

"Cissy, wait!" Riot says, coming up behind me. "I'm sorry. I'm sorry."

I keep walking, ignoring his pleas. Suddenly, he grabs my arm. I turn around ready to strike him yet again when I notice his eyes. They're glistening again. "Are you crying?"

With the back of his sleeve, Riot wipes his eyes. "Men don't cry."

"Authority help me!" I mumble, rolling my eyes. "What is wrong with your gender? You guys are just delusional, overhyped heathens."

"Fair," he says, smirking.

What in the charming world was that? Whoa, that crooked, one dimpled smirk has power. Where did my anger go? That cannot be a thing. What in the world? A man just smiled at me and all of my anger and frustration dissipated. That is thoroughly ridiculous.

"And you're wrong," Riot says, shrugging his shoulders nonchalantly.

And it all comes flooding back—the anger and the frustration—but now, it's coupled with disbelief.

"Are you kidding me right now?"

Riot shakes his head. "Not like that. You're right about everything you said—except about you and Lizzie. Lizzie was a talented powerhouse. But Cissy, from my vantage point, you are too. One, you legit kicked the shit out of me. Two, you absconded here on a Male Day, breaking a whole load of laws. And three, you just put me in my place like some tenacious lawyer determined to win her case. My dads would love you."

There's that smirk again. I don't understand this dynamic. He smiles, and my fury vanishes. That's weird. He's male and totally barbaric and bombastic. Even Cleave said that he has a temper. Yet, I'm not afraid of him at all. He seems harmless, but tightly wound. I don't really want to be around when he snaps.

"I'm kind of impressed by you, Cissy," Riot continues. "You think you're this law-abiding citizen, but you're badass." He picks a leaf off the tree and starts ripping it into tiny pieces. "Not many people—females especially—would risk their freedom for some dude they didn't know."

"It's just silly that you can't draw a picture. What kind of law is that?"

"I guess they think that art is too 'girlie' for a man," he says, shrugging his shoulders.

"That's just stupid. How can a hobby be male or female? If you like coloring pictures, then you should be allowed to color—"

"I wouldn't call it 'coloring' exactly," Riot corrects. "It's more than just coloring. When I have a paintbrush in my hand or charcoals, the whole world just falls away. I don't have any worries, problems, or pain. It all just disappears."

"I wish I had something like that," I admit. "Nothing does that for me."

"What do you worry about, Cissy?" He looks at me and his eyes are quizzical like he cannot figure me out.

"Everything."

"Tell me. I'm a rather good listener," he says, plopping down on a tree stump.

"What? You a therapist now?" I laugh, straddling a low tree branch.

"I'd totally be if men—"

"If men could be therapists," we say in unison.

"Feelings are for females," I add. "How dare a man care about his heart and his feelings?"

"Exactly," Riot agrees, rolling his eyes. "So tell me, what worries you?"

"Alright, I'll play. I worry about my Moms when I leave for higher learning. Mom works so hard at the school, and Mama still struggles with having to give Cleave up."

"Cleave?" he says, his eyes lighting up. "As in Cleave Shaw?"

"Yeah, my brother, my twin."

"Dude, that guy's a trip. He's totally the comic relief of Lakeward."

"I guess he got the humor genes, because I have none of that personality."

"Nature vs. nurture," Riot says, nodding.

"What? What does that even mean?" I ask.

"It's a scientific study in how or what people's traits

and personalities are based on if they were born that way or developed them over time, due to who raised them."

"Nature versus nurture? Hmmm, I'm not sure that has anything to do with his sense of humor," I say, speculatively. "Cleave and I are nothing alike—except that we're twins."

"Doesn't it bother you that he gets a relationship with your father and you don't?"

"A relationship with my father?" Oh my Authority, I've spent so much time berating Cleave for not wanting to develop a stronger bond with our mom, and I have not once thought about my father. "Riot, I've never considered one of Cleave's dads as my father. Never even asked about which one was the active father."

"Okay, so—"

"So? I have a father. A man who made me."

"Yeah, and I have a mom." He looks confused.

"That's just crazy that I never took the time to think about him or care about him. I have to ease up on Cleave. I'm no better than he is."

"Ahhh, but you are. You just realized it yourself that our country is screwed up and that the powers-that-be pick and choose crazy stuff to keep us safe." Riot lifts his sweatshirt up over his head. "It's so freaking hot out."

"But this morning it was freezing," I agree. "It's definitely layering season."

"Layering season?"

"Uhhh yes, wake up and put on sweaters and sweatshirts with summer clothes underneath, but by midafternoon, we're all in tank tops and shorts."

"Tell me this; if you, your mom, and Cleave want to see one another, why don't you just make plans to do so? It's not like you don't know where that can happen," he says, motioning all around. "These trees are the perfect covert for lawbreakers."

"Cleave isn't interested in Mama at all. And Mama would never break a Law of Liberty," I say matter-of-factly, shrugging my shoulders.

"Ahhh, so you're the only criminal in your family." He laughs.

"Hardly, this is the most daring thing I've ever done," I admit. "I'm a pretty 'by the book' kind of girl."

"Yet, here you are in the woods breaking our country's biggest and most punishable law," he says raising one eyebrow. "Not so 'by the book' if you ask me."

"It's terrifying being here," I say, "and pretty exhilarating."

Riot smirks again. "Are you saying being with me is exhilarating, Tree Gazer?"

I mirror his smirk with my own. "I'm not saying anything." I feel my cheeks burn.

"I think you need to be careful. I used to be where you are, and it's a slippery slope. You're going to start questioning everything now. And it sucks, because we never get any answers."

"The older I get, the more I realize I know nothing." My life has been protected and sheltered. Lately, I just feel so oblivious and curious. Why is it so wrong to want answers to the life I'm living?

"Sadly, there is so much we can learn and know, but nobody is letting us." Riot's smirk fades and is replaced with a defeated frown as his brows furrow. "Be careful out there, Cissy. I'd hate it if something happened to you."

CHAPTER 12
RIOT

"The only way to prove that you're a good sport is to lose."
(Ernie Banks)

The first time I saw Cissy, I panicked. Lizzie just laughed and acted like I was a crazy man. I remember her looking over her shoulder at the girl lying on the ground like she was something to observe, nothing to really think about. I was paranoid that she'd narc on us or that she'd shoot me for being in the forest on a female day. Lizzie simply said, "Not Cissy Maddox." She shrugged and walked away, knowing in those three words that my fears were assuaged and that I'd just follow her. Truthfully, I would have followed her anywhere.

I honestly had no idea that females were so brave and strong. I also thought—or was led to believe—that they were these cowardly, weak vessels that couldn't think or do anything for themselves. I learned quickly that women aren't these co-dependent people who relied on each other for everything and were physically and emotionally unable to handle anything. It really was eye-opening watching Lizzie try and do anything that I was interested in—excluding lacrosse of course. The girl was a powerhouse. I have teammates who Lizzie could probably outsmart, outrun, and outdebate. Never would I have thought that a woman could do anything better than a man—especially think or run.

Cissy claims to be this fearful female, but man, she surely isn't. She questions things; she challenges our way of life. She even dares to do what many women would never do. There is nothing cowardly about this female. Now that I know two girls, I wonder what else I've been wrong about.

"Hey Dads, I'm home!" I yell, throwing my backpack on the couch. The house is eerily quiet. The second I turn the corner and see my dads sitting at the kitchen table, neither speaking, I know something's wrong.

"Riot," my father says, his eyes narrow and ominous. "Have a seat."

I slowly sit, eyeing them both cautiously. This is not good. What do they know? Deny. Deny. Deny.

"Your dad told me about the girl."

Holy Authority, I'm done. He's going to kill me. "Dad! You promised you wouldn't say anything," I cry, so disappointed that I can't even trust my own dad.

"Your father and I don't keep secrets from one another," my dad says, trying to explain why he's an untrustworthy roach.

"Riot, we're done with all of this."

"All of what?" I ask, looking from one to the other.

"The sneaking around, the doing everything and anything you want without thinking of the consequences," he says, standing and pacing the kitchen. "Shit Riot, you haven't even applied to colleges yet. You're not thinking about your future at all. You're just lollygagging around without a care in the world. You need to start buckling down and taking your future seriously."

"I know, but I just don't know what—"

"Well, it's time to figure it out," he says, shaking his head at me like I'm some petulant toddler who's about to stick his tongue in a light socket.

"I know; I will."

"No Riot, I don't think you understand, son." My father walks over to his briefcase and grabs a thick file folder out of his bag. "Here are 36 college applications to schools all over our territory. I want them filled out—!"

"Father, there aren't 36 schools that I want to go to—"

"I'm sorry that you thought this was a democracy—"

"Luther!" my passive dad screams.

"Democracy?" I ask. "What's that mean?"

"Forget I said anything," he says, slamming the folder down in front of my face. "Just get these done." Both of my dads look at me, one glaring; the other sympathizing. Typical. They start to leave the kitchen.

I stop them both in their tracks. "Maybe I don't want to go to college."

The silence is thick as both men stop and turn toward me slowly. With his eyes narrow and his jaw tight, my father says, "Who in the fuck do you think you are? You, Riot, are a Logan. You abide by our rules. You do as we say —when we say it. And above all else, you are going to fucking college." He puts his face ominously close to mine and grits out, "If you don't, you will be left out on the street to beg, borrow, or do whatever you can to survive, you ungrateful dolt." He storms out and adds angrily, "A dolt is a moron. I forgot I was talking to a damn idiot."

My passive dad takes off his glasses and uses the

bottom of his shirt to wipe the lenses. With a long sigh, he shakes his head and says, "Do the applications, Riot. We love you and know what needs to happen, so you can have a beautiful life."

I hear the buzz before I feel the tightening around my wrist. "No!" I scream. "Please don't!" I reach for the buckle. It doesn't budge.

No.

No.

No.

As loud as I can, I yell, "You said that you'd never lock my tracker!"

From the other room, "You forced our hands, boy. Fill out the applications."

Prisoner. I'm a prisoner in my own home. The tracker won't move. I'm pretty sure you can't suffocate from something being too tight on your wrist, but it sure feels like I can't breathe. If I were to leave my house, the screech from my wrist would tell anyone in a four-mile radius that I'm breaking my dads' rules. Authority would be alerted, my dads' trackers would vibrate, and my own tracker would squeeze my wrist so tightly to the point that the blood supply to my hands and fingers would be cut off completely. My dads just thoroughly screwed me.

There's no hanging with Nigel.

No trips to the forest.

No art.

And if I'm being honest with myself, no Cissy, either.

I'm not certain what's worse.

"WHAT THE FUCK, Logan? Thanks for nothing." Braxton shoulders me with excessive force, sending me into the doorframe of the locker room. "Not all of us have rich daddies who pay for everything. Some of us needed that money."

"Piss off, Anderson," Nigel says, walking into the locker room. "Just go shit your pants like you did in fourth grade."

"Screw you, Nigel. That's all you got? Something that happened ten years ago when I had food poisoning?"

Nigel shrugs. "Not even close, bud. I've got more." He taps his head like he's thinking, and adds, "How could I forget that masturbation drama in the bathroom stall in eighth grade gym class when we had that silver-foxed sub. Still whacking it to gray pubes and shriveled dic—?"

Nigel's words are punched right out of his mouth as Braxton's fist plows straight into his jaw. Nigel barely flinches. Shakes his head once and dives headfirst into Braxton's stomach, sending them both over the bench and onto the hard locker room floor.

"Nigel!" I scream. "Stop!" Neither one acknowledges my plea. They're both so fired up, probably thankful for the outlet for the pent up rage they both have—toward me. They wanted this win. A lot of them needed this win. I could've given it to them, delivered a championship ring right on a platter to each and every one of them.

But what did I do?

Nothing.

My own pent up rage and anger toward my dads, my locked tracker, those damn applications, and this stifling world of homogeny stopped me. Literally stopped me.

There I was in the middle of the championship game, the game that could catapult some of these players right into the next stratosphere if we brought home the win, and I did absolutely nothing. I stood right there in the middle of the field and watched. I watched the whole thing crash and burn right in front of my own eyes—as well as the eyes of twenty-five thousand screaming fans. Coach Cox must've thought I had stage fright or something that was legitimately debilitating me from moving. It took him until well into the second quarter before he pulled me. Screaming at me on the sideline and benching me for the rest of the quarter didn't help. As soon as we took the field after the half, I once again stood in the middle of the field without any intention of giving my team the title.

It's a help yourself and only yourself society. And that's what I'm going to do. Screw this. Screw these people.

But, I certainly can't let Nigel get punished for my civil disobedience. He doesn't need to fight my battles for me. This is my war.

As I close in on their brawl, I yell again, "Anderson, it's me you're pissed at—" The pain jolts me back; my body goes rigid with each convulsive shake.

My eyes are heavy as I try to open them. "Wake up, buddy," I hear in the distance. It sounds like I'm underwater, and Nigel is calling me from the shore. The throb in my head is too much. Squeezing my eyes shut gives me no relief. "Dude, ya gotta open those eyes." I pry my eyes open.

Nigel's bloody face is staring back at me. "You look like shit," I groan.

"Decarion thinks I'm sexy." He smiles batting his lashes and raising one shoulder. "How many times you gonna get tazed? It can't be good for that concussion you're nursing."

I roll to my side, hoping to relieve some of the pressure in my head. "Where is everyone?"

"Gone. You were out for a bit. Cox didn't care." Nigel

tries to help me up, but I'm just not ready yet. "His exact words were 'let that traitor die there.' Good times. You missed one hell of a team ass-chewing. Coach was pissed. Good thing we're seniors."

"Yeah, good thing."

CHAPTER 13
VICISSITUDE

"The question isn't who's going to let me; it's who is going to stop me." (Ayn Rand)

It took me over an hour to find our one "Authority-approved" screwdriver. The tiny thing gets lost in our kitchen junk drawer like it wants to hide in the cracks of the wood for all of eternity. If something major goes wrong in our house, like the air conditioning breaks, the electrical wires short out, or the ceiling caves in, my moms have to put in a work order for Authority to get it repaired. The turnaround time is interminable. But the worst part is that we have to evacuate the house for a certain amount of time—which is never set in stone—and wait for Authority to inspect the house. After the confirmation that what we claim needs to be repaired is in fact broken or damaged, they send a male repair technician to the house to remedy the problem. We cannot reenter our own home until the male worker has been out of our house for a full thirty minutes. Our trackers indicate when we can return.

My moms get nervous with me, because I love tinkering. When something minor breaks in our house, I love being the one to figure it out. But as women, it's against our gender to build things, repair appliances, or handle any sort of construction or reworking of an item. It's sad too, because I love that sort of thing.

"What're you doing with the toaster?" Mama asks, grabbing a banana from the fruit basket.

"It's been burning all of my toast in the morning," I say, removing the bottom of the toaster to get to the heating coils.

"We can put in a request to buy a new toaster. They're not expensive," Mama says, smearing peanut butter on her banana. She looks beautiful this morning. Sometimes, I feel strange thinking Mama is stunning. We look so much alike with our black skin and braids. But Mama's features are softer than mine—her nose is so small and perfect.

Authority rations what women can and cannot buy—and how much money we're permitted to spend. Apparently, Before, women purchased frivolous items and many articles of clothing that were never necessary. Authority put a stop to that about ten years ago or so. Now, if it doesn't involve school clothes, food, or hygiene products, then females must get affirmation from Authority leaders for products to purchase—like furniture, décor, makeup, or jewelry and accessories. It's a long, drawn-out process, so we rarely do it.

"I'm pretty sure I can do this. I just have to adjust the thermometer on the heating coils." It takes me all of five minutes, and I've turned the heat down for the toaster.

"Have you talked to Marjorie?"

"Nah," I admit, putting the toaster back together, and flipping it right side up.

"I miss seeing her. Not that my vote counts." Mama is

looking at me with a small frown. She has the kindest eyes I've ever seen. All she does is care and give to others.

"It's nice that you miss her." I sit down next to her, peeling my own banana. "She's been horrible to me at school—borderline bully."

Mama gasps. "That's a pretty harsh accusation. You know the consequences for bullies."

"I definitely do, and she's one for sure," I admit with my mouth full. "Listen, I'm not going to administration or anything. I can handle it. I know she's just pissed at me and hurting. It'll die down soon enough."

"Any chance of you two working it out?"

"Not a one." I shake my head. Truthfully, I feel much lighter without her in my life. She just made things harder, heavier. "This is a 'not meant to be' kind of thing, I think."

"How do you know that? You both always seemed so connected."

"We're just not into the same things. Everything with us was just so superficial and made no sense."

"Okay, I'll bite. If you aren't into the same things, then what are you into?"

I laugh, because Mama knows me so well. She's always challenging me, making me dig deeper. "I'm not sure exactly. But I do know that nails, hair, fashion, and pink everything isn't my jam."

Mama's laugh is infectious. "That one does wear a lot of pink, doesn't she?"

"We counted once. She has four other colors in her closet—and only one of each." I walk over to the counter and open the drawer. Taking out the giant envelope, I put it on the table. "I was going to wait for Mom to be here too, but my higher learning acceptance came."

"Oh wonderful, we'll go to Gino's to celebrate this

weekend. Now, it's time to decide what higher learning avenue you want to take," she says, excitedly. "I cannot wait to see all that you accomplish. Why aren't you bouncing off the walls? You should be ecstatic."

I shrug, getting up to throw both of our peels away. "Do you want something to drink?" She shakes her head; I fill my water glass. "I just wish I could go to college."

Mama's eyes widen. "What?"

"There's so much to learn, and it sucks that I can't just do what I want to do."

"Where is all this coming from? I'm confused." Mama stands up and comes over to me. "You've never complained about the idea of higher learning before."

"There's so much to learn. Why do I have to just choose one thing and learn only that? Boys get so many options and avenues. I have no interest in being a teacher or a nurse. And I certainly don't want to be an integral nurse. Too much school," I admit. "No offense to you or Mom."

"A lot taken," she admits. "Cissy, you could be an administrative assistant, an artist—"

"I can't draw a thing," I counter. And I really know how terrible I am now that I've seen what Riot creates.

"An event planner, a hospitality specialist, a hair stylist, there are so many things you can be."

"I love math, but I don't want to teach math. If I'm being honest, then I really want to be an engineer."

Mama shakes her head. "Now that's just silly. You know that can't happen in Eka. Women don't focus on math. We just get the basics for shopping and budgeting. You don't need or want all those numbers floating around in your head like that."

"Yes, I do. And who cares what Authority says?"

"Cissy!"

"It's just dumb, Mama. Math is fascinating, and it makes no sense that females can't really study it and focus on it."

"What about being a writer? You wrote that wonderful essay last year."

"What? I wrote one essay. I'm not about to go to higher learning for writing. What would I even write? 'How to' manuals?"

"There are all kinds of informational texts that need edited and rewritten, more research to be done on gardening, cooking, mothering, and even on cleaning the house—"

"What? Yeah, I'll pass on that." This woman has known me my entire life. She knows none of those activities would hold my attention for twelve seconds, let alone an entire lifetime. "I'm just not ready to pull the trigger and make a decision that determines my whole future right now."

"Well, you have to," Mama says, matter-of-factly. "Time is running out. If you don't, you'll be stuck."

"I just wish I could take a gap year."

"A gap year?" Mama looks confused as her brows pinch together and her lips pucker a bit.

"Yeah, a gap year. Take a year off. Try some things and decide what I really want to do." It makes perfect sense to me, but what would I actually try? Waiting on tables during female time doesn't seem all that titillating.

"Sorry babe, if you don't decide before you enter into higher learning, then they'll decide for you. Based on your grades, you're going to end up as a math and science teacher or a nurse. Personally, I'd love to have you on my floor." She shakes her head and cringes. "Authority knows you'd be better than that flighty and forgetful Celeste."

"Oh, did I tell you that I think Celeste and Marjorie are hooking up?"

Mama looks at me, squinting her eyes, and nods. "Yeah, that tracks."

"Exactly."

"So what is really going on with you?" Mama asks, rubbing the back of my shoulders. "Where are all these questions and plans coming from? My little 'rule follower' doesn't usually act like this."

"I know," I sigh, kissing her hand that's on my shoulder. "It's just there are things that I want to be doing and do, and Authority just keeps blocking everything."

"Honey, I don't want you to stifle yourself or hold yourself back, but I do want you to be safe and make choices that are going to give a beautiful future." Mama opens the fridge and takes out a zucchini. "Pesto zoodles for dinner?"

~

It's time to rid my room and my closet of all things Marjorie. I need to give her clothes and other belongings back to her. No sense in holding onto everything. I don't know how that's going to go though. She's been downright evil at school. After trying and failing to make our friend group choose between us, lunch hour has been interminable. I've just been going out to the courtyard and studying by myself. With the end of our senior year approaching, there's literally nothing to study or do. I basically just stare at my notes and let my head wander. I'd rather do that than deal with the drama that is all things Marjorie. Telling our friends that I'm a bad kisser is one thing, but then telling them that my ass is getting big and my thighs rub together is just mean. Marjorie even told them all of the secrets that I shared with her in the privacy of our bedrooms. I would never do that to her. I know she's hurting, but woman, she is crossing boundaries that I'd never cross. We were friends before we started dating. I don't know why we can't go back.

After rummaging through the mementos for over an hour, I have my answer. We cannot go back, because really there isn't anything to go back to. Everything she's given me or written to me has been so superficial. The love letters she writes me are all about my body, my hair, my eyes etc. I wonder if she even knows anything about me. I wonder if she even cares.

Marjorie never called me a badass. She never told me that I was strong and courageous. The way Riot's eyes lit when he was praising me was interesting. How can it be that it seemed like he saw me with a clarity that Marjorie never did? I've known Marjorie for what feels like forever. Two encounters with Riot, and he seemed as if he could read me like a book. That's just bizarre.

And that smirk? Why in the world did it stop me in my tracks? Every fiber of my being was on high alert when that smirk splayed on his face. It's a damn half-grin. Maybe Authority is right. There is a reason men and women do not get to comingle. None of it seems normal or natural for us to be in each other's presence. It's wrong and immoral. I know that. It blurs the lines of right and wrong. Authority knows what's best. They have to. It's their job. I need to focus and get my life back on track.

All of these pink trinkets, fuzzy sweaters, and other crap need to go back to Marjorie. I need to focus on higher learning. And most importantly, I have to stay out of the forest—especially on male days.

But that smirk...

CHAPTER 14
RIOT

"I'm the rebel totally going against the grain. I always want to do the extreme. I want to get as many people looking as possible.
(Tupac Shakur)

The fact that they let me out of the house is unfathomable. Nigel's pretty persuasive though, and they can never refuse him. I swear they like him more than they like me. When we were younger, Nigel would come over and get us into all kinds of crazy shenanigans, and all he had to do was make this pouty face, and my dads would cave and soften. He's the Logan Dads whisperer. It also helped that they were going out for some guy's promotion party. Nigel was right; I did need to eat.

"Thanks for breaking me out for the night. Can't believe I haven't seen you outside of school for three weeks now. I thought I was going to die in my bedroom," I say, digging into my pasta. Decarion puts down another plate of fries. "Dude, how much food are you going to bring us?"

"This guy needs to keep his energy up. We've got big plans tomorrow." Decarion smiles and blows Nigel a kiss.

"Yeah we do," Nigel says, winking. I shake my head and make my standard gagging sound that's now a part of all conversations with these two. Nigel adds, "And get your head out of the gutter, Logan. We're babysitting his nephew. The kid is a terror. Never stops."

"Truth, last time I watched him alone, he climbed up on the fridge and wouldn't come down. Every time that I reached for him, he bit me. I ended up calling my uncles to make them come home. I couldn't do it for one more second. Kids suck," Decarion says, stealing one of our fries. "But Nigel here just has a way with that little heathen. Makes babysitting easy."

"Sir? Can I get a refill?" a man from a table across the room yells over to Nigel, clearly annoyed that our table is getting all of Decarion's attention.

Decarion sighs and rolls his eyes, "Of course sir, I'm on my way." Then under his breath to us he adds, "Because you need nine refills with one meal."

Nigel watches Decarion walk away. "Damn, he's so hot."

"I'm glad things are going so well for you two."

"I have to admit. Summer would've been epic if I would've gotten that five grand though," Nigel says, cocking his eyebrow at me.

"I know; I'm sorry. I shouldn't have blown that game," I apologize for the millionth time.

"Wish you'd come clean and tell me what happened. And no more of this 'I froze' bullshit, because you could've gotten us that ring in your sleep," Nigel says, slurping his soda out of his straw. As soon as the last drop is in his mouth, Decarion sets another full cup down. "There's a reason you didn't show up to that game. I just wish you'd tell me why. Five grand is a lot to give up."

"Don't you think it's crazy as crap that Authority pays us each five thousand dollars for winning a high school championship?"

Nigel belts out a giant laugh. "Heck no! I worked my ass off for years. Someone should pay me for standing out in 100-degree heat since I was eight years old protecting goals every damn day."

"Right, but there are so many men—and even women—struggling with money. How do they justify paying us for playing a game? People are literally broke. I think that's a problem. They give all this money to people flinging balls around."

"Their problem, not mine." Nigel shrugs. "But now, it is my problem, because I'm out 5k—just because my best bro threw the game to basically tell Authority to F off."

"That's not what happen—"

"Let's just drop it. Did you get those applications done yet?" Nigel asks, changing the topic. "I can't believe you have to fill out 36 college applications."

"I have fifteen more to go," I say, pounding my head on the table. "I don't know why there isn't one application that they all just use, and I can make copies of it."

"My dads only had me fill out three," Nigel says. "And that was way too much. Took me forever."

"Tell me about it," I say. "I'm legit drowning in essays of what makes me a perfect candidate for their school."

"Well, you wouldn't have to fill any out if we would've won that game. Elites would've been all over you to play professionally—"

"Nigel, man, come on. Can you just stop?"

"I just don't get you. Won't date. Won't get laid. People are dying to get in to the Elites. But not you. You just dump it all."

"Who cares if I don't want to play for the Elites? Who cares if I don't want to go to lake houses and parties? I'm just over it all," I say.

"It makes no sense," Nigel says. "You could have it all, and you want none of it."

"Listen, don't you just want more?"

"More what?" Nigel asks, looking at me like I've just asked him the square root of 54,006.

"Just more."

"Well, I do want more Decarion." Nigel makes a low guttural growl. "Have you seen his abs?"

Just as Nigel wipes the proverbial drool from his mouth, Cleave Shaw approaches the table. "Hey guys, you alright since that loss? Heard some dickbags at school have been pretty shitty to you all."

"Yeah man," Nigel says, shaking his head. "Nothing we can't handle. Comes with the territory."

I look at Nigel and back at Cleave. I decide right then and there that I'm just done with all of it. I'm not spending the rest of my life caring about all this Authority-driven crap. I look Cleave right in the eye, and say, "How is she?"

Cleave and Nigel simultaneously answer, "She?" Both sets of eyes are bulging out of their sockets.

I slowly exhale, feigning complete nonchalance. "Yeah, your sister. How is she?"

"You know my sister?" Cleave asks, clearly confused.

"Sure do." I shrug as if it's the most normal thing in the world for a male to know a female. "Next time you see, tell her that I said, 'thanks.' That girl really is a lifesaver."

I slide out of the booth, leaving Cleave and Nigel dumbfounded. "For what?" Cleave asks. I toss a forty-dollar bill on the table and start to walk out of Gino's.

Slowly, I turn around, look at both of them, and say, "She'll know." I shoot them a sly wink and exit the restaurant.

CHAPTER 15
VICISSITUDE

"Anger and intolerance are the enemies of correct understanding." (Mahatma Gandhi)

I've never dreaded seeing Cleave. It's usually the highlight of my entire month. But today, I'm dreading talking to him. I cannot believe how totally hypocritical I am. I have been chastising him forever for not wanting more of Mama, and I've never even asked which of his dads was the active father—my father.

My father.

The words are so strange and unfamiliar to me. I have a father. That's just bizarre. I wonder what it would be like to have a father—a man living in my house and helping raise me? A man would never tell a woman what to do or how to be, would he? I cannot even imagine a man—a father—being involved in my upbringing.

When I look up from the picnic table, Cleave is approaching, wearing the most unreadable scowl I've ever witnessed. It's almost like he's mad at me. I know I haven't done anything wrong though, except for not asking about my father.

As soon as he's about to sit down, I say, "Tell me about your active father."

Simultaneously, he says, "How in Eka do you know Riot Logan?"

We both startle at the abrupt greetingless words. He recovers before I do. "I'm not talking about my father right now. I want to know how you know Riot."

"Geez, are you working for the Authority now, Cleave, or what?"

"I'm not joking, Cissy. This is serious. Riot made it seem like you guys are friends or something."

"Riot talked about me? Like in public?"

"Cissy, I'm serious. What's the deal?"

"There's no deal. You're overacting. We met in the woods one day on a female day. We started talking and—"

"You saw a man in the forest and talked to him? Do you even have any clue how dangerous that is—and illegal? For Authority's sake, Cissy, are you trying to get yourself killed?"

"It's not like that. He was very kind."

"This is unbelievable. What was Riot even doing there that day?"

There's no way I'm going to reveal Riot's secrets—even though he revealed mine. Ours? "That, I don't know. We barely talked, to be honest."

"That guy has a temper, man, Cissy. You don't know how lucky you got. "

"I thought you liked him."

"Did," Cleave says sighing, "right up until he blew our championship. That dude's got a screw loose or something. Threw away his chances and others' chances for the Elites."

Cleave shakes his head in disbelief. "And now this. There's something wrong with him."

"I wouldn't say that," I attempt to defend Riot. I'm not even sure why.

"Listen, just stay away from him." Cleave seems to settle down a bit. "I have to admit; I didn't know you had it in you."

"Had what in me?"

"Rebellion."

"Cleave, I wouldn't call talking to a man 'rebellion.' We just talked."

"I'm sorry, but have you seen our world?" Cleave musses his hair, leaving it wild and untamed.

"Okay. Okay. You're right," I acquiesce. Deciding to change the subject, I ask, "How're things with Carson?"

"Good. He's going to college though, so who knows?" Cleave shrugs like it doesn't bother him, but I know it does. "I don't know how anyone wants to go to school longer than we have to."

"Your apprenticeship is like school," I reply. Cleave is going to be an internal pipe master. He'll handle all things concerning pipes in people's houses and businesses. If their sinks back up or their toilets won't flush correctly, then Cleave will handle their issues. Internal pipe masters make a great deal of money, but they aren't required to attend college and take academic-centered classes.

"Not like being a doctor," Cleave says. "Carson is going to be in school forever. He'll meet some hot, smart guy, while I'm digging shit out of people's toilets."

"Come on, you know that's not going to happen," I say, trying to assuage some of his fears.

"What about you? What are you and Marjorie going to do in the fall?" he asks.

"Ummm, we broke up," I admit.

"What? Why?" He side-eyes me suspiciously. "I thought everything was perfect. Isn't good old Marj the hottest girl at your school?"

"By far. Nobody even comes close to her, no lie."

Cleave sits back, his hands firmly on the table. He takes a giant intake of breath, blows it out slowly, and says, "Come clean. Are you linear, Cissy?"

"Linear? What? Why would you even ask me—?"

"The cards are on the table. You dump the supposed hottest girl at Case Academy. Now, I find out you're hanging out with Riot Logan. And everyone knows there's something off about that guy." Cleave crosses his arms and stares at me expectantly, tightening his jaw and bracing for the response.

"Are you for real right now? Are you seriously asking me if I'm falling for some guy I've just met on a random day in the woods, and if I'm risking my life—as well as both of my moms' lives? Wow Cleave, I kind of thought you knew me better than that."

"Well seems to me that something is driving you to break these laws. So, if it's not that hotheaded Riot, then what is it?"

"Don't you ever question these laws or how absurd they are at times?"

"I certainly don't. I've never seen a problem with any of the laws Authority puts in place for us."

"You may if you knew about Portia," I jibe.

"Portia? Is that name supposed to trigger something in me," he challenges me.

"Portia was Mama's sister—which makes her your aunt, Cleave," I remind him. "Portia was Mama's best friend and most reliable confidante. Someone she loved beyond all belief and would literally do anything for."

"So why is this news? Don't sisters act like they're joined at the hip at all times?" he asks, clearly bored with this so-called revelation.

"They sure were—right up until Authority killed her in Authority Central with all eyes on them."

Cleave's natural gasp encourages me. "Man, for what?"

"She fell in love with a man who helped save her and a little girl from a fire," I explain, hoping these words sink in. "He was her hero, and she fell deeply in love with him."

"Are you shitting me right now?"

"Nope, not one bit," I say, my eyes watering up, feeling the sting of Mama's loss—and my own. I would love having an aunt, someone to go to and confide in when my own moms didn't quite give me what I needed. I've heard aunts are the beautiful, rational extensions of your own moms. They expect nothing from you, but love you unconditionally. It's almost like aunts are better than moms, because you don't have to impress them, carry out their silly rules, or listen to them complain all the time. "Portia and Alex wanted to be together, live together like men and men do, or women and women do."

"That is...is...just horrible."

"I know, right?" I am so relieved that Cleave feels this way. Maybe there are more people like us, like Riot and me, who think that men and women should be able to do as they wish without Authority getting into their business.

"Damn Cissy, I don't know. This changes everything."

"I know."

"It makes me want to vomit. Like I'm legit sick right now."

"I get it," I admit, empathizing with him. "People should be able to love whomever they want—"

"We have linear blood in us," he says, his face grimacing. "I'm going to be sick. There's no way that I can handle being related to anyone linear. I am so grossed out right now."

Whoa. I completely thought he was siding with me. He is so far from seeing my point of view. Actually, the only thing I can see on his face right now is downright repulsion.

Cleave looks at me like I've committed some horrifying crime. "Now, I find out that you've been hanging out with Riot. That's revolting. You better just stay away from me," he says, shaking his head with a click of his tongue. "Ain't no way I'm going to sit by and have a linear sister. That would be end of this relationship. "

"But Cleave, she loved him—"

"No excuse. It's nauseating. Stay away from Riot," he says, getting up. He shivers and shakes his head in utter repugnance. "Linears are doomed in this country. Authority will see to it. Don't tread there, Cissy. You'll lose everything —especially me."

CHAPTER 16
RIOT

"Your kids require you most of all to love them for who they are, not spend your whole time trying to correct them." (Bill Ayers)

"Riot James Logan, get in here now!" my father calls from the kitchen. For Authority's sake, I just sat down. They've been up my ass for weeks now. I submitted my applications, but that wasn't enough. They've been griping about when my acceptances will start rolling in. My active father said that I'll be lucky to get into any school since I blew the championship. He's so dramatic —like colleges care about some dumb lacrosse game. And if they do, then I really want no part of them.

I walk into the kitchen, and there's a bottle of whisky on the table. There are three shot glasses set out. This is a trap. I'm not really sure what's up. Nigel and I haven't touched their whisky in ages. Neither one of these men would risk breaking a Law of Liberty to drink with their son. This cannot be good. They're going to kill me and bury me in the backyard.

My passive dad pulls out a chair and motions for me to

sit down. I eye the chair suspiciously as I ease myself slowly down into the seat. My father pours a shot into each glass. Each dad picks up his glass; my active father nods to signal me to pick up the third one. Hesitantly, I pick up the remaining glass.

"To Riot," my father says.

"To Riot, we couldn't be more proud of you, son," my dad says.

"Ummm, for what?" I ask, clinking my glass with theirs.

They both laugh and shoot the amber liquid into their mouths. "Riot, you got into every single school you applied to. Early admissions for every one. You can start two weeks after graduation—"

"Honors fast track," my father interrupts.

What the actual Authority? There is no possible way. I pick up my glass, and take the shot, shaking my head in disbelief as the liquid burns its trail down my throat. "You're telling me that I got into every school—like all of them? How do you even know?"

"Yes Luther, how do you know?" My dad gives my father an accusatory glare.

My father shrugs, and says, "This is my house and if things are getting mailed here, then I'm opening them." My dad shakes his head in disapproval. "Don't start with me, Atticus. You read every acceptance letter he's gotten, too."

"Wait a minute, how long have these letters been coming in?" I ask, really not wanting the answer.

"A few weeks now," my passive dad admits, dropping his eyes down and tracing the tiles on the table with his finger.

"So, you've both known for weeks that I got in, my applications were all submitted and accepted, but my tracker's still been locked?"

My father pours himself another shot and downs it quickly. "Listen here boy, as long as you live under my roof—"

"You'll listen to me and obey every rule I put into place," I finish his sentence and reach for the bottle. My father snatches it before I can grip it.

"At least, you've learned something," he says, putting the lid on the bottle and taking it with him.

"Luther, come on," my dad says, "we're celebrating." We both jump at the sound of their bedroom door slamming.

"We really are proud of you, Riot. You never cease to amaze me." He rubs the back of my hand. I glance up at his face and see the tears pooling in his eyes. "I can't believe you're going to be gone so soon. My baby." He wipes his eyes. "It seems just like yesterday that you were crawling up onto my lap asking me to tell you a story."

The buzzing is loud. We both look down at my wrist as the grip loosens around the band of my tracker. Finally, my father unlocked my parental control. "He's not good at showing it, but he really does love you."

"Could have fooled me," I reply, removing my tracker and taking it off. "Man, that feels good. I'm putting this on the charger. It sucked charging it while being attached to the wall." My dad nods in agreement with a slightly sympathetic frown. "I'm going to meet Nigel. I'm sure he's at Decarion's."

∼

It has been six full weeks since my hands have created anything. My head has been spinning and flooding with ideas, but I had no outlet to get them out. One night when my dads were working late, I actually used ketchup, mustard, and barbeque sauce to construct a design on the kitchen counter. I was elbows-deep in condiments when I heard the garage door open. It was the fastest I've ever cleaned anything in my life. I ripped off my shirt and sopped most of it up before the car even pulled into the garage. When they walked in, it appeared as if I was just scrubbing the counter with a dishrag and some soap. My father rolled his eyes and said something to the effect of never being that bored in his life. My passive dad is the clean freak.

I cannot get into the forest fast enough. My hands can already feel the mahogany box in them. I'm so excited that I can't even decide what to do when I get there. As I make my way through the woods and into the clearing, I see her. She's sprawled out on a blanket, which is odd, because she never has anything to lie on. She must've been here a while. Closing in on her, I stop in my tracks. She's crying. Not just lightly weeping, she's full out sobbing. I'm frozen in fear.

I've only ever seen a girl cry like that once, and Lizzie ended her life the very next night. Suddenly, without thinking, I rush over to Cissy, and pull her up by her shoulders. "What's wrong? What's happening?" My urgency and directness must've startled her, because she gasps and chokes. Cissy leans over and catches her breath.

"Authority Riot, are you trying to give me a heart attack?" She regains her composure and takes a few slow, calming breaths.

"I could say the same," I say, plopping down in front of her, crossing my legs in Ekian style, like an elementary school kid during story hour.

"What're you doing here?" she asks. "It's a girls' day. Figured you gave up on breaking the Laws of Liberty."

"Never. Why would you think that?" I ask.

"Haven't seen any criminal activity from you lately." She smirks, wiping her eyes. "Thought you'd gone legit."

"Grounded. Parental lockdown."

"No way! My moms would never."

"I thought that same thing about my dads," I admit. "I was wrong."

"They find out about the art?" I shake my head. "Ahhh being in the woods on girls' days?" I shake my head again, smiling. "Oh my Authority, did they find out about Lizzie?"

My hesitation sparks her interest. Cissy sits up taller and leans in closer. "Did they?"

"They already knew." Her eyes widen with surprise. "They knew I had a friend who died—who also happened to be a female." Her shocked expression makes me chuckle. "They weren't happy about it, but I didn't get in trouble for that. I basically got locked down for throwing a game, getting my ass kicked, and not filling out college applications in what they thought was a timely fashion." I roll my eyes and straighten out my legs. Man, sitting like a child doesn't feel great anymore. Kids have no idea how good they've got it.

"Ummm that's a lot," she says, tucking her braids behind her ears. "You seem to get your ass kicked, a lot. You should probably start working out." She laughs and her eyes sparkle with the watery dew in the corners.

"You're good at changing subjects. Now spill it," I say, motioning with my left hand for her to start talking.

"Oh that's what I'm going to do, tell all of my problems to some guy in the woods," Cissy replies, straightening out her own legs, making no effort to leave. "I'm pretty sure that's what horror stories are made of."

"Oh yeah, there's a big market for scary therapy sessions in the secluded woods."

"There could be. Vulnerable girl spills her guts to some random man and just when she thinks she can trust him, he carves out her guts and feeds them to alligators by the pond."

"You can trust me, Cissy," I say, quietly. "And if an alligator comes out of that pond over there, trust me on this, I'm hauling ass out of here, and you're on your own."

Cissy shakes her feet at me. "Tennis shoes." Then, she nods down at my flip-flops. "I bet Riot is a tasty snack."

"Ohhh, are you flirting with me? You think I'm a tasty snack?" Her eyes nearly bug out of her head, and her face turns a dark crimson.

"I meant that my shoes—"

"I know what you meant," I say, shaking my head, grinning. "Why were you crying?"

Cissy stares at me for a long time without speaking. She looks up at the sky, frowning. I can tell she's contemplating if she wants to really talk to me or not. I don't want to push it—force her to do anything she's not ready to do or willing to do. So I wait.

After a long pause, she says, "Do you ever feel like you're just watching your life happen, but you're not the one in charge of it?"

This takes me by surprise. I'm legitimately floored by this admission. "Ummm every single day of my life."

Cissy's jaw drops. "Seriously?"

"Not only that, but it's happening so fast, and I can't slow anything down," I admit. "It's like a runaway freight train without an emergency break." She's nodding emphatically now. "For instance, I just got into all of these colleges, and I'm going to go to one of them two weeks after graduation—and I don't even want to."

"Yes, exactly. Who says we have to be these adults right now and do everything we're supposed to do, just because Authority says it's what we have to do?"

"Finally someone who understands," I sigh with relief. "Not everyone wants to go to school, get a job, get married and apply for children, one right after another. Maybe we want to take our time and be sure of what we choose for our lives."

"Oh my Authority, you're the male version of me. Are you a mind reader?"

Before she can joke anymore, I say, "So why were you crying? What do you have to do that you don't want to do?"

Cissy groans, grabs her head with her hands, and lies back down on the blanket. "Everything."

I totally understand. I can feel her frustration and resistance. "So, what're you going to do about it?"

"Nothing. That's the problem. I'm going to end up in higher education as a stupid high school math teacher, because I'm not 'allowed' to be an engineer. I'll probably end up married to Marjorie with a ton of—"

"Marjorie?" This piques my curiosity.

"My girlfriend," she admits.

Now, this is some interesting news. "I didn't realize you were in a relationship."

Her face scrunches up as she thinks about this. "Well, I guess I'm not. We broke up."

"But, you're going to marry her?"

Cissy shrugs. "Probably. That's what everyone expects from us. Didn't you know? We're the 'perfect' couple—and people like us get married."

"I had no idea." I laugh. "Well, it's all figured out. You're good to go. Math teacher, married to your girlfriend. What's the problem?"

"That entire scenario makes me want to vomit—or pull out every hair on my head."

"Alright then, so what're you going to do about it?"

"Cry alone in the woods until a crazy madman guts me and puts me out of my misery."

"Sorry hon, I only have my paintbrushes. Fresh out of cleavers."

Her groan makes me jump. "And Cleave. I forgot about Cleave. How could you tell him about meeting me?"

"Oh shit, I'm so sorry. That happened smack dab in the middle of my rebellious meltdown," I admit. I hope I didn't cause her any problems. I am a dick. "Why? Did it get you trouble?" Now, I feel like shit. I forgot all about outing us to Cleave. It was so many weeks ago.

"Not problems actually, but it made me see a side of Cleave that I don't like. I kind of wanted him to be better than what he is." Her eyes turn down as she shakes her head slowly.

Cissy and I sit in silence for a long time, longer than I've ever sat with anyone without talking—even Lizzie—and we used to sit in silence frequently. We're both lost in our own thoughts. Occasionally, she sighs or groans. Her confusion and frustration are palpable.

Cissy sits up and scoots closer to me. "Are we in the vault?"

My eyes narrow as I shake my head, not understanding what she means. "I don't know—"

"Like whatever you and I talk about is secret, locked in the vault. Nobody can know."

"I thought that was pretty evident," I say, motioning to us, to the forest, and to the spot that I keep my mahogany box. "We've broken quite a few rules here, Tree Gazer. What's a few more? What's on your mind?"

Her frown tells me so much. She is struggling with something—something that she can't quite articulate. She keeps tucking her lips in and blowing them back out, weighing her options and trying to figure out if I'm a safe place to land. I want to tell her that I am, that whatever she tells me is safe with me, safe with us. But I don't say anything. I just wait, letting her bide her time.

Suddenly, as if it hurts to hold it in any longer, she blurts out, "Have you ever met a linear before?"

I jolt up to my feet faster than I knew I could move. My glare pierces through her. "Why the fuck would you ask me that?"

Her eyes widen and her lip quivers. The tears are back. "Just forget it." Cissy stands up and tries to snag her blanket, but I'm standing on it. It doesn't budge, nor do I.

"I'm not forgetting it. I'm serious. I want to know why of all questions in the world that you could ask me, why would you decide to ask me that?"

Cissy is sobbing again. She falls to her knees and holds her head in hands. With her shoulders shaking and gasps of sobbing breaths, she repeats, "Just forget it. I have nobody to talk to. Nobody gets it."

This has nothing to do with me, and everything to do with her. I slowly lower to my knees. I peel her hands away from her face. Her eyes are red and swollen, no longer sparkling from the teary dew. They're pained and heartbroken.

"I'm listening. I'm here. Talk to me," I say, trying my

damnedest to soothe her. She hiccups a sob. "It's okay. I promise. We're in the vault."

Then, her words come tumbling out. Her mom's sister was murdered by Authority for loving a man. Cissy's heartbroken, grieving an aunt she never had the chance to love, to create memories with—all because she loved someone she shouldn't. Authority destroyed her entire family by killing her aunt.

Without thinking of the consequences, I pull her into my arms, enveloping her into me. "It's okay. I'm here. I've got you." She clings to me so tightly that I feel like I can't hold her close enough to make her feel safe.

Once Cissy starts to settle down and surrender into my arms, I smooth the back of her head, running my hands down her long braids. "Cissy, this happened years ago. Did your mom just tell you?"

She pulls back and shakes her head. "No, a few months ago." She sniffles, wiping her nose with the back of her hand. "I thought it was important for Cleave to know about our Aunt Portia."

"Ahhh, he didn't take it well, did he?" I can see it now. People in my school are so judgmental. I swear to Authority those people cannot think for themselves. They only spout off what others tell them to think and believe.

"Not at all. He freaked," she says, her eyes growing dark with anger. "He was pissed that he had 'linear blood' in him —like it's contagious or something." Cissy swipes at her eyes, removing the black makeup that ran down under her cheeks. "I just don't know how he can't empathize with Mama. She lost her sister. All because she loved someone she wasn't allowed to love."

"Listen, we're in the vault now. Anytime you want to

talk about your Aunt Portia, you talk about her," I say. "I'll listen."

Her face crumples again. This time, no tears come. She just shakes her head and drops her chin to her chest. "It's just—it's just—"

"It's just what? Is there more?"

With her head down, she glances up at me through her lashes. She looks like a child, a scared, vulnerable child. She nods. With a barely audible response, she whispers, "Marjorie."

"Your girlfriend? Or your ex, rather?" Cissy nods. "What about her?" I ask.

Cissy looks up to the sky and shakes her head. "I don't know. I just don't."

She grips her hair in both hands and pulls. "Ahhhh, I just don't know."

"You're losing me here. How does Portia have anything to do with Marjorie?"

Cissy blows out all of the air in her lungs and says, "Marjorie is literally the hottest girl in our school—probably the world. Like Riot, nobody is more beautiful than this girl. Everyone wants her. Like everyone. Everywhere."

"I don't see the problem here, Tree Gazer."

"That's the problem! She's literally everything," she cries and rolls her eyes. "And I would rather watch paint dry on the wall than spend a day hanging with Marjorie."

I belt out the loudest laugh. I didn't mean to, but it just comes out. "That's what's got you all worked up?" I'm trying so hard to not laugh at her again, but it's so damn hard. "So you're not compatible. Who cares?"

"I care!" she explains. "If the hottest girl in the world doesn't do it for me, then what if that means that I'm...I'm...—"

Now, it's all coming together. I get it now. "You think, because you aren't attracted to her and because your aunt was linear, then that makes you—"

"Linear," we say together.

"Cissy, your aunt is not you. You're not your aunt. Linear doesn't run in your blood. That's not how it works."

"How do you know?"

We may be in the vault, but there are things in Eka we just don't talk about. No matter how much you may trust the person. "I just do."

"Ever since Mama told me about Portia, it's just got me thinking, wondering," she admits.

"If you want my advice," I offer, "then just give it another shot with Marjorie."

Cissy looks at me like I've slapped her, her eyes and mouth both wide and surprised. "Oh" is all she says.

"Listen, trust me, I love that you're thinking about how screwed up this world is. We need more people like you. Like both of us," I say, hoping to ease some of her frustration. "We can't go through life just believing everything we're told. But, in the end, Eka is a tough place, a place we're not going to change."

Cissy nods, sitting back down on the blanket. "I feel so messed up."

"That's because you have a brain. When you really start thinking about how trapped we are, it's suffocating." I sit down in front of her again. She seems to relax. "But the truth is, Marjorie is an easy choice. It's all mapped out for you. If I were you, and I know I'm not, I would just get back together with her. Forget all this nonsense."

I'm so full of shit. I know it. She probably knows it. But what is one woman going to do? Change Eka and amend all the Laws of Liberty? She'll end up just like her aunt. Just like Lizzie. Enough women have died trying to fight Authority. And I can't lose another one.

"You're right," she says quietly.

"I usually am," I joke. She feigns a smile that doesn't reach her eyes. We're both lying. But there's nothing else we can do. Lying to ourselves is the only answer.

CHAPTER 17
VICISSITUDE

"Being deeply loved by someone gives you strength, while loving someone deeply gives you courage." (Lao Tzu)

Marjorie breaks our kiss. "I knew you'd come back to me." She kisses me again. "I mean, how could you not? Look at me."

"You are gorgeous," I say, knowing that's exactly what she wants to hear.

Marjorie takes my hand and leads me over to the couch. I sit down, and she sits right on my lap. "I've missed you." She twirls one of my braids around her finger.

"Me too."

"I got into higher learning," she says. "I'm going to teach elementary kids."

"I did too," I say. "High school math."

"Oh my Authority! It's all working out." She squeals and drags me into her.

Then it occurs to me. "Uh-oh, if you're a teacher, and I'm a teacher, then neither of us can have kids."

Marjorie looks at me with a slight tilt of her head, puckering her lips. "Cissy Maddox, are you proposing to me?"

I laugh. "Of course. Let's get back together one minute and married the next. It makes all the sense in the world."

"Well, I'd marry you tomorrow if I could," she says, planting a kiss on the tip of my nose. "But, we'll wait until we're 25, just like we have to."

"But seriously Marj, what about kids?"

"Ewww, I'd never risk getting fat for anyone or anything—especially little brats who snot all over everything and expect you to do everything for them. You realize, don't you, that there are like two, almost three years, when they cannot do anything for themselves?"

"But you want to teach?"

"Yeah, like it's hard or something." Marjorie knows how hard my mom works and how much time she misses with us, because she's always at school. "I'm not trying to get 'teacher of the year' or anything. I just really want to make sure I have the cutest classroom in the school. Plus, I'll throw a few alphabet blocks on the floor and let them make some words. Piece of cake."

"So, you're going to spend all day with kids, but you don't want any of your own?' I ask, making sure I have this correct.

"Yep, as long as they don't touch me or anything, it'll be fine." Marjorie's face scrunches up like she just got a whiff of something putrid. "They're just so germy."

Marjorie has told me a thousand times that she was never getting pregnant. However, I didn't know that she didn't want children at all. "So, if I carried our child—"

"Ewww, I don't want to look at you all fat and gross," she says, crinkling up her nose. "Although, I wouldn't mind seeing those get a little bigger." Marjorie glances down at my chest with a mischievous grin.

"Now, you're being gross," I say, shifting my weight, so she slides off of me.

"You want to talk gross; how gross is it that they impregnate you with a man's specimen? There isn't anything more disgusting than that." Marjorie gets up and grabs us each something to drink. "I'm glad you decided to go into education. I thought you were going to sit around and wait for Authority to assign you a career."

"Why would you think that?" I ask, grabbing my drink and taking a long gulp.

"Well, to be honest, you're kind of lazy and never really take any initiative to actually do anything." She shrugs, cocking her head to the side. "You're lucky you're so sexy, because your boring side doesn't always do it for me."

Holy Authority, what the heck have I done? Why am I sitting here planning a future with this girl when she's the last person I want to spend my life with? I literally listened to some man that I hardly know. And did exactly what he told me to do. I've lost my mind.

"Marjorie, what do you like about me?" I ask, wondering if there really is a future at all for us.

Marjorie places her hand under her chin and taps the corner of her mouth, like she's thinking really hard. Her eyes light up when she has the answer. "You have the hottest butt at Case Academy." She walks around me and smacks my left cheek, so hard that I'm sure her handprint will be there for at least a day.

"Ow," I say, turning away from her. "I'm serious. What do you like about me?"

Marjorie sighs. "Everything," she says with more than a hint of annoyance in her voice.

"A little more specific, please."

"I want what others want. So, I want you," she says with a slight lift of her shoulders. "Every time someone mentions how beautiful you are or how perfect your ass is, I know that I've got the best."

I suppose I should be glad that Marjorie is a clueless imbecile, because right now, I'm about the most hypocritical person in Eka. If she asked me the same question, I couldn't answer with anything profound or even remotely flattering. The truth is I'm not even sure I like anything about her. Marjorie is the most brain dead girl at our school. She's probably never had an original thought.

The piano. She's really good at the piano. The Apex Music Academy was scouting her a few years ago. She interviewed with the four headmasters. After touring the higher learning center, she decided that she wasn't going there, because she didn't see one attractive person. She claims she would die if she were surrounded by ugly people all day long.

Kind of how I'm feeling right now being around her.

∽

I KNOW I'm in the minority when I say this, but I love when my moms and I all sit down together at dinner. It's such a relief, relaxing, eating, and talking with them. Most of my friends cannot wait to get away from their moms. But, I like mine.

"This is good," I say, shoveling another forkful of my mom's casserole into my mouth.

"Thanks. One of my students' moms sent the recipe to me," she chuckles. "Molly wouldn't stop talking about this meal her mom made. Finally, I just asked her mom for the recipe." I love when Mom talks about her students. Molly is a dinnertime favorite. "She was chewing her crayon and said, 'there is nothing that tastes as good as my mom's casserole.' I took the crayon away and decided that if Molly was eating crayons, then I better try the casserole she keeps talking about."

"Now, this is the same little girl who wants to marry an octopus, so she can get extra hugs each night?" Mama laughs.

"Same one."

"Hey, Moms," I ask, directing their attention to me. "What do you like about each other?" They both look at one another and smile.

Mama reaches for Mom's hand. "Well, it's cliché, but I love everything about this woman."

I roll my eyes. "Not an answer."

"I personally love that answer, Ruth," Mom says. "But this is an easy one for me. I love how this woman would do anything for anyone. She's the most caring and compassionate person I've ever known. There's nothing she wouldn't do for someone. She'd go without to give something to another person. Nobody else in this world is like that. And she's a spitfire. I love her fiery, fight for justice side. It's so hot." Mama's eyes shine. She clearly loves this compliment. "And, have you ever seen anyone more beautiful, because I haven't?"

"Gloria!" Mama leans over and kisses her. "You make co-mingling easy. You make life easy. I wouldn't want to do any of this with anyone else. The way you take care of Cissy and your students melts my heart." Mama looks at me. "Do you know anyone who is funnier than this woman? She makes everything more fun."

"I know! I know," I say, rolling my eyes. "Life is only as

fun as you make it." My mom has been feeding me that line since I was a shy child. I was always so afraid to join clubs or participate in school activities, and my mom would remind me that it was up to me to make sure I found the joy in anything I did.

Right now, I'm struggling to find the joy in anything—especially in my relationship with Marjorie. There is nothing I can do to make that more fun. I truly have more fun sitting in the woods staring at the sky than I do hanging out with Marjorie.

CHAPTER 18
RIOT

"The one who follows the crowd will usually go no further than the crowd. Those who walk alone are likely to find themselves in places no one has ever seen before." (Albert Einstein)

A mile from my destination, I pull off on the side of the road. Thumping my head on the steering wheel, I whisper to myself, "You can do this. You've got this. This is the most normal thing you've done in ages." I know my head is right. No doubt in my mind. I just don't know why my stomach and heart just can't get on board. I feel like I'm about to hurl. I open the car door, lean my head out, and wait. Nothing happens. "It's just nerves; everyone gets them. Come on, man up."

I close my door, and reach for my water. It's already lukewarm. This heat is unbearable already. Summer is going to burn my balls off. I put the car in drive and finish the last mile as slowly as possible.

Pulling into the driveway, I'm shocked at how nice the house is. It's very well manicured. The landscaping is pristine and downright perfect. That's interesting. The way the flowers are blooming and the trees are arranged, it's almost artistic. The colors blend into one another in different hues and shades. I can't take my eyes off it. Art with plants and trees. I've never thought about that. This is the most beautiful yard I've ever seen. My yard is just grass—no bushes, no trees, and definitely no vibrant colors and flowers. With my dads' schedules at the firm, they barely had time to teach me how to start the mower to cut the little lawn we do have. But now, I may start trying to add a little more to our yard. Wonder how that would go over?

As soon as I cut the engine, he comes out onto his porch. I would've gone to the door to get him. I'm no heathen. He swings the door open, and jumps in the passenger seat. "Go, go," McCarthy says, buckling his seatbelt. "Faster! No seriously Riot, faster if you don't want my dads asking you every question that's ever been asked."

I laugh, putting the car in reverse, and backing up. "Ahhh, those kinds of dads. Overbearing and protective?"

"Shit no. They don't care what I do—ever. They're just nosy as fuck. We could say that we're downing a bottle of Jack, having unprotected sex, and robbing a jewelry store, and they'd ask what brand of Jack, who initiated the sex, and what gems we were searching for," McCarthy jokes, pulling down the sun visor and checking his reflection in the mirror.

Immediately, my tension surrenders. "I definitely do not have those dads. Actually, I just got off of tracker lockdown."

"No shit?" McCarthy says. "Did you actually rob a jewelry store?"

"Not yet, but I did wait forever to fill out my college applications."

"Comparable crimes." He laughs, settling back into his

seat. There's a long pause, and then he says, "So, where are we headed?"

"Thought we'd head over to Champions for lunch, and then to catch the Authority Aces game," I say, hoping this is right up his alley. "I checked for soccer games, but no matches tonight."

"That's cool. I don't really like watching soccer. Makes me crazy that I'm not out there playing myself. Every missed goal or missed pass makes me want to charge the pitch and take over the game," he says, shaking his head. "Soccer's for playing; baseball is for watching. Give me an Aces game any day of the week." McCarthy shifts in his seat, facing me. "Can't go wrong with Elite athletes in baseball pants."

"Sure can't," I agree, holding my breath and flipping on my blinker. With a slow, inaudible exhale, I change the subject. "Have you had the loaded fries at Champions before?"

"Have I? Dude, I'd bathe in those things if I could figure out how to get all that sauce out of my ass crack."

My tension releases again. McCarthy's fun—and funny. Today is going to be good. This is exactly what I need—and what I should do. Just two guys out having fun and enjoying each other's company. It helps that he's so light, cracking jokes left and right, and is so damn good-looking, if I'm being honest. What was I so worried about?

~

"I HAD FUN TONIGHT," McCarthy says, when I kill the engine and turn toward him. "I still cannot believe you asked me out."

"Truthfully, me either," I admit.

McCarthy looks like I just slapped him in the face. "What's that supposed to mean—?"

I laugh. "No, not like that. I'm just never the 'asker.' I usually just let things happen," I admit.

"Calling bullshit there, Logan."

"Why is that bullshit?"

"Come on Riot, we're about to graduate. You've not once gone out with any guy in our entire school. Never hooked up. No one-night stands," he says, spitting facts. "We've all been waiting—hoping—but nothing. So this was quite the surprise. So no, you don't let things just happen. Not even a little bit."

He's not wrong. I love how direct and straightforward he is. McCarthy says it like it is and doesn't beat around the bush. That may be the most attractive thing about him. And trust me, there are quite a few things attractive about him.

"Touché," I acquiesce. "I guess nobody has interested me—"

"Until?" he probes.

I smile and nod. "Until now." McCarthy's smile beams.

"Where do you see yourself next year?' he asks, catching me by surprise. I thought he'd stay on this serious relationship trajectory.

"Theodore Carlson School of Broadcasting. Sportscasting most likely." What the heck? I've never said those words before—or given them any thought. Suddenly, words just fall out of my mouth now without any thought? That's just great. Sportscasting? Holy Authority, why would I say that? That's the last thing I want to do. "What about you?"

"Avery Jacobs College of Engineering at Eka University," McCarthy states, full of certainty as he sits a bit taller, clearly excited about his future. "So, we'll both be at Eka U, then."

"Looks like it," I say, grinning. "And Avery is very prestigious. Nice work, sir."

McCarthy's smile widens as he leans in just a tad closer to me. I feel my pulse speed up. It's now or never, I think. I lean over the console of the car, meeting him halfway. McCarthy closes the remaining gap, his eyes closing before his lips meet mine. My lips part, inviting his tongue into my mouth. As our tongues dance, tasting each other, his hand pulls my head closer, while wrapping his other arm around my back. McCarthy's breath deepens. A slight groan slips out of his mouth. After a few more moments, I finish the kiss, pulling back easefully, keeping our foreheads together. McCarthy smiles. I smile.

"Wow," he says, his eyelashes fluttering.

"Wow," I repeat, knowing we mean two completely different things.

~

"Well, there's a surprise," I say, standing over Cissy. "Do you have any other hobbies besides staring up at the sky?" She props herself up on her elbows. "I started calling you 'Tree Gazer,' because I didn't know your name. I didn't realize that it was all you do?"

"Sometimes, I look at water and rocks too," she says, shading her eyes from the one sunbeam that found its way through the leafy trees. "But those aren't as interesting."

"What? Water is life," I say, offended by her insult. "Fountains, lakes, pools, the ocean. All of it. How can you possibly say it's not interesting? It's ever-changing."

"Lie down," she instructs, motioning me to lie beside

her. Still hesitant, I make no move. "Come on, I don't bite." Against my better judgment, I sit down next to her and slowly lower my back to her blanket, lying directly next to her. I haven't taken my eyes off of her. "Don't look at me." She pushes my cheek and points upward. "Look up."

I do as she says. "Okay, now what?"

"What do you see?"

"Leaves, branches, that sunbeam, some blue sky—"

"Ugghh, and you call yourself an artist—"

"I never said I was an art—"

"Come on, Riot, use more than your eyes. What do you see?" she probes again.

I look up at the leaves, and really, that's all I see. The leaves are layered, one upon the other, covering the very area in which we lay. They make a canopy of greens overhead, protecting us from the blazing and unforgiving sun, shielding us from the even more unforgiving Authority as the two of us lie shoulder to shoulder on this blanket. I sigh. "Safety. Sanctuary," I whisper, understanding finally. "A place I can be myself."

"A place you can be yourself," she repeats, rolling onto her side. "I like that. That sounds like an artist's eye. Could you paint that?" She gestures to the flora-filled landscape.

"Definitely," I say, "but I probably couldn't do it justice."

"I bet if you painted what we see right now I wouldn't have to come here all the time and stare at it. I could just look at the masterpiece." Cissy smiles and rolls back over, stretching her arms over her head. "I could stay here all day and just be amazed by this beauty." She inhales deeply and closes her eyes with a small, satisfied smile on her lips.

"Me too," I concur, without taking my eyes off of her.

"I followed your advice," she says, her eyes still closed.

"What advice is that?" I ask, propping up on my elbows to get a better look at her.

Cissy opens her eyes again and turns her head toward me. "Got back together with Marjorie." She offers nothing more.

"And?" I ask, prying for more information.

"And, Authority's right. Men aren't cut out to be therapists. I guess I need to stick with my bi-monthly Authority-required counselor. Authority knows she's a fount of knowledge and help." She rolls her eyes and chuckles, but there's no humor to it. I stay silent, hoping she'll give me more. "Marjorie and I are in different worlds. We're just so incompatible. And, I don't think I really want to be compatible with someone like her anyway."

"Someone like her? What's she like?"

"Beautiful," she shrugs, "but not much else. She only cares about hair, nails, clothes, makeup, her abs, and people wanting to be her or have what she has." Cissy sits up abruptly, turning toward me, and crossing her legs. She leans in conspiratorially and says, "I asked her what she liked about me, and do you know what she said?"

"No, what?"

"One, that I have a nice butt, and two, that she likes having what others want. Can you believe that? We've been together forever and that's what she comes up with."

"Stand up," I say, "let me see. I'll tell you if she's right or not." Cissy punches me in the arm.

"Oh, I don't have to show you. I know it's a good one, but she couldn't come up with anything better—anything more profound than my ass? Come on," she groans and rolls her eyes, slumping back down onto the blanket.

"Not to be a dick or anything, but didn't you just say that all she is 'is beautiful?' Seems like both of you know it's a pretty superficial relationship, but both of you are too scared to pull the plug on it for good," I say.

"Says the same guy who told me to get back together with her."

"Good point," I say. "Care if I take this shirt off? I'm melting over here."

Cissy sits up again and looks at me. "I don't know. Should I care?"

I shrug, pulling my shirt over my head. "Just thought I'd ask. Didn't want to be weird or anything."

"Ummm Riot, isn't everything about us hanging out here in the woods weird? I don't think taking off a shirt would make it any weirder." Cissy openly stares at me. Then, her face scrunches up, and she says, "Why am I almost eighteen years old and have never seen a man without his shirt on before? Our country is what's weird. I've never even seen a picture of a man without his shirt."

"So, what do you think?"

"You look like a 10-year-old girl before her boobs came in," she says, still staring at me. "But with some hair."

"Excuse me?" I say, staring down at myself. "I do not look like—"

Her laughter echoes in the woods. "Nah, not like a 10-year-old, like when I used to play with clay and couldn't get it to flatten out. You've got all those ridges and bumps." She points to my stomach and chest.

"Uhhh those are muscles, Cissy. I've worked pretty hard for those." I motion to my stomach.

She laughs harder. "Okay Riot, maybe I should introduce you to Marjorie, and you guys can compare your abdominal and oblique muscles. I'm just screwing with you. Woman, men can be so sensitive," she giggles.

"Shit, I thought you were serious. How am I supposed

to know what you know and what you don't know? It's not like I've ever spent a day in your world."

"That's true. Can you imagine if you did?"

I don't respond. Instead, I say, "I took my own advice."

"What do you mean?"

"I told you that's it's easier if you just got back together with Marjorie. Well, I decided to practice what I preach."

"You got back together with Marjorie, too?" Cissy laughs again.

"What kind of floodgate did I open? Authority, what happened to the all-serious and rule-following Tree Gazer? Think you could bring her back to the conversation?"

"See Riot, that's what you don't know. When you hang out with females, you never know which version of her you're going to get."

"You said it; I didn't." I put my hands up in surrender. "I would never say something so sexist."

"But for real, what do you mean you took your own advice?"

"I finally asked out McCarthy McCorum."

"That cannot be a real name. Tell me you're joking." Cissy erupts in fit of giggles, grabbing her stomach and rolling to her side.

"Forget it," I say, shaking my head. "Forget I said anything."

"No, no, I'm sorry. I'll be serious. I promise. So, you took out Mc...M&M." She can't get a grip on her laughter. "Is he the blue one or the orange one?"

Watching her succumb to her giggles makes me laugh too. This is so ridiculous. But even I can't stop. Suddenly, we're both laughing uncontrollably. My stomach muscles ache, and tears roll down her cheeks. Neither of us can catch our breaths.

Man, I needed that. I haven't laughed like that in a very long time. There is something about full-out, belly laughter that heals the soul. Something that my psyche has needed for an extremely long time.

"It is a dumb name, isn't it?" I say, gasping for air.

"Like the worst," she says. "So what happened? You realized you couldn't date someone with such a stupid name?"

"Not exactly. McCarthy's great. He's smart, funny, hot, and really easy to be around. And he can have deep conversations. I like that."

"Yeah, sounds terrible. I'd dump his perfect ass, too," she says, shaking her head.

"Says the girl with the perfect ass," I shoot back at her.

"Good one," Cissy says, nodding her approval at my comeback. "So what's the problem?"

"I'm pretty sure I already found The One and lost," I admit, watching her face for recognition.

"Ahhh heartbreak. That'll do it. What happened with you and him, then?"

"Me and McCarthy?"

"No, you and The One," she clarifies. "Where is he now?"

"Oh right." I nod, taking a beat. "Well, as you know, SHE died."

Cissy sits for a moment, taking in my words. All at once, her eyes bulge and her mouth opens in awe. "She? As in Lizzie? You mean... you and Lizzie?" I can hear her swallow. Cissy's eyes dart back and forth as she grasps the gravity of what I'm revealing to her. "Riot, are you telling me that you're—"

"I'm linear."

CHAPTER 19
VICISSITUDE

"When you know yourself, you are empowered. When you accept yourself, you are invincible." (Tina Lifford)

Mending my relationship with Cleave is important to me. After all, I only have one brother—one sibling—I want this one to count. I may have overreacted to his reaction of me knowing Riot. People are very judgmental. As far as I'm concerned, Riot is no different than any of my other friends—except that he's male. And linear.

I cannot believe I actually know someone who's linear. I guess I knew two people. Nobody in the world would've guessed that Lizzie was linear. She was just so normal. Not that being linear isn't normal. Well, if I'm being honest, it isn't. Not here anyway. But, why does anyone care? I don't get it. Why is it okay for me to love and touch Marjorie, but I can't touch Riot? Or any other man. Not that I want to touch Riot. Or even other men. It just doesn't make sense that it's so forbidden and wrong.

Cleave is late. He's always late, and they never extend

our time for us. It's our own fault if one of us is late. They don't make exceptions for anything. Today though, he's really late. I'm going to wait it out in hopes that he does show, and we can reconcile our differences.

Watching each minute come and go is beginning to weigh on me. We are down to eleven minutes left of our visit, and he still isn't here. He legit cannot be that mad over my friendship with Riot. That would just be ridiculous. Imagine families being torn apart based upon whom someone interacts with.

Finally, I see Cleave approaching the gate. He walks through, has Colonel Sumter scan his tracker, and comes straight toward me. "Sorry I'm late," he says, sitting down. "My dads really wanted to talk to me, and they acted like it was a big deal."

"Is everything okay?" I ask, searching his face for answers, but he's completely blank. No emotion whatsoever.

"Yeah, no big deal," he says with a shrug. "They just wanted to let me know that when I leave for Internal Pipe Master School that they're not recommitting."

"What? Oh my Authority!" I say, my jaw dropping. "Cleave, I'm so sorry. Are you okay?"

The right side of his lip curves up as if I just asked the dumbest thing. "Of course, doesn't matter to me," he explains. "It's not like it affects me one way or another."

"You're kidding, right? This is huge news—and directly impacts you."

"It's not my business at all. If they're not in love, they're not in love anymore."

"This is completely your business. They're your dads!"

"Just not big on butting into people's lives," Cleave says, unwrapping a piece of gum and popping it into his mouth.

"They're not just 'people.' They're your parents."

"Doesn't mean that I can tell them what to do and to stay together," Cleave says, blowing a bubble bigger than his head. "Besides, I won't be there anymore anyway. Now, they'll have freedom to do whatever—or whomever—they want."

I shudder at that thought. "And that doesn't bother you?"

"Why would it? They're grown-ass men. They can make their own choices."

Then, it hits me. The hypocrisy is startling and glaring. The absurdity rattles me to the core. "Ummm just curious, but aren't you the same guy who just freaked out at our last visit, because you thought I was linear?"

"Yeah, so?"

"Well, you would care about that, but you don't care about your dads. That makes no sense."

"Cissy, that's different, and you know it."

"Maybe you should explain to me how it's different. If one is your business and the other isn't, then you must tell me how it's different."

"My dads splitting up and shagging new men is normal," he says, shrugging his shoulders. "People screwing around with the opposite sex is immoral and gross."

"Gross?"

"Absolutely disgusting," he says, confirming his statement from our last visit. "And all this badgering from you begs me to question yet again if something is going on with you and Riot."

"Not this again," I say, sighing, rolling my eyes. "We're just friend—"

The alarm blares, and Colonel Sumter screams, "Time's up." Cleave can't get to his feet fast enough.

"See ya, Cissy." He nearly sprints out of the gate.

How does he not see the hypocrisy? One minute, it's none of his business. The next minute, it's completely his business. When in reality, one is clearly his business and the other is not—but he's got them switched around.

Right?

Or do I?

I can't wrap my head around what's right and wrong anymore. Maybe my moms and Marjorie are right. Maybe I'm just supposed to do what's expected of me and leave it at that. Truly, I don't really know where all these thoughts and ideas are coming from. I never used to question everything. I used to follow every rule, every Law of Liberty by the book. But as of late, I have questions; I have concerns. And maybe that's what's abnormal. I'm not entirely sure these days. It was definitely easier and more peaceful when I wasn't trying to figure all this crap out, and I just went with the flow.

∼

THE PATH IS SOAKED and soggy. I'll have to clean my shoes before I get home. Otherwise, my moms will wonder where in the world I got so muddy. Can't possibly tell them that I was in the forest. They know it's a Male Day. It's just easier to clean my shoes prior to returning home. It'll save a bunch of lies from being told—and remembered. It gets hard keeping all of my lies straight these days.

Riot is painting today; he's covered in paint. He's also going to need to clean himself off before going home. I'm sure he just jumps in the pond. That would make everything easier. I wish we could learn to swim. It seems to me to be an important life-saving tactic. What if I fell off of something and into the water? Wouldn't it be beneficial for everyone involved if women could learn to swim? The Authority's answer is to just ensure that life preservers are attached to every dock, bridge, ledge, and wall near water. That seems silly if you ask me. Teaching women to swim seems a lot more sensible. However, I don't know any women who actually want to learn how to swim. The females I know wouldn't want to muss their hair or makeup or exert more energy than they typically do.

The colors he's using are all dark. It looks like he's covered in bruises—not paint. Everything in his painting is black, blue, dark purple, gray, and brown. I can't make out what it is though. I wonder if he knows he's painting an abstract design. Riot doesn't get the lessons I get at school. He may not know the term of what he's actually creating.

"Are you just going to lurk in those bushes and stare at me or are you coming out to talk?" he asks without taking his eyes off his work.

"How'd you know I was here?" I ask, stepping into the clearing and approaching him. I sit on a nearby fallen tree trunk, straddling it like a horse.

"When you break the Laws of Liberty, you have to be pretty vigilant of what's going on around you, so you don't get busted. When I'm out here painting, my senses kick into overdrive, listening and looking for anything that might get me caught," he says, mixing the dark purple into a light gray area.

"What're you making here?" I ask, motioning to his work. It is very dark. The painting gives me an uneasy feeling as if I'm seeing something forbidden or foreboding.

"My future," he says, using his pinky finger to smear

and blend the colors into one another. Apparently, he doesn't care about his clothes, because then he wipes his hands all over his pants, streaking his thighs with blurred lines of color.

"Your future?" I say, frowning and tilting my head. "Your future is just a dark, obscure mess with no real light?"

"Sounds about right," he says.

"Do you know that paintings like this are called 'abstract'? Do you get art knowledge at all?" He shakes his head with a slight downward turn of his lips. "Well, it is. I have some art knowledge from my classes. I've even taken some notes if you ever want to see them to learn more about what you're so good at."

Riot's eyes light up. His smile splays nearly from ear-to-ear. I don't believe I've ever seen him look so young, so light, and so happy. "You think I'm good?"

"I don't think you are. I know you are," I clarify. "You're incredibly good. I can't imagine how fabulous you'd be if you had some real artistic training too."

It's so unfortunate that he can't take more classes or even learn the mere basics that I have learned in my required art classes. It never occurred to me before I met Riot that men would even want to do art—or could create art. I think I've learned more these past three months than I've learned in all 13 years of my education. That's really not true, but I have learned a lot, and I've definitely learned to question things more.

"So Tree Gazer, what're you doing here?"

"Isn't it obvious? The answer's in my name," I say, smiling and sitting down next to him. I look up and marvel at the greenery blanketing us.

"Nah, something propelled you to come out on a Male

Day. Something more than this fine foliage." He motions to all the trees and their leaves.

"I guess I wanted you to tell me why you told Cleave about me. The last two times I've met with him, it's all that he can talk about. It's like he's obsessed or something," I explain.

"He's obsessed?" Riot asks, peering at me through the corner of his eye.

"Yes!" I confirm. "Everything comes back to me knowing you. So, why did you just drop that bomb on him? And why didn't you warn me?"

Riot laughs, throwing his head back. "Well, I didn't warn you, because I can't really call you or stop by for a quick visit. Don't think your moms would take too kindly to that."

"Fair," I agree, nodding. I pick up his paintbrush. His eyes narrow as I paint a smiley face on my leg.

"It's crazy how you can go home with a silly smiley face on your thigh for no reason whatsoever, and it's perfectly acceptable," he says, shaking his head with a scowl. "Meanwhile, I'd get the shit kicked out of me for such a thing."

"Don't change the subject," I admonish. "Why'd you tell Cleave about knowing me?"

"If you were really listening, Cissy, you'd realize that I didn't change the subject. The subject is the same. I'm fucking sick of doing what Authority wants and expects—especially when it's hypocritical and contradictory."

Riot holds up his painting, stares at it for a long time, and then places it back on the ground. He rifles through his bag, takes out his gun, checks the ammunition, and stands up. He takes the picture to a stump about ten feet away and props it up. Walking back to me, he says, "All of it is just so stupid. Ready? Hands over the ears."

I know the drill and squeeze my head, covering my ears. Riot turns around and pulls the trigger, blowing a huge hole in the middle of his painting. I jump, always startled by the sound—even though gunshots are normal in Eka.

"I like you. I like talking to you and spending time hanging with you. It's bullshit that we can't hang. So, I threw caution to the wind and just blurted it out. I'm sorry if I caused you issues. I can just feel this world closing in on me, and I'm starting to suffocate. Didn't mean to make you a casualty in my war," Riot admits, taking a granola bar out of his bag and ripping off the wrapping. He eats the entire thing in two big bites.

Riot notices me watching him, and looks down at his empty hand. "Sorry, I should've offered you some." His words are muffled through his full mouth. Bits of granola fly from his mouth.

I shake my head, waving him off. "I'm good."

Riot likes me. He likes spending time with me. That's good news, because I thought I was a total nutbag for enjoying these encounters with him. They're just so different than anything I'm used to. It's completely out of my comfort zone to break any Laws of Liberty, but being with him in these woods is the most comfortable and natural thing I've ever experienced.

"Riot, I don't want to burst your bubble, but you do realize that a war with Authority is not one you're ever going to win, right?" I ask, feeling like the grim reaper. "You're making choices that're going to land you right in the Male Confinery."

Riot looks at his tracker. He nods slowly, his eyes narrowing. "Saturday. Male Day. Ya know, I could say the same to you." He clicks his tongue, cocking his head to the left. I watch as he gets out his matches, grabs the annihilated painting, and brings it back to where I'm sitting. "I hate burning these."

"If you don't blow a hole in the next one, I'd like to keep it," I admit. "I can keep them all and just tell my moms that a girl at school painted them."

I can't read his expression. He shakes his head, closes his eyes, and sighs. "Why are you here, Cissy?"

"I told you—"

"No more bullshit," he cuts me off. "No stories about Cleave, no offers of keeping my art or bringing me supplies. Why are you here?"

"I don't know what you mean."

"If you can't be honest, then I can't explain to you why I told Cleave."

"Honest about what?' I ask, clueless to the point he's trying to make.

"Trust me, I get it," Riot says, striking the match and lighting the painting on fire. It ignites quickly, melting the colors and fabric of the canvas immediately. "You have to not only be ready, but be cognizant too."

"Cognizant of what?"

Riot smirks, and again I'm caught off guard. "When you figure it out, Tree Gazer, I'll be here. I'm not going anywhere."

CHAPTER 20
RIOT

"Any fool can make a rule, and any fool will follow it." (Henry David Thoreau)

Nigel and I have been burdened with the task of cleaning the entire locker room. Apparently, Cox blames me for our loss and for the fight with Anderson. I'd thought lacrosse and all its bullshit was behind me. But, we got notices that we can't walk at graduation until the entire locker room is scrubbed top to bottom, repainted our school colors, and two benches were rebuilt. They assigned the work. I'm to rebuild the benches, scrub down the inside and outside of each locker, and scrub the toilets and showers. Nigel has to mop the floors and repaint the walls. It's almost like they knew I'd enjoy painting, so they didn't give me that punishment.

"This is straight up bullshit," Nigel says, ringing out the mop and letting the dirty mop water drip into the bucket. "Anderson started that fight. We just finished it."

"I already told you to go home. I've got it all. It's all on me anyway."

"Nah, we're in this together, bro," Nigel says, running the mop along the baseboard by the lockers. He's putting no effort whatsoever into his task. "So tell me about all these schools you got into?"

"Nothing to tell," I admit. "Probably just end up at Theodore Carlson."

"Broadcasting? You?" Nigel stops mopping and leans on his mop. "Since when do you care about sportscasting?"

"I don't, but I gotta do something, man," I say, closing the locker door that I just finished scrubbing.

"Bet you wish you wouldn't have thrown that game. You'd be siting pretty in Elites right about now," Nigel says, thrusting against the mop. "You'd make them beg for more."

"Nope, not one regret," I say, twirling up my towel tight and flicking it at him. "Get back to work."

"Ow, dude that hurts," Nigel says, rubbing his thigh. "Decarion's going to think I'm letting someone else dominate and punish me." He winks and resumes his mopping. "Speaking of sexual domination, how're things with McCarthy?"

I nod. "Good."

"Dude, I demand some details. After all, I did get you two hunks together. I deserve the dirty deets," he says, sitting down on the bench. I swear he works for 30 seconds and sits for ten minutes. "I knew you two would be perfect together and hit it off."

"Did you, now? And why is that?" I ask, leaning deep into the next locker with my soapy towel to scrub the back wall.

"I hate when philosophical Riot comes out," Nigel groans, dunking his mop back into the water.

"What's that mean?" I pop my head out of the locker.

"I mean, if men could be counselors or therapists, you'd be one."

"Awww, that's the nicest thing you've ever said to me," I tease, coming out of the locker and standing up to muss his hair before I move on to the next one.

"It's not a compliment, Ri," he says, dragging the sopping wet mop all over the floor without draining the water first. "You get all deep in your feels. It just ain't right. Men aren't supposed to talk about all their emotions and crap. That's why women are ordered into therapy—and men play sports." He starts mopping the outside of the lockers—doing everything he shouldn't do and nothing helpful. Yeah, that's my Nigel. "Basically, McCarthy's hot. You're hot. I thought the two of you together would be hot. There's nothing more to discuss or dissect. We don't need to analyze every thought that comes into our heads."

I sigh, running my hands through my hair. "What's so wrong with talking, thinking, and feeling?"

"Everything."

"One example would be great," I say, challenging him.

"For starters, it's girl talk. So, unless you're linear, don't talk like that."

"So you're telling me that talking about feelings is linear?" I ask for clarification.

"Sure as fuck is," Nigel says, his face scrunching up like I've asked him the most asinine thing in the world.

"How exactly are one's emotions linear?"

"Oh Authority! I'm out. Philosophical Riot's here to stay, and I'm not." Nigel puts the mop back in the bucket. The mop topples out and onto the floor. "You've got this, buddy. You're the reason we're here anyway."

"Nigel! Wait!" I call out after him.

"I'm going to meet Decarion. We don't talk. We just do,"

he says, calling over his shoulder. "Because we're men and that's what men do."

∽

RIFLING through Cissy's notes tells me a lot about her. She's one of those neurotic overachieving people who needs everything perfect and in order. Every class notebook is color-coordinated, and the notes are also arranged by colors and topics. We don't even take notes at school. All of our information is printed off and handed to us. I don't even remember the last time I used a pen or pencil for actual school.

But man, this art stuff is fascinating. I have never seen photos or anything of famous artwork before. I wish I knew who the artists were. All they say at the bottom of the painting is "Owned by Authority." I feel like this blue one with the yellow swirls and sporadic lines is supposed to be someone's vision of the stars in the sky at night, but I can't be sure. I love how the brushstrokes are erratic and not smooth and precise. It's hard to tell if this was painted by a penchant child or a skilled artist with a story to tell.

"That one was painted by a man," Cissy says, pointing to the very picture I'm staring at.

"No way!" I say. "How do you know that?" This particular piece of art just got a lot more interesting to me.

Cissy shrugs, and says, "Mrs. Lyra told us. She didn't know his name or anything, but she said that there used to be a lot of different male artists. Mrs. Lyra is always saying outlandish things, so we never know whether to believe her." Cissy looks closer at the painting. "I feel like this one could be by a man though, don't you?"

"Well now I do," I confirm, running my pointer finger

along the picture of the painting, wishing I could really feel the strokes and smell the canvas. To think, if I would've lived Before, I would've had the opportunity to paint and draw or do whatever I wanted without fear of punishment and judgment. Can't imagine living in a world like that. A dream come true, really.

"Why don't you see if you can emulate it?" she asks, turning the page to another one. "I really like this one." Cissy points to the most drab-looking picture of a painting. It's impossible to tell if the person in the portrait is male or female. Is he or she smiling, or not?

"That's hideous." I laugh, scrutinizing all the dark, dreary browns. "How'd that even get in there? I could replicate that in my sleep."

"Actually, if I remember correctly from our lesson, that's probably the most famous and sought-after portrait ever."

"I wonder why. It's terrible," I say, looking closer at it. "Wish I knew who painted this one. Says it's also property of Authority. What isn't owned by Authority at this point?"

"I know I am." Cissy frowns. "Can't believe I'm going to teach math for the rest of my Authority-given life." She grabs a paintbrush, squeezes blue acrylic paint on a stick and starts painting it.

"So don't," I offer. "Do something you want to do."

"What I want isn't for females. Engineering is only for you smart, big, bad men."

"Too bad we can't switch out." I laugh. "I'll go live in your world. You go live in mine." The thought makes me yearn for so much more. "Wouldn't that be epic? What would be the first thing you'd do?" I ask, curious to what she thinks of us and our world.

"Easy. Learn to swim or build a computer for my own personal use."

"Holy Authority, I always forget that one. Can't believe you're not allowed to swim. What kind of rule is that?"

"A dangerous one," she says, shrugging. "What about you? What would you do?"

"Paint all day long out in the open and show off my work to anyone who'd be willing to look at it."

"I'm telling you, give them all to me, I'll display them proudly," Cissy beams at me with pride.

That look. Those eyes. I'm caught off guard. I close my eyes and inhale slowly, my exhale much longer than my inhale. We got here fast, faster than I even realized until this very moment.

"Why are you here, Cissy?" I lean away from the manual, propping myself up on my elbows.

"What do you mean? I brought you this manual. And why do you constantly ask me that? It's kind of rude, actually. Don't they teach manners in your world?"

"Why do you come and see me?" I ask, clarifying my question, looking for answers on her face. Something that shows recognition of what I mean.

"Well, ummm to hide, I guess."

"Hide what?"

"Not what, from," she explains. "Here, I can be myself and be left with my thoughts and questions without anyone caring what I'm doing or thinking."

"That explains why you are in these woods, but why with me?" Her face drops. I've hurt her feelings. I remember this with Lizzie. Females' feelings get hurt a lot—especially when you least expect it. "Not that I don't want you here. I really enjoy this time with you. Honestly." Her face seems to relax at that admission. A small smile pulls at the corner of her mouth. "Your turn. Truth time."

"Why'd you tell me to get back together with Marjorie?"

"Oh, so now, we're answering questions with more questions." My brows rise, challenging her.

"Yep, that's what we're doing."

"It's safer. Your relationship with Marjorie is safe. It's better to keep it safe. Anything else is dangerous," I admit. "It's nowhere you want to be. Trust me."

"Safe? Safe from what?"

"I told you about Lizzie, how I felt about her, how she felt about me," I say, still watching her face closely for the revelation. Nothing.

"Right. That relationship was very dangerous for both of you, Riot." Cissy has succeeded in painting more of her hand than she actually got onto the stick. Men and women really are just different.

"Sure was," I say, taking the stick from her. I want to add some white brushstrokes to the lower half of it. "That's why I'm not interested really in revisiting that kind of danger and pain again."

"Good to know," Cissy agrees. "I'd be sad if we didn't have our hangouts anymore."

"Our hangouts? That's what you'd miss?"

"Yeah, I like this. It's nice to talk to someone different for a change, get someone else's perspective on things. If you could just spend ten minutes with Marjorie, then you—"

"Stop," I cut her off. "Be honest. Be honest with me, with yourself. Stop hiding behind the Laws of Liberty and this relationship with Marjorie. Just say it."

Cissy bites the corner of her lip and shakes her head. "Say what? What're you trying to get me to say, Riot?"

"Come on," I sigh, rubbing my eyes, feeling the white paint smear on my forehead. "I see how you look at me."

Still, no sign of recognition shows on her face. "How do I look at you?"

"The way Lizzie looked at me."

CHAPTER 21
VICISSITUDE

"Not all storms come to disrupt your life. Some come to clear your path." (Paulo Coelho)

"This neck," she inhales my scent, "is like my favorite meal. I just cannot get enough of it." Marjorie swipes my hair off my neck and nuzzles into my neck a little more. "You taste and smell so good."

"Mmm, thanks," I reply, reaching down my leg to scratch an itch.

"Hello? Are you with me, right now?" Marjorie sits back up and shakes her head in annoyance.

"I'm right here, totally in this moment with you." I grab for her hand, and she abruptly yanks it back.

Marjorie shifts further away on the couch. "Can we be honest with one another? Like full disclosure with immunity?"

It's sad that I'm surprised Marjorie knows how to use disclosure and immunity correctly in a sentence. That is just not a kind thought—one I shouldn't have about the woman I'm destined to spend the rest of my life with. "Well, if you tell me that you killed my moms and buried them in your backyard, I doubt I'd give you immunity for that."

"I'm serious, I want to tell you something and be upfront with you."

"By all means; please do."

"When you and I were broken up," she starts, and I know where this is going. "Well, Celeste and I were kind of hooking up."

"Kind of?" I question, pursing my lips together and raising one brow.

Marjorie's head teeters back and forth. "Eh, yeah, more than kind of."

"Ummm, you do know that we go to Case Academy, right? The same place that no secret goes untold?"

"You knew?" Marjorie's eyes widen. "And you never said anything?"

"What was there to say? We were broken up. I had no claim to you," I explain. "You were free to do whatever you wanted."

"And it didn't bother you? You weren't jealous or anything like that?"

"I mean, nobody wants to see her ex move on," I admit, reaching for her foot. She lets me have it. I massage the ball of her foot. A small moan escapes her lips. "But no matter what Marj, you're my friend above all else. All I want is for you to be happy."

"Oh my Authority," relief washes over her, "I'm so happy to hear you say that."

"Well, it's true."

"Listen, I need to say this then. When Celeste and I were hooking up, it was…was…" She stalls. Finally, she spits it out with a giant breath of air. "Amazing. Like mind-blowing."

"Okay, I don't need to know—"

"No, no, you do," she says. "Let me explain. Celeste and I were crazed with a hunger for each other. Couldn't keep our hands off of each other—"

"I really don't want to listen—"

"Please, just let me get this out. It was passionate and animalistic. Couldn't get enough. And as attracted to her as I was, she's got nothing on you."

I feel my shoulders relax. As much as I question whether or not I really want to be with Marjorie, nobody wants to hear how much better someone is than you. As she was speaking, I didn't feel jealous or angry, but I did feel pain. It's hard to swallow that someone is more passionate and sexually attracted to your girlfriend than you are. That in itself is a huge red flag.

"Despite the intensity and electricity between us, Celeste could never replace you. Ever," she clarifies. "I just want us—no that's not true. I need us to be more like that. Even though I'd never choose Celeste over you, I would choose that kind of attraction and desire over what you and I have."

"Ouch, that stings," I admit.

"I know, but I have to be honest with you, so we can try to get to that same place," Marjorie softens, reaching for my hand.

"You're right," I admit, dragging her closer to me. "I've been standoffish with everything that is coming up. But that's no excuse. I should've been more affectionate and more mindful of your desires and needs."

Marjorie grabs both of my hands and grips them firmly into her own. "Cissy, do you desire me like that? Do you want to touch, kiss, and have me all the time like that?"

"I mean, yeah, sure," I say, shrugging. "Who wouldn't?"

"You."

"That's not true. Watch," I say. Taking the back of her head into my palm, I pull her toward me. I kiss her, and she wraps her arms around me. Marjorie shifts her weight forward, wrapping her legs around my back. She returns to my neck. I tighten my grip around her back. She moans into my ear as I slide my hand up the back of her shirt. Without warning, a long, audible yawn creeps out of my mouth.

Marjorie shoots back off of me like a bolt of lightning. She opens her mouth to speak, but then closes it quickly. "You can't even fake it."

"Fake what?" I ask, knowing damn well what she means.

Marjorie stands up, fixes her outfit, and readjusts her ponytail. "Cissy, I'll never regret one day or one moment I ever spent with you. Just remember that."

"What do you mean 'remember'? You're sounding as if this is—"

"Over."

~

I'VE KISSED four girls at Case Academy. Marjorie is the only one I ever dated and committed and consented to. And I'm okay with that. One serious relationship before graduation is normal. Granted, there are a ton of girls who just hop from one relationship to the next. Once word gets out that Marjorie is single again, they'll go back to fawning all over her. That's okay, because she needs it—and deserves it. She should be able to have what I clearly cannot give her.

Let's just hope with the end of the year coming quickly, that she'll go easier on me at school than after our last breakup. Her borderline bully behavior was a bit much—especially with everything else that's going on with graduation and higher learning rapidly approaching.

"How long are you going to mope in this bedroom?" Mama asks, bringing me in a smoothie with a strawberry garnish on the rim of the glass.

"I'm not moping," I groan, taking the strawberry off the glass and licking the smoothie off of it before biting through the juicy fruit.

Mama motions to my trashed bedroom, clothes strewn about, food wrappers piling up, and to my unkempt appearance. "Nothing says depression more than the state of this bedroom and the state of that hair. Do we need to schedule you an extra appointment with—?"

I shake my head. "Absolutely not!"

"Will you at least admit that you're down in the dumps?"

I nod, knowing she's right. She's always right. "I am a little depressed." I take a giant gulp of the smoothie, quickly regretting my decision as the freezing liquid goes straight to my head, forcing my eyes to squint and face to crinkle.

"Brain freeze?" Mama asks. I nod, waiting for this inexplicable sensation to dissipate. "You just seem so heartbroken, Cissy, and it's baffling your mom and me, because quite honestly, we didn't think you really ever liked Marjorie all that much."

"Oh, well that's where you're wrong, Mama."

"You did? We didn't know that—"

"No, you're right about that. What you're wrong about

is that my breakup with Marjorie isn't why I'm so down." I dunk my finger into the smoothie and lick my finger. "The breakup was inevitable. What bothers me is the why? Why didn't I like her? Why couldn't I get myself to love her—want her—like she did for me?"

"Cissy, you can't force love," she explains, taking my glass out of my hand before I can stick another finger in it. "Drink it the right way, would you?" She hands the glass back to me. I take a small sip. "Love happens naturally."

"But with someone as hot as Marjorie—"

"Nope, it's not about physical attraction either, honey." Mama stands up and pats the top of my head. "I can't explain falling in love to you or really even define it for you, but I promise you, when it happens, you'll know. It hits like a ton of bricks. There's no denying what it is."

Everything with Marjorie was so hard, so contrived, and so mundane. Was it always or did it just get stale as of late? That's what I can't figure out. I know I've grown up and changed a lot this past year, but Marjorie and I have been inseparable for years—even before we became official. Did I always feel bored or trapped in our friendship? I do know that she and I always struggled in our conversations. If we weren't talking about topics that she wanted to talk about, then we weren't talking at all. Conversations never ran smoothly and easily. It was like they were always planned out or stuck to safe topics. Marjorie hated deep conversations or Authority forbid, debates about anything. She'd clam up and quickly just tell me that I was right and drop the whole conversation.

But when I'm talking to Riot, I feel like I'm learning more, understanding things a little more, and even growing more. He's a fount of knowledge and pushes me to think more for myself. For instance, one of the things that I can't figure out and really need to probe him more about is why he told me that being with Marjorie is easier. Easier than what? Our relationship was far from easy. It was actually hard and trying, forced and superficial. How is that easy? Nothing with Marjorie is ever easy. Riot's wrong. And I need to tell him.

CHAPTER 22
RIOT

"The sound of a kiss is not so loud as that of a cannon, but its echo lasts a great deal longer." (Oliver Wendell Holmes)

Antsy. That's the only way to describe how I feel. I'm completely amped up, like I used to be before a lacrosse game—when I cared if we won or lost. There's a thundering inside of me that wants out. Yet, I can't figure out what any of it is. I'm on the precipice of something huge. I came out to the woods to paint, but even that isn't happening for me. My adrenaline is through the roof, so I can't calm myself enough to focus on what I want. Even a long swim didn't do the trick.

"You training for something," Cissy says, walking up to the tree that I'm doing pull-ups on. "What number are you on anyway? The most I've ever done is eight."

"You can do eight pull-ups?" I ask, landing back on the ground with a thud louder than I would've liked. "That's a lot for a—"

"Don't even say it," she cuts me off. "Just because I can't do 80 of those, doesn't mean I'm lesser than you."

"How long were you watching me?" I ask, alerted to her words.

"I don't know. A minute or two," she answers.

"Are you lying?" I ask, closing the space between us.

"Lying? No, why would I lie about that?"

I cock my head at her, smirking. There's something about the way she looks at me when I say something crass or challenging. Her eyes transform; they darken a bit, but there's this yearning in them that I've never seen on anyone before. "I don't know, Cissy. I just think it's awfully curious that I just did 77 pull-ups on that there tree branch, and the number you came up with is a mere three pull-ups away. That just makes me think that maybe, you were watching me a little longer and even counting as I—"

"Get over yourself," she remarks, shooting me daggers with her eyes. "Like I don't have better things to do than stand around and watch some dude pull his body weight up and down over and over again."

"Technically, you can't pull your body weight down."

"Shut it," she groans. "You know what I mean. I pulled 80 out of my ass. Random coincidence."

I walk around her. "You have any other numerals coming out of that fine rear end of yours?"

Cissy whips around, so I can't see her backside. "Wouldn't you like to know?"

"I've made it pretty clear that I'd be very interested in a bunch of digits coming out of your ass. Authority, if you can make them all prime numbers, I'd probably pay money for that." Cissy smiles and shakes her head at me like I'm someone she can hardly tolerate. "Or can you multiply them? Maybe even divide them?"

"Enough." She throws her hands up in exasperation. "I watched. Okay. Is that so wrong? I've never seen anyone do more than 30. I kept waiting and anticipating when you'd quit."

"Thirty? You know a girl—"

"Watch it, buddy," Cissy warns, glaring at me through narrowed eyes.

"So what do I owe this unexpected pleasure?" I ask, realizing instantly how much I expected her. Immediately, I notice that my antsy anxiety is gone. I no longer feel like I'm about to climb out of my own skin. I'm at ease and relaxed. Fuck. Waiting for a chance to be face-to-face with her is what had me all on edge. Damn it.

Cissy's chewing on the edge of her thumb; something I've never seen her do before. Do I make her nervous? Uncomfortable? She legit just went from carefree and fun banter to uneasy and pensive silence. I wait, wondering if she's going to fill me in on this sudden shift in mood and disposition.

"Alright, I'm just going to say it. No holding back or chickening out," she says, breathing rapidly, like she's pumping herself up for something big.

"You got this. Come on Cissy, just let it out," I joke, pretending to be her biggest fan and cheerleader. But my cheering and laughter drowned out the question. "Wait, did you just ask me if I would—"

"Will you kiss me?" she repeats. Her face is blank, completely unreadable as she watches my face for answers.

"Kiss you?" I repeat. Cissy gives me a slight nod of confirmation. "Absolutely not." I jump back up, gripping the branch. I get back into the rhythm of movements as I pull my bodyweight up. Now, I'm lifting my legs in pike lifts —anything to release this energetic surge. My anxiety is back. I'm more amped up than I've ever been. I've never been this riled up to exert energy before. I'm on fire.

"What? Why?" She doesn't look hurt or angry—just confused. "It's not like you haven't kissed a girl before. You literally told me that you were into girls."

I pause, looking down at her. I do three more L-lifts before I drop down entirely too close to her. "There's the big misconception." I shake my head at her, frowning. "Just because I fell for a girl or was attracted to a girl doesn't mean that I'm in to every single woman out there. There are girls that just don't do it for me, so to speak. Are you attracted to every female you see?" It's a rhetorical question that I don't expect an answer to. Our faces are so close that I can feel Cissy's breath on me. "I need a connection. There has to be more there than just physical attraction."

"I know but—" Cissy stops and presses a finger to her upper lip. Suddenly, her face lights up like she's just gotten the best idea of her life. "So you are *physically* attracted to me?"

"That's not what I said," I try to backpedal. "You are very stunning, and I am extremely flattered. But the truth is, I'm still in love with Lizzie."

Cissy's face falls. Her head drops, and she sighs a surrendered exhale. Then again, her head flings up and her eyes are shining bright with a mischievous twinkle. "I respect that. But, I'm not asking you to fall in love with me, commit to me, or anything like that. I just need to know. Think of it as a science experiment for my future."

"Think of kissing you as a science experimentation? Yeah, that's romantic," I say, shaking my head.

"See, this isn't about romance. It's science—chemistry, if you will," she says. "I just need to know my body's chemical, physical, and emotional reaction to being kissed by a man. And since you're the only man I know, besides my brother, it has to be you. It's for the good of mankind, Riot."

"Wouldn't it be 'womankind' in your case?" I ask, trying to lighten this suddenly very serious and strange mood.

"That's what I'm trying to figure out," Cissy explains. "It's like you've put some weird curse on me."

"Curse?"

"Yes, ever since I met you, talked to you, and heard about your past, I cannot stop questioning everything. I go to bed thinking about you. I wake up thinking about you." Cissy groans in frustration. "I even think about you in the shower. You're all I ever think about, and I can't understand any of it. It's totally bizarre and out of nowhere."

Holy Authority, did she just admit that she thinks about me when she's alone in the shower? I'm not sure of a time when I felt more flattered. Yeah, how am I going to shake this off? Every fiber of my being is on high alert right now. This cannot happen. I can't do this again. Nothing good will come of this.

"I just have to know," she begs.

"Know what?"

"If...if...I'm just curious or if there is something more going on."

"Going on with us?" I ask, stepping closer to her.

"Yes," Cissy's breath catches.

I smile. Her lips mirror mine. As I lean in, I whisper, "There's absolutely nothing at all going on with us, Tree Gazer." I place a small peck on her forehead. Her shoulders slump, and her chin falls to her chest.

As I turn to leave and leap back up onto the branch, Cissy catches my wrist in her hand, forcing me to turn back and look at her. "Please," she whispers. There's a pleading in her eyes that is downright impossible to ignore.

Shit.

Shit.

Shit.

Instinctively, I pull my hand from her grip. Flipping my hand over, I intertwine her fingers through mine. Her eyes fall to our interlocked hands. Cissy's gaze meets mine. Slowly and easefully, I tug her closer to me. Her chest and thighs are grazing mine. "Are you sure? You can't go back."

"Absolutely." She nods, sucking her bottom lip into her mouth.

Keeping our hands together, I reach around her with my other arm, easing her into me. Cissy's grip on my hand tightens. As I lean in, she sucks in her breath. I place my lips softly onto hers, a feathery light kiss. Cissy's whimper weakens my knees. Her hand flies to my chest. Thinking she's pushing me away, I pull back. Her hand takes a handful of my shirt as she guides me back to her lips. Cissy's mouth finds mine. Her tongue parts my lips before it explores the inside of my mouth. The grip on my shirt loosens as her hand trails up my chest and neck before it secures its home behind my neck. I revel in her taste, relish in the small moans that escape from her mouth, and marvel at the feel of her hands on me. There's beauty in passion. There's joy in pleasure. But this kind of passion and pleasure will only bring us pain.

Reluctantly, I force myself to pull back, breaking the dance our lips were carefully and concisely choreographing for our tongues. I'm not ready to let go of her hand or release my hand from the small of her back. I lean in, resting my chin on the top of her head. Cissy buries her face in my chest.

"This is not good." Her muffled words nearly get lost in my shirt.

"Welcome to the dark side, Tree Gazer," I say, running my hand up and down the length of her back.

"I can't go back to Marjorie," Cissy says, sniffling. "I can't go back, ever."

"I know," I console. "I know that more than anyone. That's why I can't be with McCarthy. There's no going back." She groans again burying her face back into my chest. "I don't like guys, Cissy. I refuse to ruin some guy's life by pretending to love and desire him."

"You don't think after time you could love him?" Cissy pulls back and stares straight into my soul.

"Not at all," I confirm. I grip her tighter and drink in her scent. "Not when I know *this feeling* exists." I kiss the top of her head a final time and reluctantly release her, stepping back. "Honestly, I think that Lizzie had it right."

Her gasp forces me to look at her. "Riot No!" Cissy grabs my hands in hers, but there's now unoccupied space between us, space that we both want to fill. "That is never, ever the answer. Look at all she missed out on—will miss out on." Cissy motions to the forest and then points at me. "Please don't ever think like that. There's a way for all of this to work out. I just know it."

I sit down on the grass and gesture for her to join me. Cissy plops down next to me. "Lizzie and I were together for a while, Cissy. We had way too many close calls. We were getting careless, because all we wanted or cared about was each other." As I say these words, I recall all of our encounters that our parents and even Nigel almost busted us for. "We weren't thinking; we were doing. It was dangerous. We risked too many lives."

"So, what happened just now, that didn't do anything to you—for you?"

My loud, boisterous laugh startles her. "Of course, I'm alive aren't I? That was absolutely amazing. It's just not a path I'm willing to go down again—"

Cissy's on my lap, her legs are wrapped around me in seconds, and her mouth is on mine. Both of her hands are tangled in my hair. She shifts her hips closer to me, swallowing my agonizing groan in her mouth. We kiss for a moment, succumbing to our own desire.

"Yeah, that's what I thought," she says, removing her lips from mine and sliding off of me. "Here's my problem," she admits. "For the first time in my life, I get what Marjorie means."

"What does that mean?"

"Riot, with Marjorie, it was just going through the motions. Doing what's expected of me," Cissy says, taking off her hoodie and making a pillow with it before lying down onto her back. "Kissing Marjorie's never felt like that." She peers at me through the corner of her eye. "And I'm not sure if it's you, if it's just her, or if it's...it's some taboo, dysfunctional thing in me that just wants to rip your clothes off."

I clear my throat. "You want to rip my clothes off?"

Cissy giggles a shy little squeak, a sound I'd never expect to come from her. "I do," she admits, and quickly adds in, "but I'm not going to. Marjorie was describing how she and Celeste have this energized passion, how they can't keep their hands off of each other. Marjorie and I have never been like that."

"So you chose me to be your science experiment?"

"It's more than that," she explains. "I knew I was thinking about you more than I should, making up reasons to come out here, so I figured something was 'off' with me and what I wanted."

"Cissy, it's not dysfunctional to want more out of your life or out of your relationships."

"But to want something like this? Something so taboo or disgusting?" Cissy is clearly spiraling.

"Disgusting?" I question, motioning to myself. "There's nothing disgusting about me, sweetheart." She laughs again. "And there's nothing disgusting about wanting this." Her giggles are infectious.

"Riot, I thought I was dead inside for the past year or so. But that kiss, those two kisses, they made me feel more alive than anything I've ever felt in my life." The honesty in her eyes scares me.

"Cissy, that 'alive' feeling you just got is going to kill you," I explain, wrapping an arm around her shoulder. "We have to bury it—for everyone's sake."

"But, did you feel it too?" she questions, her eyes searching my face for answers.

"How could I not? You're beautiful, smart, adorably naïve, but yet, so brave and strong—even when you don't want to be." I tuck one of her braids behind her ear. "You're a force to be reckoned with. I'd be a fool if my body and mind didn't respond to that."

My heart breaks when I see her eyes fill with tears. The pain is already starting. Why do we do this to ourselves? Why can't we just be normal?

CHAPTER 23
VICISSITUDE

"Letting go of toxic family members is painful but necessary for your well-being." (Unknown)

"Look who's the late one today," Cleave says as I sit down across from him.

"I know," I say, "I'm sorry. I was worried about seeing you, so I stalled for a bit."

"Why were you worried about seeing me?" Cleave looks confused. If Cleave were the only man I could compare men to, then I would think that all men are these distant buffoons with no real substance.

"Our last two visits were pretty volatile, don't you think?"

"Maybe, if I knew what volatile meant." Cleave laughs. Today, he's sitting atop of the picnic table. I did that a few months ago before Cleave arrived. Colonel Sumter signaled the alarm and made me sit down. Wonder why Cleave can sit up there, and I have to sit on the bench below him?

"Like angry and fighting."

"We fought?" Cleave is clearly not clued in on his emotions or other people's emotions.

"I guess not," I say, letting it go. "Mama made some muffins for you." I hand him the tin. He immediately opens the container. "She told me to tell you that she's been swamped at work, but that in the summer, she takes more time off, so she won't be shirking her baking duties for our summer visits."

"So good," Cleave says through a mouth full of muffin. "Man, I wish my dads could bake like this."

"Speaking of your dads," I say, leaning in closer to him. "How're things going on the home front?"

Cleave shrugs and unwraps the bottom of his second muffin. "Fine. My father, your active father, moved out. He's dating some guy named Vinnie. He's a cool dude. Played in the Elites for two years before he had too many concussions and had to quit."

My father. That is so strange to hear. "What's he like?"

"Vinnie?" Cleave says. "He's alright. He's kind of loud though. The man can eat more than anyone ever. I've seen him down three plates of spaghetti in one sitting."

"No, my father," I clarify.

Cleave's brows lift, like he just understood the most complicated equation. "I don't know. He's a dad. Likes sports, hates when I make a mess, really hates doing yard work, and apparently can't stand my passive dad at all anymore."

"What makes you say that?" I question, just wanting more information about my dad.

"Dude is in love with this Vinnie. They only ended their commitment last month. My—our—father is already talking about moving in with Vinnie. The guy's at our apartment every night," Cleave says, securing the lid on the muffin container. "I have to go there every other day until I —we—turn 18 next month."

"Are you bothered that he moved on so fast?" I don't like knowing that information about my father. I wonder if they'd already started seeing one another before the Deconstruction Hearing happened.

"Nah, I'd probably do the same if things weren't great with me and Carse," Cleave admits. "Like next year when he's a pre-med student, I'll probably see what else is out there if I'm getting lonely or bored. My father always says that you should never leave a relationship or a job until you have another one lined up." His laugh is almost sinister when he says it.

"Cleave!" I admonish. "How can you say that? You were just gushing about how into Carson you are."

"I am too, but I'm not waiting around for eight years while he studies books and body parts. I like when he studies my parts." Cleave pounds the table like he's made the funniest joke, yet I find it crass and inappropriate.

"Don't you want him to be happy and achieve his dreams?"

"Of course," he admits. "But not if it's going to make me unhappy."

Cleave lacks any sort of substance or compassion. It seems like I surround myself with people who are empty vessels of thought and emotion, which makes zero sense since my moms are so open, loving, and communicative. But Marjorie and Cleave are like one in the same.

And Riot, well, he's the most talkative, emotional, and accepting person I've ever known.

"Cleave, can I ask you something?"

"Sure," he says, motioning for me to give it to him.

"What do you care about?" I've wanted to ask him this

exact question for quite some time now, but haven't. I'm mainly more worried about what he might say.

"I don't get it. What do you mean?" Cleave is not bright. I assumed every guy was just like him. But now that I know Riot, it's crystal clear that not all men are created equal. Some are way more gifted and lovely than others.

"What do you love, care about? What's important to you?"

Cleave shrugs. "Well, I care about seeing Carson a lot before we go off to school. I care about making bank when I'm out of school." He pauses and thinks longer. His face lights up. "I definitely care about getting a hot husband and having an athletic son someday."

"A son? So you do want kids?" This admission relieves some of my tension. Good, he has fatherly ambition and desires. He wants to give his love to another.

"Oh heck yeah," he says. "I'm hoping to have a son in the Elites. Making cash, getting famous. I can't ball, but I'm not like my dads. My son is going to know just how important it is to be the best at sports."

"Just to clarify," I say, stopping his monologue. "You want a family to instill the importance of professional sports into your son—unlike your dads did for you?"

"Facts," Cleave confirms. "It's going to be epic. Now, if I stay with Carson that may be tricky. Neither of us is too athletic. But, we'll just start playing ball with our boy as soon as he can open his eyes."

"Open his eyes? Cleave, babies open their eyes as soon as they're born. They're not puppies." Yep, all men are not created equal. It's amazing how much I used to love these visits, thinking how exciting it was to spend thirty minutes with my brother once a month. Lately, it feels like the longest thirty minutes of my life.

"Whatever, you get what I mean."

"Alright, so what else?" I ask, probing him for a deeper response. "Do you care about anyone else? I know you don't care about your dads' relationship status. I know you care about Carson, but you're not going to work too hard to stay together. What else?"

Cleave is silent for a long time. "I care about whether my teams win when the Elites are playing."

"That's it?"

"I guess. Is there something I should care about? I feel like you want me to say something that I'm not saying."

I sigh, feeling my frown overtake my face. "Do you care about Mama? Or me?"

"Well, I guess." He shrugs, but he doesn't look me in the eyes.

"Cleave, do you love me?"

This catches him off guard. Cleave's eyes widen, but the disgust on his face tells me everything I need to know. "Love you?" He starts laughing. He's laughing so hard that he cannot catch his breath.

"Cleave! I'm serious," I plead.

"How could I love you? I don't even know you," he says, shaking his head and still laughing. "We see each other for half an hour once a month."

"For over two years. That's more than 24 times we've spent time together."

"Not nearly enough time for me to fall in love with a girl."

"I don't mean that kind of love, you moron," I quip pretty rudely. "Do you love me like you love your dads or like you love—?"

"Sure, I love you like I love my dads. Is that better?"

Cleave looks down at his tracker. We still have plenty of time left, but he's done with this—with us.

"Do you look forward to our visits?"

"Oh for sure." His smile is genuine and pure. My heart warms. "My father, well your father too, gives me fifty bucks every time I come."

"You get paid to visit with me?"

"Yeah, I never told you that?" He looks surprised.

"Why? Do you thinking hanging with me is a chore or something?"

"It's like school," he explains. "You know, you dread getting your ass up and actually going, but then once you're there, it's fine."

"That's how you feel about our visits?"

Cleave nods. "I mean, you're fine 'for a girl' and all, but I'd never want to spend more than thirty minutes with your gender. It's not you either. It's girls in general. All they want to do is talk about hair, clothes, and makeup. They're single-minded and lack substance."

"Girls? Girls are single-minded?" I ask for clarification.

"Absolutely. That shouldn't surprise you. You're one."

"First of all, you just rattled off three things and said we're singled-minded, which my guess is that you don't find that ironic at all. Number two, I've never once mentioned any of those three things to you. And finally, I am so sorry that I wanted to have a relationship with my brother. I'm sorry for being such a burden."

I stand to leave, sick of being the one who has to foster this so-called relationship with my twin brother. "Wait Cissy, are you coming next month?" I shrug, because I don't feel like I want one more minute with him. He groans. It's a defeated sound—a sound that gives me hope.

"Do you want me to come next month?"

CAROL ANN EASTMAN

"Yes, I never want to miss out on my fifty bucks."

CHAPTER 24
RIOT

"Education is the most powerful weapon which you can use to change the world."
(Nelson Mandela)

My hands won't stop. This is the fastest my fingers have created anything before. I cannot slow down; my head is working faster than my hands can paint. It's almost as if this painting is painting itself. Can art do that? This has never happened before, but I'm here for it. I haven't felt this invigorated and energized in my art since...

When I was with Lizzie, I couldn't get enough creative outlets to assuage my need. Lizzie was my... There was a word she used. Lizzie told me that she was the catalyst that got my juices—among other things—flowing. Damn it. I have to remember that word. I'd never heard it before. I should ask Cissy if she knows the word. It's right on the tip of my tongue.

Can Lizzie and Cissy both be my...? Would Cissy find it rude or disparaging if I compared her to Lizzie like that?

I have to remember that I'm at Cissy's will. If she doesn't come see me, then I'm not sure I'd see her again. I won't interrupt her anymore in the forest after our last encounter. Cissy needs time. She needs to think about what she wants and more importantly, what she wants to be. Right now, I bet she's all kinds of messed up. I remember the first time I let myself feel the way I'd been dying to feel for Lizzie. I was a mess—a disgrace really. It was penalty after penalty on that lacrosse field. I didn't know if and when I'd see Lizzie again, so I put everything I had into exerting my energy on the lacrosse field. The best is when I wore myself out and just went home and crashed. The worst is when I couldn't sleep at night, and I couldn't call her, visit her, paint her, or anything that would feed my hunger for her. Am I ready for that agony again? Am I willing to give Cissy that uncertainty and pain? Cissy has no idea what she's unleashed.

Sitting back on my heels, I inspect my painting. It's perfect. I took that strange woman (or man) from Cissy's manual and replicated her left side in the same browns and beiges, but on the right, she morphs into a vision of beauty. Cissy's face and hair are featured in vibrant hues, enhanced with highlights to recreate her high cheekbones and sparkling eyes. Her smile overpowers the lackluster smirk of the lady (or gentleman) in the portrait. Cissy is beauty in the flesh, natural and gorgeous.

"Oh my Authority, is that me?"

My shoulders release. I didn't know how much tension I was actually holding in them. She's here. She's back. My chin drops to my chest in complete and total relief. Cissy came back to me. "You're so vain. Are all women like you and think everything is about them?" I stand and turn to face her. Her eyes are nowhere near mine. She's staring straight at my painting.

Cissy steps closer. "Riot, I'm beautiful."

"I'm aware," I say, staring at her flawless profile.

"No." She slugs me in the arm. "You've made me gorgeous. I've never looked that good a day in my life." Her mouth is open slightly—in awe of what's before her.

"Cissy, that's exactly how you look all day, every day. I couldn't do you justice. Your features are perfection, so easy to paint. You're pure, untouched beauty."

Cissy blushes. Tucking a braid behind her ear, she says, "I brought you these." She hands me packs of goo. I squeeze them in my hand, and they morph into the shape of my palm.

"Thanks, I've always wanted a packet of mush," I reply, opening the packaging and taking the gray, sticky substance in my hand. It oozes through my fingers as I grip it tightly and securely.

"It's clay, you weirdo. Remember I said your abs reminded me of clay I couldn't smooth out?" She laughs and takes the gray material out of my hand. She picks a piece of it off and rolls it around in her hand. It transforms into a tiny little ball. She hands it to me and makes another one.

"That's pretty cool, but what're we going to do with a bunch of tiny balls?" I rip a chunk off and make a larger ball than the one she made.

"You can make anything with clay, Riot. You can carve images into it or sculpt items from it. Whatever you want. I bet you can even take it home without getting caught with it," she offers.

"Sculpt?" I try the word out. She nods as I squeeze more of it and think about what I could make with it. What would our lives be like if we all got to learn the same things, and it wasn't so segregated? "Cissy, do you know what carbon dioxide is?"

"Carbon di-- what now?" Her face tells me everything I need to know.

"You ever wonder what all I know and what you know and if we just shared all of our knowledge how much more we could know?" I attempt to explain.

"Is knowing more carbon dioxide?"

I can't help but laugh. Now, she's even more confused than ever. "No, that's not what I meant. I was just curious if you knew what carbon dioxide was. By the look on your face, I can tell that you don't know," I explain. "Then, I realized that if you and I shared everything we've ever learned, then we'd know a whole heck of a lot more."

"Interesting," she says, stretching the clay and rolling it between her palms. "So, are you going to tell me what carbon dioxide is?"

"Carbon dioxide," I enunciate clearly. "Carbon dioxide is basically an odorless gas. Like the waste product of the body." Cissy's shaking her head like she can't understand. "When we breathe out, it clears the carbon dioxide from our lungs."

"How'd it get in there in the first place?" Cissy asks.

"Well, it's made by our body and it travels through our blood—"

"And we breathe something out of our lungs that's in our blood? That doesn't make any sense."

"It's in all kinds of things, plants, animals, people. Maybe we need to start smaller—and not with chemistry," I say, shaking my head. "Probably not the best example. But would that interest you? Do you want to teach me things, and I can teach you things?"

"Riot, I'm going to bet that other than art and music, you get to learn everything I do. Men get way more privileges, opportunities, and education than women do. Ours is very limited. We do have some science knowledge, but we get a ton more if we go to higher learning to be a nurse. Basically, they teach us nothing."

"I bet that's not true," I counter. "We just get different ones."

"What happens when your lawn mower breaks?" she asks.

"My dads fix it—or at least they attempt to," I say with a shrug. "Why? What do you do?"

"We're not allowed to fix it. We're not allowed to have tools." Cissy thinks about this for a moment longer. "Do you have kitchen utensils, like a blender, toaster, oven, and things like that?"

"Of course," I say.

"But we get limited 'male' items. We have one tiny screwdriver, one small hammer, and 20 screws and 20 nails," she tells me.

"What? My entire garage is full of that crap," I say, completely baffled at this new knowledge.

"And we aren't permitted to have garages." Cissy laughs. "But sure, I'd be glad to learn more, but I'm not sure what I can teach you."

"Cissy, you've already taught me so much," I say, restructuring the clay in my hands. "And given me so much. Do you know that's the first painting I've made that isn't dark and depressing? I've been trapped in these dreary doldrums since—"

"Since Lizzie died," Cissy finishes my sentence.

"But this one, this painting, has light and hope. There's a promise in it that I haven't felt in a long time." And there's that look. The look that only she can give me. It weakens me; it reminds me yet again of what we cannot have, what we cannot be. "And that's a big problem for me."

"What? Why? How can having hope be a problem?"

"You don't get it, Cissy," I explain. "We don't get to hope. You and me, this can't be. You know it. I know it. The whole country of Eka knows it."

"But Riot—"

"There's no 'but.' We're screwed. The best we can hope for are a few encounters in the woods. And maybe some lessons on things Authority doesn't really want us to know. That's it." I'm squeezing the clay so hard that I've dug my nails all the way through the clay, and they're digging into my palms.

"Or." She takes a step closer. Cissy loops her finger through my belt loop and tugs me closer to her. "We just see what happens each day when we're alone in these woods. And maybe, just maybe, we stop worrying about what's going on in that messed up world of ours." Her breath is sweet and minty. She looks up at me through her lashes. Man, this girl's got game. I didn't even realize that girls could have game. She's gotten flirting down to a polished and irresistible science.

"We can't," I whisper.

"I'm not Lizzie, Riot. I'm not going anywhere," she states. "But I would like to see where this goes."

"It cannot go anywhere. That's what I'm saying," I grit out using every ounce of my restraint. "Eka won't allow it. I won't allow it." To reiterate my point, I grab the black paint and pour it all over the painting of her.

"No Riot." She lunges at the painting, but she's too late. "I wanted that one."

"Cissy, that's what you need to grasp. We can't have what we want."

"I think you're making this out to be worse than it is. We can find a way—"

"Lizzie told her moms about me, about us," I finally say, hoping to get her to understand.

"What? For real?" Her eyes reveal her total surprise. "What did they say?"

"They told her that they wouldn't risk their lives for their abomination of a daughter and that if she ever saw me again that they'd turn her over to Authority themselves," I say, my eyes watering at the recollection. "It's all in the letter she left me. She thought they'd help us find a way to be together. They always seemed so supportive of her, but they were only into the girl they thought they knew and thought they could control. When it came down to what Lizzie needed or wanted, they didn't care."

"She left you a letter?"

"She put it in my art supplies. Lizzie didn't want me to blame myself, but how could I not?" I explain, feeling my frustration and anger at the world coming back with a vengeance. "And the only thing I can do now is remember the pain that came with it all and make sure I don't make those mistakes again."

"Meaning?"

"This, you and me, cannot happen."

"But, you can paint beautiful pictures of me and teach me about chemistry?" she questions. "So, we're picking and choosing which Laws of Liberty we're willing to break now? Because if so, I'd rather not learn science, I'd rather break some laws that are little more fun. Wouldn't you?"

Cissy pulls her braids back, takes an elastic band from her wrist, and secures the hair at the nape of her neck. She's stunning with her hair pulled back. Her cheekbones and jawline are so defined, yet feminine and soft. With ease and confidence, she pulls her sweatshirt over her head. Cissy's wearing a tight, short tank top that accentuates every curve of her body. "It's kind of hot out here. Don't you think, Riot?"

I turn my head, looking up at the leaves covering us. "Yes, yes, I do." She is not playing fair. She's not playing fair one bit.

CHAPTER 25
VICISSITUDE

"We destroy ourselves when we stop feeling. If you bury your feelings within you, you become a graveyard." (Bernie S. Siegel)

I've spent a good portion of my seventeen years of life doing exactly what is asked of me and being the good girl that everyone expected me to be. Everyone in every aspect of my life calls me a rule-follower. For the past few years, I've been dating Marjorie, doing all of my schoolwork, and making my moms proud of the daughter they're raising. But all along, I knew that something was missing, something always seemed off.

Nothing is missing.

Nothing is off.

It's been in me all this time. And Riot unleashed it. Whether it's his intelligence, his artistic talent, his undeniably sexy smirk, those piercing blue eyes, the unkempt dark brown hair, those ridiculously chiseled abdominal muscles, or a culmination of everything about him, my desire's been unlocked, and I'm not playing coy or bashful for anyone. I know what I want, and this world of homogeny and over-protective control and authority isn't going to stop me from feeling and wanting what I've been missing all of these years.

I walk toward him. "I know you loved her. I also know how painful that can be," I say, stopping right in front of him. "Let me help you. Talk to me. We can get through this together." I lift my hand, and trace my knuckle along his jawline.

Riot sighs and leans into my hand, but only for a brief moment. "Nope. Nope. I'm not doing this. Can't do this again." He shakes his head frantically, trying to convince himself. He's not convincing me. "Marjorie. McCarthy. That's what we need to do. What we need to focus on." His words are shaky, despite being an attempt at finality.

"Can't happen. She dumped me." I shrug. "Marjorie wants passion, desire, and electricity. Guess what? I can't give it to her."

"Cissy, no! you have to find a way back into her life. It's the only rational and acceptable answer. You have no idea—"

"That's where you're wrong. You, Riot, have no idea," I explain, swiping a piece of hair out of his eye. He looks at me now with pleading eyes, eyes that want so much, but refuse to cave to his needs. "I thought I was dead inside. I thought there was some type of malfunctioning wiring in me that couldn't just let me be normal—like everyone else." I hook my pointer finger around his pinky. He grips it tight, giving me the courage and the permission to go on. "Everyone was always talking about their uncontrollable sex drives and how they couldn't get enough. All I ever thought was how fast we could be done and back to eating snacks and talking about the other people in our school."

Riot chuckles and closes his eyes. "It was never funny. It was sad, Riot. I was numb."

"Cissy, you don't know numb," he pleads with me, looking deep into my eyes.

"And you do?" I question. He nods, frowning. I run my finger along his chest. His eyes squeeze closed, again, a small groan throbs in his throat. "Doesn't seem like you can't feel that."

"I can feel it, but I just don't want to," he explains. "It's so hard."

"You don't think I know that. I told you about my Aunt Portia," I remind him. "Hearing her story scares the crap out of me, Riot. But it also empowers me. Portia and Alex found each other. They got to experience everything—before Authority took it away."

"They take everything away."

"No, they can't take away what we feel, what we are, and the memories we make," I say, interlacing all of my fingers with his. "Don't you realize that experiencing one moment of something wonderful is way better than a lifetime of numbness and emptiness? They fell in love Riot, real, unconditional, take-your-breath-away love. Something I've never felt."

"I have," he whispers, his eyes watering. Riot wipes his eyes with the back of his free hand.

"And are you telling me that you'd give it all up and go back to the way you were before you met Lizzie—even though you know how it ends?"

"I would."

"Bullshit," I exclaim. His eyes widen at my explicative. "No, you wouldn't. She changed you, Riot. For the better. There's no going back, because if you did, and she were still alive, it would happen with someone else."

"It's so hard. Authority makes these rules for us, and it's not fair or easy. They say that they know what's best for us, and they have no freaking clue what's best for me—or for you."

"That's what I'm saying. You taught me that. And now, it's up to us to decide, not Eka, not Authority. Us." I wrap my hands around his waist and rest my head on his chest, inhaling his male, outdoorsy scent. "I don't want to play by their rules anymore."

"Cissy," he asks, resting his chin on my head. "For now, can you just be my friend?"

This shocks me. I pull back to look at his face. Tears are running down his cheeks. "Friends?"

"Please Tree Gazer, I just really need one right now."

CHAPTER 26
RIOT

"It takes courage to grow up and become who you really are." (e. e. cummings)

Leaving Cissy alone in the woods was one of the hardest things I've ever done. I could've held her in my arms all day long, savoring her warm, honey-scented hair. We cannot venture down that dangerous path that I allowed Lizzie and I to carelessly wander. It's not fair to Cissy, to me, or to our families.

I thought I'd lost her for sure when I asked her to just be my friend. Her long hesitant pause scared the living daylights out of me. As I held my breath, wishing for a "yes," my stomach flipped and flopped until she finally relented. That beautiful woman wrapped me back into her arms, laid her head upon my chest, and said, "I'll be whatever you need me to be, Riot. There's a reason people say they're 'forever friends.' I just don't want you to be 'nothing' to me. That, I couldn't bear."

I nodded, making a silent promise. She added, "Promise me Riot, right here and right now, that I'll never be 'nothing' to you, either." I silently nodded, but I couldn't get the words out, because I'm not sure I could make that promise.

Pulling into my driveway, I'm puzzled by the sleek, chrome-colored sports car in my driveway. The EEA111 license plate gives nothing away, either. My dads never, like ever, have visitors to our house. My active father pretty much hates people; my dad never thinks our house is "company-ready." Therefore, no company—other than Nigel—ever steps foot into our home.

Unbuckling my seatbelt, I exit the car. As I walk over to this fine piece of machinery, I marvel at its beauty. I may be linear and into girls, but I can certainly appreciate a perfect specimen of vehicular luxury. I run my hand along the hood, when the car announces, "Please do not touch. Take four steps back."

Four? My laughter catches me off guard. I take three steps back, wondering if the car knows. It doesn't. My amusement stays with me as I enter my house, tossing my backpack on the bench by the front door with both of my dads' briefcases. They're both home? Holy crap, did one of my dads buy that car? If they let me drive it, I swear to Authority, I'll never disobey them again.

"Riot, is that you?" my dad yells from the kitchen. "We're in here, hon."

"Come on in, buddy," my father calls out. Buddy? Yeah, this cannot be good.

I turn the corner and see three men sitting at our kitchen table. My dads are facing toward me, and another man in an expensive, tailored suit sits across from them. There are papers laid out all across the table. Pamphlets and brochures for something. Everything feels off.

"There he is," my father jovially says, getting up immediately and wrapping an arm around my shoulder. What in

Authority is happening? My stomach churns with nerves. My father doesn't smile. He doesn't hug. And he's certainly never happy to see me.

My dad jumps up, grabbing my elbow from the other side. "We're so glad you're home, Riot. We want you to meet someone."

The handsome, well-dressed man stands and offers his hand to me. "Derrick Carkle. It's great to finally meet you."

"Likewise," I say, eyeing my dads with curiosity.

"Riot," my passive dad says, "Mr. Carkle is from Eka Elite Athletics. He's interested in you trying out for the Elite Lacrosse Team. Tryouts are less than a month—"

"I'm sorry, what?" I ask, slowly lowering into a chair next to my father.

"That's all true, Riot. After I saw your highlight reel, I started doing some digging—"

"My what?" I ask, looking between my dads for clarification.

My passive dad chuckles. "Well son, you know how I love dabbling with videos—"

"Since when?" I cut him off.

"This guy," my active father fakes a laugh, "always joking."

"That's why we call him 'Riot.' He's a laugh a minute—a total riot," my dad says. "Anyway, after I made the video of all of your lacrosse achievements, I figured why not try sending it out there and see if anyone bites?"

"You figured why not," I clarify. "Maybe the 'why not' was because—"

"And wouldn't you know it, Mr. Carkle here took a bite." My dad laughs at his humorless joke.

"Actually Riot, we were all chomping at the bit for you. You have quite an athletic resume," Mr. Carkle remarks.

"And as for that botched championship, we have plenty of professionals on staff to help assuage any stage or performance fright that you may experience in the future."

"With your talent and experience, Derrick thinks you can be on the professional field by September," my father adds, mussing my hair. "Can you believe it?"

"I...I...I really can't," I stutter, trying to weigh my options here.

"We'd like you to come out to our facility next week to take a look around, meet the coaches, and maybe hang out with the team. Tryouts aren't for over three weeks away, but we want you to be comfortable and right at home when you showcase for us," Mr. Carkle says, reaching across the table for one particular pamphlet. "This is our training facility. State-of-the-art. The housing accommodations are top-notch."

I stare at the glossy, tri-fold pamphlet. "It sure is," I compliment.

"We have massage therapists on call nine hours a day, the dining hall is stocked with healthy, high-protein, high fiber food. A five-star chef will cook all three meals for you each day during tryouts, training, and during season," Mr. Carkle beams with pride. "Now tryouts are really just a formality. If I'm here, then you can pretty much guarantee a spot with the Elites. The tryout is really for the coaches of the sixteen different teams to decide which owner is going to sign you and how much they'll want to pay for your athleticism and dedication to the sport."

"I can't believe it. You did it, Riot. You really did it." My father can't contain his excitement or shock. His son made it to the Elites. He now has bragging rights for life. I finally did something to make him proud. My father is looking at me like I've always wanted him to look at me—with pride and acceptance.

"Wow! Thank you, Mr. Carkle. This is really amazing," I say, feigning a smile.

"It sure is," my passive dad agrees. "My baby going to the Elites."

"I just...I just can't accept," I say, trying to sit as tall and as confidently as I can. "I've already committed to being a sportscaster."

"Oh no problem," Mr. Carkle says, "that happens a lot. I simply contact the college and let them know. It's never an issue. They're usually just so thrilled that someone who wanted to go to their school is now in the pros."

"See Riot, no problem at all," my father says, his jaw tight as he bites out the words.

"No, that's not what I meant. I appreciate the offer, I really do. It's quite an honor," I say, smiling as my hands and forehead begin to pebble with sweat droplets. "I'm going to stick with my original plan."

Derrick Carkle looks like nobody in the history of his career has ever turned him down. First time for everything, I guess. He fumbles around with his paperwork, muttering sounds, but no real words come out. Finally he says, "Do you realize what you're turning down—?"

"He's not turning a fucking thing down," my father bellows, the vein in his forehead threatening to break free from the confines of his skin.

"I think I just did," I say, rage boiling inside of me. "Did your dads force you guys to be lawyers?"

"Yes," my father grits through his teeth. "Because they knew what was good for us. Just like we do." I stand, readying myself to leave. "Sit your ass back down, boy!"

"Fuck off," I scream, swiping my hand over all the

papers on the table and marveling at the way they fly through the air and float in slow motion to the floor.

Both of my dads scramble to the ground, trying to collect the papers while apologizing profusely to Derrick Carkle.

"Peace out," I yell over my shoulder, tossing my tracker onto the side table, and slamming the front door.

The first time I played lacrosse with my dads is one of my best memories growing up. We walked the aisles of the sporting goods store for what seemed like forever as they held up item after item, inquiring which sports equipment interested me the most. I liked them all at the time, but the lacrosse stick made us laugh the most. I kept tossing them the ball and neither one could catch it to show me what it did. Finally, they put it down and said that I should try something else. Neither had thrown me the ball, yet, but I could instinctively tell that I was supposed to catch the little blue ball in the net of the stick. My father had already given up and was walking away. My dad told me to back up a few steps. I walked to the end of the aisle and asked for a bounce pass. I was five-years-old. Dad lightly bounced it. I never once took my eyes off that blue globe coming at me. I flipped my wrist, catching the ball in the mesh, and flipping it right back to him. I was hooked. My dads were so excited. We bought everything you could purchase for lacrosse—even things that we ended up never really needing. Both of my dads got their own sticks to help me practice. To this day, my dad has never caught one ball tossed to him. My father did get pretty good at it though.

Honestly, I loved the sport. And I relished in being so good at it. Once I started playing on a real team, it was awesome being the best at something. Having parents and fans cheer for me was invigorating and thrilling. But thirteen years of it got old. I lost my desire for the sport. It's crazy that as an athlete—a talented one—you can't just be done with it. People expect you to die on the field, clutching your lacrosse stick. That's just not what I want. And both of my dads knew that. How could they do this to me? They're constantly disregarding me and what I want.

There's only one thing I want to do now, one thing that will give me peace of mind and retribution for this stifling, horrifying world in which I live. Screw these damn Laws of Liberty. If I get caught, I get caught. If it's a life sentence in the Male Confinery, then so be it. This world feels like incarceration anyway. I can't breathe. I can't think. I can't be. Prisoner in my own world. Enough is enough.

CHAPTER 27
VICISSITUDE

"Art is not what you see, but what you make others see." (Edgar Degas)

Letting Riot walk away yesterday in the forest crushed me, took my heart and shattered it. But, I'm not overthinking it. I can see now that what we feel for one another is real—more real than anything I've ever experienced before. Probably not more real than what he had with Lizzie, but I can't let my head go to envy. It's not fair to be jealous of a ghost; I could never compete with that, nor would I ever try to. I just have to give him time, time to process what he's lost, what he could lose again, and what he wants to do from here. His touch, his kiss, his embrace tells me that we have reciprocal feelings. Time will heal him; I know it. Distance will give him clarity, and hopefully, bring him back to me.

It's amazing what a difference this is. Never have I fretted over what Marjorie was doing or thinking. I'm not sure I ever cared. My every thought leads right back to Riot—some of those are profound and full of hope for our futures, others are downright sexual and forbidden. I'm not sure who I am anymore.

I woke up today feeling refreshed and ready for the day to come. It's crazy how you just know when someone is yours and that feeling just breathes life into you, makes you feel like you can take on the world. With a grumbling belly, I walk into the kitchen. My moms are amidst a heated conversation.

"How can you say it's vulgar?" Mama asks, spreading jam across her bagel. "It's absolutely beautiful."

"What is beautiful about it? She's clearly naked. Nudity is crass and vulgar," Mom counters.

"You were naked this morning." Mama rolls her eyes.

"In front of you! Not the entire world," Mom replies.

"And you were beautiful. The whole world should get the honor of seeing what I witnessed this morning," Mama says, grinning.

"Oh you!" Mom says, grabbing Mama's bagel and taking a giant bite out of it. She growls in frustration as Mama laughs at her.

"Alright, what's this argument about?" I ask, scooping some berries onto my plate while my bagel toasts.

"You definitely do not want to know," Mom says, sitting down at her spot at the breakfast table. She takes a short sip of her coffee before deciding to blow on it for a bit.

"Sure she does," Mama says. "Someone painted a large, more than life-sized, mural on the wall of the Male Monument Center."

"What, like graffiti or something?" I ask, spearing a blueberry onto my fork and getting my bagel out of the toaster.

"Worse," Mom says, "It's a silhouette of a naked girl."

"Shut up! For real?" I ask, loving the controversy of such

a taboo occurrence in our community. Smearing grape jelly onto my bagel and sprinkling it with chia seeds, I bite into it.

"Oh yeah," Mom says. "So now there's all this speculation on who broke such an important Law of Liberty."

"What do you mean?"

"Well, it was in the Male Monument Center. So either a man is painting, which we all know is completely forbidden—"

"Or," Mama interrupts, "a woman snuck into the Male Faction and painted on the wall."

"But a man painting a woman like that would mean that he—"

"Knows exactly what a woman's body looks like naked," Mama chimes in.

"I think it's a woman, though," Mom says through a mouthful of bagel.

"Why?" I ask. There is nothing better than gossiping with my moms.

"Well, men don't get art classes or art history, and that mural clearly depicts a replica of one of Authority's well-known paintings. You know, the one with the stars that looks like a child painted it?"

Suddenly, I cannot swallow the food that's in my mouth. My saliva is gone. I take a giant gulp of my orange juice to choke down the bagel that's trying to kill me and put me out of my misery. "Can I see this mural?" I ask, looking back and forth between my moms.

"Turn the monitor back on," Mama says, grabbing the remote. "Authority's been displaying it all over our Tele-Viewer all morning long with a number to call if you have any information about the perpetrator."

Mama clicks the on switch and the mural is larger than

life. It is an exact replica of the painting I showed Riot this week. The naked, silhouetted girl staring at the painting could be anyone, but I know that it is not just anyone. The braids, the body, and even her stance are unmistakable. But the locket, the locket is not mine. The locket belongs to a ghost, but thankfully, he left her name off the small gold heart. But what takes my breath away is the caption painted through the entire mural in words more beautiful than I've ever seen.

"You will never be NOTHING to me."

CHAPTER 28
RIOT

"There is nothing I would not do for those who are really my friends." (Jane Austen)

"Derrick Carkle? Thee Derrick Carkle was at your house?" Nigel asks again, rubbing his forehead. "For the Elites? And they want you?"

"Man Nigel, he's only repeated the story about ten times. You're going to have to let it go," McCarthy says, shaking his head. "Not everyone wants to be an Elite." McCarthy opens his notebook and starts looking over his notes. Graduation is closing in, and there's no way he has work to do or things to study. I've noticed a lot of people try to distract themselves from the monotony that is Nigel.

"Yes they do!" Nigel screams. Everyone in the dining commons looks over at us.

"Keep your voice down. I can't give these douchebags anymore ammunition to hate me," I say, through gritted teeth. "Authority knows; if I get in any more trouble at school, my dads'll just kill me. They're already furious with me and not speaking to me at all."

"You're lucky I'm speaking to you," Nigel says, taking a giant bite out of his sandwich. With his mouth full, he adds, "My best freaking friend could've been an Elite, but no, he's too cool. He turns everything down without even asking me."

"He didn't turn me down." McCarthy, smiles, rubbing my shoulders. "Anyway, the Elites aren't everything, Nigel."

"The only people who think like that are those who didn't get in," Nigel grumbles.

"I think like that, and I have the offer letter." I shrug.

"I didn't get in, and I think it's awesome you turned them down," McCarthy says, reassuringly. "Not to change the subject, but did you guys see that mural in Male Monument Center before it got covered up?"

I feel my body shift in my seat involuntarily. I take another bite of my school lunch, glancing at my tracker. Only a few more minutes left of our lunch hour. I was hoping we'd avoid this topic today, but it's all anyone wants to talk about. I never intended to tell Nigel or McCarthy about the Elites, but knew the Elites would keep us busy most of our lunch break. And I was right.

"Heck yeah, I did," Nigel says. "It was disgusting."

"Disgusting?" McCarthy and I both question, simultaneously.

"I thought it was extremely sexy," McCarthy says, taking a grape from my tray and popping it into his mouth.

Slowly, I turn to face him. "You did?"

"Absolutely. The art was perfection, but that body was pure beauty."

"I'm sorry, what? You thought a woman's body was beautiful?" Nigel asks, his face revealing nothing but disdain.

"Oh for sure, I can appreciate the beauty in all bodies.

Men, women, tall, short, black, white. Doesn't matter. The human body is just perfect." McCarthy surprises me with this new revelation. Actually, he's always shocking me. He's a lot smarter and deeper than I ever gave him credit for. "My dads taught me to appreciate all bodies and all walks of life."

"They did?" I ask, wishing I had dads like that.

"Yep, they're pretty progressive—for Eka anyway," McCarthy explains.

"Not me," Nigel chimes in. "I think the mural was awful. Showing those chest balls like that—"

"Breasts," McCarthy corrects, rubbing his temples—something I've noticed him do a lot when Nigel is around. It's like he's attempting to rub Nigel's stupidity out of his head.

"Same thing," Nigel says. "They just sit there like volleyballs waiting to be served. But, I'll tell you that it was quite ballsy. I didn't think females had it in them?"

"Had what?" I ask.

"Courage. Can you believe a girl would sneak into our town center and paint their pornography all over our walls?" Nigel asks. "I mean, they'll burn for it for sure, but it certainly was ballsy."

"If they get caught," McCarthy adds. "But I don't think it was a girl."

"You don't?" Nigel and I ask together.

"Nope. Not one bit," McCarthy says.

"There's no way a guy knows that much about a girl's body. Unless. Oh, yuck. No way!" Nigel says. "You don't think there are guys and girls around here hooking up, do you?" He pushes his empty lunch tray away from. "I just lost my appetite."

"There's nothing left on your plate," McCarthy points out. "And man up, there are linears everywhere, Nigel. It's not like it's a big deal."

"Not a big deal? It's like the biggest deal," Nigel says, incredulously. "It's the only time that I think Authority really knows what they're doing. Guys and girls together may be the grossest thing ever."

"I don't know why anyone cares," McCarthy says, shrugging.

"You don't?" I ask, treading very carefully on this topic.

"No. It's none of my business. Plus, Authority shouldn't dictate who should be together and who shouldn't. At least, that's what we think at our house."

"I think girls and their big volleyballs should stay on their own side of town and steer clear of what doesn't belong to them," Nigel says, standing up and grabbing his tray. "I mean, I get why they'd want us. Look at us, but no thank you. Give me Decarion and his big di—"

"Nigel!" I stop him.

"Dimples. His big dimples," he says, swinging his backpack onto his back. "Get your heads out of the gutter, boys." He walks away, leaving his tray on the table per usual. Now, it's up to me to dump both of our trays.

∽

"Thanks for dropping me off," I say to McCarthy. "I'm not sure when I'll be allowed to drive again—if ever."

"No problem, man. Anytime," McCarthy says, turning the car off and facing me. "I just want to tell you that I'm really having fun hanging out with you."

"Me too," I admit, shifting in my seat a tad closer to the

door and putting my backpack on my lap. "Hey McCarthy, are your dads really that progressive?"

"Oh Authority, almost too progressive." He chuckles. He shakes his head, looking off into the distance. "Can I tell you something?"

"Sure," I say, dropping my backpack back onto the floor of his car.

McCarthy looks around. I'm not sure what he's looking for or trying to check out. But then, he takes a deep breath and exhales it all out slowly and deliberately. "My passive dad hooked up with a girl back in high school," McCarthy states, blowing my mind.

"What?" I cannot contain my total disbelief. "No way! He just told you that like it was no big deal?"

"Not so much. I heard my dads fighting about it once. My active father still has a problem with it from time-to-time, but he's mainly gotten over it," McCarthy explains. "But sometimes, when he's drinking, he starts spouting off about it. I think it bothers him more that it doesn't really bother him—if that makes any sense."

"I bet it's just like any other ex. You never want to know that someone you love has been with someone else," I say, trying to sound speculative and not excited at this admission.

"Maybe, but either way, they still fight about it sometimes. My passive dad told me that he and his friends wanted to try out this place that let men and women hang out together," McCarthy recalls. He doesn't look upset or repulsed. He's just retelling a story. "My dad met this girl. They hit it off, and the next thing ya know, they were fooling around. He'd never done anything with anyone before, so it was all new to him."

"What did he say about it?"

"Nothing more than that. It was a one and done kind of thing," McCarthy reveals with a shrug.

"How do you feel about it?"

"Relieved."

"What do you mean 'relieved'?"

"I heard they destroyed the place they met. I'm relieved my dad didn't get caught and killed. I'm relieved he married my father, and that I'm here," McCarthy says. "I don't care one way or another that he hooked up with a girl. I'm glad he told me."

"You really are amazing, you know that?" I say, rubbing my hand along his forearm.

"Back at you." McCarthy smiles. His smile is perfection with his precisely straight and pearly white teeth. "And Riot, I'm completely happy being friends with you."

"Friends? What do you mean?" I'm confused. I'm pretty sure he and I are in the beginning of a relationship.

"Yes, friends." He laughs, grabbing his water bottle out of the console and taking a long drink. After a slow swallow, he says, "Listen, you're great Riot. And you are incredibly hot. You know that, but this, you and me, it's not going anywhere."

"What? Why do you say that?" Now, I'm completely clueless—and kind of offended. I've never had anyone break up with me before or even turn me down gently. This is new.

"You may not know this, but I'm a pretty hot, sought-after guy," McCarthy says with a confident chuckle. "People want this." He motions to his body and makes circles around his face. Then, he winks at me.

"I'm sure they do."

"And I also know when people do not want this," he adds.

"You're not saying that I don't—"

"Stop it! Riot, I've been kissed by many men, many." He runs his hand along the steering wheel. "And it's quite obvious when they want me. And you, Riot Logan, have no real desire for me. That kiss, no matter how much I wanted it to be the hottest thing ever, was anything but."

Crap, I thought I played my part so well. I was convinced that I was making this hot, perfect man melt. Apparently not. Then, McCarthy adds, "And that's fine, because I like you. I like hanging with you. So just because we're not going to end up in this passionate love affair, doesn't mean that I don't want to keep hanging out."

"I...I...I don't know what to say," I admit.

"Don't say anything. There's nothing to say," he says, turning the key in the ignition. "I'll pick you up for school in the morning." I open the door and start to get out. "And Riot, since we're being honest, I love being with you; Nigel's a bit much sometimes."

My laughter carries me out of the car. He's one hundred percent right. Nigel is a bit much—most of the time. Not just sometimes.

After I get out and shut the car door, I watch him back out of my driveway. It would be so much easier to fall for him. He's just wonderful. He's honest, open, wise, and so easy to be with. But no, I have to choose the hardest path in life to journey down. But that thought right there; that's the problem. It has always been the problem. I didn't choose this. I certainly didn't wake up and decide that I want the hardest life I can think of for myself. If I could choose, I'd choose McCarthy and go on with my life. But after experiencing passion and pleasure with Lizzie, and this new feeling of hope and possibility with Cissy, I can't possibly choose a life of suffocating mediocrity. Nobody could. How could I? It's not fair that anyone—not my parents, not Authority, and not even Nigel—would believe that I should settle for a life lacking passion and desire.

CHAPTER 29
VICISSITUDE

"Love is like water. We can fall in it. We can drown in it. And we can't live without it." (Unknown)

Watching Riot work is fascinating. He's able to talk to me, but his eyes never leave his product. He's clearly struggling with the clay. It may not be his forte, but paint, lead, charcoal, and colored pencils surely are. "Damn it," he says, squishing the clay back together again. It's getting hard and crusty—probably impossible to mold and shape the way he wants.

I take out my water bottle and drip a bit of water onto his clay. "If you moisten it, then it gets pliable again."

Riot pauses, nothing moves—not his hands, his arms, his shoulders, or his eyes. He's completely statuesque. Finally, he looks up at me and asks, "How long you been keeping that information from me?"

Sucking my lips into my teeth to avoid laughing, I look down at where my tracker should be, and say, "A little longer than thirty minutes."

"Ahhh, I see how you are," he says, standing up and wiping his hands on his pants. Grabbing a tube of paint, he squirts a small dollop into the palm of his hand, and says, "Come here."

"So someone thinks I was born yesterday," I say, grinning. Hopping to my feet, I dash by him, grabbing a tube of paint myself. After putting a large glob of paint in my hand, I say, "You come here."

"Because you think getting paint on me scares me," Riot says, walking confidently toward me. He stops inches from me. When he gets close like this, my heart refuses to calm down. It pounds out of my chest like it has somewhere it needs to be. "Your move, Tree Gazer." He smirks. That damn smirk.

"I don't know what you can possibly mean," I say, coyly with a little bat of my lashes for effect. "I was just thinking that I could use a little color. Didn't have time for makeup today. I lightly dab my index finger into the green paint in the palm of my hand and begin smearing it along my lips. "Always thought I'd look good in green lipstick. Don't you think, Riot?"

Riot's face is hysterical. His jaw drops, and his eyes widen. It's hard to not laugh at him. Just when I think he's completely stumped and caught off guard, I add, "But not as good as you'd look with green blush." I swipe my hand all along his cheekbone, rubbing green paint all over the left side of his face.

"Oh, you did not," he yells, reaching for my hand. I'm too fast for him, and I bolt past him before he can grab me. But my speed and endurance are no match for an Elite athlete. Riot quickly catches up to me, and he lifts me up, tossing me over his shoulder with one arm and one fluid motion. He's protecting the paint in his hand.

"Now, what part of you is going to look good covered in yellow paint?"

"My feet," I yell. "My feet would be gorgeous if they were yellow."

"Nah, definitely not your feet," he says, still not releasing me to the ground. "How would you look with yellow hair? Did you ever want to be a blonde?"

"If you touch one strand of my—"

Riot slowly eases me down, keeping me tight to his body as I slide down every inch of him until my feet meet the ground. "You'll what?" he challenges. His breath is hot on me.

"I'll..."

Riot grins. He kneels before me and places one hand on the hem of my shirt. He looks up at me, asking permission, before he lifts my shirt. Revealing my stomach, he uses his pinky finger and dabs it into the yellow paint. With quick motions and perfect precision, he paints a yellow flower on my stomach. Then, he reaches up, takes some green paint off of his face, and creates a stem for the flower. My belly button is the middle part of the flower. He only used two fingers and smeared paint, but still created the most intricate and beautiful flower ever—right on my stomach.

"You can breathe," he says. I exhale all the breath I was holding. Had I really held my breath that long? No way. I had to have taken a breath or two at some point, but honestly, I can't be sure. "Cissy, you are the most exquisite canvas I've ever painted on." I'm about to thank him, when he adds, "But then again, I've only ever painted on drab canvases, sticks, rocks, and paper. But yeah, you are much better looking than most rocks."

With that, I jump into his arms, wrapping my arms and legs all around him. "Whoa, where'd that come from?" he asks, holding me tight. Then, I start squirming and rubbing my torso on him. "Oh for Authority's sake." He laughs, trying to get me off of him. I refuse to budge. I'm latched on like a koala bear, certain to transfer every bit of my belly paint onto his shirt.

"Hold on," I say, squirming into him. "I'm almost done." I'm laughing so hard that tears are forming in the corners of my eyes. Finally, I realize I'm fighting a battle with no opponent. Riot's arms are extended out wide—not wrapped around me. He's standing perfectly still, eyes closed, with his teeth biting into his bottom lip. "Whoa," I say, jumping down off of him. "Did I hurt you?"

Riot takes a deep breath and sighs it out slowly. He's motionless. No part of him is moving at all. Frozen in stillness. Finally, he says, "No Tree Gazer, you didn't hurt me. I'm perfectly fine." He lifts his shirt over his head, revealing the most flawless stomach and chest in the world. Using his shirt, Riot wipes the green paint off of his face.

"What was that all about, then?" I ask. "I thought we were playing and having fun." I'm suddenly very uncomfortable and self-conscious.

Riot smiles and says, "We were. We are." He winds his t-shirt around his head, making a tight-looking hat with his shirt.

"That's an interesting little hat ya got there," I say, pointing at his head.

"Do-rags make it easy to keep my hair and sweat out of my eyes."

"A 'what rag?' That can't be a real word."

His laughter is infectious. "I've got a lot to teach you."

"Start with why you got all weird and stoic when we were just having fun," I say, drinking out of my water bottle.

Riot's face blushes, and he looks at me with a surprised expression. "I forget sometimes that you aren't clued in on all things...ummm...male."

"What does that mean?"

"It's kind of hard, no pun intended, to goof around with a girl writhing on your junk, if you know what I'm saying."

"No, I have no idea what you're saying. Should I know what you're saying?"

"Let's just table this for now," he says, shaking his head.

"Why? What did I do?"

"Not a thing," Riot says, unbuttoning his pants. "But for now, let's just go for a swim. Hopefully, it's frigid in that water." He turns his back toward me and drops his pants. He's wearing tight shorts under his pants.

"I can't swim, you know that."

"Well aware," he says, walking out into the clearing where the pond is. "Let's go, Tree Gazer. It's time you learned how to survive if you ever fall into a lake."

"I don't have a bathing suit," I call after him. "Are those your underwear? What am I supposed to wear?"

After a large splash, I hear, "I don't care what you wear. Go naked if you want."

"What if someone sees us? I'm not supposed to be here right now."

"I'll teach you how to hold your breath underwater."

Shit. What am I supposed to do now? My bra and underwear match, but they're not exactly sexy. Marjorie used to get so mad at me for my practical undergarment choices. You could always count on her underwear being some sort of pink lace or silk. Right now, I'm sporting a light purple bra and light purple cotton underwear. Typically, they never match, but today, the purple panties were the first I grabbed. They just coincidentally matched the bra I'd already grabbed to put on.

Here goes nothing, I think. I pull my shirt off, noticing the yellow paint on it for the first time. I slide my shorts down and kick them off. I hate walking in the woods with bare feet. I'll keep my shoes on until I hit the water's edge. When I approach the lake, Riot's swimming in toward the shoreline. "Come on in," he says, before he submerges completely under the water. He pops out only a few feet from me, shaking his head, spraying water everywhere.

"It's freezing," I complain, wading into the water up to my ankles.

"You just have to dive in; you'll get used to it," Riot urges.

"Dive in?" I question. "Yeah, because I know how to do that," I say, rolling my eyes. "You do recall that I can't swim."

"Do you at least know how to hold your breath and go under water?" he asks, staying low in the water next to me.

"No, I've never once put my entire head—or body—in water like this," I admit.

"What about the bathtub?"

"Never under the water," I explain. "I can hold my breath and put my face in the shower stream. Does that count?"

"That absolutely doesn't count." He laughs, offering me his hand. "Here, grab my hand. I've got you."

"No chance, I don't trust you," I say, backing away. Immediately, I regret my word choice. Riot looks hurt by my words. I certainly didn't mean to offend him. It's just not normal for women to be in water like this. I'm not comfortable right now at all. As a matter of fact, I'm scared.

Careful of my footing, I take a step deeper into the

water. Riot backs up away from me. "It'll start to feel warmer the further you get into the water. Were you allowed to have a baby pool when you were a little kid?" I shake my head. I've never even heard the diction "baby pool" before. Riot continues, "Eka is cracked for sure, but this has got to be up there with one of their dumbest rules ever. Why can't women swim?"

"You're asking me? Like I know anything. We just think that Authority believes our lives aren't as valued as male lives," I say, stumbling. I can't catch my balance, and I'm going down. Riot's there in a flash, catching me before I go under. Being pressed against his wet, bare chest is pretty much the greatest place I've ever been. I would've fallen much sooner if I knew this was my reward. But, he can't know that. After all, we're just friends. The worst two words in the Ekian language. Just friends. Translation: Complete torture.

"Well, it's time that you and I break yet another Law of Liberty, Tree Gazer," Riot says, still holding me up. He walks backwards, taking me deeper into the water.

"Is this going to be too deep for me to touch the bottom?" I ask with a quiver in my voice. I'm not sure if the tremble in my voice is due to the chill in the water, the fear of drowning, or the nervousness of having Riot's arms wrapped around me.

As he holds me tighter, Riot looks me in the eyes, and says, "I can promise you this right here and right now, I will never—ever—let anything happen to you, Cissy. Because whether Authority gets it or not, you and your life are extremely valuable and incredibly precious." His words make me catch my breath. The words are so powerful and so final that I believe him, and all of my fears are completely assuaged. The deeper we go into the water, the tighter I cling to him, and the more I relax, feeling nothing but safety and sanctuary in his arms.

"Alright, I am going to hold your hands. I want you to extend your arms out long and kick your feet," Riot says, letting go of my back. "Cissy, you're going to need to unhook your legs from around me."

"I'm pretty sure that's not going to happen," I say, squeezing my thighs tighter.

Riot chuckles and sighs. "You have to trust me."

"Have you ever taught anyone how to swim before?"

Riot pauses. He looks up through the corner of his eye as if he's giving this some serious thought. "Have I ever taught anyone to swim?" he repeats the question. "As a matter of fact, I have taught exactly zero people to swim."

"Well, perfect," I say, "What could I have possibly been afraid of?" I curl my lips in to hide my laughter and smile. I'm pretty sure this guy could convince me to do anything.

"I mean, how hard can it be? What's the worst that can happen?"

"Exactly," I say, grinning. "It's not like drowning is that big of deal."

"Or alligators," he adds. "They don't usually bother us anyway."

"Alligators?" I wrap my arms and legs tighter around him.

∼

TWO HOURS LATER, we're lying on a blanket, completely spent. I cannot believe women aren't allowed to swim. It is legitimately the most exhilarating and freeing thing I've ever experienced. Once we took it back to where I could touch the bottom of the lake, I felt much safer and able to listen to his instruction. By the end of our lesson, I could go under the water, holding my breath while the water surrounded me. It was a sensation I've never felt before. There were times when I didn't even want to come back up, but my lungs couldn't handle it anymore. Riot taught me to swim underwater for a few feet right into his arms. I couldn't quite get the hang of swimming with my head above the water. Riot said that it'll come with time and practice. "I'm not sure what I'm going to tell my moms about my hair. You clearly have no idea what water does to a black girl's hair."

"You're right, I have no idea, but I admit, I like what you've got going there." He laughs, ringing out my braids. "It actually doesn't look much different."

"Riot, when this hair dries, I'm going to be able to wash a dishpan with how brittle and wiry the fuzzy pieces are going to be," I say, trying to smooth down the flyaway wisps.

"If you're interested in swimming again, I can always bring you a swim cap, so you don't have to worry about your hair," Riot offers.

"Oh my Authority, I'd love to do this again and that would be perfect. A swim cap would be an Authority-send."

We both lie in silence with a small portion of the sun coming through the leaves, warming and drying us. My hand brushes up against Riot's as we're basking in the afterglow of our water-induced euphoria. I really want to hold his hand, but since my promise of being "just" his friend, I simply let the back of my hand linger against the back of his. I can't recall a time when I yearned to interlock my fingers with Marjorie's.

"Hey, Riot," I ask, turning on my side to look at him. "How'd you do it?"

"Do what?" he asks, not turning toward me, but gazing up at the sky like I typically do.

"The mural. Male Monument."

I watch as his eyes widen. Slowly, he rolls over and looks at me. There's a fear in his eyes that I've never seen before. "What mural?"

"Lying is not your forte, my friend," I say, rolling my eyes. "Like I wouldn't recognize Lizzie's locket. Or the painting that I just showed you a few weeks ago. Or my own braids and silhouette."

"Valid."

"So, how'd you do it?"

"It was actually much easier than I expected. Truthfully, Authority has us believing that we'll get caught and killed if we do anything we're not supposed to," he says, his eyes alight with excitement. "That mural took me four hours to paint, and I never had to go hide or anything. Nobody ever patrolled the area. It was just me, my art, and that giant wall. Cissy, I loved it. I never felt more like myself."

"Aren't you worried that you're going to get caught?"

"Not now. I got away with it."

"What if Lizzie's moms recognize her locket? That could be a giveaway," I say, hoping he'll be more cautious in the future.

"Can't happen. Her moms still have quite a bit of time on their sentence in the Confinery for her suicide."

"What if they let them watch the news in the Confinery and they see it? Then, what if they think something more happened to Lizzie and suddenly, you're getting blamed?"

"You've got yourself a wild imagination, Tree Gazer, but trust me, it was easy to get away with," he says, lying back down. "I'm dying to do it again."

My groan tells him all that he needs to know regarding

how I feel about his future plans to paint in the Male Monument Center.

Riot quickly changes the subject. "Have you ever seen the movie, *Summer Salsa*?"

"Yes! I didn't know we saw the same movies." I love *Summer Salsa*.

"Next time we go swimming, I want to try the lift that those two guys do in the water--lifting you above my head. That's another thing that's stupid. They stopped letting men dance after that movie, but yet, they still let us watch it. Makes no sense."

Slowly, I sit up. I stare at him. "Riot, do you mean the two girls in the lake who do the lift? The one they practice before the final scene where Joanna lifts Baby into the air?"

Now, it's Riot's turn to look at me like I've lost my mind. "Johnny lifts Buddy at the end."

We both shake our heads in disbelief. "You mean to tell me that they change genders for every single movie and just remake it. I knew that women weren't in my movies, but I had no idea that you all saw our movies with different people playing the parts," Riot says. "I hate it here."

"Marjorie's moms told her that Before it was a boy and girl in that movie."

"No way!" Riot exclaims. "Are you sure?"

"I'm not sure, but that's what Marjorie told me." Riot scoots closer to me, intrigued by this newfound knowledge. "Actually, Marjorie's moms tell her all kinds of things from Before."

"And you guys aren't on speaking terms any longer, right?" he asks.

"Not really, why?"

"Cissy, I want her knowledge. I want to know everything her moms tell her."

"I'm pretty sure they make most of it up. They're really weird."

"Or, they tell her the truth. And we just think the truth is weird, because we're not used to it," Riot offers, definitely making me think. "You know what I really wish? I dream of breaking into the Kendyl Corporation."

"Riot! Don't you even think about—"

"Can't help it. I think about it all the time. I want to know everything about Before. It makes no sense that we can't learn about our history. Why does Eka want to keep everything a secret? It's dumb. I want answers."

I shake my head. I grab his hand, and say, "Riot, you can't live in the past. If you do, you'll have no future."

"That's where you're wrong, Cissy. The past is our truth, our life. We need to know where we came from and how we all got here."

CHAPTER 30
RIOT

"If you want to make beautiful music, you must play the black and white notes together." (Richard M. Nixon)

"Riot, look at his," my dad says. "It's a brochure for your dorm. What kind of room do you want? A quad or a double?" I didn't realize either dad was talking to me again. That's good news, I guess. The last thing either of them said to me was that I needed to take out the trash. I took it out. That was the end of it. And that was a week ago.

"I didn't know that was something I chose," I admit, sitting down next to him. I start leafing through the brochures. The dorms are fire. They have everything. It's like they're these all-inclusive resorts. Why would anyone graduate? Seems like living in one of these places is the dream. "Is that a workout room?"

"Room? It's a whole facility—in each dormitory. They certainly didn't have it set up like this when I was in college," my dad whines. "I may have had more fun in college and gotten myself some of those abdominal muscles you and your father have."

I laugh. My dad has never been into fitness. He hates all exercise, all activity actually. That's what has always bothered me about him forcing me to play sports—just to agree with my father. "I'm not sure that would've done it." I laugh. Don't get me wrong; my dad isn't fat or anything like that. Obesity isn't permitted in Eka. He's just not chiseled and muscular; he's more soft and gooey than anything else. The man has zero definition.

My dad grabs his small belly and gives it a loving rub. "Your father loves me the way I am."

Flipping through the pamphlet, I say, "I guess I'd like a single."

"A single? Uh no!" my dad cries. "That's so sad and lonely. How will you meet people? How will you make friends? Meet a husband?"

"I'm sure I'll manage," I mumble, thinking that the last thing I want to do is hang out and party with a bunch of college guys guzzling beer and ogling each other. And meeting a husband isn't high on my priority list as of right now—or ever.

"Riot, you must get at least a double—if not a triple."

"Triple what?" my father asks, strutting into the kitchen. He must've won his big case; he's nearly floating.

"Our antisocial son wants a single for his dorm room," my dad says, folding his arms across his chest. "And congratulations, babe." My dad smacks my father's ass. My father leans down and kisses him.

"Sounds like the first smart choice that boy has ever made," my father says, glancing at one of the pamphlets, before tossing it on the table and grabbing an apple. That boy? Gee, thanks dad.

"Luther, he can't go to college and hole himself up in his room, day in and day out. He needs to get out and meet people. Have a little fun."

"Kid needs to study and focus on his future."

My father's voice is beginning to go up a few octaves. Before this turns into World War IV, I decide a compromise is in order. "How about a double? One roommate should be fine." This seems to calm them both down. I haven't really talked to either one of them about anything serious in a while. I decide to take my chance since they're both in a pretty good mood and being abnormally jovial. "Hey, can I ask you guys something?" They both look at me without saying anything. My passive dad finally nods.

"Have either of you ever been inside the Kendyl?"

My father rolls his eyes. "Of course. We have access cards." He takes a bite of his apple. With his mouth full, he asks, "Did you really not know that?"

"You have access cards to the Kendyl?" I ask, my eyes giving away my disbelief. My father pulls it out of his wallet and flashes it at me.

"Sometimes, our cases require us to know more about Before—for evidence and further facts," my father clarifies.

My dad adds, "But every time we argue a point using Before as a precedence, it doesn't really help our clients. It's best just to keep the past in the past."

"So you can basically just walk right in there and look up anything you want to look up?" They both nod. "Do you do the research on a computer or in books?"

"Either," my father says. "Whichever has the most information."

"And neither of you want to tell me anything about Before?"

They both shake their heads. "Not a thing."

My father adds, "Riot, the full consequences for delving into the past are too harsh. It's not worth it. Way too dangerous."

"How about this?" I offer, hoping I can get even a little something out of them. "Is the answer to why men and women not being allowed to interact inside the Kendyl?"

My dads nod.

"What about why men make more money than women?" They nod again. They eye each other cautiously. I can tell that they're not going to give me much more information. "Okay one more, what about the reason why we can't read real books, use computers, and why men can't paint or women can't be in sports?"

"It's all in there," my father says.

"That's more than one," my dad chuckles.

~

"I JUST DON'T GET IT," Nigel says, throwing another gutter ball.

"Baby, you have to aim for the middle pin," Decarion says, jumping up and rubbing Nigel's back as he comes back to the chairs.

"I know that. Can't bowl well since I broke my thumb last year at that playoff game," Nigel says, shrugging Decarion's arm off his shoulder. Nigel doesn't lose well, and gets overly cranky and defensive. "That's not even what I'm talking about. I don't understand why they're not dating."

"Why does it matter?" I say, grabbing my ball, and tossing it down the lane. After knocking down eight pins, I wait for my ball to return. "We're just friends. What's so wrong with being friends?"

"It's just bullshit," Nigel says, stuffing a handful of

nachos into his mouth. "You two spend a ton of time together. Why not just be more?"

"I'm not sure it works that way," Decarion says, drawing Nigel down next to him, wrapping his arm around him. "Look at us. We can't be 'just friends,' because we can't get enough of each other. They can't force themselves to be something they're not."

"But they're so—"

"Hot," Decarion sighs. He shakes his head, rubbing his forehead.

"Dude, there's more to a relationship than how hot someone is. Sure, Riot is smoking hot," McCarthy says, smiling. "But there has to be chemistry—something more."

I point to McCarthy, agreeing with him. I roll my second ball, knocking down one of the two pins left standing. Trying to convince Nigel of anything he disagrees with is futile. The man can't ever see another side of any argument.

Decarion's tracker blares and vibrates. "Shit, my dads need me. I gotta roll." He stands, extending his hand for Nigel.

"You have to go; I don't," Nigel says, taking a long drink of his soda. Decarion sighs and crosses his arms over his chest. Decarion is about the most patient boyfriend on the planet. Sometimes, I don't know how he does it. Putting up with Nigel is tough—a full time job. Nigel looks around at all of us, slurping the end of his drink, getting every last drop. "What? What'd I do?"

McCarthy and I shake our heads. Decarion gives Nigel an all-knowing and enduring look. Nigel groans, rolls his eyes, and stuffs another handful of nachos into his mouth. As they walk away, McCarthy calls after them, "Easy killer, now that you're not playing lacrosse, they're going to drop your caloric intake." Nigel doesn't turn around. He just merely flips him the bird. McCarthy laughs. "Right back at you!"

"It's so nice to see you two getting along," I joke. McCarthy rolls his third strike of the game. "Dude, why're you so good at this?"

McCarthy shrugs, a blush covers his face. "I'm kind of good at everything." He stills, his eyes darting back and forth. "Wanna come over? I want to show you what I'm really good at."

"Ummm." I have no words.

"Shit man, I thought we already covered this. I'm not about to jump your bones."

∼

"Who is this fine specimen of a man?" Mr. McCorum says, circling me like a vulture assessing its weak, helpless prey.

"Riot, my dad. Dad, this is Riot," McCarthy mumbles, grabbing my wrist and dragging me through the living room. "See ya, going to my room," he calls, moving faster than he ever has before.

"Wear a condom!" his dad yells after us.

"Not like that. Already told you that."

My laughter erupts as McCarthy closes the door. "See. What did I tell you?"

"He seems fun. My dads are all business," I reply, looking around his room. I stop in my tracks, marveling at the sight in front of me. "McCarthy, what is all this?"

"Paraphernalia. Contraband. Forbidden items. Illegalities," he announces, reaching under his bed, grabbing a case that looks like a storage box for a ten-year-old to be hidden in. "Basically stuff that Authority would execute us for."

"How did you get this stuff?" I ask, spinning in circles, feeling like I just hit the jackpot of knowledge.

"My dads love defying Authority. It's kind of their thing. But they keep it minimal, so we fly under the radar. Basically, they work to simply buy forbidden things."

"Holy Authority," I say, running my hand along a poster. "What's The Vibrant Quakes?"

"A band," McCarthy says. "Wanna hear them?"

"Hear them what?" McCarthy takes a square-shaped machine out of his closet. Thumbing through another box, he takes a round, black disc out, and places it on the machine. The black disc begins to spin. Suddenly, the room is filled with sound—a wonderful, upbeat, and toe-tapping sound.

"Music? You have music?"

"Sure do. And listen," he says, opening the ten-year-old kid's transportation case. He removes a shiny, wooden object with a few buttons and long wires on it. McCarthy positions it on his lap, listens to the song playing, and then out of nowhere, starts mimicking the sounds coming from the music machine. Then, he starts singing along with the words. I'm shocked, nearly dumbfounded. And completely excited.

"Shit, McCarthy! That's incredible."

McCarthy gave me a crash course in everything music, and I was hooked. It was amazing. We ended up listening to every record he has. I was complete shit at the guitar, but I still enjoyed trying to make it sound like he could. He was really good at it. I couldn't tell the difference between the bands playing and McCarthy. To my utter amazement and total envy, his dads even came in and hung with us for a while too. His father played this gold-looking pipe thing, a saxophile or something, and we had what was called a "jam session." My job was to pound the heel of my hand on this wooden circle with metal discs on it. When McCarthy nodded at me, it was my cue to hit it. So I did. It was the most fun I've had in ages. It was like being a kid on the lacrosse field again when everything was new and fun—just for enjoyment.

Lying on his floor after hours of playing and listening, I say, "I loved tonight, man. This was awesome."

"Your turn," McCarthy says, rolling to his side, peeking at me over the side of his bed.

"For what?"

"Tell me your deep dark secret."

"What deep—"

"Dude, you're not getting out of it. I literally just showed you everything that could get me and my entire family killed. You've gotta give me something. Everyone has something he's hiding."

McCarthy's right. It's not like I don't trust him. I just don't trust our world. Eka is a breeding ground for judgment and hypocrisy. He could show me all this, and then turn on me for not abiding by the Laws of Liberty just to save him and his family.

"I'm waiting," he says, tapping his fingers on the bed.

"Fine," I agree. I stand up and grab a pen and the record folder. I open it up to a blank part of the cardboard. With McCarthy watching over my shoulder, I sketch a fast, and pretty awful, picture of him playing his guitar.

"Well look at us," McCarthy smiles, nodding. "Just two criminals sharing their crimes openly and freely." He jumps up and reaches for a box in his closet. Pulling it down, he opens it, and tosses me a giant book. "Read this."

"What the fuck? You have a book?" I say, running my hands along the brown, soft cover. "Is this leather? Like from animals." There's a shine to his eyes. He loves this. "McCarthy McCorum, you're a hoodlum. You love breaking the law."

"Damn straight." He laughs. "What are rules for if you can't break them?"

"So what is this book?" I ask, leafing through it.

"Just read some of it, and report back what you think," he says. "I'm curious about your thoughts on it. Just don't fucking get caught with it. We'll burn for sure. I have another one too. Different kind."

Staring at him in all of his mischievous glory, I feel more courageous than I've ever felt before. "So how much criminal activity do you condone?"

"What do you have in mind? I'm not killing your father," McCarthy states.

"We'll talk about that later." I laugh. "But seriously, there is something that I'd really love to do."

"Ohhh, I'm listening."

"So, my dads have access cards to the Kendyl Corporation. I want in there. I want to know all the shit they're hiding from us."

"The Kendyl? You want to break into the Kendyl?"

"Sure do," I admit, trying to replicate the poster of The Vibrant Quakes on the inside cover of the Justice for Us folder. "And I need a lookout man."

"You want to break into the Kendyl, the most guarded and protected building in our town, and you want me to be your accomplice?" McCarthy asks, again.

I nod.

"Fuck yeah," he says. "I'm in."

CHAPTER 31
VICISSITUDE

"It is not our differences that divide us. It is our inability to recognize, accept, and celebrate those differences. " (Audre Lorde)

There is no reason that I can possibly come up with that I'm not allowed to be in this lake, submerged in this water, and entirely enjoying myself. It's relaxing and serene. Why would Authority not permit women to do this? There is no rational answer other than the fact that they make up ridiculous and minute rules to control us. Swimming is unbelievably soothing. The feel of the water all around me, making me nearly weightless, transforms me. I feel like I can be anyone and do anything. I don't even care about my hair.

I take one last little lap before getting out. Just as I step onto the shoreline in my bra and underwear, I hear footsteps approaching. Slowly, careful to not make too much noise or splashing sounds, I work my way back into the water, dunking myself so only my head, eyes, and nose are above the water. Suddenly, the person walking toward me emerges from the forest and steps into the clearing. I dunk under the water, praying that my lung capacity can outlast the person's curiosity.

Please don't come swimming.
Please don't get in this water.
Please don't see me.

I can feel the waves and water as the person enters the lake. My lungs are giving out. I have to resurface. I turn around, my back toward the shore. Gasping, I come up for air.

"Well, at least you learned something," Riot says.

Holy Authority, thank you! Thank you for being Riot.

His voice is music to my ears. I turn around, and he's closing in on me. "You do realize that you're right out in the open, in the lake, and it's a Male Day, don't you?"

"I have been here in this water every Female Day since you taught me to swim. I can't get enough of it," I admit, falling backwards with my arms spread out wide. "This is the greatest thing ever."

I splash him, and he goes underwater before my deluge covers him. He brushes past my leg. I feel him swim around me. The tap on my legs makes me open them. Riot swims under me, lifting me up onto his shoulders. "Oh no, whoa! Riot, you're going to drop me!" I scream.

"That's the fun part," he reassures me. "Are you ready?"

"Ready for what?" I ask, squeezing his head with my thighs and gripping his hair in tight handfuls.

"You're going to go backwards," he announces, beginning to count and bounce at the same time.

"Wait, wait, wait," I yell, pulling his hair harder.

"Just trust me," Riot begs, wrapping his hands around

my ankles. "It's fun. I promise." Then, he counts to three and flips me backwards off his shoulders and I tip back into the water in one fluid motion.

The water welcomes me as I plunge deeper into the lake. Using my new knowledge and technique, I kick my feet and basically flail my arms until I realize that I can touch the bottom. Standing, I emerge from the water, laughing, coughing, and gasping for air. "That was fun— and a bit terrifying," I admit, wiping the water off of my face. "Got any other fun games you want to torture me with?"

"I sure do," Riot says, swimming toward me. "Here, put your hands on my shoulders," he instructs. I place my hands on the middle of his shoulders. His hands grip my waist firmly. "On my count, bend your knees, push off of my shoulders, and jump up over my head, okay?" I nod, bouncing on my toes, ready to leap over him. "One, two, three," he yells.

I take off, using all of my leg muscles to get up over him. I begin to soar—that is, right until my head collides into his face. "Ow," Riot screams, dropping me in the water. Once I come back up, I see the blood.

"Riot, oh crap! Are you okay?" I swim-run toward him. His shoulders are shaking, his breath is heaving.

Finally, I realize he's laughing, and relief washes over me. "I guess it's harder than it looks—or you're a lot heavier than Buddy in the movie," he jokes through groans of pain and fits of laughter.

"I am so sorry," I say, prying his hands from his bleeding nose. "Let's get out of here. I have an extra sweatshirt in my bag that we can use to stop the blood flow."

Once the bleeding stops, and we're sitting on my blanket, Riot reaches for his backpack. "I want to show you something." He looks around as if what he's about to show me is the most valuable secret he's ever had. Pulling a rather large book out of his bag, he shows it to me.

"A book? Where in the Authority's sake did you get a book?" I ask, grabbing for it. He pulls it back before I can touch it. I snatch it right out of his hand. "Holy crap, is this leather?"

"I'm pretty sure it is," he says.

I guide it to my nose. The smell is inviting and pleasant—a scent I've never experienced before. I trace my fingers along the words that are engraved into the soft brown material. "*The New Testament*. What is it? What's it say?"

"I've only read a small bit of it. Just started flipping through and reading a few pages. Kind of hard to read and understand," he says, taking it back. "They're little stories with lessons or something."

"Where'd you get it?" I ask, flipping through the thin, nearly transparent pages.

"Listen to this one," he says, stretching his hand out for me to place the book in it. Riot thumbs through the pages and finds a small folded piece of paper. "I liked this part, so I marked it with this. 'Do not conform to the pattern of this world, but be transformed by the renewing of your mind.' Then it goes on about some other stuff that I can't figure out."

Riot's eyes are shining; his smile spans the entire width of his face. "That's just like us," I say, leaning in to see the pages. "We're not conforming, and we're learning so much —or renewing our minds like it says."

"That's what I thought too," he says excitedly, flipping more pages. "There's a lot of talk about Jesus and God."

"What?" I shrug, trying to see the words.

"I'm not sure yet. I haven't gotten that far, but it's on almost every page," he says, still staring down at the pages.

"Where'd you get it?" I ask again, taking the book from him. I can't get enough of the scent of the cover and the feel of the smooth texture.

"I wonder how long it would take me to read the entire thing," Riot says, inching closer to me to see the book more clearly. "Or understand it."

I glance over at him, cocking my eyebrow. "Twice now, you've skirted my question, Riot." He fidgets and runs his hands through his hair. "Where'd you get it?"

Suddenly, there's a sound of a branch or a stick breaking, followed by the crunching of leaves. Riot throws the book in the bushes, shoving me behind him. "Run," he whispers as I bolt toward the bushes.

"She doesn't have to run," a guy says, emerging from behind the largest oak tree in the forest. "I gave it to him."

"Fuck McCarthy, you scared the shit out of us," Riot says, bending over and blowing so much air out of his mouth that the front of his hair flies up. His hands are on his knees as he catches his breath. Coming up, he puts a hand on his heart, and says, "It's okay Cissy; you can come out."

My feet are frozen. I can't move. Twice in one day, I've been scared out of my mind and terrified of being discovered. What am I even thinking? I'm in the woods. On a male day. Swimming. Reading some book. And now, there's not one, but two guys, within ten feet of me. Am I trying to get myself killed? Do I want my moms in the Confinery for the rest of their lives?

Riot spreads the bushes apart. "It's okay. You're safe."

My heart is pounding. My body refuses to budge. Without warning, I can't catch my breath. I place my hand on my chest and gasp for air. My lungs won't fill. My heart feels like it's going to explode out of my chest. "I... I...can't..." I shake my head, each gasp harder and shallower than the last.

Beginning to panic, I double over, panting. Riot rubs my back. "It's fine. It's McCarthy. He's cool." His words sound miles away, drowned out by the pounding in my ears and the short gasps of my breath.

The guy walks over and kneels in front of me. "Cissy?" He looks at Riot. "That's her name?" Riot nods, stepping back. "Cissy," the guy says with a gentle and soothing tone. "You're having a panic attack. It's okay. You're going to be okay."

"A panic attack? What's a panic attack?" Riot asks. The guy ignores him.

"Cissy, listen to me. Look at me," he says, placing his hands lightly on my wrists. I look at him, my heart racing. "My father has these all the time. It's going to be okay. We're going to breathe. That's all, slow easy breaths." I shake my head. My hands are shaking and flailing around. "Yes, just breathe. Inhale through your nose, slowly, nice and slow. Now exhale, slow, slow slow," he soothes. "This time, inhale for four, three, two, one. Hold it; don't exhale. Now, let it out slowly for one, two, three, four. Again, inhale."

My heart starts to slow; my focus comes back. I listen to his words, and do exactly as he instructs. He's breathing with me, slow and controlled. His thumbs are making small, rhythmic circles on the backs of my hands with the tempo of his counts. "Now, tell me what you see," he says. I shake my head, not understanding. "Just tell me three or four things that you can see right now. Keep breathing."

I inhale slowly, and say, "Trees," and exhale out. "Bushes," I inhale again. I hold my breath. "My blanket," I exhale. With another inhale, I say, "Riot." Everything slows and calms. My pulse no longer feels like it's in overdrive. My heart no longer feels like it's trying to explode out of my body. And most importantly, I can pull breath into my lungs without gasping for air.

"Shit, Riot," he says. "We've got a problem."

Riot's right by my side. "What?" His eyes are wide and stricken with fear. "What's wrong? Is she going to be okay?"

"I'm not sure," he says, "but the way she smiled, and her face lit up when she said 'Riot,' seems like she's just like every guy at Lakeward." He laughs and backs up. "But, I'm not sure she's going to strike out like all of them did. She seems like she's got one up on all those guys."

Riot's eyes widen. My chin drops to my chest. Riot clears his throat. "It's not like that. Cissy and I are—"

"Feed me a bullshit line like 'just friends,' and I'll kick your ass right here in these woods," he says. He sits down on my blanket with an all-knowing smirk on his face. "Truthfully, this makes so much more sense now. I mean, you turned *this* down." He gestures to his face and body. "At least, I know that I'm still as flawless as ever." His laughter echoes through the trees.

"McCarthy McCorum, this is Cissy Maddox." Riot points between us. "Cissy, this is—"

"M&M, it's nice to finally meet you," I say, trying to be funny and charming, but feeling very apprehensive and shaky.

"M&M? So," he looks at Riot, "she's got a nickname for me. I've been talked about. Good to know. Good to know. What sort of things has Riot here been saying about me?"

Riot visibly relaxes and walks over to the blanket. He sits down facing McCarthy. He waves me over. Reluctantly,

I take a few steps toward them. But thinking better of it, I redirect and sit on the tree root near them, ensuring a safe distance.

"I just told her that you're—"

"Trap it! I want to hear it from her," McCarthy says, pointing to me and trying to cover Riot's mouth.

"Ummm," I stall, looking to Riot for help. He just nods, encouraging me to go on. "Uhhh, he said that you're friends. You're smart. Easy to talk to," I say, hoping that's enough to give him.

"Keep going." He smiles. "This is fun."

"Open-minded, athletic, and…and…"

"And?" he says, motioning for more.

"Really hot!"

"I knew it." McCarthy claps, beaming from ear to ear. "And what do you think?" He looks at me expectantly.

Riot's right. He is funny and charming. "Riot's right," I agree, grinning.

"About what?" he goads.

"Since when are you such a compliment hog?" Riot asks, shoving him to the side. "Ignore him, Cissy."

"Hey, you owe me this," McCarthy says. "I mean you turn me down for a girl. That's tough on the old ego."

"I didn't—we aren't—"

"Actually, wait a minute," he says, pointing to both of us. "No, it's not. I am hot. Kind of perfect, if I'm being honest. It's not a blow to my ego. It's not like you wouldn't choose me over Nigel or Decarion—or even Braxton. I'm clearly the best guy around. But, if this is your kink, then I can't compete with a girl."

"We're not—"

McCarthy rolls his eyes. "Save it. I mean; this chick is beautiful." I feel my face flush. "Those braids are sexy as hell. And her body is exquisite. She's a masterpiece." McCarthy clasps his hand over his mouth and his eyes bulge. Once he takes his hand off of his mouth, he looks at Riot and says, "Holy fuck! Riot, you son of a gun. You're more hood than I thought."

"What do you mean?" Riot says, shifting uneasily. His eyes lock with mine. Terror mirrors both of our faces.

"The Male Monument Center," McCarthy responds. "That's her! You painted her. I kind of thought you were all talk. But you really are badass." McCarthy pumps his fist in the air. "Oh baby, it's on. We're doing this. Kendyl Corp, here we come!"

Riot stands up, shaking his head and motioning for him to stop talking. "McCarthy, I didn't tell—"

I walk over to them. "You didn't tell me what?" My eyes narrow. I can feel my heart begin to speed up, yet again.

"Nothing," Riot says in a whisper, closing his eyes.

"Riot, talk to me," I say, maneuvering my head, so he has to look me in the eyes.

He sighs and his shoulders slump. Riot looks so defeated and forlorn. "I don't want you to worry."

"Worry about what?"

"We're breaking into the Kendyl Corp. to find all the shit these assholes are hiding from us," McCarthy blurts out.

"You're going to do what?" I exclaim. "No way! I'm not letting you. No chance."

"Cissy, listen to me," Riot says, grabbing my hand. McCarthy's low whistle forces Riot to drop my hand quickly as he clears his throat again. "I have access cards. My dads will never know they're gone. We won't get caught. I promise. We're going to be fine."

"Then, I'm going with you," I announce, crossing my arms petulantly across my chest.

"No chance," he says, shaking his head.

"If she goes, then she can be the lookout, and I can actually go inside with you. Two of us inside rummaging around would be much faster," McCarthy offers, siding with me. "It'd be safer with her."

I walk over to McCarthy, wrapping my arm around his shoulder. "I like you. I like this guy."

"Ohhh," McCarthy says, clapping his hands. "Did you see Riot's nostrils flare and his eyes darken when you touched me? Man, I never stood a chance. He's got it bad," McCarthy laughs. "And I love it. '..each man should have his own wife, and each woman her own husband.' That's Corinthians, friends. You follow my book, and no damn laws are broken." McCarthy thumps Riot on the back. "She's in, dude. We'll both be there. She'll be safe."

Riot stares at me, shaking his head slowly. "Cissy, please."

I shrug, lifting my hands. "I'm going."

Riot shakes his head slowly. "Yeah, I figured."

CHAPTER 32
RIOT

"Civil disobedience becomes a sacred duty when the state becomes lawless or corrupt." (Mahatma Gandhi)

There's a tremble in my hand as I place my tracker on the charger. Breaking rules lately has become second nature to me, but this one is beyond risky. It's downright dangerous. And now, I've gotten Cissy and McCarthy all wrapped up into my world of rebellion. If this goes down badly, I'm the dickhead that caused it.

My house is eerily quiet. My dads went up to bed hours ago as I sat on the couch waiting for 1:00 a.m. Part of me wants to go alone and leave McCarthy and Cissy by the path in the forest wondering where I am and if I chickened out. That would be the smart thing to do. This is my mission—not theirs. But knowing McCarthy, he'd come to the Kendyl to find me. Cissy would be tight on his heels. Actually, the smartest thing would be to just go upstairs, get into bed, and not think about the Kendyl, my art, music, or Cissy ever again.

But, I never said I was smart.

Slipping out the front door, there's a small creek to the door that suddenly feels like the loudest noise I've ever heard. I brace myself for my father's booming and irate voice. Silence. There's no pounding footsteps, no thundering bellow—just a complete lack of sound.

Pulling up to the path of the forest, McCarthy and Cissy are already there. As soon as I kill the engine, Cissy's at the door, opening it. "Riot," she pants. "Please reconsider this. Please." She wraps her arms around my waist and buries her head into my chest. "We don't have to do this. We can just hang out. That's breaking enough laws as it is."

Inhaling the scent of her hair and rubbing her back, I say, "I know, but I just can't help it. I have to know. You know I can't stand the secrets and hypocrisy." Cissy squeezes me harder. I can hear a small sob escape her. Looking over her head at McCarthy, his face is expressionless. I can't read his thoughts at all.

Cissy pulls back. "I can't do it. I can't go with you."

Relief washes over me. "Oh thank, Authority." I pull her back into me and hug her tighter. "I'm so glad." I kiss the top of her head. "Will you wait here? We'll come right back afterward, and you'll see that we're both safe and sound. Okay?" Cissy nods, tears flowing freely down her face.

"Okay." She nods, swiping the tears from her cheeks.

"All right, you two friendly friends," McCarthy mocks, emphasizing friends and thumping us on the back. "We gotta go."

Cissy hugs me again, and says, "Be careful."

"You got it, Tree Gazer," I promise, twirling a finger around one of her braids.

"You too, M&M." Cissy looks at McCarthy, and then wraps her arms around him too. McCarthy smiles down at her, not saying anything. He hugs her back, reassuring her.

McCarthy and I park two blocks from the Kendyl, choosing to walk the alleys toward the back of the building. Neither of us speaks as we go, nervous energy forcing a quick jog from both of us. Stopping at the back entrance where the all-access keycard panel is, McCarthy and I collect ourselves.

"We're really doing this?" I ask, wondering if we've both lost our minds.

"Looks like it," he says, bouncing on the balls of his feet.

"You armed?" I ask. McCarthy lifts his pant leg, revealing his holster and Glock secured in place. "Loaded?" He nods.

"You?" I nod, pointing to my ankle as well. "Mask?"

Reaching in my back pocket, I pull out an old black t-shirt I made a mask out of. McCarthy shows me his makeshift blue plaid mask. We are far from the professional criminals the movies portray. We look like ridiculous bank robbers from a slapstick comedy. But, this is the best we could do.

Nodding, we pull the masks over our heads, turning on our flashlights. Clasping hands, we half-arm a hug, pounding each other's backs. "Let's roll," McCarthy says, just as I take out the access card and swipe it along the security panel. The red light blinks once, twice, and a third time. A green light appears and a three-bell ding unlocks the door.

McCarthy opens the door and motions me forward. "After you," his muffled whisper is barely audible through the mask. McCarthy nudges me. I turn around to see him pointing to the video camera in the corner. We duck our heads, ensuring our identity remains unknown.

Not knowing exactly where we're going, we jog around aimlessly, trying to read the signs on each door. Splitting up on each side of the hallway, we check each door for something indicating old records or past documents. Floor one was a bust.

Once we're on floor two, McCarthy snaps his fingers at me, pointing to the door in front of him. I shine my flashlight on the sign, "Religious History." I wave him in. There are books similar to the one McCarthy gave me lining all of the walls. A cabinet in the back has the same access panel that dons the back door. I swipe my card and each drawer's green light illuminates. Stuffed file folders make it hard to open the drawers. I grab a handful; he grabs more.

McCarthy starts flipping through the documents. I take out my father's pen camera, snapping pictures of the informational texts. "This shit is crazy," he whispers. "Wars broke out all over the world all because people believed in Jesus—that guy from my book—and some didn't."

"There's so much information here," I marvel. "Now, I guess I know what 'Jesus' and 'God' are."

"Who they are," he corrects. "Keep reading it. Jesus is the son of God," he says, skimming more and flipping through the pages. "It's my favorite thing to read."

"It says here that Eka was founded for religious freedom," I say, trying to read as fast as I can. "Not sure what 'religious' means, but they killed people for it. Like lots of people believed in that God from the book, but they killed people who didn't believe in it—or him. Or whatever."

"That doesn't make any sense," McCarthy says, now looking over my shoulder. "Let me see." He grabs my file from me. "I've read that book cover to cover a few times now. That book is all about loving each other."

"Well, that may be what that book is about, but these people sure didn't care what that book said," I say, pointing to the wars and persecutions that occurred from their different beliefs. "They legit executed and alienated people for not doing what the book says."

"How can that be? Everything I've read in it is all about loving your neighbor, helping those who are less fortunate," he explains. "Unless I'm reading it wrong and missing something."

"I don't know, man," I say. "Seems like the more we know, the more confused we get."

"We gotta get moving," McCarthy says. "Think we can just take a few of these?" He gestures to the folders. "I mean; we're in enough shit as is. What's a little more?"

Grabbing my stack, I stuff the folders into my backpack before we leave the room. McCarthy grabs more files, shoving them into his backpack. There's not much more on floor two, so we head up to the third floor.

"What the—?" McCarthy says, lifting his mask to get a better look. He ducks his head away and pulls his mask back down when he turns toward the camera. We're spinning in circles marveling at what's before us.

The third floor isn't a hallway with offices bordering it. The third floor is one giant room with stacks and stacks of shelves lining the perimeter. Each shelf is chock full of books. The books are crammed together so tightly that it's hard to extract them from the shelves.

I take one down. There's a red stamp across the front. In red, bold, block letters the word **BANNED** is splayed over the front cover. I can't even make out the title. McCarthy takes another book down. The same stamp is emblazed on his too. Every book we pull down has the same stamp.

McCarthy grabs a couple of books and puts them in his backpack; I follow suit. "Let's go." He points to the stairs. I don't want to. I want to read what's in these books to uncover what got them banned. This is the most fascinating room I've ever seen. I want to read every word on every page.

"Wait," I say. McCarthy turns. "Were people allowed to read all of these books Before?"

He shrugs. "I have no idea."

"But...why can't we now?"

"Dude, that's why we're here," he says, pushing me toward the stairs. "Let's go."

The fourth floor was too much for us. We're sitting in the stairwell, lost in our own thoughts, unable to wrap our heads around what we just discovered. The fifth floor looms ahead, but we can't muster up the energy—or maybe even the courage—to continue up.

Occasionally, one of us starts to talk, but the words don't come. Finally, he says, "So men with men was forbidden? Women with women was forbidden? And the preferred coupling was men and women together. I mean it says in my book and all, but I didn't know any of it was real."

"That makes no sense," I say, shaking my head, dying to take my mask off. "How did we get here, then? It's a complete 360."

"One-eighty," McCarthy corrects, and adds, "Ummm, and the baby-making. You don't think...I mean that can't..." He doesn't finish his thought, because neither of us can figure out what our thoughts are.

"So, you're telling me, that if I put—"

"That's exactly what that anatomy book said—and showed. Almost like it was supposed to go—"

"We cannot talk about this right now," I say. "It's too much. We've got to get out of here."

"But wait," McCarthy says. "It said that babies happen

naturally. They didn't have to apply for them Before. They just popped in there like magic."

"And sometimes, people didn't even want them."

"And they—"

"Killed them!" I finish his sentence. "And that was okay. Why would that be okay?"

I cannot wrap my brain around this at all. We have all kinds of applications, forms, classes, and registrations we have to go through to even get approved to donate our sperm. It takes years before they grant us children. We have so many regulations and rules to follow before we can be parents. People test us. We go through mock parenting trials to prove how fit we are to be fathers. But in the time of Before, you could just BAM create a baby. And that was that. What in the world?

"So Riot." He scoots down a few steps and sits right next to me. "If you and Cissy were to, ya know?" He gestures toward my junk. My eyes widen at his statement. "Then, she could just grow a kid right inside there without anyone's permission."

"Nah, I'm sure they fixed that," I say, having no idea what I'm talking about. "That's how it worked Before. It can't be like that now. Right?"

"I don't know, man," McCarthy says, standing up and flinging his backpack onto his shoulder. "It's kind of cool though, don't you think?"

"Kind of terrifying if you ask me," I admit, ascending the stairwell to the sixth floor.

Each floor is more shocking than the last. Apparently, having each person carrying a firearm at all times is new. There were people all over Eka who didn't even know how to hold or shoot a gun. How could that be safe? Not only that, but they didn't even want a gun.

"Look at this," McCarthy says, handing a folder over to me.

I read where he's pointing. "Guns could shoot multiple bullets at once?" He nods. "That's awesome. Can you imagine? We could take out a whole slew of people in one sitting."

"I think that's why they got rid of them," he says, tossing another folder at me.

This folder has that same red, bold, block lettering on it. Across the whole front of the folder are the words: **SCHOOL SHOOTINGS**. He points to a cabinet. "What's that?"

"An entire cabinet of folders that say the same thing," he says, his mouth turned down. "With pictures. Mainly kids."

"Kids?" I ask. "What do you mean?"

"Go look for yourself," McCarthy says, clearly rattled by what he just found.

The folders are gruesome and completely unbelievable. Armed men walked into schools and killed children. And it happened all the time. Nobody stopped it. The government of Before just gave them more guns—the guns that could shoot over and over again. Kids went to school in the morning and never came back. The teachers, the staff, and the students had no way to defend themselves. They just sat there and got shot.

I thought Eka was bad, but man, I'm not sure about Before either. It sure seems pretty screwed up too. I glance over at McCarthy. He's not looking so good. "You ready to get out of here?' I ask. He nods. We grab a few more files and put them in our bulging and overly stuffed backpacks.

Our excitement and energy entering the Kendyl was usurped by the melancholy, sepulchral discoveries of what we uncovered about Before. I always believed that Eka was stifling us, but maybe, all along they were protecting us. I don't even know anymore.

On the first floor, McCarthy notices a door we hadn't seen the first time. "Let's check it out," he says.

I'm not sure if I'm ready for what's inside this door. My heart and head can't handle any more of this. There isn't a plaque next to the doorjamb like all the others. With reluctance and uncertainty, I push the door open, shining my flashlight throughout the room.

"Jackpot," McCarthy says, grabbing a guitar. "This is awesome." The entire room is full of musical instruments, records, and pictures of bands and male singers. There are male singers and male instrumentalists depicted on nearly everything we see. "Look at all of these guys."

"Wow," I say, not responding to McCarthy. There's an entire section of artwork, art supplies, and art history books. Most of the artists in the books are men—very few women are highlighted or discussed. I want to steal every single thing in this room, but I settle for an art history book and a sculpture "how-to" book.

McCarthy takes two records. "I can't believe men sang in bands." McCarthy's records at his house are only women singers and instrumentalists. "This is gold. Wish I lived Before, man. I could've been famous."

I'm glad his mood increased. I hated seeing him so down—so unlike himself. But is he crazy? Would I want to live in Before? Man, I don't know. I'd love to be free to create anything I wanted. But everything else seems so messed up. But they did get to be with women. Cissy and I could be free to do or be whatever we wanted. But Nigel and Decarion couldn't.

"Oh wow! I'm grabbing this for Cissy," I say, stuffing a box in my bag with the words *Dirty Dancing* on the cover.

Marjorie was right. Our movie used to star a boy and a girl. The lengths that Authority goes to in order to hide us from any knowledge of the past knows no bounds.

Closing the door with our backpacks secured to our backs, we creep toward the back exit. Suddenly, we hear the three beep chime alerting the unlock of the door. The back door opens and McCarthy and I dash toward the front entrance.

A security officer screams, "Freeze," but we keep hauling ass to the door. He's old, but he's fit and fast.

"Go. Go. Go," McCarthy yells, shoving me forward. We're athletes, so I know he's not going to gain on us. We've just got to make it to the door. With him fast on our heels, we charge through the front door, tripping the alarm system. Lights flash, alarms blare. "Keep going," McCarthy pants. "Around the back."

We sprint toward the back. Picking up momentum, we're closing in on my car. "Faster," I yell, still a block from where I'm parked. Authority-issued officer cars come screeching down the road. The gunfire pierces my ears. We duck behind another car. "We're not going to make it."

"The fuck we aren't." McCarthy grabs me by my backpack and pulls me to the next car. Bullets are whizzing by.

A car speeds by, slamming on its brakes. The vehicle jerks to stop. The passenger door flies open. "Get in," Cissy yells. McCarthy and I dart for the door. I jump in the passenger seat, leaning forward for McCarthy to get in. A loud gunshot rings in my ears. An animalistic scream causes every hair on my body to stand on end. I look around as I close the door, and Cissy speeds off.

"Fuck," I yell. "You gotta go faster." Cissy floors the gas pedal as we hightail it out of the Kendyl Corp. property. She's driving like a maniac, but nobody is behind us. I search in each direction, expecting a line of Authority officers gaining on us. None are in sight. "We did it," I say, leaning back on the headrest, panting. "Wow Cissy, you saved us."

Cissy doesn't look at me; she's still driving at breakneck speed. "Let's just get out of here first. I'm just glad you guys are safe."

"I'm not," McCarthy groans.

"What?" I say, turning around. McCarthy's hunched over on his side with his hand wrapped around his back. His skin is pale; his face is scrunched in agony. He pulls his hand away from his back. "They shot me," he says, revealing his entire hand covered in blood.

CHAPTER 33
VICISSITUDE

"Have mercy on me, Lord, for I am faint. Heal me, Lord, for my bones are in agony."
(Psalm 6:2)

"I couldn't stay in the forest. I tried; I really did. Look at my fingers. I bit my nails all the way down to the quick. Then, I started biting my actual skin. Look! Look, I drew blood. I was legit eating myself. So, I drove over near the Kendyl, knowing that I wasn't allowed to be over there, but I don't think anyone saw me. I just had to make sure you guys were okay. I was so worried. But then I heard the sirens, saw all the officers and…and…and I just knew—knew I had to get to you guys. I couldn't just let you get caught. I knew I had to do something. I had to help. I had to. I just did. And I wasn't fast enough. The gunshots were so loud. Sounded like they were coming from everywhere. I saw you guys running, and I was like, 'Oh my Authority, I have to get to them. But I wasn't fast enough. Now McCarthy's got a bullet in him, and there's blood. Oh no, there's so much blood. What're we going to do? I mean; he's going to be okay. I know it. We just have to get—"

Riot reaches over and rubs my shoulder. "Cissy, breathe. It's okay." Riot turns around. "You okay, man?" McCarthy groans. I turn around, and nearly run us off the road. "Keep your eyes on the road. Stay focused, and speed up a bit."

I do exactly as Riot tells me to. "Where are we going?' I ask, checking McCarthy's face in the rearview mirror. "He needs a hospital."

"We can't take him to the hospital," Riot says, trying to remain calm. "Let's get back to the forest, and figure out everything there."

We drive in silence for a good bit. The only sounds are McCarthy's groans that force me to jump and jerk the steering wheel every time I hear it. "Not much further now, man," Riot says, attempting to comfort McCarthy. "We need a plan."

"He needs a doctor," I reiterate, starting to get my bearings back. "Like now." I pull next to Riot's car. "Are you taking him back to the clearing?' I ask.

Riot motions for me to get out of the car. I kill the engine and get out. Riot meets me at the back of the car. "I don't think I can get him back to the clearing." He looks around, hoping the answer is right in front of him. It isn't. Riot starts thrumming his fingers on the hatchback of my car. He's biting his bottom lip. "I don't know, Cissy. I just don't know." There's terror in his eyes. He's beginning to unravel.

"All right," I say, ready to take over. "Do you trust me?" Riot looks apprehensive, but his slight nod is the only affirmation I need. "All right, put McCarthy in the back of your car. Try to pull further into those bushes there to sort of hide your car a bit—just in case anyone comes by. Stay in the backseat with him," I say, taking my hoodie off. "Use this to apply as much pressure as you can to help stop the bleeding, but don't push the bullet in any further—"

"I don't think I can do that, Cissy," Riot says, his eyes wide as he shakes his head. "Come on, Riot, you have to. I'll help you get him to your car."

After we get McCarthy positioned in the back of Riot's car, I grab my keys, pulling Riot over to my car. "Listen, I'll be right back. Trust me."

"But where are you going?"

"Just trust me, Riot," I say, getting into my car. "And Riot, be careful. Stay vigilant."

∼

"Mama." I tap her lightly. Her eyes flutter, and she groans before she rolls over. "Mama," I say again, shaking her a bit.

Mama opens her eyes, rubbing one of her eyes with her fist. "Cissy, what time is it?" she asks, reaching for her glasses. "Is everything okay?"

"No Mama, it's not," I admit and all the fear, pain, and worry start pouring out of me as tears soak my cheeks. "I need your help, please." Mama throws the blankets off of her and swings her legs off the side of the bed. "We have to hurry." As a nurse, Mama understands when things are urgent. She grabs her pants off the floor and throws them on, grabbing a sweater off the chair. "And Mama, get your medical bag," I say. She runs into the other room where she keeps it. "And the one that has the major emergency stuff in it."

Jumping into the car as she's putting on her shoes, Mama says, "Cissy, who's hurt? You're scaring me, baby."

"I know, Mama. I am too," I say, struggling to get the car

started. "Can we please just wait to talk until we're there? Please." Mama snaps her seatbelt, and motions for me to grab mine. I pull it on one-handed as I'm speeding out of the driveway.

"Whoa, honey. Slow down," she says, bracing herself with her hand on the dashboard.

"Mama, I love you, I really do," I say, beginning to cry harder. "Please don't be mad at me. But someone needs our help. And we can't not help."

Mama nods, watching me intently. I have no idea what's running through her head. Compassion is Mama's middle name. She'd lie down and die for anyone at any time. She gives everything to her patients. I just hope that when we get to Riot and McCarthy that her heart is bigger than her fear of Authority. And more than anything, I hope we're not too late.

Please don't let us be too late.

Mama interrupts my thoughts. "Cissy, I'm staying quiet now. But when this is over, you're going to have a lot of explaining to do."

"Yes, Ma'am," I say, pulling down the road to the forest. I slow the car, careful not to make too much noise on the rocks and gravel. We certainly don't need to alert any more people to our situation.

Riot's car is dark. There's no sign of movement. Please let them be okay. Please let him be okay. And then it occurs to me that I'm not sure which "him" I'm referring to.

The back door opens and Riot gets out, running over to us. I jump out of the car. "Cissy, he's not doing too goo—" Riot blanches, staring at Mama. "Ummm Cissy, what did you do?" he asks, his head shaking slightly back and forth.

"Cissy, who's your friend?" Mama asks, not taking her eyes off of Riot.

"Mama, Riot, Riot, Mama," I say, pulling her by the wrist. "We don't have time for that now. This is urgent."

Riot falls in step with us. "What're you doing? What's happening?"

"Mama's a nurse; she's going to help him."

"Him? There's another man somewhere around here?" Mama asks, her eyes wide as she turns around looking for another person. Riot throws open the door. Mama gasps at the sight of McCarthy, but then morphs into the professional I hoped she would. "Cissy, in the bag, there's chloroxylenol in the inside pocket. It's a blue bottle. You, rip up your shirt in strips and pour the liquid on the shirt." She walks around the car and opens the other door, near McCarthy's head. "Hello, I'm Nurse Maddox, but you can call me 'Ruth,' that's what my friends call me." Mama snaps on some latex gloves. "Okay, what's your friend's name?"

"Ummm, McCarthy. McCarthy McCorum."

"Okay McCarthy, I'm going to take good care of you. I promise. But I'm going to need you to be very—very brave. This is going to hurt, honey, but I need to assess this injury." Mama starts to roll him forward. McCarthy's agonized moan stops her. "Alright Cissy, there's a syringe and a vial of hydromorphone in my extra bag. Grab it. He's going to need something to ease this pain."

I rummage through the bag. I can't find it. "Here," Riot says, shining his flashlight into Mama's bag.

"Found it," I yell, louder than I anticipated.

Mama breaks the seal and fills the syringe, flicking it a few times before injecting the medicine into McCarthy's upper arm.

"Okay, you, on my count, I'll need you to help me roll him to his side, so I can get a better look." Together, they easefully maneuver McCarthy over. Mama's eyes darken and flash with a rage and fear I've never seen on her face before. "A bullet. He was shot?" Her voice is shrill. "That would've been pertinent information. Who shot this boy?"

Riot and I look at each other. Neither of us answers.

"Who shot him?" she grits through her teeth with slow, clipped words.

"Authority security," Riot answers, his head hanging heavy.

"Authority? Authority shot this boy?" Mama stands up abruptly and shakes her head. "Dammit, Cissy." Mama closes her eyes, mumbles something under her breath, takes a deep intake of air, and says, "We've got to get it out. Those bullets have GPS trackers in them. Normally, we just clean the wound and stitch it back up. We don't remove the bullets." Mama checks our surroundings again. "I don't hear anything or see anyone. They're probably waiting for sunup since they know exactly where he is right now. We've got a little bit of time. But we need to hurry."

Riot and I are both equally surprised. Bullets have trackers in them? And doctors don't typically take bullets out of people's bodies? "So what do we do?" I ask, knowing the last thing Mama wants is to talk to me right now. I bet she'd rather not even look at me.

"Give me a hemostat," Mama says, squeezing onto the floor of Riot's car. Indicating that I don't know what that is, I shrug my shoulders and flip my palms. "Tweezers. It looks like long tweezers."

"Got 'em," I say, handing them to her.

Before she grabs them, Mama says, "You, pour the chloroxylenol all over the hemostat." He does exactly what he's told. Mama takes the antiseptic and pours it directly into McCarthy's bullet hole. The agonizing bellow that escapes McCarthy's mouth makes us all wince.

"Cissy now, grab the Celox-A," Mama instructs as I rifle through her medical bag. "It's a red and white—"

"Found it," I announce, dropping the plastic bottle before I give it to her. Picking it up, I hand it to her. "Sorry. What's that do?"

She glares at me. "It speeds up the clotting of the blood after a gunshot wound." Hearing her perfectly clear enunciation of "gunshot" makes me want to hurl. That was intended for me.

"You, I'm going to need you to hold him, because even with the morphine, he's going be in extreme pain when I start trying to dislodge this thing." It's not lost on me that she hasn't once called Riot by his name.

McCarthy's screams shatter me. Riot's eyes are squeezed shut as he's whispering soothing words of encouragement into McCarthy's ear. After what seems like forever, Mama announces that she removed the ammunition. Keeping the bullet in the tweezers, she presents them both to Riot. "Take this—just like this—very carefully into those woods and dispose of it. Make sure it's where nobody, other than Authority, can find it." Riot nods and delicately takes the hemostat from her. "And, do not tell me—or Cissy—where you hid it."

"Yes, Ma'am." Riot walks quickly and carefully, but with purpose, into the woods.

Mama sits with McCarthy for quite awhile, insisting that I wait for her in the car. Riot sits outside of his car. I watch Mama from the car. Every so often she takes his blood pressure, checks his pulse and temperature, and dabs a wet cloth onto his forehead. Twice, she's changed the dressing she placed over his wound, using the sterilized strips of Riot's shirt. She's incredible at her job—calm, collected, and precise.

Right before daybreak, Mama gathers her medical supplies, says something to Riot, and walks back to the car. Motioning for me to slide over, Mama gets into the driver's seat. Letting her head fall with a thud against the headrest, Mama sighs audibly with her eyes tightly closed. "Don't say a word. Not one damn word," she instructs. "We will talk about this in the morning. I mean after we get some sleep."

"But, is he going to be—?"

"I said 'not one word.' I mean it." Mama starts the car, checks behind her, and backs out of the parking spot. "And yes, I think he'll recover. But that bullet was awfully close to his spine. He's very lucky."

CHAPTER 34
RIOT

"There is nothing more vital to the bond you share with someone than simply being there for them." (Suman Rai)

I used to be a normal guy, spending my time on the lacrosse field, hanging with my friends, and watching live sporting events with my dads. When I discovered that Jase Johnson could get us certain forbidden goods for a cost, I knew I wanted to see if I could actually do what my hands and imagination were itching to do. Realizing that art was my personal outlet for frustration and worry was a tough lesson, because I knew at that point that my love for it was going to cause some serious problems in my life. My art brought Lizzie to me. And then, our relationship drove her to complete suicide. You'd think that would be the wakeup call I needed to force me back to a legitimate and acceptable lifestyle—free of crime.

But did I learn anything from losing Lizzie? Apparently not. I walked my ass right back into those woods and resumed my life of selfish crime. When Cissy Maddox kicked me in the balls and head, I wish it would've knocked some sense into me. Getting tangled up with Cissy was not only stupid, but it was also downright dangerous. And if that wasn't enough, why in Authority's sake did I get McCarthy ensnarled in all of my antics, too? If McCarthy dies, his blood is on my hands—no doubt about it. This is nobody's fault, but mine. And now, Cissy involved her mom. Everybody is in peril, because I just can't be satisfied. Who do I think I am?

"Agghhh," McCarthy groans as he begins to stir. He seems agitated and uncomfortable. I don't have anything to help him relax or take any pain away. I don't know how long his painkillers will last. McCarthy sticks his tongue out and smacks his lips.

"You okay, buddy?" I whisper, running a damp towel over his forehead.

"Agghh, thir...thirs...thirsty." His words are barely audible. I lean over the front seat to grab his water bottle from earlier out of the passenger's cup holder. When I sit back down, McCarthy is out again. With his mouth barely ajar, there's a slight snore escaping his throat. His breathing seems regular and even, which makes me a little more at ease.

I pull the metal straw out of McCarthy's water bottle, suctioning my thumb over the top opening to keep the water in the cylinder. "McCarthy." I shake his shoulder lightly. "Hey buddy, wake up. Let's get some water in you."

McCarthy's eyes flutter. "Agghh," he groans, "fuck man."

Lifting his head, and placing it in my lap to elevate his head, I say, "Don't try to move yet. Just open your mouth a little, so I can drip some of this in it." He shifts a bit, licking his lips. "Good, now open." There's a small sliver of space between his lips. I dribble the water into his mouth. He licks his lips again and opens his mouth more. I repeat the process. "That's good, buddy."

The sound of gravel kicking up on the road freezes me in my action. "Shit." I lean over McCarthy, shielding us both from the eyes of whoever is speeding down the road to the forest. "Please. Please. Please," I whisper, hoping we're not about to be surrounded by Authority. The approaching car is close—too close. The car screeches to a halt. I want to look up, but know that I can't risk giving us away. Hopefully, they just think my car is parked here for an early morning sunrise walk or left over from a night of camping or an alcohol-binge. When the car door swings open, my heart speeds up, and I tuck McCarthy closer to me, holding him for dear life. He moans, and I loosen my grip as not to injure him further.

There's a quiet tap on the window. I squeeze my eyes shut tight before facing my imminent doom. Slowly opening my eyes and turning my head toward the window, Cissy's mom's concerned eyes are staring back at me. Relief washes over me. "Thank Authority," I whisper, shifting my body to place McCarthy comfortably back down onto the seat. She steps back a few feet when I open the door.

McCarthy begins to mumble again. His words are unclear and seem like gibberish to me. "Greater love has no one than this: to lay down one's life for one's friends." He moans. His words are coming out in groans. "That's from John. It's Chapter 15. It's verse 13."

"What's he saying?' she asks.

"I'm not sure," I say. "He's been talking like that a lot. And I don't really get it."

Cissy's mom places a calming hand on McCarthy's forehead. "How's he doing?" she asks, nodding toward McCarthy.

"I don't know," I admit. "Every time he groans or moves, it scares the shit—crap—out of me. I don't know what I'm doing."

Her mom nods knowingly. There's a look that passes over her face. Was it sympathy? "Let me take a look, check his vitals." She starts opening her bag. "I also brought a few oral painkillers. Just a few. But he can take one every six hours. I provided you with four of them." She hands me the bottle. I want to grip her hand in an appreciative grasp or hug her, but I know better.

She takes her time with McCarthy. This woman is even more gentle and kind than the hospitalists at Male General who took care of me. She's kind and encouraging. Her words are soothing, and McCarthy seems to respond well to her, settling more comfortably in his sleep. Removing her stethoscope from her ears and neck, she puts it back into her bag. "His temperature is a bit elevated. I'm going to give him a shot of some strong antibiotics to stop any infection that may be setting in and some acetaminophen to bring down the fever."

After she's done tending to McCarthy, she motions for me to meet her over by her car. "He's not out of the woods yet," she explains. "Keep doing what you're doing. Keep him hydrated." She opens her car door and throws her medical bag on the passenger side seat. "You're not safe here. Not for much longer. You need to get him out of here."

"Yes, Ma'am." I nod, glancing over at the car. "Thank you, Mrs. Maddox." I run my hands through my hair, not knowing really what to say next. "And please, thank Cissy for me, too."

Her eyes scan over my face, and her eyes narrow. "Ryan," she starts with a sigh.

"Riot," I correct. When I see the rage flash in her eyes, I

realize that wasn't my best choice. I should've just let her call me "Ryan."

"Riot," she grits out. "I have no idea what's going on with you and my daughter—"

"There's nothing—"

"Save it," she stops me, throwing her palm up, not too far from my face. "I'm a grown-ass woman, and I can definitely read a room. And I know my daughter. Whatever this is or was is now over. Understand?"

"Yes, Ma'am." I nod, dropping my chin to my chest in apologetic remorse. She's right. There's no refuting that. How can I possibly argue with her? I just got my friend shot in the back. Cissy needs to stay as far away from me as she can. If I were Cissy's mom, I'd report McCarthy and me to Authority and just be done with it. I'm not sure why she hasn't yet.

I watch her pull out and wait for her to be out of sight before I walk back to my car. Opening the car door, I'm happy to see McCarthy's eyes are open. "Hey buddy, you okay?" He nods, and I slide into the back with him. He's able to take three sips out of the straw, which I find encouraging.

∽

I'M SITTING in McCarthy's bedroom, listening to a record, marveling at how different our dads are. McCarthy hit some sort of parental jackpot. I pulled into their driveway, left McCarthy in the car, and went inside to explain everything that happened. Both of his dads were terrified and for some reason were thankful for me. Can't figure that one out. His dad said that there's no stopping McCarthy when he gets an idea in his head. His father is now hopeful that this "little stunt" as he called it will knock some sense into him. They keep stopping in and giving him protein shakes to sip and applesauce to eat. I was shocked as shit when they told me that McCarthy had already told them that he was planning a mutiny with a linear. Yep, he told his dads. And here I am inside their house without being thrown out on my ass for being linear and for nearly getting their son killed.

"How's he doing?" Mr. McCorum asks, sitting down next to me.

I shrug and shake my head, not really knowing what to say.

He runs his hand along McCarthy's forehead. "Isn't this the most beautiful boy you've ever seen?" I smile and nod, because that's an easy statement to agree with. "Did he tell you that we weren't permitted to father?"

"What? Then how—?"

Mr. McCorum shrugs and chuckles. "We learned ages ago that rules are meant to be broken or at the very minimum, bent to our will." He smiles and brushes the hair off of McCarthy's forehead. "We know a guy who forged all of our paperwork. Thank God we did too, because this boy is a miracle. Between this boy and our Bibles—"

"Your what?" I ask, shaking my head in confusion. He motions to *The New Testament* on my lap.

"Bibles. We have *The New Testament* and *The Old Testament*. We read them regularly and trust in God. His father and I just continued to pray and pray. McCarthy here is our miracle. God granted us the greatest joy in life." He stands, kisses McCarthy on the forehead. "I have some work to get done. Try reading and praying, Riot. It does help." Mr. McCorum leaves the room, and I'm left leafing through the Bible—wondering what any of it means.

"What's in the folders?" McCarthy's raspy and pained voice pulls me from my thoughts.

I scramble up from the floor and stand over him. "You okay?" I grab his most recent shake and offer it to him. He shakes his head.

"The folders?" he asks again.

"Unimportant," I say, fluffing his pillow and feeling useless.

"I didn't get a bullet to the back for something unimportant," McCarthy says, barely audible, with a groan.

"You're right. You're right. I'm sorry," I say.

"Tell me you're sorry again, and I'm going to shoot you in the back," he says, trying to smile. "After what we uncovered, we did the most important thing." McCarthy's eyes flutter as he mumbles, "My flesh and my heart may fail, but God is the strength of my heart and my portion forever. That one is from Psalm chapter..." He doesn't finish his sentence before falling right back to sleep. There's a small smile on his face. That smile settles my worry a little more. McCarthy's not mad at me.

I'm glad I finally figured out that he's been quoting that *Bible*. He must get comfort from it. At first it was scaring the crap out of me. He was speaking in weird phrases and such, but then I finally got it. Every time he recites a passage, he calms down and sleeps more softly. So I am all for it. If it helps McCarthy, then by all means, who am I to stop him?

I rummage through my backpack, grabbing one of the folders. It is enormous. Next time he wakes up, I'm going to have some information for him. Hopefully, this folder labeled: **Slavery/Racism Part 1** won't be too horrifying.

CHAPTER 35
VICISSITUDE

A lot of parents will do anything for their kids, except let them be themselves."
(Banksy)

The knock on my bedroom door makes my stomach churn. I'm not ready for the deluge of anger and punishment that is about to rain down on me. I wish I could hide under these covers until the storm blows over, and my moms don't hate me.

"Come in," I call from under my blankets. I hear the door open, and two sets of footsteps walk in. They do everything together. I wish Mama could have kept this between her and me and not tell Mom. No such luck.

I feel a tug on my comforter. I groan, holding it tight over my head. "You have to face the consequences. That's the problem with growing up and learning lessons," Mom says in her teacher voice that is rarely used on me.

Reluctantly, I emerge from my cocoon of comfort and security. "I know what you're going to say, and believe me, it's not anything I haven't already said to myself," I start, trying to lessen whatever blow is coming my way.

Mama motions me to scoot, so both of my moms can sit on either side of me. "We're talking," she says, sitting on one side of me while Mom sits on the other. "You're listening."

Mom starts first. "You have no idea how lucky you are. We could be identifying your body at Authority morgue right now." I nod, feeling the tears filling my eyes.

"Teenage rebellion is normal, Cissy," Mama adds, "but this was downright reckless." My head falls back against the wall. I know they're right. "How did he even contact you to know that they needed help?"

Well crap, they don't know I was with him when he was shot. Truth or lie? Truth or lie? Lie, always lie. "They didn't contact me," I explain. "Riot's an artist, and I've been sneaking him art supplies. The hiding spot we use is far into those woods by that parking lot. I'd just dropped off some canvases when they came speeding in."

"What were they even doing that they got mixed up with Authority?" Mom asks. I shrug and shake my head, indicating that I have no idea.

"Why are you illegally supplying art materials to that boy?" Mama asks.

"How do you even know him?" Mom asks at the same time.

I explain everything to them without telling them anything. It's a monologue of truthful lies and false truths. He was Lizzie's friend. She introduced me well before she died. I knew he was safe. She used to supply him with materials, but he ran out. I told him that I could help. We never talked or spent time together other than exchanging art supplies. The only reason I decided to help him and

McCarthy was because I knew Mama would never want me to just let someone bleed to death. She taught me that much. Compassion is more important than the laws.

"Cissy, I'm sure it goes without saying, but you are not seeing that boy again," Mom says, giving me her sternest teacher eye.

"Well after today," Mama corrects, shooting Mom a side-eye.

"Ruth," Mom sighs, shaking her head.

"Gloria, he needs these; I cannot have a dead teenager on my hands." Mama pats her pockets. She reaches in and takes out two bottles of pills, handing them to me. "I already stopped over this morning, but that boy is going to need more. You have to get these to him. One is a strong antibiotic. The other is a nerve block that should help alleviate some pain."

"Get them to him and tell him that you won't be seeing him or talking to him anymore," Mom directs. "If he isn't there or you can't see him, leave him a note. But get in and get out." They both stand to leave.

"Yes, Ma'am," I say, putting the bottles in my backpack. "Moms?" They stop and turn to look at me. "I'm sorry."

"We know you are," Mom says, "but you can never do something so stupid again." She kisses the top of my head and walks out. Mama stays. She closes the door.

"Cissy, to love that boy is to wish for death," she says, placing her hands on my shoulders and kneeling down to look me in the eyes. "And don't feed me any lines like you're 'just friends,' because you wouldn't risk your life, our lives, and all of our reputations for some boy who wants to paint pictures."

"Mama, I swear—"

Mama shakes her head, waving me off. "Stay away from

him. And if you can't, then be honest. We'll get you into therapy—a different type of therapist than you regularly go to. It's confidential, and Authority doesn't punish those who seek rehabilitation."

"What? Therapy for what? Rehabilitate what?" I ask, confused.

"Conversion therapy. To get the linear out of you before it's too late," Mama explains. "I wish every day of my life that Granny Meredith could've gotten Portia into conversion therapy. She'd still be here today if she would've gone and cured her urges." Mama hugs me and kisses the top of my head. "I can't bear to lose you, honey. You mean too much to me. If need be, we can get you the help you need."

⁓

WHEN I HEARD THE SIRENS, I couldn't possibly sit there and just hope that Riot and McCarthy were okay. I had to help them. And I don't regret it one bit. I do wish I would've been faster and been able to get to them before that bullet did. My moms raised me to be someone who helped others. Well, I did. Why does it seem like there were stipulations on teaching me to be a good person? It's almost as if they only want me to be loving, kind, compassionate, and generous to those they approve of—those they deem worthy of my love, kindness, compassion, and generosity.

This wait feels interminable. Typically, I don't have to sit here this long for Riot to make an appearance. I'm not about to go back home without seeing him. I hate that I don't know if he's okay. I hate that I can't just go check on McCarthy and him. How can checking on someone's safety and well-being be unacceptable and illegal? Riot's right; this world is so damn screwed up. The fact that I never saw any of it before this year is unfathomable. I was just going along, following any ridiculous rule they put in place without ever questioning it. I'm not doing that anymore. Those days are over.

"Cissy, what're you doing here?" Riot shakes me, waking me up.

"I must've dozed off," I say, rubbing my eyes. There's a pink and purple hue to the sky. The sun was shining and blazing when I got here. Just another infraction on my moms' list.

"What are you doing here? Your mom explicitly forbade me to see you, and after all that she did for McCarthy, I'm going to honor her wishes," Riot announces with finality, stepping back from me, creating distance. "I'm just here to hide some of these document folders in the spot."

"Gee thanks, nice to see you too," I say, sitting up. "Mama wanted me to get these to you. After she saw you this morning, she stopped at the hospital to restock her bag. Aka, get more meds for McCarthy."

"Awww man, she's the best," he says, taking the bottles from me. He holds my hands in his. "And Cissy, thank you. For everything. I'm so grateful to you and to your mom." He opens his backpack and puts the bottles in them. "I'll never forget this." Riot turns and leaves, walking back toward his car.

"Riot," I call after him. He stops, but doesn't turn around. "Aren't you going to tell me anything that you found?" His head falls back as he looks at the sky, running his hand through his hair. Riot shakes his head and starts walking. "So that's it?"

"Yes." That's all he says, and he doesn't stop.

"So this is 'goodbye,' then?" I ask, catching up with him.

Riot turns, his eyes glassy and pained. He walks toward

me, wraps an arm around my back, and pulls me close to him. He looks me in the eyes. Then, his eyes travel all over my face. Finally, he lowers his head and kisses me softly on my lips. The kiss doesn't linger. There's no passion. There's no promise of anything. Riot pulls back, nods once, and says, "Goodbye, Cissy."

CHAPTER 36
RIOT

"We crucify ourselves between two thieves: regret for yesterday and fear of tomorrow." (Fulton Oursler)

Mr. and Mr. McCorum were so grateful for the extra pills. When I got back to McCarthy's house, they were all in his room. McCarthy was awake and alert. Breathing a sigh of relief, I only stayed for a bit—not wanting to interrupt their family time. After all, his dads are in caregiver mode right now, catering to his every need.

Driving back to my house seems anticlimactic. The last time I was here, I was just about to embark upon a mutiny for understanding and knowledge. Now, I'm more confused, desolate, and frustrated than ever before. The facts are simple: the world was screwed up Before. So our Authority tried to fix it, but that resulted in screwing it up even more.

Pulling into my driveway, my heart drops, and I lose all saliva in my mouth. There are two Authority sedans parked in my driveway with the lights flashing. The sirens are off. I don't know whether I should throw my car in reverse, hightailing it out of town, or get out and surrender peacefully. As I sit and contemplate my options, my front door opens. My father escorts the Authority officers out, shaking both of their hands. I reverse the car, backing up into the road to let them out. Each officer waves to me as he leaves.

What in Authority is going on?

My father is still on my front porch, his arms crossed over his chest. The vein on his forehead is trying to break out of his skin. He's clearly waiting for me to get out of my car, which makes me just want to shrivel up and die in here before facing him right now. Authority officers don't just drop by the house. This is not good.

Killing the engine, I unbuckle my seatbelt as a wave of nausea washes over me. I have to play this calm and collected. "Hey, Dad," I say walking to the front porch, "what was that all about?"

"Give me your wallet," he says.

"My wallet?"

"Give me your fucking wallet, Riot," he yells. This makes me jump. I shove my hand in my back pocket, retrieving my wallet.

"Here," I say, wondering what in Authority is going on. My father pulls every last item out of my wallet. He throws some of the contents onto the porch stand that used to have a plant on it, searching for something. "Dad, what're you looking for?"

"Where were you last night?" he asks, still rummaging through every sliver and pocket of my minute wallet.

"Where was I?" I repeat, because I don't know what to say, what to admit to, or what to deny. He glares at me. "I was here with you."

"Did you leave this house?" he asks, handing me back my wallet with nothing left in it.

"No, of course not," I lie. "Did you check my tracker?"

"I'm not an idiot, Riot. You don't think I know that you kids charge that damn thing when you want to go do shit that you know you wouldn't be allowed to do," my father states, making me realize that I'm not as clever or stealthy as I thought. "I'm going to ask you again. Where were you last night?"

"I was here. Man, Dad, why? What's going on?"

What does he know?

How bad is it?

How much shit am I in?

"Apparently, I scanned in to the Kendyl with my access card last night at 1:30 a.m., and didn't leave there until 2:45 a.m. You wouldn't know anything about that, would you?"

Holy Authority, I'm dumber than I thought. How could I not think about the fact that my father's card would be linked back to him? Anyone in his right mind would realize that whomever was swiping in with an access card would be logged into the computer system.

"No sir," I whisper, refusing to make eye contact with my father.

"I'm going to hope my son isn't dumber than a box of rocks. My son can't possibly be the stupidest man in Eka. He can't be." My father walks into the house and slams the front door, leaving me alone on our front porch.

Sorry Dad, but your son is a complete moron, a reckless imbecile. Oh man, I'm not sure what to do now. Coming clean is not an option. Absconding north can't happen either. I've spent much of the last year believing Lizzie made a kneejerk reaction to our situation. But it's evident that Lizzie knew that there's no way out. So she found one.

Man, did her decision wreck me. If I followed in her footsteps, would anyone really care?

Cissy.

～

"Wake up," my dads say, barging into my room.

"What's going on?" I ask, trying to get my bearings.

"Do you know McCarthy McCorum?" my father asks, pulling the blankets off of me.

"I...I..." Stalling is the only thing I can do.

"Well, his father just called here and said that you do. So organize all of your lies and figure out what you want to say right now," my father yells.

"Riot, we need you to be honest with us, honey. Your friend was arrested this morning at his house for breaking and entering, tampering with evidence, treasonous intent, and failure to uphold the Ekian Laws of Life and Liberty."

"Well, you don't look surprised at all," my father states.

"Apparently, he had an access card—"

"He fucking had ***my*** access card, Atticus, and how in Authority do you think he got that card, Riot?" I shake my head. "Oh the kid doesn't know. There's a shock."

"Luther, you have to calm down—"

"Tell me calm down one more time. Try it, I dare you," he yells at my dad. My dad just sits down on my bed, defeated.

"Dads, listen—"

"No, you listen. I want that card back. I want you to start talking. And I will not tolerate one more lie coming out of that mouth of yours."

"Luther, honey, we don't have time for this right now. We have to get to the courthouse," my dad says. The growl that comes out of my father's throat is threatening and ominous. I'm pretty sure he's never been this irate with me before—and he's always angry about something. This is next level.

"Oh that's right. I'm going to save your friend. You better hope to Authority that what we uncover in this case doesn't have your name and fingerprints all over it."

"Save my friend? What does that mean?"

"Your father is going to represent McCarthy," my passive dad explains. "When his father called, he said that would only be fair after everything that went down."

"And since we don't know anything that 'went down' as he stated, I agreed, because something tells me that saving his ass is going to end up saving yours as well." My father slams the door as he leaves.

My passive dad jumps, shakes his head, and reopens the door. "You knew I was right behind you." He waves to me and leaves the room, closing the door behind him.

This shitshow cannot possibly get any worse. How many more people are going to suffer, because I can't get my head out of my ass? McCarthy's been arrested. His dads know everything. There's no way they'll stay silent to save me. McCarthy's the pawn to get to me. Soon, my dads and the rest of Eka will know that my brilliant idea got my friend shot and arrested—and for what? My own selfish curiosity.

CHAPTER 37
VICISSITUDE

"A bird cannot love freely when caged." (Matshona Dhliwayo)

The house is eerily quiet. The sun is shining through the crack in my curtains, creating a glimmer of light. My moms didn't stop in to say "goodbye" before they left for work. It's the start of the last week of school, and I have no desire to get up and go. I can't face seeing Marjorie today and deal with her hanging all over Celeste Peltzer. With everything going on, I can't take that too. It's just too much. Sounds like a perfect time for a self-induced senior skip day. Just the thought of heading out to the woods to swim and relax makes my spirits immediately lift. They always say that self-care is super important. Well, that's what's on my agenda for the day. And hopefully, Riot's calmed down and come to his senses. After all we've been through, he can't possibly shut me out now.

Deciding some breakfast is exactly what I need to get this day off to a good start, I head into the kitchen. Both of my moms are seated at the kitchen table, drinking their coffee in total silence.

"Hey," I say, grabbing a loaf of bread. "I thought you both left for work already."

"Have a seat." My mom gestures to the table.

When two women are this quiet and reserved, you know you're in for a world of hurt. I lower my butt to my chair, bracing myself for whatever is about to come tumbling out of their mouths.

"You're not telling us everything," Mama starts.

"About what?" I ask, knowing not to incriminate myself. There are so many teens that just cave without finding out first what their parents know. I'm not about to fall into that trap.

Mom rolls her eyes. She's not one for teenage antics. She can see right through adolescent bullshit. "Your friend was arrested last night."

"Who?" I ask, feeling bile surface to my throat.

"McCarthy," Mama clarifies, watching me intently. I'm careful not to show my relief that it's McCarthy and not Riot. She already suspects too much.

"For what?" I feign ignorance.

"There are a whole slew of charges being brought upon that boy," Mom explains. "But mainly for breaking into the Kendyl and stealing classified documents."

"Oh no!" I cry, cupping my hand over my mouth.

"You were never a good actress, Cissy. Stop playing dumb. It's very unbecoming," Mama says, losing patience with me. "You're playing with fire here. Authority doesn't screw around. If you had any part of their crime, they'll find out."

"Are you trying to kill your mother?" my mom asks rhetorically. "She's already lost a sister due to a linear lifestyle. We refuse to lose you, too."

"McCarthy is going to stand before Judge Greer first thing tomorrow morning."

"Is that bad?" I ask, looking between the two of them, wanting inside information.

"He's the meanest judge in our district. Your friend won't see the outside of the Male Confinery for a long, long time, Cissy," Mom says, stirring her coffee. She doesn't even put anything in her coffee, so I know this is just a nervous action. There's absolutely nothing but plain black coffee in her cup. "We're just praying to Authority that you're not going to end up in the Female Confinery too."

"McCarthy is injured. How can he appear in court?"

"Do you think Authority cares about that? Have you not been paying attention?" Mama yells. "Cissy, you're in grave danger. Don't you see that?"

Mama's right. I know that. But Riot's in more danger than any of us. "I have to warn Riot," I announce, standing up and heading to my bedroom.

"I'm sorry, but have you lost your mind?" Mom asks, following me to my room.

"He needs to be careful. I have to see him."

"You will do no such thing. We've already told you that you are not to see him ever again," Mom says, standing at my door.

"It won't take long. I promise. I'll be right back." I slide on my shoes and grab my car keys.

"You're not listening," Mom states, shaking her head. "You're not going anywhere."

"No, you're not listening—"

I hear the sound before I feel the tightening around my wrist. "No!" I screech. "Please! No! No! No!" I reach for the wristband, trying to put my finger under the wristband before it tightens and I cannot get it off. It doesn't move.

"Are you kidding me, right now? You know how important this is."

"You forced our hand, Vicissitude," Mom says, closing my door. Through the closed door, she adds, "This is for your own good."

In third grade, Evelyn Daniels made fun of my skin color. She told everyone that I was a vanilla fudge ice cream cone. When it got back to me, I was naively flattered. I'd always loved a twist cone—and nobody before that moment ever even mentioned my appearance or skin as something different or noticeable. When I wasn't upset or angry, Evelyn gassed up her insults, tearing me down each and every day. Evelyn had derogatory comments about my hair, my skin, and even my intelligence level.

At first, I wasn't bothered by Evelyn or her ridicule, but as time wore on, it got to me. People would snicker or whisper to one another when I walked by. Marjorie, who was my very best friend at the time, would often tell Evelyn to shut her mouth and then try to cheer me up. But there were times when Evelyn would say something belittling to me, and I'd notice Marjorie scrutinizing me. It almost seemed as if Marjorie was wondering if Evelyn could see something she couldn't. Kids were beginning to turn on me and side with Evelyn.

Marjorie hated it. Evelyn was stealing the limelight, and Marjorie couldn't take it. So, she took matters into her own hands—in a very diplomatic way. It was actually Marjorie who told my moms about Evelyn and her offensive remarks.

Mama was ready to go to war with anyone who hurt me or caused me any sort of pain. Mom, being a teacher, knew how schools and students reacted to a tattletale at school— even for things as serious as bullying. Mom had a different plan. Nightly, Mama, Mom, and I spent hours role-playing ways in which I should react to Evelyn's degradation. Basically, they taught me how to fight fire with fire. We had a comeback or a reaction for anything that Evelyn threw my way.

It was two weeks later, when Evelyn walked by me at lunch and quite loudly asked me if my hair was real hair or made out of a dead horse's tail. I smiled, armed and ready. Then, Evelyn laughed and said that I was so stupid, because I didn't even realize she was making fun of me. All the kids laughed. One snotty girl neighed.

Just like we'd practiced, I reached into my bag, pulled out a carrot, and handed it to her. Taking the carrot, she looked at it and then asked what it was for. I smiled and said, "Rabbits like carrots." Then I made my teeth buck out like hers and chomped my lower lip with my over bitten top teeth. Evelyn threw the carrot across the lunchroom and ran straight to the office, crying hysterically. The bully certainly had no problem dishing it out, but woman, she couldn't take it herself.

It wasn't long before the headmaster and Authority-appointed liaison wanted to see me in the office. They asked me what transpired during our lunch hour. I recounted the events word for word, event by event, revealing Evelyn's part as well as my own malicious comeback. They asked me if Evelyn had ever treated me poorly before. I admitted that she had. Immediately, the liaison and headmaster wanted to know if anyone had ever witnessed her mistreatment of me. I revealed that nearly everyone in our class had been privy to her behavior. They questioned each student. Back then, nobody ever lied to an adult. It was too terrifying. Everyone recounted all of Evelyn's wrongdoings.

Evelyn was immediately removed from our school. I was the third grade hero for standing up to the class bully. I knew in that moment that I'd never hide anything from my moms again. My moms knew what to do, how to handle it, and how to come out on top. I followed their advice to a tee, never faltering. From that moment on, whenever anything was awry at school, they were the first people I confided in. They had the answers and my best interest at heart. Their unconditional love for me was never clouded or masked by their need to fulfill society's view of what or how a daughter should behave. It was the three of us against the world—Team Maddox for the win.

But that was then.

This is now.

Clearly, my parents are currently misguided by their fear of what Authority could or would do to me if my transgressions were uncovered. They're reacting as terrified moms, just trying to protect their only daughter from harm. But this time, they're wrong—completely and utterly wrong. They have no idea what's best for me. If they did, this shackle wouldn't be cutting off my circulation as it threatens to report me to Authority every time I get close to the front porch.

But mark my words. One way or another, I am getting out of this house and off of this porch.

CHAPTER 38
RIOT

"Dads are most ordinary men turned by love into heroes, adventurers, storytellers, and singers of song." (Unknown)

"I can't believe they shot him right in the back," my dad's saying as he walks in the house. "That boy is the sweetest, most charming—" His mouth clamps shut when he sees me siting on the couch, waiting for them.

"Was school optional today?" My father rolls his eyes, hanging his hat on the coatrack and dropping his briefcase on the foyer bench. "Are there any rules you follow anymore?"

"What happened? How's McCarthy?" I ask, ignoring his snide question.

"Riot, you know we cannot talk about this case with you—"

"What do you mean 'how's McCarthy?' Surely, you have no idea that he was shot by Authority after his B&E at the Kendyl, now do you?"

"Ummm I uh just meant how'd the meeting with him go?" I stumble on my words, trying to play dumb.

"That lovely boy is so—"

"Atticus, can I please have a moment alone with my son?" my father asks.

"***Your*** son?" my dad questions, glaring at my father. "Oh, so now he's ***your*** son? I'm so sorry that Authority didn't deem me acceptable to father—"

"Whoa, whoa, sweetheart," my father backpedals, "that's not what I meant. I just meant son, my son, your son, our son. I wasn't laying sole claim to this kid. Trust me, not my intention."

My dad gets ultrasensitive about being my dad. When he applied for fatherhood, Authority denied his application, stating that he was "too feminine" and didn't display enough "masculinity" to use his genes for fatherhood. My active father always makes sure that my passive dad does most of the parenting. Otherwise, my passive dad feels excluded and unworthy.

"Well, that's how you made it sound," my dad pouts, placing both of his hands on his hips with his chin turned up. This argument is a common one in the Logan household. My father does a great job of making my dad feel better about it most of the time.

My father envelops him in a tender embrace. "I'm sorry that it came across that way. I promise there was no spiteful intent. I just want some alone time with Riot. Is that okay with you?"

My dad sniffles and nods his approval. "Fine. But I get extra back rubs tonight then." My father mumbles something and agrees to these terms. My dad walks toward the kitchen and says, "I'll get started on dinner. It's been a long day."

Walking back toward the front door, my father opens it and commands, "Out." I jump up and follow him out, hoping he'll let me back in this house after this so-called talk. But I'm not dumb. There's no way this is going to be a "talk." This is going to be an all-out tirade—a monologue of disgust, disappointment, and rage.

My father motions for me to sit. I do so. "Full disclosure and immunity," he starts, using my dad's phrase that often relaxes me. When my dad says "immunity," I tend to feel safer to speak the truth. But now, with my father offering it up, it only feels like a trap. "Did you steal my access card and enter into the Kendyl with the McCorum kid?"

"Dad, I'd never do something like—"

"Riot James, cut the crap," he yells and then lowers his voice. "You're my kid." He's pacing back and forth on the porch, shaking his head from side to side. "You're all me, kid. Every bit of you is me. Why do you think I wanted to be a lawyer?"

"You like to argue with people," I reply honestly.

"Well yeah, I do, but it was more than that. I wanted in that Kendyl. I wanted those files. Just like you, I needed to know the truth about this fucked up world." He sits on the outdoor table facing me. "I hate the law, hate being an attorney. Hate everything about it."

"What? I never knew that." Who is this man? Someone swapped out my father with this impostor.

"Of course you didn't. I don't tell you shit like that." He reaches into his pocket and pulls out his smokeless pipe and ignites the vapors. Inhaling he says, "Apparently, when you were begging for answers to all of your deep questions, I should've been honest with you. It would've saved us from all of this."

"Dad, I didn't—"

"Yeah, you're probably right to keep denying it. You don't know anything. You were at home the entire night," my father says, blowing foggy air out of his mouth. "Your Grandfather Britt caught me breaking the Laws of Liberty and forced me to be a lawyer. Did I ever tell you that?"

"What? No!" This new information is crazy, and I can't quite wrap my head around it. "What did he catch you doing?"

"I suspect you're more like me than I imagined, Riot. I'd always hoped that you'd have more Atticus in you if I let him take the reins and raise you, but it doesn't appear that way." He dodges my question. "The truth is I wanted to be in a band. I love singing, songwriting, and playing the drums."

"I'm sorry, what? You write music and sing?"

"Don't look so surprised. The first year we had you, my voice was all that soothed you at night." He leans over and places his head in both of his hands. "Remember that wooden fort in the back of my dads' yard that they built for me when I was in elementary school?" I nod, recalling all the times I played in that fort when I'd visit Grandpa Brit. "Well, in high school, I started going back there with different guys—and well, you know. So, one of my boyfriends had a drum set and some records. Illegal stuff. And we experimented."

"Whoa! And Grandpa Britt caught you?" I ask, my shock evident on my face.

"Sure did," he admits. "Next thing I knew I was in law school, learning the laws and the history of our laws inside and out. And I never touched a drum or sang a note ever again, because I know how severe the consequences are. But just between you and me, I do quite a bit of songwriting still."

"So you had a love, a passion for something illegal—and you still write songs?"

My father nods. This newfound knowledge gives me hope—hope that I can someday be upfront and honest about my art.

"But Riot, Authority means business. They don't go easy on anyone ever."

"I know," I say, closing my eyes, feeling the gravity of my situation.

"The problem is we, Logan men, are wired differently. We push buttons, teetering over the boundaries. We aren't satisfied until we're completely fucked." He runs his hand along his bald head and down his face. "And Riot, I think you're fucked. They're going to find out it was you. And I don't know if your dad and I can protect you from them."

CHAPTER 39
VICISSITUDE

"You can waste your lives drawing lines. Or you can live your life crossing them."
(Shonda Rhimes)

And women can't tinker? Screw you, Authority. I could be the best damn engineer you've ever had. Guess you'll never know now, will you? Woman, my adrenaline is in overdrive. I feel like I can do anything. I'm an unstoppable badass.

Sliding into my car, I feel freer than the day I earned my driver's license. I tap my wrist, and the little green bubble that represents me depicts me right at my house. I start the car and back out of the driveway. No sirens. No blaring alarms. My tracker is loose and comfortable. As I turn the corner out of my neighborhood, that beautiful green bubble is still right on my house. Take that Authority—and you too Moms. There is no holding me back. There's no holding women back. We can and will do anything we so damn desire. You can watch. Or you can resist it. Either way, we can do it all.

Approaching the cavern where Riot keeps his materials, I crawl into the briars and grab his box. I need to leave him a note about McCarthy and give him a heads-up on what I think he should do. Pulling the box out, I notice there are files under the box, so I grab those too. The top folder is labeled: **Slavery/Racism Part 1.** My curiosity gets the best of me. Opening the folder, I begin to read.

Holy Authority, in the time of Before, there were thousands of people with the same mentality and beliefs as Evelyn Daniels. If I lived Before, people who looked like Marjorie and Riot could have *owned* me—like I was property. What? That doesn't even make sense. How did they even do that? Nobody is going to own me. That's just ridiculous. Why didn't the black people just leave and walk away or say, "No thanks?" I would never let someone treat me that way. The images of the slaves are heartbreaking. The people in the white hoods were ruthless and vile, burning and hanging black people for their own enjoyment.

And then years and years later, there were still reports of police officers who were supposed to "serve and protect" their society ended up killing people who looked like me. Sometimes, there was justification; but other times, these officers just used their strength, power, and status. How did the people of Before know which police officers were the good ones and which ones were not? Did people with my skin tone just walk around afraid all the time? When I see an Authority officer, I feel safe, secure, and completely protected—unless I'm driving a getaway car with two forbidden criminals inside. However, I can't imagine a time and place when an Authority officer would judge me for the color of my skin or the texture of my hair.

Men and women during this time were encouraged to get married and have children—the way my moms described to me. But black women and white men or vice versa weren't allowed to comingle or cohabitate. It looks like there's no time period where Riot and I would be permitted to love one another openly and easily. Maybe we really are taboo and immoral. It doesn't seem like anyone has ever accepted what he and I have—or could have.

Closing the folder, I decide to ignore the next folder **American Revolution 1776.** I'm not even sure what something in the 1700s has to do with Eka. I know Eka was founded in the mid-2030s. I'll read this folder later. I shove it into my bag, and grab my notebook out to write Riot a letter.

Folding the letter, I open Riot's box to place the letter on top. I've never rifled through his box before out of respect and privacy for him. But, I notice a snapshot and can't resist moving some supplies to get a better look at the picture. I snag the picture, discovering six more are underneath. They're all of Lizzie. I'm not sure if Riot took these pictures or if Lizzie gave them to him, but either way, it's clear that he kept them for a reason. I can pretend all I want that there's something brewing with Riot and me, but the truth is, his love and adoration for Lizzie is still very real and very deep.

One picture in particular pulls at my heartstrings and colors me green with envy. Riot had to have taken this one. Lizzie is dressed for all intents and purposes with everything covered, but there's an allure and sex appeal to this picture that's not apparent in the others. Lizzie's lying right on the sand, half in the water and half out. One hand is behind her head in a lazy nonchalant manner. Her other hand is just resting on the top of her jean shorts with her fingertips dipping in slightly to the waistband. She's wearing short—extremely short—jean shorts and a white men's shirt tied into a crop shirt with no buttons secured. The shorts are unbuttoned and unzipped halfway down. Lizzie has on a bright blue lacy bra that's completely visible through the water-soaked white shirt. Her hair is drenched, but the wet ringlets around her face are sexy and glamorous. Her lips are pursed in a pucker, like she's trying to blow a kiss to whoever is on the other side of the camera lens. I knew Lizzie Griffin most of my life, and I never once saw her look this stunning and desirous. No woman—or man I guess—would turn down the beautiful woman in this picture.

"Cissy!" Riot calls, scaring me half to death. I startle so easily that the file falls off my lap, and I throw the picture about a foot to the left. "What're you doing here?" He runs up alongside me and starts reorganizing the pictures and folders.

"I had to come check on you and warn you—"

"You've got to get out of here. They arrested McCarthy," Riot says, cutting me off. He's frantic, shoving all of his things back in the box and tossing them all into a duffel bag he brought with him. "I know I'm next."

"Riot, what're we going to do? I can't just sit by and watch Authority lock you up."

"Cissy, you've got to forget that you ever met me. You really need to just—" Riot looks back at his duffel bag and looks at the folder on top. "Did you read that folder?" I nod, my frown showing my disdain for the information I uncovered.

"Listen to me," Riot says, zipping up his duffel and dropping it at his feet. He grabs both of my hands. "If we lived Before, Cissy, I wouldn't have cared one bit about our skin colors. I would've openly befriended you—not caring what anyone thought."

"Befriended?" I ask.

He smiles and nods, wrapping me into his arms. "The best of friends," he adds.

"Because you would've been in a relationship openly with Lizzie," I say without thinking and releasing myself from his embrace.

Riot looks confused. He glances back down at the duffel bag. Smirking, he looks back up at me. He chuckles, and it downright infuriates me. He curls his lips under and tries to hold back a laugh. Now, all I want to do is smack that smirk right off of his face. "Oh Cissy, I can't tell you what would've happened in our make-believe life of Before. But, I can tell you this: you are beautiful, smart, brave, and just perfect. If there was a way, and there's not, but if there was one, you and I would be together in the here and now."

I can feel my face pink and burn with embarrassment. "I didn't mean—"

"It's okay," he says, patting the bag. "There are some provocative pictures in here. I admit, I'd probably go a little crazy if I saw you with a guy or something like that."

"Riot, I just want you to know that whatever happens, all I want is for you to be happy—and safe."

"And that's what you need to know, Cissy. I can't live happily or safely knowing I put you in any type of danger. So can you please, please, just pretend that you never met me, so I know that you're going to be okay?"

With tears streaming down my face, I nod, crossing my fingers behind my back. Riot wipes a tear from my check and pulls me into his chest. He holds me there for a long time while I sob into his chest. "I don't know what I'm going to do without you," I say, gripping his shirt in my fists by my face. "These four months have been the most exciting and wonderful months of my life."

Riot kisses the top of my head. "Mine too." But the jealous teenage girl in me refuses to believe that. If he really felt that way, then he wouldn't be holding on to those pictures of Lizzie and sending me away. Riot may have enjoyed the time with me as a distraction from his grief, but they weren't life-changing like they were for me—or like the time he spent with Lizzie.

CHAPTER 40
RIOT

"This is what the LORD Almighty said: 'Administer true justice; show mercy and compassion to one another'." (Zechariah 7:9)

"All rise," the bailiff calls to the courtroom. We all stand as Judge Greer walks into the courtroom. He's a large, white-haired man, closing in on his late seventies or early eighties. He lumbers as he climbs the two steps to the judge's bench. I can hear him huff and puff when he situates himself in his chair, pounding his gavel for order. That little action was all for show, because nobody was talking or rustling around. This dude is totally on a power trip, which cannot be good for McCarthy.

McCarthy looks like shit. They shaved his head. His smooth, bald head breaks me. McCarthy had the nicest hair. What's the point in shaving it all off? When I walked in, he smiled, but I know McCarthy's smile and that wasn't it. He looks like he's in so much pain. Has anyone tried to help him get medicine or take away his pain since Mrs. Maddox did? My dads are sitting next to him, whispering to one another as they look over their briefs.

The prosecution won't let up on who the other person is that's caught on camera. McCarthy continuously shrugs his shoulders and refuses to give the name of his accomplice. The fire in my stomach threatens to burn through my body. Every time a new picture of the two criminals in the Kendyl is displayed on the giant screen in the courtroom, both of my dads' shoulders and backs stiffen. Neither one glances back at me.

The prosecution promises McCarthy that he'll go easy on him if he'll just reveal the name of his "friend in the video." McCarthy's silence is deafening. The prosecution reminds him of the consequences of being found guilty of treason and conspiring to overthrow Eka.

After the prosecution interrogates him and finally rests, my father approaches him, delicately and confidently. I've never watched my father in court before. He's cool, calm, and collected. He's prepared and poised. I'm truly impressed. Grandpa Britt knew exactly what he was doing forcing my dad into law.

One of the questions my father asks McCarthy, makes the entire courtroom guffaw in uproarious laughter. Judge Greer pounds his gavel until silence returns to the courtroom. My father asks again, "McCarthy, you're not too smart, are you?"

McCarthy nods. "No sir, I'm not."

"Isn't it true that you were close to not graduating from high school?"

"Yes sir," McCarthy confirms.

"But yet, you got into school for engineering. Isn't that right?" my dad questions.

"Yes sir. My dads know the admissions counselor. Otherwise, I would've been denied. My grades are bad."

"So you're no mastermind. You don't have some grand scheme to overthrow our government, do you?"

"No sir." McCarthy shakes his head emphatically. "I wouldn't know how to do that." This gets another chuckle out of the courtroom.

"Do you deny being in the Kendyl?"

"No sir." The courtroom erupts in chaos, giving Judge Greer another opportunity to thump his gavel as hard as he can. Once decorum is restored, McCarthy adds, "I just like knowing things. I just wanted to know stuff about Before. That's it. I had no malicious intent. Just curiosity."

"Just curiosity," my father reiterates. "But you do realize that a curious mind is grounds for confinement in Eka."

"Objection," the prosecution interrupts.

"Sustained," Judge Greer agrees. "Strike Mr. Logan's last statement from the record."

The questioning continues. My father finally rests. Judge Greer sighs and takes over. "Mr. McCorum, please stand up." McCarthy does so. My dads stand too. "Did I tell you two to stand?" My dads look at each other, shake their heads, and sit back down, confused. This doesn't appear to be protocol, but my dads are rolling with it.

"Mr. McCorum, please tell me what you would like from me today," Judge Greer asks, sneering at McCarthy.

"Your Honor?" McCarthy asks, indicating that he's unsure of the judge's question.

"In your fairytale world, what would you like me to do today? What do you think your punishment should be for breaking into our most sacred and respected building?"

"With all due respect, your Honor—" my father begins.

"Mr. Logan, am I speaking to you?" the judge asks. My father shakes his head. "Then, please sit back down." My father does so without another word.

"Ummm," McCarthy stalls.

"Boy, I asked you a question, and I'd like an answer."

"I'm not sure," McCarthy admits. He glances at my dads and looks briefly over his shoulder at me. "I guess I'd like to pay a fine. Maybe do some community service—"

"Oh, that's what you want. You break into our building. You run from Authority. You steal documents that have not surfaced as of yet. And...and...you're tampering with evidence by not revealing who that strapping gentleman is in these photographs," the judge snarls. "And you think a good punishment is a hefty fine and some highway trash service." The judge nods condescendingly at McCarthy. This is not going well. "Here's what you're missing, young man. This is my courtroom. This is my town. And I will not —absolutely not—be made to look like a fool in front of my constituents. I am in charge here."

"Yes sir." McCarthy nods, his shoulders slumping.

"For your crimes Mr. McCorum, you're looking at a life sentence in the Male Confinery. Do you understand what that means?"

McCarthy's response is barely audible, but his head is nodding affirmatively. I can see his shoulders shake. Watching him crumble is too much. I have to do something. I can't let him go down for me.

"You have one more chance, Mr. McCorum. Reveal the name of your partner in crime, and your fate won't be as bleak," Judge Greer declares, his eyes narrowing.

McCarthy wipes his eyes and glances at my dads as he does so. Their faces give nothing away. They're stone cold stoic and unreadable. My dad wipes sweat from his forehead. My father clasps his hands in his lap.

McCarthy stands up tall and says, "Behold, God is my salvation; I will trust and will not be afraid; for the Lord

God is my strength and my song, and he has become my salvation." The courtroom gasps. The McCorums groan, clinging to one another. One of his dads starts panting and gasping for breath. A panic attack. I see my own dad reach for my father's hand.

"McCarthy McCorum, you give me no other option. This is my town. I will not tolerate disobedience and treason. We will not be threatened by juveniles looking for some fun, trying to overthrow our way of life. You will be punished by my terms and my terms alone. I don't care what the law books say."

"Your Honor," my father stands, "this is not precedent—"

"Not another word from you, Mr. Logan," the judge growls. Judge Greer looks at one of the Authority officers and nods. The bailiff stands, puffing his chest, and approaches the bench. "Mr. McCorum, please come forward." McCarthy turns and looks at me, his eyes full of tears and terror. He walks carefully toward the judge and the bailiff. "I hereby sentence to you to two life sentences in the Male Confinery for treason." The bailiff shoves him forward.

Slowly, I ease myself from my seat. It's now or never. Three words and McCarthy is off the hook. All I have to say is "It was me." Just as the words form in my mouth, four Authority Select officers enter the courtroom. Everything happens so fast. The guns are raised. McCarthy's eyes widen in fear as his hands fly to his face. The four blasts are loud, shaking the room. McCarthy's obliterated body slumps to the ground. His fathers shriek and run toward him, but the Authority Selects detain them at the table, refusing to let them near his body.

"Noooo," I scream, dropping to my knees.

"Ladies and gentlemen of Eka, any form of insurrection will not be tolerated in this country. All traitors will be punished to the fullest extent of the law. Let this boy's body hang in Male Monument Center for 48-hours, reminding Ekians who is in charge," the Authority Select officer announces. The four Selects march in precise unison out of the courtroom.

Wild-eyed and frenzied, Judge Greer stands, thuds his gavel three times and announces, "Peace and obedience are restored. Court is adjourned." His words are hard to hear over Mr. and Mr. McCorum's wails.

The Authority officers descend on the two grieving men. "You have the right to remain silent—"

My father yanks me up. "Let's go." My dad is on the other side of me, wrapping his arm around my waist. They're nearly carrying me out of the courtroom. I can't breathe. I can't think. And I can barely walk. Grounding down my feet, I shake my head. My hand clasps over my mouth as I rush to the trash receptacle. All the contents of my stomach are emptied into the trash. The dry heaving won't stop.

My dad says, "Come on son, we have to get out of here."

Looking around, I notice that all eyes are on me. They know. They all know. The McCorums are being dragged into custody for raising a criminal. I did this. Their son is dead, because of me. This is all my fault.

CHAPTER 41
VICISSITUDE

"A child seldom needs a good talking to as a good listening to."
(Robert Brault)

The TeleViewer broadcasts McCarthy's death over and over again, from every single angle. Hearing his dads scream brings me to my knees every time I hear it. Seeing Riot in the background standing up, I can tell what he's about to do. Each time that I watch him ascend from his seat in the courtroom, my stomach roils as I whisper to myself, "Don't do it." The blast from the pistol stops him from his public confession. I'm a monster for the relief that I feel from knowing that Riot is in the clear.

For now, anyway.

"I can't watch this anymore," I say, leaving my moms in the living room and walking back to my bedroom.

Entering my room, something seems off. My curtain is blowing. I never leave my window open, but I notice that it's slightly ajar. Goosebumps pebble on my skin as my hair stands on end. Someone was in my room—or at least tried to get into my room. Before I yell for my moms, I rush over and close the window completely. On the floor of my bedroom, there is a sketch, a fast, messy sketch of the clearing, our clearing, with the word "midnight" written on it.

Was Riot here? How did he get in here? I put my name and address on every art supply I gave him, so the alibi that he found them in the woods would be believable. I never thought in a million years that he'd ever come to my house. How can he be so reckless? He's going to get himself killed.

And I will tell him so at exactly twelve o'clock.

∽

TREKKING through the dark and treacherous woods in the middle of the night isn't something that I'm comfortable with. It's terrifying. There are so many things that could eat me right now, and I wouldn't even see them coming. My flashlight isn't bright at all, so it's eerily dark and foreboding. The only thing that keeps me going is knowing that I get to see Riot and make sure for myself that he's okay.

When I step into the clearing, Riot is sitting cross-legged on the ground, clicking his flashlight on and off repeatedly.

"Riot," I whisper as not to startle him. His tearstained face turns toward me. I've never seen anyone more heartbroken and grief-stricken in my life before. I run to him, wrapping him in my arms. He holds onto me and sobs into my shoulder.

"It's all my fault," he cries over and over again. I hold him, letting him grieve as I soothe him and stroke the back of his head. Rocking him back and forth, all I want is to comfort him and lessen his pain. "Stay with me tonight." It's not a question, but a mere statement, one I couldn't refuse if I tried.

We lay out the one blanket that I keep in my backpack. The hot, humid air won't be as bad as the mosquitoes that will attempt to eat us alive. Riot starts a small fire in hopes to deflect some of the blood-sucking insects. Lying by the fire, he recounts the entire story of the courtroom. Hearing it from his mouth and his perspective is gut-wrenching. I didn't even realize I was crying until he reaches up and wipes the tears from my cheeks.

"My dads took me to McCarthy's after the trial," he explains. "Once I saw that they arrested his dads, I begged my dads to at least let me go to their house to get some stuff out of there before Authority uncovered it."

"All the music stuff?" I ask, and Riot nods.

"But now, it's all hidden in my Grandpa Britt's backyard in my dad's old fort. I told them that they should just burn it down, but my father has other plans for it. Plans he's not telling me about."

"Riot, what's your plan?" His shrug doesn't help my anxiety. "You're going to need one. You know that, right?" He nods and pulls me into him.

"Can I just hold you tonight and figure it out tomorrow?" he asks, his arms tightly wrapped around me. It's mind-blowing how everything just seems better when we're together. There's no way I'd leave him now. Riot needs me, and I need him. That's the bottom line. You can't walk away from people who are suffering and struggling—especially those who need you.

"Absolutely." I look at my watch. "But I do need to get home before my moms wake up."

"Cissy, why is your tracker on?" He sits up slowly, looking around. "They're going to find us. You forgot to charge—"

Smiling, I show him my tracker. "Look at the green bubble," I brag. "Where is it?"

Riot looks down. His eyes widen in surprise. "It's at your house. Whoa! What did you do?"

"I told you that I'd be a good engineer." I smile, proud of myself for my ingenuity.

"You rigged it?" I nod. "That's incredible, Cissy." He's visibly impressed. Riot stares at me with wonder. "I wish I could've known you Before." Riot's head is in my lap.

"Did you read the file on racism and slavery?" I ask, running my hands through his hair. He frowns and nods. "I want to read more of it, because I don't understand it."

"So much of what we found doesn't make any sense," he explains. "Cissy, they legit lynched people for being black. One young, black boy told a white woman she was pretty, and white men brutally killed him for no reason."

"Who decided that was okay?" I ask, knowing neither of us has that answer.

"Yeah, like why would the white people be in charge? Who decided that they were better than the black people?"

"I guess the same people who decided that men were superior to women in Eka," I reply.

"But we're not," he says. "I couldn't have rigged my tracker. You did though."

"And I'm a woman," I say, smiling. "And black."

"And perfect," he says.

"Riot, do you think we're wrong?"

"Wrong about what?"

"Well, Before, black people and white people were segregated and not permitted to interact, let alone be in a relationship."

"Right, but that folder says that one court case, Brown

something or other, finally let black people and white people go to school together."

"Yes, but then they switched the rules and men and women were no longer permitted to interact. So, all the rules and regulations are constantly forbidding this, you and me. So, are we immoral?"

Riot stares at me for a long time. He reaches up and tucks one of my braids behind my ear. He runs his thumb along my jawline and over my bottom lip. "Nothing about this feels wrong, Cissy."

My eyes close. My heart fills. I take his hand in mine and kiss his palm. I switch my position, so I can join him on the blanket—both of us facing one another. We lie together in silence. We're fighting sleep, but we both know that we're going to need some rest to face whatever's in store for us. His rhythmic breathing and the rise and fall of his chest finally lulls me to sleep.

~

THE SUNLIGHT STREAMING through the canopied leaves pulls me from my slumber. Checking my tracker, I know that I have to get home before my moms get up for work and realize that I haven't been home.

As I'm trying to disentangle myself from Riot's embrace, he rolls closer to me, holding me tighter. Maybe they won't be too mad if I'm not there. I'd much rather stay right here all day long, hidden in these woods with this incredibly brave and beautiful man.

Riot sniffs my hair and makes a satisfied sound. As much as I don't want to move or leave we have to. I need to make sure he doesn't get himself into any more trouble. He's already in a world of peril.

"Riot," I whisper, "we need to get out of here." His eyes snap open, and he looks around frantically. Releasing me, Riot sits up and scans the scenery, looking for an incoming threat. "Nobody's here," I explain. "We just need to get home, so we can figure out our next step."

After packing up our things and walking toward the lot where we park, we make a plan to meet at the same time and place tonight after our parents are asleep. "Oh fuck," I say, stepping into the parking lot with Riot right next to me.

"Good morning, Cissy," Mom says.

"Riot." Mama nods at him.

Neither of us speaks.

Mama points to Riot's car. "Go, you've done enough damage." Riot's head falls. He walks to his car and gets in. He doesn't look back at me, doesn't say a word. He starts his car and drives off without even a glance backwards.

"You are ours until your 21st birthday and you've earned your higher learning certificate," Mama starts, walking toward me. "That means, you do what we say, when we say it. You get no choice in anything. Those are the rules. We've been too lenient. And now, you're jeopardizing all of our lives, Vicissitude."

"You will never see that boy again, and if you do, we will turn him in. There will be no ifs, ands, or buts. This was the last time that you will ever lay eyes on that criminal. Do you understand us?" Mom is pissed. Her stern, clipped teacher voice is even more threatening than it usually is.

"If you don't want that boy shot in broad daylight in the middle of Male Monument Center, then you need to listen to us. We will turn him in."

"And your new tracker arrives today. Whatever you did to that one," Mom gestures to my wrist, "will not happen again."

CHAPTER 42
RIOT

"A friend is someone who understands your past, believes in your future, and accepts you just the way you are." (Unknown)

When I get to my house, nobody's home. My dads are already gone, and for that, I'm thankful. Small victories. Just as I'm exiting my car, Nigel's rusty old truck pulls in behind me. I don't have any patience for Nigel right now. My little win just turned rather rapidly into a big loss. I'm not interested in pretending with him today. I just want to go inside, take a long hot shower, and sleep for days.

Nigel taps on my window. I motion for him to hold on as I turn off the car, unbuckle my seatbelt, and get out of my vehicle. "Hey Nige," I greet him with no sense of gladness to see him whatsoever.

"Can we talk?" he asks, following me up to my porch.

"Of course," I agree, motioning to the chairs on the porch. He shakes his head and gestures that he'd rather go inside. It's hot as balls, and for someone as robust as Nigel, I wouldn't want to sit out in this sweltering heat either.

Nigel and I head right into the kitchen. I grab beverages out of the fridge; he goes straight into our pantry and pulls out a variety of snacks. This is our typical after school routine. Apparently, we're both skipping the last week of school. Can't believe we graduate next week and McCarthy won't be there with us. Will I be there?

Sitting down on my couch, surrounded by snacks, Nigel says, "Man, I'm sorry about McCarthy."

"Thanks man, it sucks," I agree.

"I should've butted out and let you do your thing," he laments. "But no, I had to keep pushing you and pushing you. Next thing, I know, you're getting serious with a psychopath, and it's all my fault—"

"We weren't... I mean, what?" Most of the time, I have no idea what Nigel's talking about. But this is more confusing than Nigel's normal cracked out philosophies.

"You said you weren't interested, yet I wouldn't let up. I wanted you to find someone who makes you as happy as Decarion makes me. Now, McCarthy's dead. You're sad. And the only guy you've ever fallen for happened to also have a few screws loose."

"Nah man, you've got it all wrong. McCarthy is—was —" I correct myself. "A really good guy."

"Yeah for a nutjob who breaks into the Kendyl. I should never have gotten you into that mess."

"Damn it Nigel, do you ever listen?" I ask, slamming my hand down on the coffee table. "McCarthy was the best. He really was. And not because I had feelings for him or anything like that. He was fun and spontaneous. And just loved life." I can feel the tears spilling out of my eyes, but I don't stop. "And now he's dead. He's dead, because the fucking Authority think they know what's best for us."

"Ummm Riot, Authority does know what's best for us. That's their only job."

"They can't possibly know, Nige. Don't you get that? We're being controlled. Nothing is ours and ours alone. We are all property of Authority."

"Shit man." Nigel takes a long drink and then throws a handful of nuts into this mouth. "McCarthy got to you. Brainwashed that pretty little head of yours. Don't worry, buddy. This will get easier with time. And I'll be here for you the whole way."

"Why aren't you listening to me? You don't understand. Authority has our entire world all fucked up. We can't even love who we want or do what we love."

Nigel nods. "Because they shot the man you loved. I get it, bro. We'll get through this. You know what they say about getting over someone." Nigel winks and chuckles at his own joke. "I gotta take a leak." He stands, thumps me on the back, and disappears into my bathroom.

How has his moron been my best friend for nearly sixteen years? What I wouldn't give to have McCarthy here. He can at least formulate a coherent and interesting thought. Could. Could formulate a coherent thought. I don't want a world where I have to think or speak of McCarthy in the past tense. He was the most vibrant person —full of life and personality, intelligence and sarcasm, wit and wonder. And now he's gone. He deserves more. McCarthy deserves to be recognized for how truly wonderful he was.

And I'm going make sure he is.

My dads are up late tonight. It's well past midnight, and I'm still fake-sleeping in my bed, ready to head out. Yet, I can't sneak out until they go to bed. They've been talking and planning all night in low, hushed whispers. When one of them has a big case, their noses are buried in files as they both search for answers to help the client. Other than McCarthy's case, I don't know of another big one they have coming up. But this one must be a doozy. They worked right through dinner and didn't even care that I sat on the couch while I ate my meal. Usually, my passive dad is pretty strict about all three of us sitting down together for supper and not letting anything interrupt us. Tonight, it was every man for himself.

Finally, fifteen minutes after two o'clock, I see the light under my door go out and hear their bedroom door close. I give it twenty more minutes before I get up and slip on my shoes, grabbing my keys and duffel bag.

Late night driving like this may be my new favorite thing. Being the only one out on the roads is nice—therapeutic almost. I love the feeling that everything is serene, and I'm free to roam wherever I want. Granted, it's a feeling —not the reality.

Pulling up to Authority Central, the public square where the Kendyl is, where the courthouse is, and where the west side of Male Monument Center is, I feel my tension heighten. There's no way, I'm actually going near the Male Monument Center. I refuse to see McCarthy's body hanging in the square. I've already heard that many people have come to deface his corpse. I'd probably take it down and bring him home with me. It's evident that I'm spiraling and sound choices aren't really my thing these days.

I grab my duffel and head into the square, marveling at how pristine and unblemished the courthouse is. The four large, white pillars are the foundations of our society, the pillars of strength that uphold all of our Laws of Life and Liberty in Eka. Yesterday, I didn't notice their height or girth. Standing next to them now, I feel small, overpowered by their significance and symbolism. I should strike a match and just let this entire square burn. But arson's not my thing. My weapon of mass destruction is much more evolved than that.

CHAPTER 43
VICISSITUDE

"The aim of art is not to represent the outward appearance of things, but their inward significance." (Aristotle)

With two more days of my senior year left, I figure that I should show up at least once this week. Despite not sleeping at all last night, I'm going to make an appearance at Case Academy before they put me on the truancy list. My moms are already irate enough with me; I guess I shouldn't do anything more to rile them up. Luckily, I didn't get caught again last night when I went back into the woods.

Riot never showed. I waited well into the early hours of the morning for him in the forest. Admittedly, I'm pissed—and worried. In that order. He knew how frightened I was the night before in the pitch black with all the creepy crawly things surrounding us. He also knows how worried I am that he's going to get hauled in to Authority Central and indicted for the Kendyl break-in. Leaving me alone all night in the woods was ruthless, not to mention rude and disrespectful. When I see him again, he's going to get an earful.

If I see him again...

Checking my reflection once again in my mirror before leaving my bedroom, I'm pleasantly surprised with how good I look—even though I got about two hours of sleep last night. I probably won't go back into Case Academy the rest of this week. The next time I'll be in my high school will be next weekend at graduation. I've never been more ready for anything in my life. I'm ecstatic to rid myself of all things high school and high school drama and stupidity. It's time to get out and move on.

"Well, well, well, look who decided to grace us with her presence," Marjorie says when I walk into Informational Texts and Composition.

I smile, dropping my backpack next to my desk before sliding into my chair. "Hey, Marj," I say, trying to sound easy and carefree. It's hard though when she's sitting on Celeste's lap—right in front of everyone. "Hi, Celeste! Are you interning at the hospital again this summer?"

I can't quite make out what her response is since she's basically sucking on Marjorie's neck for every classmate to watch. Mrs. Kerrick is nowhere in sight. I guess it's not just seniors who slack off at the end of the year.

"Looks like she moved on pretty quick," Hannah Gray says, twirling her hair around her finger. "Does this mean that you're on the market—?"

"Teachers, please power on your TeleViewers. There's breaking news coming from Authority Central," Mrs. Vogel's voice from the main office booms through the public address system.

"Again?" someone groans.

"Like, who cares?" Celeste mumbles.

"Not one person," Hannah Gray says, sitting on my desk and crossing her legs in front of me. Her skirt rides dangerously up her thigh.

Mrs. Kerrick rushes into the room, grabs her remote control, and turns on the classroom TeleViewer. A female reporter is outside Authority Central, Selects and officers are everywhere in the background. The reporter is barricaded away from the male reporters, the Selects, and the Authority officers. Authority forbid, they work together on a breaking news story.

Mrs. Kerrick increases the volume. "...no known suspects at this time. If you or anyone you know has any information regarding this heinous crime, please come forward. This disgraceful act will not be tolerated in Eka. The vandal will be punished to the fullest extent of the law."

The scene cuts away from the face of the serious reporter and scans the four pillars in front of the courthouse. Her voice narrates the visual before us. "This is a photo of our immaculate courthouse yesterday morning. Today, the scene is quite different." The camera closes in on the four pillars—each with a different image painted on it.

Immediately, my thumb goes into my mouth as I begin chewing on the side of my nail. My heart is thudding in my chest. The middle two pillars have vibrant portraits painted on them. One portrait is of McCarthy with his infectious smile and perfect hair. He's wearing his school soccer uniform with a guitar strapped over his chest. He looks young, happy, and so full of life. Just like he was only three days ago. There's a cross of some sort on his arm, but I'm not sure McCarthy had ink on his arm. That must've been added for dramatic, artistic effect.

The worst part of the painting is that there's a noose

around his neck, and he's hanging from a branch. But it's not just a regular branch from a tree, it's made to look like a branch, but it's actually #9 of the Laws of Liberty. He's hanging from, "No individual is permitted to worship any false idols. The Authority is the only guiding leadership of Eka." The words are made to look like the markings of the bark on the tree. But when the camera zooms in, you can clearly make out the words.

Shit Riot, what did you do?

The next pillar is of Lizzie in all her fiery red hair, adorned in her ballet costume and ballet slippers. Lizzie's beautiful and polished to perfection—like she looked in that provocative picture I discovered of her. Like she appears in Riot's eyes. She, too, is hanging from what looks to be a branch, but she's hanging from #2. "Males and females are prohibited from congregating, conversing, cohabitating, or co-mingling." He changed her locket. And my heart drops. He painted "Riot" on her gold locket.

"Oh my Authority, that's Lizzie Griffin," Hannah Gray gasps and covers her mouth.

"What? Lizzie was linear?" Celeste questions.

"Ewww, that's disgusting," Marjorie groans.

"If she looked like that every day, then she wouldn't have had to go 'linear.' I'd have done her," Hannah says.

The other two pillars are painted only in black and gray, silhouettes of two people. One is a man hanging from #2. The same words that make up Lizzie's branch are on Riot's too. I know it's Riot too, because the only color on his pillar is in his hand. He's holding a colorful paint palette—complete with every color he used in these portraits. The last pillar, a female silhouette is hanging from #5, "No person will obtain a career that does not fall into his/her gender at birth."

I have to get out of here. I can't be here anymore. Not in this school. Not in this place. Not in Eka. I risked everything for him. Everything. And all that I am to him is a time killer, someone to bide his time while he's grieving his loss and planning his attack on Authority. He promised me he'd never hurt me. He swore I'd never be a casualty in his war.

Isn't that exactly what I am right now?

Riot publicly proclaimed his love for Lizzie right in the middle of Authority Central—and revealed her love for him, too. But me, all I am to him is some silly girl who wants to be an engineer, a girl who dreams of having a "male job." After all of this time, that's the profound impression I made on him.

I just want out. Out of all of this.

CHAPTER 44
RIOT

"When my father didn't have my hand, he had my back."
(Linda Poindexter)

My dad rushes over to me when I walk into the house. He envelops me into a tight hug that seems to last longer than it should. "Uhhh Dad," I say, "is everything okay?"

"Far from okay," my father announces, walking into the hallway with a suitcase. He drops it on the foyer floor next to another fully stuffed duffel and a few bags of groceries.

"Are you guys going somewhere?" I ask, wondering if my dad is ever going to let go of me. My dad starts crying, squeezing me harder. I guess we'll be in this embrace even longer.

"Atticus, that's enough. We have to go over everything. Riot, there's a breakfast casserole in the kitchen. Go sit at the table. We'll be in there in a moment." My father pries my dad off of me. "Come on, Atticus." I eye the luggage and stare at my dads while they whisper quietly in the hallway.

The kitchen counter is full of food. All of my favorite breakfast foods are splayed out on the island with various morning drinks that I also enjoy. This can't be good. They know something. They're turning me in. I can't really think of anything else this could be. The last time they made a spread like this, it was when I made captain of the lacrosse team as a sophomore, which was unheard of at the time. Underclassmen were never captains. I was the first at Lakeward. My dads made the biggest deal out of it, celebrating me for weeks. I've clearly done nothing for them to commend me at this point.

My parents enter the kitchen. My dad's eyes are red, swollen, and wet. It even looks as if my father's eyes are a bit bloodshot and puffy too. My father clears his throat. "First of all," he says, scooping some breakfast casserole onto his plate. "You're an amazing artist, Riot. The details, the precision, and the creativity and depth to your work are exceptional."

"Really beautiful, baby," my dad adds and starts crying again.

"I don't know what you're—" I begin to negate their compliments. My father holds up his hand and waves me off.

"Atticus, you've got to hold it together. You know we're running out of time." At that my dad begins to cry harder. My father sighs and says, "If you can't control yourself, you need to go to our room to compose yourself. We don't have time for this right now. Just pretend he's one of our clients."

Client? What? Fuck, I'm going to the Confinery. Or is my lifeless body the next one to be displayed in Authority Central? My breakfast is stuck in my throat. I can barely swallow. I take a gulp of my cranberry-infused orange juice just to choke down the food lodged in my esophagus. Losing my appetite, I push my plate away and wait.

"In the time of Before," my father starts, "there was something called the 'Underground Railroad.' It was established—"

"To get black people, or slaves rather, to the north where they could be free," I finish his statement.

"How in Authority do you know... scratch that. Do not answer that." My father gets up, grabs his whisky, and pours a lot of it into his own orange juice. He guzzles the whole glass in three seconds flat. "Well, it was resurrected more than a decade back. But this time, it gets people across Eka's northern border."

"What people?" I ask. "Like criminals?"

"No, not criminals," my dad says, finally composing himself and embracing his attorney-client disposition. "It's been used as of late for people to abscond north. People that Authority would deem 'undesirable.' You know, artists, musicians, linears. Mainly people like—"

"Like me? Is that what you're saying? I'm an undesirable? That's what you're saying," I start getting defensive, rising out of my chair.

"Stop," my father says, pushing me back down. "There's no time for teenage angst and bullshit. You're an incredible artist. We get that. We can also gather that you and that girl who killed herself may or may not have had something going on. Whatever. All that is water under the bridge. What matters now is getting you, our son, to safety—where you can live and be happy for the rest of your life. That's our only concern right now."

"But, what am I—?"

"We've got it all figured out, Riot. You just have to listen to us carefully, and we have to move quickly. You painted your damn name on that girl's locket. They know you're my son—and that you used my access card to get into the Kendyl."

Man, that access card. How could I have been so dumb?

"Baby, from here on out, you have to listen to us completely. Do exactly as we say. We've mapped out an itinerary for you to follow," my dad says, tossing a file folder in front of me.

I open the folder. There are maps, instructions, addresses, and names. I don't recognize any of the names or places they have starred and highlighted on the map—nor do I even know how to read and follow a map. Thankfully, my dads have even detailed how to use the map and follow it precisely. I'm not even sure what I'm looking at. It's all mumbo jumbo to me.

"What's 'the Wog' mean?" I ask, flipping through the pages.

"The Underground Railroad is basically called 'The Wog' now, because Sofia Wogland brought it back to help the people of Eka. Sofia's house is the first sanctuary you need to get to—"

My father interrupts my dad. "If you make it to the Wog, we're pretty hopeful that you can make it up north and across the border. Sofia's got a lot of connections."

"And Sof's expecting you."

"You need to finish eating, take a good shower, because we don't know when your next one is going to be, and get on the road," my father explains, scooping more food onto the plate that I discarded. I'm about to protest when he adds, "You need your energy. And we're not sure how safe it's going to be for you to stop and eat. We filled the bags with easy, grab-and go foods, and the car you're using is stocked too."

"The car?" I ask, more confused now than ever. "I'm not taking my car?"

"Oh honey, Authority knows everything about you—including what kind of car you drive. They'd snatch you up the second you got on the highway." My dad looks at me. "And eat. You have to get going."

"Geez," I say, feeling uneasy. "It's like you can't wait to get me out of here."

"We can't," my father confirms. "It's important that we save your life, Ri. I'm surprised they're not here already. We pulled some highly illegal strings. We've got two cars waiting in our garage for us."

"Us?" I ask, wondering what in Authority is happening.

"Your father and I are heading south," my dad explains. "Oooh which reminds me." He walks over to me and takes my tracker off and places his adult tracker on my wrist.

"When you get outside of the city, put this tracker into someone's pickup truck or hook it to someone's car in some way. We'll do the same with this one," my father says. "Our trackers will be going in opposite directions of where we're actually going."

Whoa, they've thought of everything. That's what they've been doing in their hushed voices late hours into the night.

"And Riot," my father says, "bring the girl with you."

"What?" I ask, my eyes giving away everything.

"She's not safe here. You painted her, honey. They'll use her to get to you. She can't be here." My dad's eyes are small and sad. "Now finish up and jump in the shower."

Thirty-four minutes later, I'm stuffed, showered, and standing outside of a strange, nondescript car. This car is the most boring-looking vehicle I've ever seen. It's a light blue sedan with four doors. There's normal wear and tear on the outside and inside. With the exception of a few rust spots near the back bumper and a small crack in the windshield, the car is in pretty good condition.

There's a similar maroon-colored automobile next to it in our garage. The maroon one is a bit nicer. Of course, they're taking that one. Both cars are loaded with luggage, food, maps, and camping gear.

"It's about six hours by car to Sofia's. The entire Wog knows you're coming. Sof has it all mapped out and will tell you whose houses along the Wog where you'll both be staying." My father shows me the map again. "Whatever you do, just keep driving and stay the course. No major detours. We've put the Authority-approved travel permission logo on your windshield." He motions to the Ekian travel logo in the top left corner of my windshield. "It expires in 90 days, so you won't be able to get back here."

"Where did you even get—?"

"Take this. Only use it for extreme emergencies," my dad says, placing a small rectangle in my hand. I have no idea what it is. "That's a cellular phone. It's all tracked. We've tried to turn the tracking off, but we can't. Keep the phone off at all times unless you need it to tell us something." My dad shows us his and then gives me a piece of paper with a number on it. "That's the number to this phone. One ring and we'll know something happened. We'll call you back ten minutes after that one ring. That way, we can make sure we're both in safe places before we talk."

My father hands me a small case. I take it and open it. "I have my own gun. Why do I need this?" The new gun in the safebox is a high-powered piece of weaponry. It's much more ominous than the one in my anklet.

My father rolls his eyes. "Number one: your gun and

ammunition are tracked. So, hand them over; we can toss them along our drive to throw Authority off your trail." He extends his hand out. I bend over and release the gun from its lock on my ankle. I place it in his hand. He sighs, running his hand along his smooth head. "Number two: you have a civilian weapon which won't help you if you're facing off against Authority."

"A civilian weapon?"

"We don't have time for this," my father groans, his annoyance increasing. "Your gun will get locked if you try to use it against Authority. Authority-proofed weaponry has capabilities that if you try to engage in gunfire against them, they can lock and disengage your weapon. It won't shoot, Riot. You're a dead man then."

"What?" This is brand new information to me.

"Hence the Authority-issued weapon." My dad nods to the gun in the case.

"How did you even get—?" I start, but my father shakes his head, refusing to give me any further details. "Do you guys have one?" I ask, wanting to keep them as safe as possible too. My father nods. Relief washes over me.

I hug them both. This is surreal, but none of us have the time to say everything we want to say. So, all I get out is, "I'm sorry. I am so sorry."

My dad immediately grabs me, pulls me close, and wraps me in his arms. My father joins in the first Logan family hug I've ever had in my life. My dad's face is wet and streaked with damp lines.

"We love you, son," my father says, wiping one lone tear from his cheek. "I'm sorry we can't do more."

∼

PULLING down Cissy's street in the female faction in broad daylight feels like the most dangerous activity I've ever partaken in—even though I know otherwise. There's something about being cloaked in darkness when you're committing a crime that makes it seem so much safer and acceptable. With the sun blaring and women out walking, I feel like a dude in an ordinary car is a dead giveaway for misconduct. But, nobody looks my way. At the last minute, my dad put a floppy hat on my head and told me to wear my sunglasses while driving through the Female Faction. I did so, and it appears to be working. Apparently, we stopped keeping track of how many Laws of Liberty we're breaking, because a man wearing women's clothing is right up there on the list as a major crime.

As I spot Cissy's house, I'm surprised to see her get out of her own car and lock her door. I'd hoped that we'd get to talk inside with the four walls of her house masking our conversation. I tug the hat further down my forehead as I pull into her driveway. Immediately, Cissy turns to look at me. The bewildered look on her face gives me hope that my disguise can get me all the way through the Wog.

Cissy walks carefully toward my car. Hasn't anyone ever told this girl to never approach strange cars? That's a universal rule, right? Nobody should walk toward a stranger's vehicle. Cissy is peering into the car with her hand blocking the sunlight and her eyes in tiny slits as she squints, looking for recognition. Finally, her face reveals that she knows who's in the car. I smile and wave as I unbuckle my seatbelt. Her eyes narrow even more as she spins on her heel and walks to her porch. She unlocks her front door and walks inside, closing the door behind her.

What in Eka just happened? Cissy clearly knew it was me, but she ignored me and went inside without a word.

She can't possibly be angry with me. Two nights ago, we slept in one another's arms. That was the last time I saw her. We even made plans to meet again last night.

Which, I never showed. Oh okay. She's mad at me. But why would she walk away? If I didn't show up for plans with Nigel, then he'd tell me that I was an ass. I'd explain myself. He'd get it, and we'd move on. Cissy didn't even give me time to explain. She just stormed away. Why would someone do that?

After banging on her front door for over five minutes, I decide that I have to enter—without permission. If I walk in there, and she doesn't want me to do so, Cissy has every right to shoot me between the eyes. All she'd have to do is call Authority, tell them that an unwanted intruder entered her house, and they'd remove my body with no questions asked. She'd be completely in the clear. That's how it works in the male faction anyway. I'm not sure what happens here —especially if a male were to enter a female's home.

Authority values male lives over female lives. It's a well-known and accepted fact. However, men are not permitted in this area of our community, so I'm not even sure what the consequences or reactions would be if she killed a male in her home.

Opening the door, I call out, "Cissy, hey! I need to talk to you. Please." She appears at the end of the hallway, eating an apple as carefree as anyone in the world could ever be.

Biting into the apple with a loud crunch and juice on her chin, she says, "It's forbidden for you to be in this house. And Riot, I'm no longer tempted by you and your wicked ways."

"I'm sorry," I say, walking toward her. She puts her hand up, stopping me.

"Sorry for what?" she asks. "Are you sorry that you

came in here uninvited? Or are you sorry that you left me alone in the woods all night by myself?" She leans on the wall, sizing me up. "Or Riot, are you sorry that you don't feel something more for me than you actually do?"

"Feel something more? What do you even mean—?"

"Shut it, Riot. Don't you dare patronize me. Your heart is Lizzie's. Okay fine, I get that. But really Riot, all I am to you is some **girl** who wants a **man's** job? After all of this," she motions to us, back and forth, "I'm just some engineer wannabe?"

"What is even happening right now? I'm not sure what you're talking about, Cissy."

"Those portraits. I'm just a black, silhouette, wannabe science and math girl, right? And Lizzie, she's the beautiful, vibrant, dancer that you love. Both of you breaking the laws to be together." She turns and walks away, presumably into her kitchen.

Now what? Do I follow her? Does she want the rationale of why I painted her as such? I think I should just leave. But my dads said that if she doesn't come with me, then I'm putting her in harm's way. She'll be a pawn in Authority's game to finish me. Her words ring back to me "...dancer that you love."

Walking into the kitchen, "I loved Lizzie. I've made that very clear," I say, choosing my words very carefully. "That love for her got her killed. And I know she ended her own life, but if she and I had never met, that beautiful woman would be dancing on a stage right now. I carry that with me daily."

Cissy pulls her lips in a tight line, refusing to let herself speak. Tossing the apple in the garbage disposal, she turns it on. The grinding is loud and screechy before she cranks the faucet for the water to rinse into it, subduing the crunching and scraping sound. She's drowning out my words with the disposal.

Reaching around her, I turn off the disposal. I place my hands lightly on her hips, turning her toward me. "Cissy, it's terrifying how much I feel for you. My love for Lizzie brought me to you—to this moment right now. I'm not ready to qualify what this is," I motion between us, "just yet. But I do know it's something. I couldn't paint you the way you've seen me paint you before. It would be your death sentence. Do you want me to have three people's blood on my hands—and on my conscience? I'd love to broadcast all over Eka what you and I are feeling and growing into." Her face finally softens. The stiffness in her shoulders releases and they lower. "But, I—we—can't risk that. You know that. You saved me from myself. You also didn't even hesitate to risk everything for McCarthy and me when we were in danger. You are so much more than an 'engineer wannabe' to me. So much."

Cissy's chin drops to her chest as she sighs. When she looks back up at me, her eyes are glistening. "It hurt."

"I admit; I never tried to see those portraits through your eyes. I'm sorry for making you feel insignificant. But the truth is, you're the most important person to me, Cissy Maddox."

Cissy wraps her arms around my neck, and I lower my chin to her head, where she fits in perfectly. "Thank you for saying that."

"I'm not just saying it," I say, running my hand up and down her back.

"But Riot, people are going to ask my moms who the lady was in the funny hat. So, you should probably get out of here. You know, they'd kill you if they found you here."

Her hands push at my chest. "Can we meet up tonight and talk more?"

"Actually Cissy, do you trust me?" I say, sliding my hands down her arms and holding her wrists in my hands. Her eyes narrow. "I need you to come with me. Can you pack some stuff?"

"Ummm yeah, not going to happen. Start talking, Riot." She wiggles out of my grip and leans onto the other counter with her arms crossed over her chest.

After I explain everything to her, Cissy's wide, terrified eyes fill with tears. She fists her hands and rubs the tears away before they can fall. Rubbing her hands along her face, she looks around the kitchen. There's a long pause as she takes it all in. Opening the drawer behind her, she grabs a notebook and a pen. With her back toward me, she's frantically writing on a piece of the paper. After nearly eight minutes, she closes the notebook, slides it under her arm, and leaves me alone in the kitchen. When I realize she's not coming right back in, I follow in the direction she went.

I find her in her bedroom, throwing clothes and other items in a flowery, quilted bag. She grabs a smaller one that matches the pattern on the bigger one, and starts tossing in bathroom items and a bunch of things that I've never seen before. Items that clearly women use and men do not.

In the midst of all of her packing, she looks up and asks, "What about graduation?" Neither of us speaks. She's not looking for an answer. It's a rhetorical question that we both know can't happen. We don't get the ceremonious commencement into our adulthood. We won't get to cross the stage with our peers and turn our tassels with our fellow graduates. Our choices as of late have ripped us from this tradition. But Eka's rules and regulations forced those decisions.

Cissy opens her safebox and removes the gun from its case. "Don't bring it," I say, shaking my head.

"Riot, you're crazy if you don't think we need protection—"

"I'll explain all of it in the car," I say, grabbing her biggest bag. "Need anything else?" Cissy takes a final look at her room and shakes her head. She turns the opposite way down her hallway and opens the door on the end. Ripping out a page in her notebook, she walks into her moms' room and places the letter on the blanket in the middle of the bed.

Cissy runs her hand along the pillow by the headboard. She picks it up, smells it, and places it back down. "Okay, let's go," she says and starts for the door. Stopping abruptly, she pivots on her heel, grabs the same pillow, and says, "It'll keep them close to me."

CHAPTER 45
VICISSITUDE

"To bring about change, you must not be afraid to take the first step. We will fail when we fail to try." (Rosa Parks)

"So you're telling me that our guns are like childproof or what...Authority-rigged?"

"Afraid so." Riot nods, barely taking his eyes off the road.

We've been driving for about twenty minutes at a moderate speed without any traffic to slow us down. Contrastingly, I've been talking a mile a minute and bombarding him with more questions than a four-year-old at bedtime. "So, if Authority is after me, and they're about to shoot me, and I go to shoot one of them first, they'll lock my gun, leaving me defenseless until a bullet plunges into my forehead?"

Riot visibly winces at my description. "Yep." I probably shouldn't have created that visual in his head—especially since he just witnessed the same thing happen to his friend two days ago.

"As much as that pisses me off, it really is rather brilliant," I admit. "It's such bullshit though. Why wouldn't we know that? That's pretty valuable information."

"My guess is that Authority started that due to the school shootings of Before."

"The school whatings?"

"Man, we have so much to talk about," Riot says, flicking on his blinker before changing lanes.

"Well didn't you say that we have hours and hours in this car before we get to Sofia's?" I ask, reclining my seat more and propping my feet up onto the dashboard.

"It's some pretty jacked up stuff, Cissy. Are you sure you're ready for this?"

"Absolutely. Enlighten me oh wise one." I laugh, bowing to him like he's my guru full of knowledge.

Riot's words infiltrated my mind and won't let me relax. In the time of Before, people would just randomly walk into schools and start killing kids—sometimes little elementary school kids. If my mom were a teacher from Before, she could've been shot by a random gunman right off the street. And nobody—not one person in the school—had any form of weapon to defend him or herself. That's just bananas.

My teachers have often mentioned how there used to be teacher shortages. Well, no damn wonder. Who would be a teacher if it meant that you might get shot? And they didn't just get one bullet to the forehead. Apparently, in Before, they had these crazy guns that shot off a lot of bullets at once. Killing one kid with one bullet wasn't good enough; they needed to be able to shoot many bullets at once.

"You're right," I agree. "Authority childproofed our guns to make sure we couldn't do stupid stuff like shooting up schools and whacko stuff like that." But then it dawns on me, "But wait, you know all that racism and slavery stuff?"

He groans and nods. "We talked about it a little bit."

"Right, but there's a problem with our Authority-proofed guns," I explain. "We already know that Authority goes too far. We sometimes need to fight them. Remember those innocent black guys who were killed by their police officers—and they didn't even have any guns?"

"Yeah, like that one guy who couldn't breathe, because they were kneeling on him."

"Yes," I say, remembering the detailed account of the file. "He had every right to shoot that officer who was unlawfully cutting off his air supply. But if he would've tried, they would've locked his gun—"

"And given them a reason to shoot him lawfully."

"But if I remember correctly, he didn't do anything to warrant being killed—just arrested and maybe jailed for a bit," I say, noticing that Riot is a million miles away—lost in thought. "It's not like he broke into a top security building and stole all of their precious secrets."

Riot shakes his head, coming out of his reverie. "Too soon, Cissy, too soon."

"Riot, we're never getting out of this if we can't joke a little and take some of this weight off us," I say, scooting closer to him and massaging the back of his neck. "You've been white-knuckling that steering wheel for almost an hour straight. You're going to get early onset arthritis and give yourself a heart attack."

"Fair," he says. "Are you hungry?"

"Not really, and you just said you were full about half an hour ago," I remind him. "Are you ready to stop or something?"

"I just think we need to get rid of one of my dads' trackers."

"That's cool with me. Let's stop at the next charging

station and get rid of it," I say, sitting back up. "Let's stop at a female charge stop and do it there. It would be more confusing that way."

"Good plan," he says, reaching for my hand. He takes it in his, gives it a squeeze, and then lets it go.

Men are confusing. I never know what he wants or what he's thinking. The low, satisfied moan that escaped his throat when I rubbed his neck gave me a glimmer of hope. But this cool dude hand squeeze shattered that hope instantaneously. However, we are running away together to cross Eka's border. You don't do that with just anyone. Riot did ensure that I knew his dads made him bring me along for my own safety. They made him. That didn't feel too good on the old self-esteem, but he did care enough about me to want to keep me out of peril.

When we get to the charging station, I get out and hook the car up. There's an attractive girl walking into the bathroom with a large handbag slung over her shoulder. I nod to Riot and follow her into the bathroom. While inside my stall, I call out, "Hello, anyone in here?"

The girl announces that she's next to me. I simply explain my stall is out of toilet tissue. Immediately, her hand is under my stall with a wad of paper in it. Thanking her profusely, I grab the tissue and quickly flush it. I wait a few moments after she exits her stall and leave mine. "Thank you so much."

"No problem," she says. "I love those braids." My hair is always a conversation starter with women in restrooms.

"Thank you," I say, smoothing some of the flyaways down. "It needs redone." As we chat about hair and makeup, I walk next to her to the door. Opening the door and holding it for her, I say, "Let me return the favor for bailing me out." She nods her acceptance as she walks through the open door. When she passes in front of me, I drop Riot's father's tracker into her large bag, hoping it finds its way to the very bottom of the purse.

Approaching the car, Riot is back in his floppy hat and ridiculous sunglasses. His head is tucked, so she cannot get a clear glimpse of his face. "This is me," I announce, pointing to the car.

"What's your name?" she asks, stepping a bit closer to me.

"Ava. Ava Treyfield," I say, pulling the name out of the clear blue sky.

"Well Ava, do you think I could call you sometime?" she asks, smiling at me.

"I'd like that," I lie, reaching into my own purse and getting out a pen. I jot Gino's telephone number down on the palm of her hand. At the very least, she can order a good meal when she realizes I gave her a fake number. "And who's going to call me?" I bat my lashes at her and smile.

"Jane Blackbottom," she says, extending her hand. We shake hands, and she lingers a little, tracing the back of my hand with her thumb. The horn startles us both as we jump back.

I roll my eyes and sigh. "My sister is always in such a hurry."

Jane nods. "Trust me, I get it. Can't wait to talk to you again, Ava."

I watch as she walks away before getting into the car. "Authority Riot, are you trying to get us noticed?"

"Sorry, was I cramping your style there?" he says, starting the car. "You want me to come back and get you after you two have gotten to know one another a little more?" Riot pulls out onto the highway. He glances over at me and back to the road. Looking at me again, he asks, "What? What's the smile all about?"

"Nothing. Not one thing," I reply, feeling much better about running away with him. After all, there's no way he'd be so worked up and freaked out if he weren't jealous, and we were "just friends."

CHAPTER 46
RIOT

"For nonconformity the world whips you with its displeasure."
(Ralph Waldo Emerson)

Cissy has been asleep for the past forty minutes. Her face cracks me up when she sleeps. I've watched her sleep three times now, and she always looks the same. Most people have that peaceful, angelic calm to their face when they're sound asleep. Not Cissy. She looks like she's in pain. Her face is always scrunched up with her mouth agape. Truthfully, she's the most unattractive person that I've ever seen sleep. It looks uncomfortable and sepulchral—like she's dreaming of horrific happenings yet to come. For some reason though, I love it and can't get enough of it. Everything about Cissy is just different than what you'd expect. She's always surprising me with what she does and says. I should wake her up, but I'm going to give her a few more minutes.

We've been driving up this same hill for over twenty minutes. The winding road to the top keeps getting more and more narrow. The pavement ended almost two miles ago, forcing us to now nearly crawl at a snail's pace up the dirt and rocky road.

The address on the dilapidated mailbox matches the one on my paper: 3716 Torrey Fern Way. This is it. I'm not sure what I was expecting, but this certainly isn't it. There's a shanty adjacent to the mailbox at the end of the drive. The old shack has no front door or wall. There are shelves built in it as if it's an open closet with no doors. The little house is full of fruits and vegetables. I'm not sure if people have left them here or if Sofia Wogland leaves produce for others to take. Either way, it seems weird.

Turning down the driveway and around the bend, there's a wrought iron gate. Upon approach, the gate doesn't move. There's a keypad. I scan the paperwork, but can't seem to locate a code for access. I attempt the address. The red light blinks three times and goes out. The four digits of the address are not the passcode to open this gate. I keep looking, but find nothing. I start punching in the numbers of the address in different orders, hoping one of them opens this damn gate. Nothing.

"Just push the call button," Cissy says, looking over my shoulder.

"Shit, you scared the crap out of me. I thought you were asleep," I say, settling back in my seat.

"Those constant beeps, and your 'fuck' after every try woke me up," Cissy says. "Much like when you got us lost three hours ago and kept pounding your hand on the dashboard. Wasn't it much easier to wake me up and let me show you how to read that portion of the map—instead of acting all macho like you didn't need my help?"

"Valid," I say, looking back through the papers. "What'd you say about a call button?"

"That big silver button at the bottom of the numbers is

a call button. Just push that." It cannot be that easy. She's delusional. I press the silver button.

"Yes?" comes a voice from the box.

"Hi. Ummm, yeah, I'm Riot Lo—" A loud buzz goes off, and suddenly, a loud rattling comes quaking from the gate as it begins to shake. Then slowly, the rickety old metal door begins to slide to the left, opening barely enough for my four-door sedan to fit through. "Huh, I can't believe that worked."

"I can't believe the things that men don't know," Cissy says, dropping the passenger side visor to check her reflection in the tiny, clouded mirror.

Traveling up the dirt pathway to the house, I notice that the driveway gets wider. The landscaping becomes more and more visually pleasing. The trees are trimmed and the lush greenery is cut back and primed in a pristine and polished manner. The yard is manicured and beautiful, reminding me of the McCorums' landscaping. The memory pulls at my heart.

"Wow, this is beautiful," Cissy exclaims, scooting to the edge of her seat as she looks around at the scenery.

"It sure is," I agree. We round the corner to the front of the house, and both of us gasp. "Holy crap."

"Uhhh your friend Sof must be doing pretty well for herself," Cissy says, staring at the house in awe.

"What in the world? I've never seen a woman have a house like this," I say, just as Cissy clobbers me in the arm. "What? You know what I mean." Only the men in Eka have large, extravagant houses. Most of the women live in smaller, modest homes with little to no luxuries.

"Where did she get money like this?" Cissy asks, gawking at everything.

Shrugging, I stop the car and say, "Beats me."

The front door flings open and a heavyset woman bounds out the door onto the large wraparound porch, clasping her hands at her chest. "Owen, doll, they're here." Sofia claps her hands and comes barreling down her four front steps to greet us at my car. Adorned in what I guess you'd call a long, oversized dress or muumuu, she's all bosom, hips, and butt. Her earrings are large, bright orange circles that just about touch her shoulders. With bright orange hair and bright orange lips, she looks like a cartoon character. This woman is larger than life, but is rather short. She's about as tall as she is around.

Sofia whips my door open, leans in, and hugs me. "Oh loves, you made it. I'm so happy you're here." Standing back, she yells again, "Owen, get their things. Hurry now."

Cissy and I get out of the car and start to grab our bags, when Sofia smacks our hands away. "That's Owen's job. Lord knows he doesn't do much around here." She rolls her eyes and laughs. "You know how men are." She herds us onto her porch and yells for her husband again.

Owen comes out, and the sight of him takes me by surprise. He's Sofia's polar opposite—where she's short and stout, he's tall and lean—almost too tall and too skinny. His pale skin is thin and translucent, showing roadmaps of veins all throughout his skin. His slight, gray hair is combed over a large bald spot. Sofia grabs him by the arm. "Hon, these are our new guests, Riot and Sassy."

"Cissy," I correct her. Cissy sidles up next to me, pressing close to me.

Owen mumbles and nods at both of us. Sofia directs him to the car, walking down the steps toward my car. "Ummm Sofia is not a 'she' is she?" Cissy asks.

"It doesn't appear as such," I whisper. "And did she say 'Lord?' Do you think she read the *Bible* that McCarthy read?"

Cissy shrugs. "I feel like we're in a whole different world."

"I think we are."

∽

Sofia and Owen made an elaborate dinner for us. We ate out on the patio with lights strung overhead. A small fountain with a light up waterfall made the entire dinner experience seem like a dream. When they showed us to our room, Cissy's discomfort was evident. Sofia looked between the two of us and cut quickly to the chase. "Why does she look like she just sucked lemons? Girl, what's got you all tizzied up in here?" Using her index finger, Sofia pokes on the side of Cissy's head.

Cissy hems and haws without answering. "Cissy and I are just friends. We don't actually sleep together in one bed," I explain, hoping this eases some of Cissy's misgivings.

"You don't? You two could've fooled me. This girl here looks at you like I look at chocolate sauce-covered ice cream on a hot August day. But you do you," she says, dragging Cissy by the arm. "You can take this small bedroom at the end of the hall then, sweetheart." Cissy's relief is evident as she walks in and drops her small, fabric-quilted bag on the small, twin-sized bed.

Feeling guilty, I say, "Cissy, you can have the other room. The one with the big bed and bathroom attached."

She shakes her head, lies back on the small bed, and

says, "I'm good here. Feels homey." I see the sadness flash on her face, but she shakes it away and smiles.

"You two get comfortable, and meet us downstairs in about half an hour, so we can go over some details. I made carrot cake to eat while we discuss your plans. Everything's always better with cake." With a wave, Sofia pounds down the staircase, leaving us alone in Cissy's room.

"I don't get it," I say, motioning to my room. "We've slept together on the blanket in the forest, literally wrapped around each other. Why is this any different?"

"It's completely different, and you know it," Cissy says, peeking out the window. "This whole thing is crazy. We just ate dinner with two men—one who's dressed as a woman. Excuse me if I'm acting a little bizarre here. I'm not exactly in my comfort zone, surrounded by a bunch of men."

Wow, her distrust of men is either learned or inherent. To think, I never even shared with her what McCarthy and I discovered in the Kendyl about men and women. Never once did I tell her about what can happen between a male and female. And I certainly didn't share with her about how men used to take whatever they wanted from a woman with or without her consent. That was just too disturbing for me to learn. I can't imagine what she'd think about that. I wonder if her moms warned her about men and how they could hurt her in ways she'd never fathom.

"You're right. You're right," I say, raising my hands in surrender. "I get it. I really do. If you want, I can sleep in the hallway outside your door. Whatever you need."

"No, it's fine. I just need some time to process all of this. Remember, this morning, I was in my last class ever at Case Academy, and now, I'm standing in some man—woman's

—house in Authority knows where on the top of some mountain six hours away from my moms."

Cissy starts breathing hard, panting. Her eyes widen as she gasps for air. Her hand starts flailing and tapping at her chest while she tries to catch her breath. Her face looks frightened. Shit. Last time this happened, McCarthy took care of her. What did he do? How did he calm her down? Something with breathing and counting. What though? What do I do?

"Cissy," I say, sitting on the bed in front of her. I reach for hands. She gives them to me. "Breathe." She shakes her head, eyes wide. "It's okay. We've got this. Count with me." Her breaths are frantic and rapid. No, it wasn't count with me. "Okay, inhale while I count." I count to five, and she inhales as I do so. She's looking at me like I have all the answers. I have no idea what I'm doing. I'm grasping at straws here. "Okay, now slowly blow that air out." I squeeze her hand, and she slowly releases the air. We do this same thing a few more times. I can sense that she's calming down more. Then I remember, "Tell me what you see." She starts naming the things in the room, focusing on everything other than her fear and uncertainty.

Cissy looks me in the eyes, and finally says, "You," and with that, her breathing evens out and the panic in her eyes disappears.

∽

When we get back into the kitchen, Cissy and I are both surprised to see Sofia without her pumpkin-colored wig and her face freshly cleansed. Sofia's salt and peppered hair is a stark contrast to the wig from earlier. Neither of us mentions the transformation.

"Oh yay, you're here." Sofia cuts us each a large slice of cake and puts a plate and fork in front us. She puts two pieces on her own plate and a small sliver of cake on Owen's. "This one here eats like a damn bird." She thumbs in Owen's direction.

The plan is rather simple for the time being. We are to lay low for almost a week, staying with Sofia and Owen until they get word that Authority is hunting for me in other parts of Eka. Once we hear the coast is clear, we're to head to the next destination. We only stay at the next house for two nights until we travel further north.

"But who are you in contact with?" Cissy asks, her leg bouncing nervously. I place my hand on her thigh, and it immediately stills. Sofia notices this and a small smile splays on her lips. She gives me a wink.

"Oh, we have many people who support the activity of the Wog. But they like remaining anonymous. Sometimes, they don't even give you their real names," she says, taking a large bite of her cake. "All of our houses are very difficult to find. Once you leave, it's hard to find us again if you don't have a map to the house. And Riot, when you leave, you must turn that map over to me. You can't reroute your way back to us. Understand?" Cissy and I both nod. I squeeze her hand under the table.

"Not that he could figure it out again, anyway," Cissy jokes, easing the tension in the room.

"Very funny," I reply, pretending to pout.

"Sofia, if you don't mind my asking, how did you get involved in all of this?" Cissy asks forwardly.

"Easy," she says, proudly. "I killed Bradley Casey years ago. Pushed him right off a cliff when he was hiking. They never did find his body." Sofia guffaws and slaps the table loudly. Cissy fidgets in her chair uncomfortably.

"Was he...was he...your husband or something?" Cissy asks, taking a slow sip of her iced tea.

"No sugar, Bradley Casey was me. Or rather, I was him. I hated that nobody would listen to me when I told them that I was no man. I've known my entire life that something happened to me in that birthing center." She shakes her head disgustedly. "I may have been born a man with a penis and all, but there ain't nothing manly about me. Is there, baby?" She turns to Owen, who quickly shakes his head. Sofia leans over and kisses him. "I had to keep playing those dumb sports and mathing all that math. When all I really wanted to do was dance, sing, do my hair, and wear my makeup."

"Finally, I couldn't take it anymore," Sofia explains. "I needed to be me. And Owen here, he loves me no matter what my name is. So, I shoved that Bradley Casey off a cliff. Owen mourned my death. He was the perfect, grieving widower. With all of my life insurance money—"

"Life insurance?" Cissy asks, looking at all of us.

"Poor girl," Owen mumbles, shaking his head.

I clear my throat. "When a man dies, if he's married, Authority pays his spouse a great deal of money, Cissy."

Her eyes narrow and one brow raises. "For real?" We nod, ashamedly. "Like how much?"

Owen grumbles an answer none of us can hear.

Sofia says, "Enough." She motions to everything around her.

"Enough to purchase all of this?" Cissy asks incredulously.

We nod. Cissy shakes her head in disgusted disbelief. "Do you know what we get when our spouses die?" We all know. Our heads hang in shame. "Two weeks paid off of work." She slams her hand onto the table. "Oh wait, we also get our spouse's salary for one year—until we can find another wife to share the bills with."

"That's why the Wog was started, baby girl," Sofia says, placing a comforting hand on top of Cissy's. "We're fighting all the hypocrisy that plagues Eka each and every day. We can't just stand by and let Authority screw us day in and day out. Sometimes, we need to screw them first. So welcome to the Wog."

CHAPTER 47
VICISSITUDE

"Be not afraid of going slowly. Be afraid of standing still."
(Japanese Proverb)

Sitting on a large boulder, looking down the mountain, I'm torn between how beautiful this part of Eka is and the ridiculousness of how it's illegal for me to travel here with my moms. Mama especially would love it here. I can hear the gasp that would escape her throat when she saw the vast landscaping and the beauty that stretches for miles and miles.

A branch snaps, and I jump to my feet, nearly falling off the rocky ledge. Stilling myself, I grab at a ledge above to balance. My heart races. Did someone follow me out here?

Riot said that he was going to sort through the plans with Sofia while she explained each person we'd come in contact with. He noticed my uneasiness and asked if I needed a break. I definitely needed a break. "Riot," I whisper, hoping to see his unruly head peek out of the brush. Silence.

Then suddenly, the leaves jostle, and I freeze. There's

movement coming toward me. A doe and her fawn come out of the plush greenery. All three of us freeze. The mother bolts to the left with her baby behind her. Simultaneously my heart drops and melts. The fear is gone, but I'm left with a yearning for my own mothers to come and save me from danger.

Lowering my butt back to the boulder, I tuck my knees up under my chin and bawl. I cry for McCarthy. I cry for my aunt and Alex. I cry for Riot. I cry for my mothers. I cry for my lost graduation. I just cry. There's no stopping the tears. I don't even try to hold back. I need this. This release will allow me to rid myself of the worry and pain I'm harboring. I need to let this out. I've been pretending for days now to be courageous when I just don't want to be anymore.

I long for the days that I crawled up into Mom's lap and she'd hold me, smoothing my hair and telling me that everything was going to be okay. Something deep inside me tells me that it will not in fact be okay. This is the calm before the storm. Living in the south, I understand that just as well as anyone.

The sobs come harder as my shoulders quake. Snot's just falling out of my nose at this point. I'm a faucet of tears, mucus, and pain. Using the sleeve of my shirt, I wipe my nose and face, but the tears won't stop.

"Cissy, my Authority." Riot comes running toward me. "Are you okay? What happened?" He's scanning my face and body for injuries.

"Nothing," I whimper. "Everything," I correct.

Riot understands. More than anyone he understands. "I shouldn't have asked you to come," he says, rubbing his forehead and holding me. "I'm such selfish dick. You should be at home getting ready for graduation and forgetting all this bullshit."

His remorse snaps me out of my pity party. We do that for each other. When one of us crashes, the other steers for a bit. When one crumbles, the other picks up the pieces. This is just such a new phenomenon for me—nothing I've ever experienced.

"Riot, can I say something honest and true, please?"

"Of course, anything." He brushes my braids out of my face and holds my face in his hands, waiting for me to speak.

Closing my eyes and taking a deep breath, I say, "I'm scared—"

"I know. I know. Me too," Riot admits, releasing my face and holding my hand. "But I promise, I'm going to do all I can to get us north. Everything I can."

I shake my head. "No, that's not it. I want to say this, just in case it doesn't work out." He stares at me and gives me an encouraging nod to go on. "I'm afraid, because of Eka, of this place, and it's all so dangerous. But the truth is Riot, I think I'm falling in lo—"

Riot puts a finger over my lips and cuts me off in midsentence. "Please don't say it. Please don't finish that statement."

"But Riot, I need—"

"No, listen to me," he says, shaking his head frantically. "When we cross that border and we're safe and completely free, say it then. Say it loud. We'll paint it on the first open space we see. But for now, let's just focus on our safety. We can't get careless. Okay, Cissy? Please."

Riot and I spend the day in this new forest, close to Sofia's house as to not get lost or turned around. The trails are narrow, the mountains high, and the area overgrown. Not like what we're used to. We walk in hopes to discover a swimming spot, but find nothing nearby. Wading in a small creek is the most that we can do. But just our bare feet in the cold, crisp water gives us a sense of normalcy and serenity—feelings that we haven't felt in a while.

Sofia and Owen refuse to let us cook for them. Instead, Owen makes us a pasta dish that is probably the best food I've ever eaten my life. Riot and I both scrape our plates clean and neither of us turns down the offer of seconds, which makes Owen blush. The only words he mutters during dinner are "I grow all of my own ingredients." Sofia beams at him with pride and adoration. Riot smirks at me, and my heart leaps. The power of that smirk is dangerous.

When Riot walks me to my bedroom, he stops at the door and says, "I wouldn't mind just spending the rest of my life living here with you in this house."

~

IN THE MORNING, I pad down the hallway to Riot's bedroom. His bed is made, and he's not in the bathroom. The towels and washcloths are folded and neat in this bathroom. I don't see his bag. His bag is gone. Where is his bag?

Running downstairs, I collide right into Sofia. "Riot's gone!"

"Oh honey," she says smiling. "He'll be back at noon. Owen took him into town."

"What if someone sees him?"

"All covered. We disguised him pretty well. They're going to check the Ekian news and get some supplies that I don't think Riot's dads realized you all would need. Navigating these hills and this area requires much more than what those southern boys use to glamp. Rookies." She rolls her eyes and waves her hand. "It's much more treacherous up in these parts. Now come eat. "

Sofia and I sit down for breakfast. She clearly loves doting all over people. "Did you want kids?"

"I certainly did. Authority didn't deem us suitable. They said that I was too feminine and that Owen was too meek to father a son. We were denied every time we applied. We didn't give up until we aged out of the application process," she explains, stirring her coffee. "Then after we knew we couldn't parent, that's when I killed Bradley and became who I've always been destined to be." Sofia smiles and waves her hands in the air, her bracelets orchestrating the sounds of her symphony.

"Well for what it's worth I think Authority missed out on some wonderful parents. You two would've been perfect." Sofia hugs me and gives me another honey-covered warm biscuit. Feeding people is clearly her love language.

"Sofia, if up north, you and Owen can do and be whatever you both want, then why do you both just go up there too?" I ask, wondering why she's hiding high in the mountains for the rest of her life.

"Easy sugar, I love it here. This place is my home—my sanctuary," she replies, looking out the window. "There were a few years there that Owen and I considered going north, because I can get surgery up there to remove my genitals and become a real woman."

"I'm sorry, what? That's a thing?"

"It sure is. Used to do it here, Before. But people didn't like that," she explains, scowling. "They said it was wrong and unnatural. So we were heading north to be with people like ourselves."

"But what happened?"

"My heart happened," she says. "I realized I had all this money. I had this place high up here and away from everything, and my heart is just too big and too soft to spend all that love on myself. I decided I was too old to become the woman that's in here," she says, pointing to her chest. "So, I stayed the gregarious and flamboyant woman I am today and remained right here to help people like you. Remember, it's always better to help others before you help yourself."

"Oh Sofia," I say, tearing up.

"No 'Oh Sofias' here, baby girl," she says, patting my arm. "I'm as happy as apple pie on a sizzling July afternoon right here with Owen. I have no regrets."

We finish the rest of our breakfast lost in our own thoughts. It really is a shame that Sofia and Owen weren't granted permission to parent children. They're both oozing with love and respect for one another, and I just know that would've overflowed into total adoration for their son or sons.

As Sofia and I clear the table and rinse the dishes, she stops, dries her hands on her sundress, and says, "I just want you to know, doll, that you and your ***friend*** have a long road ahead of you. It's going to be scary and dangerous to get north," she says. Sofia turns and leans on the sink, facing me. "You still have twelve more hours by car—and with people after you." She wipes her hands again and grabs my head, pulling me in close to her. "But remember this, when it's for love, it's worth it. There is nothing more important than love. Nothing."

Sofia releases my head and hugs me. "I can promise you that." Her embrace is exactly what I need, but her encouraging words fill me with more motivation and determination than I've felt since the first time I brought art supplies to the forest for Riot. Her inspirational approach to life is infectious; she makes me want to do better and be better.

"How did you get so wise?" I ask her, wishing some of her wisdom could rub off on me.

"The answer isn't one you're hoping for, doll," Sofia says as she starts wiping off the counters. "Wisdom comes with experience and usually those experiences are setbacks, hardships, pain, and suffering. But once you endure those types of hardships, you can do one of two things: you can fester, dwell, and become bitter." Sofia pauses for a second, letting her words sink in. "Or, you can force yourself to embrace the pain, work through it, and come out on the other side of it with knowledge of how to turn your pain into something positive and helpful for others."

I nod, knowing she's right, but I also wonder how exactly I'm going to do that. It's hard to see how I'm going to come out of this better than I was last year at this time. Back then, I was oblivious to everything—even my own emotions. And I certainly had no clue about all of the new information I now have regarding Before. How can I possibly spin this to help others or inspire someone else?

Truthfully, I can barely see how we're going to ever get out of this unscathed. How can two teenagers outsmart the Ekian Authority? I wish I had some of Riot's optimism. If this ends badly, then I never get to tell him exactly how I feel about him.

"Oh my Authority," Sofia exclaims, her hand clasps over her mouth as her eyes widen. I whip around quickly; my mouth drops open. "What have you done?"

CHAPTER 48
RIOT

"I remember those who showed me kindness even if it was a risk to themselves." (Helen Rieder)

"What?" I ask, running my hands through my hair. "You don't like it?"

"Oh honey, don't you know that everyone loves dark hair and blue eyes? This, this, bleached blond look isn't you. It's not you at all," Sofia responds. She motions Owen to the den, and they head out of the kitchen.

Owen walks past me and mumbles, "I think it's very nice, son."

I'm waiting for Cissy's response, but so far, her open mouth and bugging eyes are her only reactions. "Well?" I ask, gesturing toward my hair and motioning for her opinion.

"Riot Logan, why? Why would you do this to yourself?" she asks, walking around me in circles. Cissy stops, feels the texture of my hair, and shakes her head in disbelief. "You had the most beautiful hair. I can't even wrap my brain around this one."

"I figured it could buy us some time," I explain, catching my reflection in the microwave. "I don't think it's that bad. It's kind of cool, don't you think?"

"Nope, no I certainly do not," she says, erupting in a fit of giggles. "It's certainly going to take getting some used to." She keeps fluffing my hair and blowing me kisses. "You kind of look like Maggie Philips. She bleached her jet black hair, and it came out this exact yellowy, orangey color."

"It's not orange," I say, jerking my head away from her.

"Ummm, it's pretty orange, but that's okay, pumpkin, I'll still run away with you." Cissy laughs and adds, "I'd never run away with Maggie and her bright orange, beach ball head though."

"Oh for Authority's sake," I say, grabbing a biscuit out of the basket and pulling a chunk off the top to toss in my mouth. "It's a perfect disguise. And you're next, blondie." I reach in the bag and pull out the hair color for her.

"No chance," she says, backing away. "You can just forget it. There's no way that stuff is touching this hair."

Sofia yells from the den. "That girl is not bleaching her hair."

"Stay out of it," Owen says, walking back into the kitchen. "Cissy dear, we think it's much safer if you two don't fit the descriptions of the two fugitives that are running from Authority."

"What descriptions?" she asks, eyeing Owen and me. "What did you two find out when you ventured into town?"

Owen takes off his ball cap and rubs the top of his head. "Well, it's not good—"

"It'll be fine once we alter our appearances a bit," I explain, frowning.

"Are we on the TeleViewer?" she asks, approaching me and narrowing her eyes. I nod, and her head drops. "Shit."

"But you look lovely up there," Owen says, trying to ease her worry.

"Like that's going to help make her feel better," Sofia says, coming out of the den with a large case. "And Riot, that girl is not bleaching that hair."

"Sof darling, they need to be incognito," Owen says, running his hand along her back.

"Well I know that," Sofia scoffs. "But bleach isn't the answer."

"I've got it," Cissy yells, "let's just shave all of my hair off!"

"What?" the three of exclaim at once.

"Cissy, you can't just shave—"

"Shut it, Riot," she cuts me off. "I most certainly can—and will. It's hair; it grows back. And, I'd rather be bald—than orange."

"It's not orang—"

"You know, if you did, we could throw you in some jeans, an oversized shirt, trainers, and a baseball hat, and you'd be able to pass as a boy," Sofia says, thoughtfully.

"Then, you two could travel together and actually go inside stores and restaurants together," Owen adds.

"Let's do it," Cissy bounces on her toes. "Let's boy me up."

Cissy and Sofia disappear upstairs to turn the most attractive woman on the planet into a man. My protests landed on three sets of deaf ears. Obviously, I understand the importance of Cissy and me trying to fly under the radar, but ruining that girl's appearance is the last thing I'd ever want to happen. I was struggling with bleaching her hair, but shaving her head is well beyond my original intentions.

Grabbing another biscuit, I sit down at the table and pull a file out of my backpack. I haven't touched these folders since the day after McCarthy and I stole them, which was less than a week ago. But still I had to have them, but yet, I haven't looked at them. That's messed up. I got my friend killed over something that's just been sitting in my bags for days now. My selfishness knows no bounds.

I pull a folder out entitled **World War II/Holocaust 1939-1945**. Well, this one can't be that bad or that relevant since it was nearly 140 years ago. Let's hope it's some light reading to take my mind off of the beautiful woman upstairs shaving her luscious locks for a chance at survival. One of the beauties of women is the creative ways in which they wear and style their hair. It's always so unique. Shaving a female's head seems cruel and unjust, but Cissy is her own person. Who am I to stand in her way of the choices she wants to make? I wonder if she's going to be the first female in history to have her head shaved.

"Riot," Owen says, sitting in the chair adjacent to me. "What's wrong?" He reaches for the folder that I closed and had been banging my head on for the past five minutes.

"Owen, has the world always been fucked up? Is that what I'm understanding?"

"Ahhh the Holocaust," Owen says, shaking his head with his eyes downtrodden and sympathetic. "One of Eka's most treasured secrets."

"How could...I mean...what?" I can't even formulate my words into rational questions.

"Riot, that one is a doozy. There's a ton to unpack in that folder. But the one thing good about that one is that it wasn't here," Owen says, rubbing the back of his neck.

"But we didn't do anything to stop it until so many people were murdered," I say, opening the folder back up and immediately closing it again.

"It's a shame that they no longer teach this to kids in schools. It's a horrific part of our past that never should have happened. Kids need to learn this stuff so we never repeat it."

"No way! Kids have no business learning this stuff," I counter. "This shit is terrifying. Why would we subject children to these images and the darkest parts of our history? I think I understand now why Eka banned this stuff from us. It only makes me sad."

"Ahhh but sadness is a normal part of life, my dear," Sofia says, sitting on the other side of me. "You can't shelter the world from the truth, because look what happens. Two wonderful kids understand the importance of knowledge and start to search for answers themselves—and then they end up putting themselves in danger."

"But this is some whacked out shit," I say, shaking my head.

"True, but that doesn't mean that putting our heads in the sand and ignoring its existence is the answer either," Sofia says, patting my arm.

Sofia gets up and pours us each a tall glass of lemonade. Handing me a glass she says, "That's why we need people like you—people like us—to question Authority and call them out on it when they venture the wrong way. If that dictator taught love and acceptance, then how many lives would've been spared? He taught hatred, intolerance, and bigotry. That's no way to run a country—or to live a life."

"Ahem," Cissy clears her throat behind me. My head whips around to see her. Every last strand of her hair is gone. Her scalp is a mocha, smooth, shiny globe of perfection. Her eyes are bigger, brighter, and more pronounced. Her ears are adorned with large gold hoops that I'm assuming belong to Sofia. Cissy's applied makeup to her eyes and lips, accentuating all of her most striking features.

My shock is palpable. Everyone is anxiously awaiting my response. I'm floored by how much more intoxicatingly gorgeous she is. She's shaved away society's notion of what defines beauty and has surmounted that beauty with her own natural exquisiteness. I didn't think I could find her more attractive, but I was clearly wrong. Evidently, I spend my entire life in a state of erroneous beliefs and thoughts.

Standing, I walk toward her. Grabbing her hands, I splay her arms out long with my own, and say, "You are breathtaking. The most lovely person I've ever seen."

Sofia chuckles behind me and says, "I just love how friends talk to one another nowadays."

I hear Owen smack her and say, "Leave them alone."

CHAPTER 49
VICISSITUDE

"Some days I wish I could go back in life. Not to change anything, but to feel a few things twice." (Drake)

I can't believe how much cooler my body and head feels without all those braids creating more heat and weighing me down. Men are so lucky. Short hair, shaved heads, and fresh, no makeup skin are the ways to go. Who knew?

Men.

Men knew.

However, I do need to sit further under this tree, because I could feel the sun scorching the untouched skin on my head. Opening my notebook, I look around, making sure nobody's around before I start writing. As I begin to write and express my thoughts, feelings, fears, woes, and hopes, my eyes burn with tears. The teardrops pellet the paper, but I swipe them across the notebook, smearing some of the ink.

I write until I can write and say no more. "Cissy?" Riot calls from the trail. I close the notebook, but not before he sees it and my tearstained face. "What're you doing?" he asks, glancing down at the notebook.

"Nothing," I attempt, but his one raised eyebrow tells me that my answer isn't going to suffice.

"Cissy, we can't have secrets from one another if we're going to get through this. We have to be honest all the time. Are you having second thoughts? Because if you are, we can have Owen get you back home—"

"No, it's not that," I admit, holding my notebook against my chest. "I just...it's so beautiful here. This is the kind of stuff my moms love. I was hoping maybe that I could send them a letter. Tell them I'm okay, tell them all about the kindness we're receiving, and how pretty it all is." He's shaking his head before I even finish my words.

"You know we can't—"

"But Sofia could mail it," I say, hopefully. "She can do it in town, not using her own mailbox."

"We can't put the Wog in more danger than we already have. You know that," he explains softly and rationally, and I know he's right, but I hate him for it. "How about this? Why don't you start using that as a diary and you journal everything that we do and see. Then, when we're safe and happily up north, you can mail them the entire thing. They'll see the journey through your eyes and know that we've made the right choice."

This makes me pause and think. Grinning, I reply, "You're good. You know that, right?" He winks at me and offers me his hand.

"Of course I do. But Cissy, I came here to ask you if you'd accompany me on a proper date."

"A what? How? We can't do that," I say, confused and a little excited.

"Sure we can. Owen and Sofia arranged it all with

some of their nearby friends in the Wog," he explains, pulling me up from my tree-covered boulder. "One of the members of the Wog has a small diner that we can go to for a late lunch. We'll sit in a small room off the kitchen meant for storage, but still. Then, one of Sofia's childhood buddies, or would that be Bradley's buddy, I'm not sure how that works," Riot admits and scratches his head. That makes me laugh. He shrugs, visibly confused with how to refer to Sofia's life before she became Sofia Wogland.

"Anyway, Sofia's friend from when she was a kid owns a zipline that's closed on Thursdays. He said that we are welcome to come by and give it a whirl. Sofia trusts him with the knowledge that she's still alive, so she trusts him completely with this—with us," Riot says, his eyes eager with anticipation. "What do you say? Can I take you out?" He senses that I'm teetering. Riot knows I'm wavering on my desire to spend a day out and about with him and the fear of what this could mean for us. "Plus, my new hot boyfriend, Victor Mattrix needs to get out of the house." His mischievous smirk seals the deal.

Surrendering I say, "Eww, can we work on the name?"

"Nope, what's done is done, Vic my boy."

"Fine, Tucker Breeland," I say, skipping ahead of him.

"What? How did I become 'Tucker Breeland?' That's a ridiculous name," Riot yells, trying to catch up with me.

Stopping I turn around with my arms wide as I shrug. "Do you think a blond-haired, blue-eyed pretty boy, would have the name 'Riot?' Now come on Tuck, your golden locks scream 'Breeland' through and through. Let's have high tea and macarons at noon," I announce in the most elitist accent I can muster.

"Wow, that was really bad. Acting is not your forte."

"I'm going to die! I'm going to die! I'm going to die!" I scream, gripping my cable so hard that my hands are cramping and my knuckles are white. "How did you talk me into this?"

Riot's behind me, controlling his speed, so he doesn't plow into me, sending me flying over the trees and into the side of a mountain. "Just lean back, enjoy the view, and feel the exhilaration of the wind blowing through your hair—"

"Very funny, asshole," I yell, wishing I could punch him in the arm.

Closing in on our next ledge, that takes us toward a different direction, I slow the line as I screech to a halt, lengthening out my legs to land my feet on the platform. I have never loved firm structures more in my life. I grab the pole, hugging it as I step up onto the small landing to make room for Riot to land. His dismount is flawless. Is there anything he doesn't do well? "Nice job, Tucker," I say, thumping the top of his helmet, preferring to muss his hair.

A beeping comes from his leg. Sofia's buddy, Mason Judall, gave us these things, Walkie Somethings, to communicate with him while we're up here. Riot's eyes widen, and he shrugs as he gets the device out of his anklet—where he usually keeps his weapon.

Riot presses the button with the mouth image and says, "Hey, it's Ri...Tucker." I cover my hand to suppress a laugh.

"Hey Tuck, we've got snow." Riot's eyes widen. My mouth drops. Snow is code for Authority-officers since they're donned in white uniforms.

"Where?" he asks, his head whipping around. "How many?"

"Not here. In town. Man, to be honest, it's a blizzard.

They're doing a lot of questioning. I want you to camp up there for a bit until the coast is clear," Mason says through the crackling static.

"What do you mean, 'camp up here?' How is that possible?"

"On lift six...are you on three or four now?" Mason asks.

Riot looks confused. I hold up my fingers. "Four," I say, knowing exactly how many more times I have to endure the terror of this contraption.

"Alright, when you get done with six, clip out of the gear, leave it up top, take the ladder down—"

"Oh heck no!" I say, shaking my head in refusal.

"Go on," Riot says, waving me off.

"Take the ladder down, and about twenty feet behind you is a small creek. Walk toward the falls. You can hear which way they flow. You'll come to a part that has three waterfalls. Two waterfalls go down. On the backside of the waterfall that's coming from the top of the mountain, there's a cavern. Go in there. Don't get the walkie-talkie wet. Keep it near you. I'll let you know when the snow melts."

"Sounds good," Riot says, his shoulders tense and his jaw tight.

"And Riot," Mason says. "Be vigilant."

∼

THE DISTRESSING CRAWL down the ladder of platform six was enough to send me into a frenzy of fear and anxiety. With Riot two rungs below me, he talked me through each step as I descended down the ladder. Placing both feet on the ground was the greatest feeling, knowing that I was safe. For a moment.

We immediately sprinted to the waterfall, wading into the water while holding the walkie-talkies above our heads. It was tricky to get under the stream of the falls into the cavern without getting the devices soaked. But with a makeshift sleeve of sandwich baggies from our leftovers at the diner, we were able to waterproof the devices.

Panting and sopping wet, Riot and I climb up onto the driest ledge of the cavern, waiting for word from Mason. "Do you think that thing will work inside here?" I ask Riot, realizing how old and worn it looks.

Riot shrugs. "He said to keep it nearby, so he must have some faith in it."

"I just hope that all of this is worth it in the end," I say.

"We have to stay positive. We knew Authority was going to search high and low for us. They hate losing, you know that," he says. "I just thought that we'd have more—"

"More time," I finish. "They got here fast, don't you think?"

Riot nods. "Why do they care? I mean, I get that they're pissed that I have their documents and vandalized the pillars. But why do they care if we travel, if we run away together, and if we're in lo—" He trails off without finishing the sentence. Shaking his head, he wipes the water dripping from his hair. I really wish he would've finished that statement.

"You know, Riot. We may not make it, and I'm going to be so disappointed if we don't do this again," I say, turning toward him. Leaning in, I pause right before my lips meet his. He groans and closes his eyes, but he doesn't stop me.

Finally, after what felt like ages, Riot's lips are on mine, and his tongue is exploring my mouth. Riot's hungry moan gives me the courage and confidence to pull him closer, shifting myself onto his lap. His arms wrap around me while his hands slide up under the back of my shirt. The feel of his strong hands on my bare back sends shivers down my spine.

This feeling is unsurpassable. Nothing in my life prepared me for how I feel right now. I can't get close enough to him. A part of me wants to crawl inside of his skin and become one with this man. If we die in this cavern, wrapped inside one another, then I'll die a happy woman.

Riot's mouth travels down my neck and toward my collarbone. "Oh Authority," I moan. "Oh yes." His hand is on my head while his tongue and lips explore every inch of my neck and ears. I claw my hands into his back, trying to pull him closer to me.

A faint beep and a low vibrating sound jerks us back to reality. I quickly jump off Riot's lap as he reaches for the walkie-talkie, unwrapping it from the makeshift plastic sleeve we constructed for it. He punches the button, and says, "It's Tuck."

"Shesw cloesred outf," comes Mason's voice through the static.

"What?" Riot says, shaking the mechanism. Riot jumps in the water with the walkie-talkie above his head. Going closer to the waterfall, near the opening, he says, "Say that again."

"Snow cleared out," Mason repeats, and Riot and I both sigh with relief as our heads fall to our chests.

CHAPTER 50
RIOT

"When we love, we always strive to become better than we are. When we strive to become better than we are, everything around us becomes better too." (Paulo Coehlo)

Supposedly, there's a feeling that people get when they know something bad is going to happen and the end is near. I haven't been able to shake that feeling all day long. Taking Cissy to lunch and zip lining was everything I wanted it to be. We were two teenagers on a real date, holding hands, laughing, and just enjoying being with one another. It was everything. A day I'll never forget as long as I live.

But through it all, my stomach was in knots. I could feel a heavy lump of dread in my gut. It was like doom just lingering overhead waiting to engulf us in the consequences of our actions. I refused to acknowledge it or even speak to Cissy about it. I wanted to bury that ominous feeling deep inside, so Cissy could feel free and have a day worth remembering.

When we got back to the Wog, Sofia and Owen were panicked. Mason had contacted them, informing them that the Authority officers were patrolling in town, searching for us. Sofia wanted to feed us, but we both declined. It'd been a long, tiring day. We were spent and ready for bed.

Lying on the bed while Cissy showers, I know we have to start discussing what comes next. Sofia and Owen think we need to move to our next destination tomorrow night— three days earlier than we were supposed to. I asked them if they thought I should call my dads. They both said that it wasn't time yet. I was disappointed. I really wanted to hear their voices and make sure they'd gotten further south.

Cissy exits the bathroom with a white towel wrapped around her, her body glistening in droplets of water. "I usually put my hair in a towel or shower cap. This felt great." Her smile is genuine and infectious as she strokes the top of her smooth head. "Smell my head. I bet it smells so good." She leans over to put her head by my nose. The scent of vanilla with a hint of honey tickles my nose. I place a small kiss on the top of her head.

Cissy and I do not go to bed. After talking to Sofia and Owen, we spend the next hour repacking our bags, getting more supplies from the Wog's fallout shelter, and rehashing our new travel plans. We head out in the morning.

"I'm just going to miss you two," Sofia says as we ascend up the stairs to our bedrooms.

"It's not like you won't see them in the morning to stuff them full of food," Owen grumbles before he waves and retreats to the kitchen.

Cissy runs back down and hugs Sofia for the fifth or sixth time. "I can't thank you enough."

I walk to Cissy's door and wait for her. She comes up the steps, grinning from ear to ear. With one wave, Cissy disappears into my room. "Oh boy," I sigh, stalling by her door.

When I walk into the room, Cissy's lying on the bed, wearing her oversized t-shirt and pajama bottoms. Despite the casual look of her clothes, there's a serious—almost seductive—look to Cissy's face. I lean against the armoire and fold my arms against my chest crossing my legs at the ankle. She shakes her head and pats the spot on the bed next to her.

"Cissy listen—"

"No, you listen." She hops up, grabs my hand, and drags me to the bed. "I just want to be in here with you tonight. I want to feel you next to me. Is that too much to ask?"

I shake my head and pull my shirt off over my head. As I start to get into the bed, Cissy shakes her head. I stop. She points to my pants. "There's no way you sleep in jeans."

"You're not making this easy, you know that, right?" I unbutton my pants and push them down. Kicking them off of my feet, I lift the blankets and slide under the covers and into the bed.

Cissy scoots over toward me. I open my arms, and she comes inside, resting her head on my chest. "This is all I want, Riot. Nothing more. Don't worry."

"That's not what I'm worried about," I admit, running my thumb along the smooth surface of her head.

"Then what are you so uptight about?" she asks, propping up on her elbow to look me in the eyes.

"Remember when I told you that Lizzie confided in her parents about us?" I ask, hoping that the subject of Lizzie while Cissy and I are lying together in a bed doesn't enrage her. She nods, interested, and with no sign of anger. "Well, first of all, you need to know something. Men and woman can have—like—you and I, we can—"

"Have sex and make babies," Cissy finishes my statement.

"What? How did you know that? I didn't show you that folder." I'm shocked that she knows.

"My moms explained it all to me when they told me about Aunt Portia and Alex," she says. "Wait, there's a folder on it? I want to read it." Cissy sits up and looks around like she's going to get it now.

"Not now. Later, okay?" Cissy frowns and lies back down with her head resting on my chest. "One of the things that Mrs. and Mrs. Griffin kept asking Lizzie was if I raped her." Cissy's face is blank with no recognition of the word. "Well, I didn't know what that meant and neither did Lizzie. But when I went to the Kendyl McCarthy and I quickly learned and understood the gravity of that word."

"What is it?" Cissy asks lifting her head to look at me.

"In the time of Before, I guess men did whatever they wanted to women whenever they wanted." Cissy doesn't understand my explanation. How could she? This is inexplicable. "Basically, men would force themselves on women whether they wanted to have sex with them or not."

"So, they didn't have consent contracts?" Cissy asks, shocked. "Marj and I signed ours about three months into our relationship—with our moms' approval."

I nod. "That's what most people do I think. But Before, there were no contracts. People would just assume—or hope—that both parties were interested. And I guess a lot of times, the men didn't care if a woman wanted to or not."

"That's awful," Cissy says. "Riot, I don't know about

Before. Eka is a messed up place for sure. But Before doesn't sound any better, does it?"

"With some stuff no," I agree. "The thing is: I can't believe Mrs. and Mrs. Griffin would think I'd ever do anything to Lizzie that she didn't want to do."

"So Riot, did you guys, ya know?"

"Did I have sex with Lizzie?" I ask, making sure I know exactly what she's asking. "No, not really. At the time, I hadn't read those files, so I didn't even know she and I could do that." I can feel my face heat and redden with embarrassment. I'm glad the lights are dim, so Cissy doesn't see my naivety. "We did some things though—things we'd done before with others. But nothing more than that."

"Why are you telling me this?"

"I just want you to know that I would never force myself on you—or anyone," I explain. "That's abhorrent and something I'd never do."

"Well thank you for telling me that," Cissy says. "And Riot, you wouldn't be forcing anything on me. When you and I are ready, we'll both know it and consent to it. I know that." Cissy sits up on her knees and looks at me through the dark room. "But the way my moms talked, there's no real explanation for how many times you do it or when you do it that makes a baby grow in there. Sometimes, it can happen the first time."

"Yeah, according to the folders, there were a ton of unwanted babies Before, and people did all kinds of things to not be parents of those babies."

"Like what?" Cissy asks. "Because in no way do I want to be a parent right now."

"Well, our best bet then is to just hold each other like

this to make sure that we don't put a baby in that belly of yours."

Cissy moans and snuggles in closer to me. "Sounds good to me." Her voice is getting quiet. She yawns. "Good night, Tucker." She kisses me softly on the lips and lies back down.

"Night, Victor."

CHAPTER 51
VICISSITUDE

"What we have once enjoyed we can never lose. All that we love deeply becomes a part of us." (Helen Keller)

"Alright baby girl," Sofia says, holding me close. "You take care of him. And yourself. Stay out of trouble."

"I will." I nod, squeezing her harder one more time.

"Do you have enough snacks?"

"Sofia, you filled their entire backseat with food. They only have four hours to Eli Sadie's house. I'm sure they'll manage," Owen says, coming in for his own hug. I hug him tightly. "It's that damn rat dog Eli has that they should be the most worried about."

"Oh stop, that dog's fine," Sofia says, smacking Owen upside his head.

"Everything in that house is personalized with 'Olivia' all over it. Who names a dog 'Olivia' anyway?" Owen grumbles and shakes his head. "The dog's name is even on Eli's welcome sign. It says, 'Welcome to Eli and Olivia Sadie's House. Please wipe your paws.' I mean really."

"I think it's cute. If you weren't allergic, I'd have a thousand little Olivias running around since we couldn't have kids," Sofia says, looping her arm through his.

Owen winks at me and mouths the words, "I'm not allergic."

Laughing, I hug them both again, wishing we could stay in this beautiful cabin up in the mountains, protected by the trees and the iron gate forever. But the more time we spend here, the more danger the Wog will be in.

Riot opens the door for me. Reluctantly, I walk toward the car, continually waving to Sofia and Owen. "Until next time," I say, refusing to say goodbye.

"Authority weapons?" Owen calls. Riot lifts his pant leg to reveal the Glock in place. Owen's head bobs up and down. He spins on his heel and walks toward the house, leaving Sofia in the driveway, wiping tears from her cheeks.

"Be good you two," she calls. "Remember, if it's for love, then it's all worth it." She blows us each a kiss and watches us back out of the driveway and through the iron gate.

"Ready, Victor?"

"Born ready, Tucker."

~

THE DRIVE IS LONG, boring, and anticlimactic. There's nothing to look at. It's all open roads and nothing but trees and fields. I'm glad I don't live up this way. I bet people go crazy from boredom. Authority knows, I'm about to.

The only plus to this drive versus the drive here is that Riot hasn't let go of my hand once. "You know what I miss?"

"What?" he asks, glancing over at me.

"You calling me 'Tree Gazer.' I liked that."

"Well Vic, those days are gone." He laughs and rubs the top of my head. "But why? That's a terrible nickname. Why'd you like being called 'Tree Gazer?' It's pretty lame, ya know."

"Nobody ever gave me a nickname before," I say, chomping on pretzels.

"Isn't your name Vicissitude? Wouldn't that mean that 'Cissy' is in fact a nickname?"

"Oh shut it, you know what I mean," I say, feeding him a pretzel. "What's the first thing you want to do when we cross the border?"

"Easy," he says, pulling me to him. Leaning over, he kisses me on the cheek. "Kiss you in front of everyone."

"Now, that's something to look forward to." Tracing the back of his hand with my thumb, I say, "Can you believe my moms didn't look up what my name meant before they named me?"

"Why? What does it mean?"

"Are you ready for this?" I shake my head and recite the exact words I learned in eighth grade. "A vicissitude is a change of circumstances or fortune, typically one that is unwelcome or unpleasant."

"No way! Are you kidding me?" Riot laughs and covers his mouth with the back of his hand.

"Nope. When I got home and told them, they were just as appalled as I was. Next thing I knew, 'Cissy' was my new name." I shake my head. "Apparently, my mom heard the word around the hospital, and she thought it sounded exotic for a name. They never bothered to find out what it meant first."

"That's perfect." Riot looks over at me, thoughtfully. "But it is kind of crazy how we changed our circumstances. But let's make sure that it doesn't end badly, then."

"Says Riot, who may or may not have started his own riot against Authority."

"Look at us. Just two unwelcome troublemakers out on the open road," Riot says. "Who knew? Life sure is crazy."

"Sure is," I agree. "So after everything you've read and researched, do you think Ekian Authority is better or worse than the leaders of Before?"

Turning on his blinker and changing lanes, he says, "Honestly, I'm not sure. I know that when I read *The New Testament*, I liked the words and the way it comforted me. There were some parts of it I didn't understand, but more often than not, I liked what I read."

"We have it with us, don't we?" I ask. Riot nods. "Good, I want to read more of it then. Where is it?"

"The files are in a box secured to the bottom of the car. My dads rigged it up there, so even if you looked under the car, you wouldn't see the lockbox right away. *The New Testament* is with the files. I also liked the *Bhagavad Gita*. It was different, but it also made me feel lighter and peaceful."

"Why do you think Authority doesn't want us to read them?"

"All I can gather is that there used to be fights over whether or not what was in any of them was real or not. Some fought, because they wanted people to follow their book, but others wanted to follow a different belief system. So fights broke out. Not just here either—all over the world," Riot says, shifting in his seat. "Here's what I think though, who cares if any of it was or wasn't real." He tries to glance over at me, but swerves the car.

"Eyes on the road, Tucker. You can stare at Victor all you want once we get north."

He chuckles and continues. "All that matters is that

some people did believe in it, and they liked it. I loved how I felt when I read all of them. Who cares if some did or some didn't believe? If any of those books and stories give them peace, why does anyone else care?"

I shrug. "I have no idea. I want to read things that give me comfort and make me feel serene. But it's kind of like how I don't get why people cared if my skin was black or white." I recline the seat all the way back, placing my forearms over my eyes to block the sun.

"Yeah that makes no sense either. In Eka, nobody cares if you're black."

"But everyone cares that I'm a woman and forbids me to do the things I want. And the things you love."

"Right, like painting," he says.

"What do you think Sofia and Owen are going to say when they see the mural you painted on the bedroom wall last night?"

"They're going to love it," Riot says, proudly.

"It really was beautiful. You captured them and their love perfectly. But you really should've gotten some sleep. We do have a long drive ahead—"

"Fuck. Fuck. Fuck," Riot yells, pounding his hands on the steering wheel. His expletives jolt me upward.

"Riot, what're we going to do?" I ask, scanning the line of Authority-issued vehicles blocking the road. "We can't just bust through that. Should we back up and see if we can outrun—"

"Cissy, listen to me, listen carefully," Riot says, slowing the car. "They want me. They don't want you. They don't even know you. As far as they know, you're Victor Mattix, some dude I met on my way down here."

"Riot, what're you saying?" My heart is racing. I can't catch my breath.

"Be brave, Cissy." He turns to me and kisses me, placing his forehead against mine, he says, "Please."

"Riot wait! What're you doing?" He reaches under his pant leg and releases the gun from his anklet and kicks it under the driver's seat.

"You need the gun. Use the phone. It's in the lockbox under the car. Call my dads in an hour," Riot instructs. "Take the maps and keep going north. Find liberty, Cissy."

"Riot, I am not—I can't go without you," I cry, my words catching in my throat.

"Please Cissy, you have to. Otherwise this was all for nothing. Please, for me." He squeezes my hand. "And McCarthy. And Portia."

"Riot—"

"Promise me, keep going."

The car is surrounded. Officers in white and silver armor encircle our car, guns drawn. I pull my ball cap down over my eyes with my hands up. The lead officer yells, "Riot Logan, you're under arrest for treason. Get out of the vehicle with your hands in the air."

"There's something in the glove box for you," Riot says. With one hand in the air, he opens the car door. "I surrender, and I'm unarmed," he announces loudly.

Officers are on him in seconds, throwing him to the ground and prying his arms back. One officer cuffs him while another shoves his head to the ground. Another kicks him in the side. Riot screams in pain. A different officer pounds his nightstick against Riot's head. Riot's bloodcurdling bellow rings in my ears.

"No!" I yell, crawling over the console to get to him. When I try to get out, an officer grabs me and throws me back against the car. My head hits the doorframe. Then, I see him. Over by the barricade, near the Authority Select officers in their threatening all black uniforms, Mason Judall is accepting money from one of the Selects. He turned us in. And for what? Money. Everything is always about money. How can I let Sofia and Owen know their friend is a traitor? How does money trump human life?

Riot looks up at me, tears streaking his face. "I love you," he whispers. Another officer kicks him in the head. Riot's head falls to the ground. He's out.

"No please," I whisper, unable to breathe. "Wait!"

"What's your name, boy?" a uniformed officer asks, shoving my face onto the hood of the car. I can't catch my breath. "I said 'what's your name, boy?' Don't make me repeat myself."

"Victor, Victor Mattix," I choke out.

"Victor Mattix, eh?" Another officer types my name into this gadget. Two officers look over his shoulder while Riot lies motionless on the ground. I can't even turn my head to see if he's breathing. "How do you know this criminal?"

"I...I...uh just met him at a charging station," I lie, panting for air.

"Well you sure can pick 'em, kid. This guy here is a dangerous fugitive. Wanted all over Eka," a cocky officer with a limp says. "He might be pretty, but he ain't worth the trouble." With that, he kicks Riot again and begins walking back toward the trunk of our car. He motions for the other officers to get him. They pick Riot up. I can hear his faint groan as they drag him across the road in the direction of the barricade. Tossing him like a ragdoll into a car, they slam the door and high-five each other.

An officer pounds on the roof of the car. The driver turns on the sirens, and the car speeds away, taking Riot away from me. "I love you," I whisper as the car shrinks in the distance. I never got to say it. He never heard my truth.

My eyes burn with tears as they begin to trail down my cheeks.

"Where's the girl?" An Authority Select officer approaches me.

I shake my head, pretending I have no idea what he's talking about it. "The girl," he asks again, striking me in the low back with his nightstick. I fall to the ground; my scream is high-pitched and all too telling.

The officer with the gadget shows the screen to another officer. They both nod. "Well, looks like you got lucky, Mr. Mattix. Once we search this car, you're free to go."

The files. Oh please, please, don't find the files.

Or the paints.

Or the gun.

Or the phone.

I am fucked.

Watching the officer go through Riot's clothes makes my stomach churn. My luggage and clothes are strewn all over the road. Sofia made me leave all of my clothes at the house. She packed my luggage with Owen's pants and shirts. There's not one female article of clothing on the street. Thank you, Sofia. And I just thought she wanted my makeup for herself. Instead, she found another way to protect us.

The sun is beating down on me and sweat is pouring into my eyes. Standing on the side of the road watching this violation of our privacy is infuriating. I just want to jump in this car and follow Riot.

With an armful of art supplies, an officer says, "He must've hidden the documents somewhere else. That car is clean. Other than these."

The Select looks at me. "Where are the files? The weapons?"

Wide-eyed, I just shake my head. Are these the dumbest men in Eka? How could they miss the gun that's right under the seat?

The lead officer calls to the gunmen and says, "Call ahead and tell them not to execute him until the files are found. He'll tell us. We'll torture him until he caves. Either way, he's a dead man, and we're getting those documents."

Execute him? Dead man?

"Alright Mr. Mattix, you can go," the cocky officer with a limp says. "And in the future, try to pick 'em better." He shoves me against the car as he limps toward the others.

Immediately, I double over and vomit. The officers laugh. One says, "That guy was good-looking. What's he doing with that wimpy little shit?" They all laugh as they get into their cars, leaving me heaving and crying in the middle of the road.

I glance back at Mason, making direct eye contact with him. He grins and winks at me before getting into his own car and speeding off.

It takes me a good while to calm myself enough to even get back into the car. Distraught, I slide into the driver's seat and pull the car off to the side of the road. I have no idea what to do. If I go home, they'll arrest me. I don't want to put my moms through that. I can't possibly find my way back to Sofia and Owen's cabin. I have to warn them about Mason. How many more people will he knowingly send to their deaths? Can I go to Eli's house alone? He's a complete stranger—and a man. After what Riot told me, would that even be safe?

Remembering Riot's words, I know that I have to drive somewhere secluded and call his dads, signaling them to return the call with only allowing it to ring once. I drive north on the highway for exactly sixty-one minutes until I pull down a road with no traffic or businesses. I need to use the restroom and call the Logans. Parking in an abandoned lot near an old charging station, I get out and walk around. There's nobody in sight. I walk down a small embankment and crouch behind a tree.

Feeling safer since nobody saw me go to the bathroom, I walk back to the car, crawl under it, and search for the lockbox. It takes me a few minutes, because I know literally nothing about cars. But once I find the box, breaking into it is easy. I don't know the code, but I'm able to pick the lock pretty quickly.

The files and phone are neatly organized in the box. I find the paper with the number on it. Turning on the phone, I wait for the lights to indicate that I can start dialing. I punch in the numbers and wait for the ringing to start. It rings once. I want to stay on the phone until they answer, but those are not the rules. I hang up and wait. Time slows to a near standstill. Finally, the phone rings and vibrates, scaring me to death.

I press the green telephone icon, and before I can say 'hello,' a man's voice says, "Riot, are you okay?"

I take a deep breath and say, "Mr. Logan, this is...ummm..." I decide against using my name. "They arrested him," I announce instead.

"Fuck," he says. Another voice in the background begins to wail. "Atticus, walk away. I need to hear the details. So Cis...ummm, so are you okay?"

"I don't think so," I admit. "I'm scared." The sobs start. I have no control over my tears or shaking body.

"Shit," he says, whispering something to someone else. There's commotion on the other end of the line. "Alright, listen to me. We're going back. We'll take care of Riot. We'll do everything we can to get him a fair trial." There's more movement and whispers on the other end.

"Hello honey," a different man says, choking on his words. "Can you read that map?"

"Yes sir," I say, leaving out that I was the only one who could read the map.

"You need to stay the course."

"Sir?"

"Listen dear, Riot wants you safe. You mean something special to our boy. So, we need to get you north. That's the most important thing right now."

"But I can't go by myself—"

"Yes, you certainly can. You've gotten this far. You can get the rest of the way. You just have to be brave. We'll get word to your moms and let them know." I can't stop crying. My resolve is weakening. "You call us and keep us updated. Same plan. Just keep going."

There's noise on the other end. The other voice is back on. "He's right. You need to keep moving. It's too dangerous for you to stay put or to even think about coming back here."

"Okay," I acquiesce.

"It's what Riot would want," he adds, ensuring that I heed his warning.

"For Riot," I say, closing my eyes and squeezing the phone.

"Yes," he says, his voice cracking. "For Riot."

~

I can't believe this is happening. Vicissitude Maddox, rule follower, the girl voted most respected and admired by her graduating class is now all alone, heading for the border for a chance at survival. With Authority on my tail ready to arrest me—or worse. They say you learn a lot about yourself during your senior year. I learned a lifetime's worth about myself in less than six months. I just hope I live long enough to talk about it and use what I learned to save more people like me.

Heading north, I'm closing in on Eli's house. There's been nothing but cornfields for miles and miles. I've never seen so much corn and so many open roads and fields. When I'm about ten minutes from the Sadie house, I pull off the road to gather my bearings and grab a snack. I have one more thing to do before my second sanctuary along the Wog.

Opening the glove box, I see an envelope with my name on it. I take it out of the compartment, grab my water and a small bag of nuts, and exit the car. Sitting on the hood of the light blue sedan, I open the envelope.

The first thing I find is a small sketch of Riot and me in the lake performing a perfect lift. His details are exceptional. Each of my braids is precisely constructed with small differences between each of them. He captured his cocky smirk perfectly as he's holding me with pride above the water. He may have been a little too generous with his bulging muscles or with my chest size. I wish I could tell him so. But I can't. I hold the drawing close to my chest as I let my tears fall. Finally, I read the words he wrote underneath the sketch. His caption at the bottom makes me laugh. "Even though we never figured it out, it was perfect to me." We sure didn't figure it out. We didn't figure anything out.

I place the sketch on the hood of the car and open the other paper. I cry harder when I see my name written across the top. And then I read:

Dear Cissy,

Fuck, if you're reading this, then I'm either dead or somewhere in some Authority-guarded cell. Either way, I want you to know one thing: I regret nothing. The world I uncovered in your arms is worth a million lifetimes. Cissy Maddox, I know I never let you say it, but I want you to know that I love you. I have loved you since the day you kicked me in the balls and then waited to see if I was okay. If there is anything that defines you, then it's that. You're a fighter with a compassionate and loving heart. Loving you was easy. And Cissy, I know. I know you loved me. I could see it in your smile, in your eyes, and most importantly, in your bravery. Only a courageous person could love someone like me. Cissy, you're the bravest person I know. So please, don't give up. Keep going and find freedom—find it for all of us.

All of my love,
Riot.

Ps. I found this in my dad's things in the fort at my grandpa's house. Did I ever tell you he wrote songs? I think this describes us.

People Like Us
People like us look for truth behind the lies.

PEOPLE LIKE US

> People like us hear the agony in their cries.
> People like us question and ask what it's all for.
> People like us hide in the dark afraid of who we are.
> People like us still bleed beneath our wounded scars.
> But in the end...
> People like us must retreat from the dark and come into the light.
> People like us need to come together and unite.
> People like us will reveal the hypocrisy and flaws.
> People like us can tear down these oppressive walls.
> People like us can no longer accept the silence and quiet.
> People like us are riled up and ready to riot.
> People like us can change world.
> People like us—one boy and one girl.
> People like us.

Riot's words and his dad's lyrics rip through me, shattering my heart. Holding them both against my chest, I cry for the beautiful boy who wanted so much. I cry for the girl who didn't know what she wanted—until it was too late. Mourning the loss of what I never got to experience, I sob into my hands, letting every emotion wash over me. The agony of loss crushes me, but I let it. These feelings are mine and mine alone. They define me and empower me. Once the final tear is shed, and there are no more tears to fall, I fold the letter and the song together and secure them back into the lockbox.

Once I strap the box in its spot under the car, I fall into the driver's seat, double-check the map, and start the car. If my calculations are accurate, I'll arrive at Eli's in less than fifteen minutes. I head north to Eli's—and to freedom. Every ounce of my being wants to turn this car around and run into my moms' arms, but I know that's not possible.

You can never go back. You must always keep going forward. The past is a fleeting shadow of what once was. The future is an optimistic sunbeam of light and hope. Please let me find my way out of this dark, dismal place in the present. Taking a deep breath and letting it out slowly, I whisper, "For Riot," as I continue our journey to freedom alone. "For Riot."

SNEAK PEEK

ENJOY A SNEAK PEEK INTO VICISSITUDE'S JOURNEY TO FREEDOM AND RIOT'S FIGHT FOR HIS LIFE IN CHAPTER ONE OF THE SEQUEL TO PEOPLE LIKE US.

Jaynus
One

After fifteen years of being a lawyer, I've prosecuted over 35 criminals, each ending in his public execution. The whole faction comes out and watches as the man begs and pleads for a pardon, but none is ever granted. The audience waits with bated breath until the man's feet stop jerking and flailing about. The hanging used to be fast and painless, but the onlookers never enjoyed that. The public wanted a stricter punishment for the crimes committed against Authority. The sentencing specialist decided that a tight brace around the neck while the criminal's hands were bound behind him would work more favorably for the crowd. Now, the prosecuted hangs by his neck with his feet dangling, but death does not come. Death comes slowly and painfully as the executioner tightens the brace around the man's neck—one centimeter at a time until the life drains out of him and justice prevails once again.

"Mr. Greer, the Judge wants you in his chambers," my assistant announces as he knocks simultaneously on my doorjamb. Lassiter Vlaneer is one sharp and efficient paralegal, but he struggles in decorum and etiquette. Lassiter once propositioned me after hours, knowing the price of work-related sexual misconduct. He claimed that the fine would be well worth it for one night with me. I agreed. And it was worth every penny. We now pay our fine about once a month, because a night with Lassiter is better than drowning my stressors in bourbon. But, it's never anything more. Just a release between friends—or between boss and subordinate.

"Mr. Greer?" I question, wondering why he chose such a formal greeting.

Lassiter's gaze doesn't meet my own. "Um yeah, I just want to keep things professional, ya know, while we're at work?"

"Of course I do. This doesn't have anything to do with the new solicitor the firm hired last week, does it?" I joke, winking at him. "Listen Lass, our secret is safe with me. You know if my father found out, he'd have both of our asses." Lassiter and I shiver simultaneously.

My father is a world-class dickhead. I'm pretty sure there's nobody in this entire country of Eka who likes him or respects him. The man's borderline evil. After each criminal I've sent to the brace, I heave my lunch in the first container I can find. Watching their deaths never sits well with me. My father, the infamous "Judge Grotesque Greer," does a shot of bourbon for every minute it takes for the brace to end the guilty man's life.

And that's the other thing. In my father's career, there have been sixteen people found "not guilty" by him. Only sixteen. Those sixteen accused men were as innocent as a doe in a pasture at sunset. I couldn't even discern why any of them were actually on trial. Not all of them were during my career here, but I did the research and studied the cases. My father is relentless and unforgiving. I'm fairly certain he knew they were innocent all along as he delayed their trials over and over while they sat alone in the Confinery for months. One man sat in a cell for two years before my father would hear his case. My father just loves to assert his dominance.

I'm definitely much more lenient and tolerant. I get my compassion and trust from my passive dad. Authority, rest his soul. When my passive dad died, my father became even more cruel and inhumane.

"Judge Greer," I say, entering his chambers, quietly and softly. After closing his door, I walk over to his desk, where he's typing frantically on his keyboard, punching each key like it's a "fuck you" to whomever the recipient may be. It probably is, too. "You summoned me—"

My father raises his hand, gesturing for me to wait. After close to ten minutes, he pushes a final key with flair and finality.

"I want him dead," my father cuts to the chase as he closes his laptop with a thud. It's amazing that thing doesn't shatter daily. "And I need answers before he's in the brace."

"You don't think I know that?" His glare silences me immediately. f only he was the father who suffered from ALS and died so abhorrently. Instead, my loving and kind dad had to face an end that nobody should ever endure. And now, I'm stuck with this sinister man as he terrorizes the Male Faction.

"Get answers today! I don't care how you have to do it, just do it!" His face and tone tells me I'm dismissed. "And I want him braced by the end of the week."

Fuck.

Riot Logan hasn't said one word since they threw him in the Confinery. Not one. Nor has he eaten one morsel of food. There hasn't been one torture tactic that's worked on this kid. But I have one final idea up my sleeve that I know will give me what I need. I hope, anyway.

∾

The guard motions me through the metal detector that blares as I walk through the arch. "Metal rod in my back," I mumble as the guard waves the wand over me. The screeching gets louder near the middle of my spine. "Hector, why? Why do we do this dance every single day."

"You know the rules Jaynus," Hector shrugs, gesturing for the next person to walk through. "Authority knows, I'm not about to piss off your father."

"Why does everything come down to my father?" I ask rhetorically, knowing there's nobody to commiserate with, simply because no one in Eka would dare to rile up Judge Greer.

It was tough growing up with a father like him. There was no wiggle room for anything. Any misstep resulted in severe punishment—especially if my passive dad wasn't in the house. Since I have access to the Kendyl, the establishment where our country's secrets are hidden, I know that parents used to face consequences for punishing their children. I have no idea why Eka stopped doing so. Some of my consequences were so severe and debilitating that I couldn't see out of one of my eyes for weeks at a time. I spent most of my high school years trying to hide my bruises and black eyes. Luckily, I played hockey, so my excuses were always believable.

When the prison guard opens the cell door, I see him—siting in the same place as always, knees to his chin, arms draped over his knees with his forehead resting on this forearms. Slowly, his eyes meet mine. He's battered, beaten, and bruised—a look I know all too well. His head falls right back down on his forearms.

"I pulled some strings. Think these might get you out of your funk," I say, dumping the contents of my bag onto the floor. Cells used to have actual beds and mattresses, but in Eka, once you're found "guilty," and moved to the Confinery, men are stripped of their "human" identity.

Guilty confines are nothing more than mere animals and treated as such. Confines are given two meals a day in a metal bowl on their cell floor. They do get as much water as they want, but are only given five trips to the bathroom in a 24-hour period. Most men urinate right on the cement floor of their cells. A few even defecate there too, proving they are just animals. When confined, men are given one blanket to use to cover up or as a pillow—the choice is theirs. They get walked twice daily around the outdoor arena, collar, leash, and all. The public loves their daily viewings of the confines as they're marched—and sometimes even dragged—around the arena during lunchtime and before dusk.

I wouldn't believe it if I didn't see it with my own eyes. Riot Logan's eyes light up and a smile splays across his face at the sight of the various paints and brushes strewn all about his cell floor.

"Yes sir, these are all yours," I can tell that he's using all of his restraint to not reach out and grab a brush. "What're you waiting for? Grab one. Start painting. You have this entire cell, um room, to paint. Have at it." Riot doesn't move. His face reveals nothing. "I'll stop back later this evening and see whatever masterpiece you've created."

Exiting the cell and just as the door is about secured, I hear, "Are my dads alive?" With most confines, I'd let the door slam behind me—not offering even the slightest glance to let him know I heard him in the first place.

I turn, jamming my foot in the door to stop it from closing, nearly crushing my foot with the weight of the metal door. Leaning against it to shove the door back open, I tilt my head inside. "Riot, I wish I had that answer or any information for you, but both of your fathers are still at large and on the run. Nobody has heard anything from them."

Riot's eyes drop. "The Maddox moms?" He questions without looking at me.

I nod, "Separated, in different Female Confines. Word is they're both fine."

Riot's head falls back onto his forearms as I exit the cell.

AFTERWORD

Author's Note

Wow. I am honored and humbled. Thank you so much for reading *People Like Us*. This novel has been in my head for over a decade. I was worried that I wouldn't be able to figure how to approach the topics and themes in a way that wouldn't offend anyone. But as time progressed and our society became more and more divisive, the storyline and characters kept getting louder and louder in my head, refusing to be silenced. Once Roe was overturned in June of 2022 and states began passing the "Don't Say Gay" law, I couldn't stop the novel from writing itself in my head; I just needed to open my laptop and allow the characters to finally be heard, and the story to be told.

In my honest opinion, I am worried for our country and especially for our children. Lately, it seems as if we are sheltering our children so much so that we are no longer allowing them to think and evolve as individuals. But yet, somehow we've given them all the freedom in the world to explore the Internet and only find comfort and solace in social media. And trust me when I admit this, I love posting on Facebook, bragging about my family, sharing pictures, and watching hours and hours of TikTok videos. I fully understand the amusement. However, how can we stop our children from reading certain books, refuse to let them explore their own sexuality, prohibit them from hearing about the past and present horrors that minorities have endured, and prevent them from losing a competition or failing a class, and yet, we won't stop them from disengaging and focusing all of their attention (and happiness) on social media? We are hurting our children. And we're just ignoring their cries for help.

Our children, our adolescents, are human beings. They have real thoughts and feelings. They are not our baby dolls, our Barbie dolls, or our pets. We have to give them freedom to succeed—and fail. Most importantly, we have to give them the freedom to think for themselves. When did it become acceptable—and even the norm—to refuse to allow our children to experience life? Why are parents living their children's lives for them? How did we get here?

Granted, I am 51-years-old. My childhood and adolescent years were in the 1970s, 1980s, and 1990s. I definitely had more free reign of my neighborhood than I'd ever let my own children have now. I roamed my neighborhood like Ponce de Leon searching for the Fountain of Youth. I slept on the back dash of my mom and dad's car. I knew my grades when progress reports and report card came out. That is also when my parents learned of my grades. I was permitted to live my life without my mom and dad dictating my every move. They never ever tried to ingratiate themselves into my life and live it for me.

As a whole, our society has chosen to shelter our children—not from outside dangers, but from knowledge and from accepting others' lifestyles. This decision is only hurting—more like destroying—our children. Our children have the opportunity to be better than we are. Why are we regressing and making them less intelligent, less informed, and less accepting and tolerant than we were? I am so confused and so disappointed. I want to help. I want to help make a difference in the world. But, I'm not a politician. I'm not a leader. I'm not a warrior. I'm just an English who cares and loves her students. And, I have a vivid imagination, Therefore, this book, *People Like Us*, is the only way that I know how to help the future adolescents of the world. I want you all to know that there are so many people who are just like you. You are not alone. There are also thousands upon thousands of people who like you just the way you are.

ACKNOWLEDGMENTS

A special thank you to my "full spectrum" of Beta Readers. I enlisted the help of people from the entire political and religious spectrum. I did not want to offend anyone. I had far far liberal left readers and far far conservative right readers. The feedback was paramount to the evolution and sensitivity of this book. Thank you to: Jennifer Burba, Brock Eastman, Emersyn Eastman, Mike Eastman, Hal Foster, Michelle Gaither, Carla Grasso, Angela Hall, Deanndra Hall, Jordan Horstmyer, Michelle, Kelling, Amanda Kuebler, Jennifer Manion, Mary Ellen McAvoy, Lisa Nesline, Jennifer Otterman, Polie Pavlova, Beth Smith, and my White Gables Book Club (Debbie, Jane, Mary, Marybeth, and Patti.) Thank you for taking time out of your lives to provide honest feedback of my novel.

Angela Hall, thank you for always being my biggest fan and for always viewing me as a "real author." You know how much that means to me.

Virginia Carey, I truly appreciate your knowledge and expertise. Thank you for editing my novel (twice) and for your encouragement and support. I am lucky to have met you in the book world fourteen years ago.

Christine Ticali, you will forever hold the title of my "writing bestie," but you are so much more than that. I love you and I am so thankful for our friendship that has withstood so much in our lives. When we met, our children were just little kids. Look at us now. Our friendship still survives and thrives. I owe you everything—my friend, my therapist, my comedian, and my saving grace in my writing world of disappointments and setbacks.

To my family, thank you for always supporting me in every crazy endeavor I embark upon. No matter what new idea I have or wild journey I begin, you are all there to cheer me on. And I do realize that I tend to flit around with new experiences a lot, but that never seems to deter you. I love you all. Carla, I love your newfound passion for reading and sharing books. I love that you are my sister and biggest support ever. Emersyn, please keep reading and most importantly, keep being the open-minded, accepting person that amazes me every day. Brock, you inspired the religious aspect of this book. You gave it a whole new layer that this book needed. Brevin, one day, if you should ever choose to read a book, maybe read this one. You inspired the athletic portion of this book. You gave Riot his sensitivity and athleticism—both of which you possess. Mike, you are my "claim to fame." People can change their viewpoints. People can grow and evolve. You certainly have, and I am so thankful that you are my ever-changing husband. I am so lucky.

And finally, to my former students, thank you for always allowing me to be your safe space, the person you feel the most at home and comfortable sharing your truths with. I pray that someday all individuals can share their truths with everyone without judgment or fear.

Made in the USA
Coppell, TX
09 August 2024